ROLE SHIFT: THE OUTCOME

ROLE SHIFT: THE OUTCOME

Amador Amado

ISBN: 979-8-9876421-2-2

Thank you, Alicia Cole, for creating the stunning book covers!

TABLE OF CONTENTS

CHAPTER 1
A SURPLUS OF BETAS

The year was 2069. The feminist equality empowerment movement had had a negative impact on society. The roles had been reversed to the point women now sustained a dominant position and had the responsibilities of males. The agenda had backfired on them. Most men had become stay-at-home dads, husbands, or boyfriends. There was a sixty-five percent drop in pregnancies and childbirths. The economy had crashed on multiple occasions due to the demand for physical strength required to endure blue-collar occupations. The system was in danger, vulnerable to the consequences of the outcome. Women had begun to miss their past positions because of a vast scarcity of alpha males. Most men were in favor of the idea and contested for a resolution not benefitting their current status. Testosterone was in high demand and was only found in minute dosage in supplements outside the human body—incrementing in value. Estrogen was the leading factor fueling America at the moment. The exclusion of chivalry was the first sign they failed to observe. Military, law enforcement, and every title previously predominantly maintained by men were now at the mercy of women. Correctional facilities had seen a surflux in female confinement. The government took action, forming a complex group of scientists, doctors, and psychologists to study the culprit behind the epidemic.

In the midst of it all comes a story of a couple, struggling with the new norm: Mercedes, a mid-twenty-year-old woman holding a job at a call center, and Jesus who was around the same age and worked in construction. They had met at a nightclub where Jesus presented himself as an alpha, only disguising his true nature in order to obtain commitment from his victim. They danced the night away, and afterward, Jesus repeatedly requested for her phone number, which she denied multiple times until she felt empathy and pity for his intent and succumbed to his courting. They began dating after she subsequently responded to his text, ignoring it for days. She was in search of a real man, and he vigorously deceived her. Unaware of the changes taking place in society, she fell for his plot. She had no idea she was being fooled, and she defended her partner against the opposing advice from her friends and relatives. It wasn't until marriage became a topic of their relationship that she kinda began to suspect. Jesus argued he wanted a big wedding and he wouldn't turn himself sexually over to her until then. There were more conditions to be fulfilled; she had to bend on one knee and ask for him to marry her, offering a diamond engagement ring and wedding band to him. She also had to ask for his hand from his mother in person. Mercedes was a single mother of two and just wanted a male figure in the lives of her children, so she accepted. They tied the knot in their early twenties and became a family. He insisted on changing his last name to hers, but at that time, it was a taboo—another tall-tale sign she didn't take into consideration. They continued on their journey in a hectic spiraling relationship until they conceived a child together. A male with low testosterone was born, and as he aged, he flourished femininely. They were now in their mid-thirties as their current situation at hand began to unravel.

Jesus was at home watching over his feminine son—Jr.—who was about four years old. Mercedes was at work and her older kids were attending school. Jesus had resigned from his occupation after a strike came into effect, initiated by his coworkers pleading for equality in men's rights, as women had overtaken their positions. He went outside to attempt to change a tire on his vehicle. He stood there for a while, holding a screwdriver in his hand—observing the tire and scratching his head. He couldn't comprehend the procedure required to change the flat tire on his car. He walked back inside his home and grabbed himself a glass of wine instead, as his son played with his older sisters' dolls. He placed his glass on top of a living room table and sat down on the floor to play with his son. Jesus grabbed a doll and, while pretending it was working on a construction site, said, "It's time to head back in from break after eating those two burritos that messed up my stomach. Oh look, a hammer to nail the Sheetrock to the structure." His son laughed as Jesus made the doll hammer a shoe carton box.

His son replied, holding another doll in his hand, "Let me help you with that. This is a job for a hardworking woman. Move out of the way!" He took the hammer.

Jesus noticed the time of the day and remembered he had to go buy some ingredients for the meal he was going to cook before his wife and stepchildren came home. He threw a small fit recalling he had no means of transportation as he had a flat tire on his ride. *If only I had been born more masculine,* he thought as he got his kid dressed and ready to walk to the food chain market. Once they both were properly fitted to trek down to the store, they exited the residence and made their way on foot. As Jesus exited the house, he flipped off the tire giving him trouble, as he blamed it for having to walk to get groceries. During their commute, they were sexually harassed by several passing cars. Some were masculine men getting a laugh, but most were women in search of a partner. Upon arriving at the market, a male subject chuckled at him and his son.

Jesus had slipped into a pair of pink sandals and was wearing short white shorts with a tight purple top—revealing his abdomen. His son wore the same but in different shades and had a man purse slung over his shoulder. Jesus gave an unpleasant look at the man and turned to the shopping carts in order to grab one. He and his son then proceeded to obtain the much-needed items on his list. They went through every aisle in search of the ingredients and became easily distracted when they came across the fruits and vegetables. He picked up a cucumber and inspected it—not because it was on his list but because he desired it in his rectum. He turned to gaze at his son and wiped the smirk off his face as he placed the cucumber down. His son looked at him and asked, "Dad, can you buy me some nail polish?"

Jesus responded, "I have plans to ask your mom to pay for us to get some manicures. How about you help me convince her when she gets back home?"

His son uttered with a gleam of happiness in his eyes, "Yeah! That would be much better than painting them myself."

They continued down the aisles, grabbing the products on their list. They walked to the self-checkout counters and began scanning the items in the cart. He then took out his debit card—the account to which his wife was the sole contributor—from his sports bra and paid for the products. His son helped bag the purchases. They grabbed the receipt and placed the bags inside the cart, then made their way out of the front door. There were three bags, possibly weighing only around fifteen pounds total, yet he decided on taking the cart all the way to their home because he didn't want to carry them. A female employee gathering the carts outside noticed his intentions and shouted, "Bring the cart back! You can't take it! It has a ..."

He and his son began to run with the cart as the woman tried warning them of what would happen. The cart had a technological mechanism that made the cart's wheels freeze up after leaving a predetermined radius. So as Jesus dashed with the cart and reached the perimeter, the cart's wheels came to an immediate stop, causing him to slam into the cart and fly over it—toppling out all of the contents inside the bags. Bystanders burst into laughter as he lay on the ground, while his son grabbed the items on the ground to place them back in the bags. A woman who was there to shop exited her vehicle. She walked over toward him and asked, as she helped him up to his feet, "Are you alright? You took quite a spill there."

Jesus commented, "No, my knees are bruised, and I may need medical attention." There was a sour expression on his face, as he whimpered.

The woman replied, "From the looks of it, I don't believe your injuries are serious enough to dispatch an ambulance. You're clearly standing and walking on your feet without issue."

Jesus said, "You're right; plus, I won't be able to file a lawsuit because there's a warning notice on the shopping cart, which I didn't read. Thank you." He and his son walked away embarrassedly, carrying their bags home.

Josefina, Mercedes's younger sister, who was living at home with their father, had just woken up from her sleep. She was working the second shift at an assembly plant that produced men's supporting underwear that had a bra-like cup to hold the crotch. The company was currently in jeopardy because men's testicles were continuing to shrink across the Western Hemisphere. Her father, Danny, saw her exiting her room and making her way toward the restroom. Danny was a retired fireman. He was in his room lying down, talking on the phone to one of his girlfriends; he was one of the male population in high demand—a real man. He put his cell down and yelled at Josefina, "How did it go last night on your date? Did you finally strike gold with a real man unlike your sister?"

Josefina was urinating and shouted back, "No, Dad. It went horrible. The more I try to find a real man, the more I'm disappointed." There was a pause as she expelled gases from her body, which sounded like a trumpet out of tune, and then continued, "He freaking pretended to be very masculine throughout the night until a lesbian punked him, and his little feminine voice came out apologetic in a cowardly fashion, embarrassing us both. I was about to stand up for him but realized he wasn't worth it, so I just walked away and left him there."

Danny responded, "I'm sorry to hear that, baby. But I'm proud of you for deflecting those sissies out there you keep running into. The last thing you want is to end up with a pansy guy like your sister. If it wasn't as common as it is, she'd be the joke of the family. Hey, whatever happened to that other guy you were talking to?"

Josefina uttered, "I asked him to send me a dick pic, and when I received it, it looked more like my clitoris. The guy had a micropenis. I'd show it to you but I erased it."

Dan commented, "Are you serious? Ha, ha, ha! No, thanks, honey, I wouldn't want to see it even if you had it still. I'll take your word for it."

He resumed his conversation with his twenty-seven-year-old chick who was obsessed with him. Josefina wiped her vagina, lifted her underwear and shorts up, and then walked to the sink to wash her hands. As the water hit her fingers, she looked at her reflection in the mirror, observing how she had begun to grow a thicker mustache and beard. Females were beginning to transform.

Jesus and his son had made it back home and removed the items from the bags, and he began to chop up some ingredients to cook. As the contents of the meal simmered over the stove, he decided to sweep and mop before his wife got back from work. His son got back to playing with the dolls and watching little girls play with cars on a social network channel. Jesus swept the entire house and began preparing the mop bucket to mop right after. He went over to the kitchen to make sure the food wasn't burning. Once clearing his worries, he got to mopping the home. As he was about to finish, he slipped and fell on his rear, shouting "ouch!" in a feminine manner, which was comparable to a moan.

His son was not around to render aid, and even if he was, he'd be too preoccupied observing little girls play with what once were boy toys on his tablet. Jesus attempted to rise to his feet, utilizing the mop as support, but he fell once more. He managed to stand up finally and picked up the mop from the floor to continue with his chores. He knew time was running out, and Mercedes would be arriving home shortly. The last thing he wanted to do was displease her since she was the provider. So he continued his duties and went to check the food again. The meal wasn't quite ready yet, so he began to wash the dishes after putting on his apron. He scraped off the remaining food on the dirty dishes and began to clean up the sinks to use them for washing and rinsing. As he washed, he pondered on how his scalp's follicles had been falling off as he was going bald. His condition had only worsened since his early thirties when it began. At first, he'd mask his hair loss by using baseball caps prior to the new norm. He gathered the ones in the sink and tossed them in the trash.

Josefina got out of the restroom and walked over to her bedroom to retrieve some clothes to wear after a shower. She was getting ready to go to work. Danny was on the phone now conversing with another of his girlfriends, a thirty-year-old who he had just met the other day. He asked her, "Do you have any kids?"

She replied, "I have one boy who I've been raising on my own because his father left us to be supported by some older woman, who buys him just about anything he could dream of."

Danny responded, "Wow, he left his family to be a stay-at-home guy? I've heard how this is only getting out of hand with these feminine men. They no longer want to work and would rather stay home doing chores and playing video games. I'm glad I was raised in a different era. I'd hate to join the masses and take part in the destructive nature toward masculinity."

The woman uttered, "There are less and less real men out there to track and hunt down. I was surprised when I met you that you'd even pay any attention to me, given you're at the top of the food chain right now and could take your pick from a hundred or more women—even despite your unwavering decision to keep a few at hand who'll have to share you."

Danny commented, "Well, since you brought it up, I actually am enforcing those standards. If you'd like to continue getting to know me and dating, those are the actual requirements to do so." He giggled.

The woman stated, "Back then I'd disagree with sharing a man, but due to the current circumstances, I'd rather divide a real man than a fake one. So if you have other girlfriends, I'm alright with being part of your admiring group in hopes you'll one day choose to keep only one till the end of days."

Danny said, "I'm glad to hear you're on board with the concept of modern dating and the competition for males."

Mercedes had finally gotten home after work. She walked in and greeted Jr., who was happy to see her. She then turned to look at Jesus with no affection. Jesus, on the other hand, ran up to her, attempting to give her a kiss, but she moved away and stuck her hand out so he'd kiss it instead. He did so, and she then hung her purse on the coat hanger by the front door and walked over to the kitchen to see what was for dinner. She lifted the cover off the pan and observed some burnt rice in it. In the other pan were some undercooked pork medallions. She fumed and inquired, "What the hell have you been doing all day, Jesus? What's this you undercooked and overcooked? I fucking wish I had listened to my friends and relatives who clearly advised me against marrying you! Had you not fooled me to believe you were masculine, I'd probably be happy without having the stress of providing for you along with my kids. You're an incompetent excuse of a man."

Jesus was about to give his alibi to cool her anger, but she smacked him across his face and ordered him to call a restaurant to place an order for carryout, which he'd have to pick up. She then grabbed the pans and tossed the food in the trash. She asked, "What the heck is that on your face and why're your knees scabbed?"

Jesus flinched, believing she was going to strike him again, then responded, "I fell coming back from the store earlier. We had to walk over there because I was unable to change out the flat on my car."

Mercedes once more fumed. "Are you fucking serious? What a useless person you've become. Give me your car keys so I can change it for you while you order some food on your phone!"

Jesus uttered, "OK, just don't hit me again. At least not in front of Jr. I don't want him to grow up thinking it's alright to let women smack men around."

She turned around to see if their son was watching, and since he wasn't, she swung her palm on his face once more before heading outside to change his car tire.

Her older kids walked back home from school while she was outside replacing the flat with the spare. They both greeted her as her older son asked, "What're you doing out here? Changing out your wife's car tire, Mom?"

Mercedes replied, "Son, I hope and pray you don't turn out to be like him and your younger brother. This world needs more men to survive and thrive as nature intended." She finished tightening up the last lug nut and dropped the vehicle off the jack.

Her son responded, "Don't worry, Mom. When I grow up, I'll take care of you so you can leave that dumbass." She embraced her son, and all three walked back inside the house.

As they entered the dwelling, she was admiring her oldest son for being masculine. Her youngest then awoke her to reality by asking, "Mom, can you pay for daddy's and my manicure? I want to paint my nails."

She uttered, "Are you kidding me? Why can't you be more like your older brother? You know your father isn't someone to look up to." Jr. started to sob, so she picked him up and played with him a little to distract his thoughts. She observed Jesus getting off the phone and slowly walking up to her.

He said, "I ordered some pizzas for us. Were you able to change out the tire?"

She replied, "Good, and yes, I did. Now go get those pizzas and take the tire down to the tire shop before you get the food so they can have it ready when you're on your way back."

Jesus inquired, "I overheard Jr. asking if you could pay for our manicure. Will you be able to?"

She placed Jr. down and told him to cover his ears as she commented, "Why can't you be more masculine? Have you looked for a job to help around? He's almost going to be enrolled in school, and you'd have no excuse to sit around at home when he does. I don't want to spend the rest of my life supporting you and your feminine wants and needs."

Jesus responded, "I haven't looked for a job. He still has a few months to go to school, and if you don't want to get us a mani, it's alright." He put his head down dejectedly.

She stated, "No manis. Now go do what I told you to! Or should I go do it myself as well?" He replied, "Well, It would be better if you did, don't you?"

She fumed, "Bullshit! Get your ass out there and get the tire fixed and bring us back the food, you fucking incompetent pansy." She raised her hand up to strike him, but he darted out of the house to follow her orders before he could be assaulted.

Josefina had gotten out of the shower, after shaving off her beard and mustache. Her father had taken off to go see the thirty-year-old he was speaking to earlier. She was getting dressed while searching for potential candidates on an online dating site. She was putting on her pants when she came across a handsome-looking man who appeared to be macho. She liked his profile and began writing him a message that read, "Hi there, handsome, I'd like to get to know more about you after reading your bio and feeling enticed by your self-description. Get back to me if you're interested in telling me more about your hobbies." She hit send and put on her blouse. Just then she received a phone call, and she thought it was the guy she had just written to. As she reached out for her phone—which was in eyesight but not in arm's reach—she realized there was no possibility of that being true since he didn't have her number and hadn't even replied to her. When she grabbed her phone from her dresser, she saw the contact read "Mom." She answered the call, "Hi, Mom, how're you doing?"

Her mother responded, "Hi, *mija.* I'm alright, just here having a late lunch by myself at home, and you?"

Josefina uttered, "I'm OK, I guess. Been having a hard time locating my shining prince in armor, but I'm not giving up and settling for a simp like my sister."

Lucia, her mom, commented, "Yes, *mija,* don't make the same mistake your sister did. I bet right now she's doing everything he should be doing, plus working and providing for her family. It's a disgrace to mention her in such a manner, but I warned her. It also doesn't help how things are now with more men like him to choose from. Speaking of which, where's your dad? He was supposed to come by to pick up some food I made for him."

Josefina responded, "I'd hate to end up like my sister with a useless man around, who I'd have to support and maintain. As far as Dad, he left without letting me know where he was heading. Maybe he'll drop by later on to pick up the food. Have you tried calling him?"

Lucia stated, "I called him, but he's not picking up. I sure miss having a man like that around, even though he was complicated to please with such high testosterone levels. Granted, had I known things would unfold as they have, I'd do my best to keep him happy. Now it's just wishing I could go back in time and know what lay ahead. Anyhow, *mija,* I know you're probably getting ready to go to work, so I won't interrupt you any longer. I hope you have a great day at work and that you find your king soon. I love you, take care."

Josefina said, "Thanks, Mom, I appreciate your best wishes for me. Let me know if Dad goes for the food. If not, I'll swing by for it after work. I love and miss you; take care too." Then she hung up and headed out of the home to work.

Her mother and father's marital situation was that they were divorced. They had been married for approximately thirty years and had two children—Mercedes and Josefina. As the modern crisis came into effect, Lucia had begun her menopause and neglected Danny's needs. He eventually found someone to meet his demands, a younger one-legged woman with enough beauty to make up for her missing limb. His reason was that besides being generous, she wouldn't be able to run away from him. He was correct about the sprinting part but failed to realize she would be able to hop off, as she did. This all took place after he had filed for divorce with Lucia and was living away from home. Lucia had started dating a one-armed man when the case was finally over. One time they had met up with their new partners at a family gathering. The one-legged woman and the one-armed man met and fell in love. They eventually left Danny and Lucia for each other and started a new relationship, believing their common distinctions would better suit them both. The one-armed man began assaulting the one-legged woman soon after due to the lack of trust he faced. He wondered when she'd do the same to him as she had done to Danny. They eventually separated as well, and the girl tried to get back with Danny, but it was too late. Danny had become aware he was a rare find and rejected her as he entertained a few gals. He had become a GILF or "Grandpa, I'd like to fuck," because of which he now wouldn't settle for just anything out in the field. He was a real man with high testosterone and the power to attract any woman he desired. Lucia gave up on dating, and she just remained alone with the dream of getting back with Danny someday. He would still keep in touch with her and bang her from time to time for good old time's sake, as he'd call it. But he had plenty of prospects competing for the title that he wasn't interested in filling out anymore. Marriage was out the window for him as well as having children. He had experienced that life already and didn't miss it one bit.

Jesus had gotten back home from the tire shop and the pizza joint. He was walking up the walkway to his house when his neighbor saw him and greeted him, "What's up, bro? How's life treating you?"

Jesus replied, "Hey, what's up, Nick? I'm alright, just tired of how violent women have become and their high expectations for men with low testosterone. Why can't they just understand us and accept things as they are now instead of comparing us to other guys from their past?"

Nick uttered, "I hear you, broskie. I too am on the same boat with my wife. Hey, have you heard the government is looking for volunteers for their studies on men? They are paying top dollar for those who are selected. I'm going to apply, man."

Jesus said, "No, I haven't, but shoot me the information so I can check it out please, when you get a chance." Their wives yelled out both their names and told them to head inside.

Jesus ran and opened the front door just as he heard Mercedes ask, "Who were you talking to outside? I saw you arrive a few minutes ago but didn't come in."

Jesus responded, "I was approached by Nick, and he was telling me about this study paying top dollar for men who are selected. He's thinking of registering and is going to send me the information so I can check it out and maybe register myself."

Mercedes inquired, "What's the study on or what?"

Jesus said, "I think it's on figuring out the source for the decrease in male testosterone or something like that."

Mercedes stated, "Oh, I've heard. Sounds like a good idea, and I support you registering so the government can find out why you're so feminine. Now go call the kids over to eat and sit your ass down in the living room so I won't have to see your pansy face while I enjoy my food!"

Danny had gone over to the thirty-year-old's house and was having his way with her while her kid was still at school engaging in after-school activities. He had her standing on her hands while holding her feet up. He was asking her, "Who's your daddy? That's right, that's right, just take it all in and shut up. Enjoy the feeling of having a real man inside you. Be a good girl, and daddy will buy you an ice cream." She came while listening to his toxic dialogue.

She lost her balance as she felt an internal eruption and slumped over, causing his penis to bend inside her and pop out rapidly. He screamed out of pain, "FUCK! Damn, I think you broke daddy's dick!" He grabbed his cock in his hand to review it.

Carla stated, "I'm so sorry, daddy. Please forgive me. It was unintentional, and I was unable to keep my strength after having an orgasm. Let me massage it so you could feel better." She grabbed it in her hands and began gently massaging it.

Danny felt her touch and flinched a bit, causing him to take a step back. He felt the carpet in her room wet under his feet and looked down past her attending his shaft. He had made her squirt as well, and that turned him on. He shoved his membrane in her oral cavity and pushed her head in, making her gag. She placed her palms on his legs and tried pushing him off but was unable to do so. She gave in and threw up all over his penis. Danny heard her spewing; he removed his penis from her mouth and jumped back. He grabbed a pillow from her bed and began cleaning off the vomit dripping down his leg. He said, "Damn, baby, I must have not shaken the bottle correctly, and your stomach didn't like the milk I fed you."

Carla said, as she got up and helped him clean his shaft, "I'm sorry, daddy. It wasn't that; it's your hung cock that made me throw up. Please forgive me once more for my poor performance."

Carla then cleaned herself and tossed the pillow outside her room. She laid him in her bed and was about to place his dick back in her mouth when he said, "Hell no, baby! You need to brush your teeth if you want to keep sucking me off. I don't want you to get more vomit on it." She agreed and ran to her restroom to grab a wipe to clean the rest of her mess.

She gargled some mouthwash as she headed back to her room. She wiped his penis first and then the floor. She ran back to the restroom and threw the wipe then spat the wash out her mouth. She then went back to her bed and climbed on top of Danny, riding him until he came and then left.

The day was coming to an end; at Jesus and Mercedes's residence, the whole family had finished eating and were about to go to bed. Mercedes was in Jr.'s room tucking him in and following his request to read him a book. He asked her to read him a story of a little girl who wanted to be a boy. As she got halfway through the story, he fell asleep. She quietly got up from his bed and walked out of his room. She then went to her bedroom and saw Jesus applying his nightly facial cream that he had purchased from a guy selling it on Craigslist. The cream was composed of the man's male dog's semen, but Jesus was unaware of the actual ingredients. Mercedes shook her head and walked over to the kitchen to make him a testosterone-infused drink that she had been feeding him for approximately three months, with no success. When she got back to the room, he was lying down in bed, having already fallen asleep. She shook him up and made him drink the potion. After he did, she took the cup and placed it on top of the TV stand and lay in bed next to Jesus. She tried fondling him to get some sex, but he refused to cooperate, giving the excuse he was sleepy. She finally gave up—a bit irritated—and fell asleep herself.

CHAPTER 2
FEMNS NETWORK

The following morning, Mercedes woke up early as usual to head off to work. She got ready and took off as Jesus continued to rest his eyes. On her way to work, she dropped off her teens at school and then drove to her job. She had been at the same company for some years and was now a manager. When she arrived at work, she saw the female groundskeeper going around the garden at the front of the building, making sure the sprinkler system was functioning properly. She headed inside to begin her day. She walked over to the break room to make herself some coffee and then went to the floor to make sure everyone had arrived on time and had begun to take in calls. The phone lines were surging with male callers requesting more television channels for their paid programming. A new hire raised her hand for assistance. Mercedes walked over to her and asked for the issue. The employee stated, "This man on the line wants to know if we can offer him a package of only soap opera, cooking, shopping, and FEMNS Network?"

Mercedes told the employee, "Let him know we are not offering that package at the moment, but I will advise our corporate office about it so they could take it into consideration and make a decision since he's not the first to ask." The employee went ahead and informed the customer.

Mercedes was about to walk away and head over to her desk when she overheard a conversation taking place in the next cubicle. She turned her headphones on to the call and heard a male telling the employee, as he sobbed, "I want my money back. I've been trying your guys' product for a month now, and I can't grow any hair on my chest or rectum. I'm disappointed in your product, which I bought following favorable reviews online of previous clients whose testimony sold me."

Mercedes and the employee looked at each other. They wanted to laugh, but the employee replied, "Sir, you're calling a cable television customer service line. We don't sell any hair growth products, but I could assist you in anything related to your cable service."

The man responded, "Oh, you mean to tell me I dialed the wrong number?" The employee uttered, "Yes, you did."

The man said, "I'm really sorry and ashamed I just shared that with you. Would you be kind enough to keep that confidential?"

The employee commented, "No problem, mister. No one else listened to this conversation other than me." As she turned to look at Mercedes with a smile on her face, she then continued, "If there's anything else I could help you with, please let me know. Otherwise I hope you fix your issue and have a great day."

The man replied, "No, that was all. Thank you and hope you have a great day too." He disconnected the call just in time to not hear Mercedes and the employee laugh out loud.

Danny rose out of bed and checked his phone. He had an unopened text from Lucia, which informed him of the food Josefina had gone to pick up after work to take to him. He texted back, "Thank you, and I'm sorry I didn't answer your call yesterday. I was busy running errands."

His penis was sore, and he walked over to the kitchen to get an ice pack to place over his shaft. He checked the fridge and saw Lucia had sent him some flautas with rice and beans, which were his favorite. He also observed a note on the bagged food. He took it with him to his room along with the ice pack. When he got to his bed, he lay down in it again and placed the ice pack over his dick. He began to read the note Lucia had written to him:

Hello to the most wonderful man on earth. I tried getting a hold of you hoping you'd answer and visit to pick up your favorite food I made you. There's nothing else in this world that satisfies me more than being of any help to your life. I hope this meal cheers you up and keeps you content. I still reminisce about those days I cooked for you in our humble home as we raised our two beautiful daughters. I have a special place in my heart for you and always will. Love, Lucia.

Danny smiled on reading the note and said quietly, "Yup, she still wants the D." He turned on the television set after placing the note down next to him so he wouldn't have to stare at the ceiling while he iced his cock for ten minutes.

Jesus woke up and removed the sleeping mask from his face. He stretched in bed as he yawned, then looked outside the window at the brightness of the sun entering through the curtains. He sat up in his bed as he heard the front doorbell ring, getting up to go check who it was. When he got to the door, he peeked through the peephole and saw a delivery van driving off. He opened the door to find a package on the floor, which he picked up to take inside. He walked to the kitchen with the package that had his name on it. He placed it on top of the counter and opened it. It contained three pairs of shoes he had ordered online and a wig. He had forgotten about them, but on seeing them in front of him, he was happy. This reminded him he wanted to purchase some shirts, and so he went ahead and made the purchase online, which awaited him in the shopping cart. Mercedes had already warned him to stop buying so much unneeded stuff since he was paying with her money, but he didn't care. He felt irreplaceable since most of the real men were either already married or remained single as they didn't want commitment. He put his shoes away; then he tried on the wig and walked over to Jr.'s room. Jr. was lying in bed hugging a stuffed bear dressed in a flowery dress with a summer hat. Jesus smiled at his son, and then he walked back to the kitchen to serve himself some cereal to eat. He turned on the television set and saw a commercial from the government looking for male subjects for a study—the same information Nick, his neighbor, had shared with him the day before. Jesus grabbed his cell and dialed the number given in the ad. He spoke to an individual who asked him some questions and told him he'd send him a package for him to review and send back. Jesus hoped things would work out so his wife could get off his lazy feminine ass. His son woke up after listening to his call and came to the kitchen to greet his dad. Jr. said, "Good morning, Dad. Are we going to get our manicures done today?"

Jesus replied, "No, *mijo,* your mother said she wasn't going to pay for it, so we're out of luck. But we can paint them ourselves, if you don't mind."

Jr. uttered, "Alright, I guess we can." He walked over to his older sister's room to retrieve her nail polish bag, which she hardly used anymore.

When Jr. got back to the kitchen, he observed his father looking at dildos on his phone and asked, "What's that you're looking at, Dad?"

Jesus replied as he closed the window on his phone, "Oh nothing, Son, just some back scratchers I've been meaning to buy since I have a hard time reaching my back."

Jr. responded, "Can you get me one too, Daddy? I want one to scratch my back as well." Jesus said, as he put his phone away and looked at his son, "You know what, Son, I think I'll get us some later because your mom has been getting on my butt about buying too many commodities."

Jr. said, "I'm hungry, Dad. Could you serve me some cereal in my pink bowl and spoon?"

Jesus said, "Sure, Son." He got a bowl and spoon and served him some cereal to eat.

Jesus was watching his son eat when his phone received a notification. It was an email, and he opened it to read. It was the government package for the studies. He read it and began filling out a questionnaire. It took him as long as his son took to finish eating to fill it out and send it back. He and his son then began to paint their nails together while sitting at the kitchen table.

Josefina had woken up and walked out of her room to find her father lying in bed with an ice pack over his privates. She asked, "What the heck are you doing, Dad? Why do you have an ice pack over your junk? Did you hit yourself or something?"

Danny replied, "Yes, *mija,* I hit myself this morning on the couch when I woke up." Josefina said, as she walked back into her room to get dressed, "Ouch, hope you feel better."

Josefina and two other friends of hers had made plans to go drive around construction sites to see if they could spot any real men working after breakfast. Their plot was to hit up on those men in order to find themselves a mate. She heard a honk outside and ran out the door, letting her father know she'd be back later on before work. Josefina jumped into her friend's car, and they sped off. They arrived at a small diner soon after and took a seat by a window. They began chatting about their failed attempts in finding a man and compared tactics. They placed their order and ate. From there, they drove down to a nearby construction site. They pulled up on the site and searched for men at work. They saw some, so they exited the vehicle and walked over to them with some burritos; they had bought extra for such a case. Josefina was the bravest of the trio and walked up to a guy who was installing some plumbing for a building. She told him, "Hi, sorry to disturb you, but I brought you some food, just in case your wife didn't send you with lunch to work."

The man stopped what he was doing and said, as he continued working, "I don't have a wife but thank you for the gift. You can lay it down right there, and I'll eat it later."

Josefina placed a burrito next to his toolbox and stated, "So, how's the weather treating you today?"

The plumber responded, "Same as it is treating you, I guess."

Josefina uttered, "You work many hours here? What's your favorite part of the job?" The plumber commented, "What's with all the questions? Anyhow, I work a lot of hours, and my favorite part of the job is getting paid and going home."

Josefina was nervous to be in front of a real man and couldn't seem to gather the correct words to lure him in. Her friends too were terrified, and they just kept quiet as they watched her try to court him. Josefina said, "Wow, mine too. So, do you have any plans for tonight?"

The plumber replied, "Yeah, go home and get some rest."

Just as he finished replying to her, a group of female construction workers chased Josefina and her friends off. They yelled at them in a threatening manner, "Get the hell out of here! Leave our men alone and find your own!" The girls ran to the car and jumped inside, then darted out of there before they became casualties.

One of the female construction workers grabbed the burrito they had given to the plumber and threw it at the moving car. It flew right above the driver's side door and ripped apart, hitting the driver as the window was down. The rest flew over the roof and onto the front windshield. Josefina's friend shouted, as she swerved the vehicle almost crashing into a cement truck, "Ah! Fuck, they hit me with something. I can't see."

Josefina screamed, "Go! Go! Go! Watch out for that truck!" The driver had just about time to remove the food from her eyes and manage to avoid an accident.

Jesus was inside his house gossiping on the phone with one of his friends. He walked from his room to the kitchen to see what he could cook today. While searching through the fridge, he found some ground beef. He looked through the pantry to see if they had some spaghetti pasta and sauce. To his surprise, there was some, so he knew he wouldn't mess up this meal, and he got to preparing spaghetti. He told his friend on the phone while cooking, "Ay, I think Hugo is going to get eliminated from the show since he's been whoring around with all the girls." He was referring to a famous television show called *Mens-trual Season Three*, which just about every pansy was watching on the FEMNS Network channel. He continued, "He just banged Marcy, and her husband found out. Did you see?"

His friend Sam replied, "Yes! I saw that. Oh boy, he's been causing a bunch of problems with the rest of the guys since he's masculine. I kinda hope they kick him out of the show before he breaks more marriages and the network doesn't have a show to air. By the way, did you get your nails done after all?"

Jesus uttered, "No, Mercedes doesn't want to pay for them. Wish she was more like Nick's wife. She pays for everything without a complaint on what it is or what it's for."

His pal said, "How's Nick doing? I haven't seen him in forever. I don't even remember when was the last time I was at your house."

Jesus said, "He's alright, better than I am. He told me about this study the government is doing on guys, and if you get elected, they'll pay you well."

Sam said, "Oh yeah, I saw an ad on that. I was thinking of calling to see if they'd take me. I'd be honored to participate and find out why I'm so feminine. Like I'm always hungry and yet I don't know what I want to eat."

Jesus laughed and commented, "That happens to me too, ha, ha! I called and they sent me some documents through email. I filled them out and returned them earlier. Hopefully, they pick me so I too can find a cure to being so feminine. Like I like it in a way but then again I don't, you know?"

His friend said, "Yeah, I understand you absolutely." There was shouting in the background followed by two thuds.

Sam's wife had gotten home from work and smacked him around because he was on the phone gossiping, which she detested him doing. Sam uttered, "I'll call you back because she's mad at me. I'm going. Babe, stop. Stop hitting me, I'm going." There was a click at the other end of the conversation. Jesus still had his cell phone to his ear when he saw his wife walk in from work. He looked up at the ceiling and began to pray that she wouldn't beat him up like Sam's wife had done to Sam.

Lucia went over to Danny's house after Josefina had left for work. She was outside knocking on the front door. Danny knew she wanted to get her rocks off, but his penis was still in pain. So he decided to pretend he wasn't home. Lucia called his cell, and he rejected her call. She knew he was home since his truck was outside, and there wasn't another vehicle present there to indicate he may have company. She walked over to his bedroom and peeked through the window. She saw him standing by the door looking at it. She knocked at his window and said, "I can see you standing there, Danny."

Danny was startled, and he jumped, hurting his privates a bit as he squeezed his legs together. He turned around and saw his ex at his window. Walking over to the window he had left open, he said, "Hi, Lucia. How've you been? I'm sorry I didn't open the door. I thought it was some Jehovah's Witness. What brings you here though?"

Lucia replied, "I came to see if you had eaten the food I sent you and pick up the Tupperware if you're done with it. I was nearby paying some bills and decided to drive by to see if you were home. That's why I didn't call you because I saw your truck outside. You look good, Dan, always so handsome."

Danny stated, "Oh, well, go to the front door so I can let you in." She followed his directions.

Danny opened the front door and let her inside. She embraced him right away, smelling his chest and uttering, "You smell delicious."

Danny said, "Thanks. Now let me go grab those containers so you can be on your way." Lucia replied, "I'm not in a hurry. No need to rush. Why're you walking funny though?" She observed that he was walking bowlegged.

Danny said, as he got her trays out of the fridge, "I hit my nuts on the couch in the morning."

Lucia inquired, "Aw, I bet they hurt and need some soft caresses, huh?"

Danny responded, "Nope. You'll only agitate my pain and I want it to go away. Here is your Tupperware." He handed her property to her after keeping the food away inside his containers and putting some food in the microwave to warm up for consumption.

Lucia uttered, "So since you're in pain, there's no way you could fuck me, right?"

Danny stated, "Of course not, Lucia. Can't you see I'm hurting, and you want me to fuck you still? Stop being dick greedy. Maybe some other day but not right now. I know that's all you came for anyhow, with the excuse that you came for your containers. You probably planned it since yesterday; that's how sneaky you are."

Lucia took her trays from him, saying, "That is a lie, Dan. I did not plan anything out. I simply got turned on by looking at you right now and wanted some, but never mind. I can see you're not in a good mood. Thanks for returning the Tupperware. I'll see you some other time." She walked out and left.

Mercedes asked Jesus, "Who're you talking to on your phone and why're you looking up at the ceiling?"

Jesus answered as he placed his phone down, "I was talking to Sam. I was also praying you wouldn't come home to beat me."

Mercedes replied, "You better not be calling your mom and complaining to her that I mistreat you. She informed me the other day you told her I threw the TV remote at you. She also said you wanted to file a report for spousal abuse to the Husband Protective Services. Or are you ordering more junk that you don't need with my money? If I find out you've been shopping for stuff, I'm going to be pissed."

Jesus replied, "I wasn't talking to my mother. Please don't hit me or get mad at me. Look, I cooked some spaghetti—your favorite, honey."

Mercedes responded, "Did you burn it like you did yesterday's meal?" He stated, "No, babe. I didn't burn it. Want me to serve you a plate?" She uttered, "Where's Jr.?"

He commented, "He's in his room playing."

She said, "Serve me a plate then, while I go change in the room."

She walked to the back of the house and stopped at Jr.'s room to greet him, and then she went to change. Jesus grabbed a clean plate and served her some spaghetti. He then served himself and Jr. too. He placed the plates on the dining room table and took a seat to eat. He called out his son's name so he would join him. Jr. walked over to the table and took a seat to eat. Mercedes came back from the bedroom and questioned, "Why's there some shoe boxes in your closet? Didn't I warn you to stop buying junk?" Jesus's mouth was full, and as he attempted to speak, he began to choke. Mercedes said, "Why're you mumbling like an idiot? Answer me, why did you buy those shoes?" She then realized he was choking.

After a pause, Mercedes told him, "Better look up at the ceiling and ask God for help because I don't know what to do in these situations."

Jesus put his hands on his neck and looked up at the ceiling, asking for mercy. His maker answered by allowing the food to go down his esophagus and clearing his airway. He then grabbed some water and drank it to help flush down the rest. Mercedes saw he was better and took a seat at the table to eat. She told him, "I want you to return those shoes as soon as possible and get my money back."

Jesus responded, "OK, honey. I wanted to tell you also that I contacted the government study, and they sent me some forms to fill out and I sent them back. Hopefully they pick me so I can have some money to help out and get you something nice."

Mercedes uttered, as she ate her food, "That's good. Hopefully they do call and pick you. As far as getting me something, I'd rather they find a cure for your femininity and make it go away."

Danny sat down to eat the food he had warmed up. It was delicious, so good that had he not been hurt, he'd fuck the shit out of his ex. He turned on the television and observed a commercial regarding a study on men to be conducted taking place. He dialed Mercedes to inform her, "Hey, *mija,* I'm here watching TV, and this commercial came on about the government conducting studies on pansies like your husband. You might want to have him call."

Mercedes replied, "Hi, Dad, he's well aware of the studies and contacted them already. He says he's waiting on them to pick him or not."

Dan commented, "That's good, *mija.* Hopefully they find a cure for those sissies so this world can go back to normal. How're my grandkids doing?"

Mercedes stated, "Yes, I hope so too. They're doing good, Dad. Jr. is here eating with us, and the other two should be back from school in a bit. How have you been?"

Danny responded, "I'm alright, *mija.* Just here eating some food your mom made for me."

Mercedes inquired, "Is Mom there with you?"

Dan uttered, "No, honey. She was here earlier, but she left."

Mercedes said, "Oh, and what have you been up to?"

Danny replied, "Nothing, same thing as usual, you know. Well, I just called to inform you about the study. Say hello to the kids, and I'll talk to you later."

She commented, "Will do, Dad. Thanks for keeping Jesus in mind. See you later." They then hung up.

Jesus had finished only half of the food he had served himself. Mercedes asked him, "Why didn't you finish the rest?"

Jesus stated, "I don't want to keep gaining weight. I look fat as is. Just look at my flabby arms and stomach. I feel gross with myself. I always want to eat and I don't know what, but then I remember I shouldn't because I'm getting fatter. Hardly any of my clothes fit me comfortably anymore."

The older kids came back from school and took a seat to eat at the table with them. Jesus got up and began serving them as

Mercedes asked them how their day had gone. Danniel, the daughter, said, "Today we were making fun of men and their feminine children they've been producing." She looked at her little brother sitting across from her at the table wearing a dress and makeup.

Mercedes replied, laughing, "What men are you talking about, *mija*? It's only a title now without the work that goes with it. Just look at your stepfather and little brother. Don't they make the cutest mother and daughter ever?"

Jr. uttered, "Yes, we do, Mommy. Dad and I are super cute."

Chris, the eldest, commented, "Exactly her point, little bro." They laughed while Jesus's lips trembled as he tried to stop himself from sobbing.

Mercedes told Jesus, "So did you change out that light bulb in our room that went out?" Jesus responded, "No, but I'll get to it right away, honey." He placed the plates in front of Chris and Danniel.

Jesus walked toward the bedroom to see if he could fix the bulb. He turned on the light switch, but that didn't work. He looked at the switch and kept switching it on and off for a second. He then walked under the bulb to see if he could see anything wrong. Then he held a conversation with the bulb, saying, "Hey there, little buddy. How about you turn on, since the one in my head is off too and you're making it feel uncomfortable?" He then walked to the garage to see what tools he could find to carry out the task.

Jesus walked over to where the tools lay in the garage. He opened the toolbox and looked at them, wishing he knew which one to use. He had a small anxiety attack trying to figure out which tool was required for the job. He randomly grabbed a hammer and went back to the room. There he lightly hammered the light switch, hoping that would fix the issue. He turned it on, but there was no light. He then walked back to the garage to switch tools. He grabbed a wrench and walked back to the room. There he stood, scratching his head with the wrench as he was puzzled as to how he'd make it work. He went back to switch tools, and this time he had a screwdriver in hand. He saw the screws on the switch cover and began removing them, feeling satisfied that he'd figured it out. After unscrewing the switch cover, he removed it and looked inside. He observed the steel case housing for the switch and the wires hanging out of it. He poked the wires and tried turning on the switch, but nothing was gained. He saw the housing had screws too, and he began removing them as well. Just as he was about to remove the last one, Mercedes walked in and asked, "What the fuck are you doing? That's not how you switch a light bulb. Put the cover back on and screw it all back together, you fucking moron." He began to put it all back how it was.

She then went to the closet to retrieve a new light bulb and got a copper pot from the kitchen, informing her daughter to follow her and record the outcome. When they got to the room, Jesus had finished and was waiting for instructions. Mercedes told him, "You're going to get on top of the bed and remove the light cover, which has screws around the rim." He began following her instructions as she spoke, "Then you'll remove the cover and carefully place it down safely. From there, you're going to unscrew the bulb with your hand. You might want to place this copper pot on your head for safety purposes. After the bulb is removed, you're going to stick the screwdriver in the bulb housing to make sure it has current."

When Jesus did that, he got an electric shock and flew a few feet off the bed. He landed by their feet, with smoke coming out of his scalp. The girls laughed, as Danniel who was recording it said, "It's not Christmas yet, and you're already lighting up like a Christmas tree."

Mercedes laughed. "I've never seen the light bulb in your head shine as bright as it just did."

Jesus looked at them, crying and saying, "You guys are mean. You tricked me into hurting myself for your own enjoyment." Mercedes then got up on the bed and finished the task at hand, as

Danniel walked out to share the video while Jesus whimpered on the ground.

Josefina got out of work and met up with this guy she had met online, the one she had messaged on a dating app. They were to meet up at a bar and have a few drinks as they got to know each other better. Josefina showed up there to find the guy sitting at the bar, waiting for her. She knew who he was since he had shared his description with her prior to the appointment. She took a seat next to him and said, "Hi, are you my hot date?"

The guy replied, "Hello, yes, I am, and you're my future sugar momma, I mean baby momma, right?" They held quite a long conversation while having some drinks.

Josefina ordered some tequila shots, but he was reluctant to take his. He stated, "I don't like tequila."

She uttered, "Come on, show me you can handle a shot so I'll know you have chest hairs." That was a sign of masculinity most men lacked at the time.

He responded, "Alright then." He took the shot, and his lips puckered up—wanting to spew. He rapidly grabbed a lime from the counter and sucked on it.

Josefina laughed as they continued to drink and converse, till she asked him to follow her back to her home. They arrived at her residence and quietly snuck in without waking up Danny. She escorted him to her room, then threw him on her bed. She began taking off his clothes and hers as well. He whispered, "I see you're in a hurry, huh? You don't want to maybe drop it a notch so I can feel comfortable enough to perform?" She ignored him and lay next to him after undressing herself and him.

She began to touch his penis, which wasn't erect. He was perspiring with nervousness and kept taking her hands off his part.

She kissed him all over his hairy chest, and then it came off. He was wearing a chest weave in order to pretend he was a real man. She thought it was weird, but she was drunk and horny; plus, she had spotted their drinks all night and wanted sex in return. She grabbed his pecker once more and hopped over him to introduce it inside of her vagina. He pushed her off and said, "Sorry, I can't. This is my first time with a woman."

Josefina replied, "You mean to tell me you're a virgin? But you're in your thirties already. I mean I've seen an old film with the same storyline but never actually met one in real life."

The guy uttered, "Well, I'm not a virgin, virgin completely. I mean I've had anal before. Wanna try that?" He plopped himself up and bent over, giving her his back.

Josefina realized he was like the rest, a beta pretending to be alpha. She got up and grabbed her clothes and threw his clothes at him, ordering, "Get the fuck out of my house, you pansy. Why couldn't you just be honest and say you're fucking feminine?" The guy got up and took his clothes before running out of the room and home because Josefina had picked up a big dildo she had and was threatening to hit him with it.

The guy ran out with his clothes in his hands, naked down the street, and was out of sight as she closed the front door. She went back to her bedroom and used her sex toy for her pleasure. Once she came, she put her pj's on and went to bed.

CHAPTER 3

A RACE FOR A CURE

Jesus woke up in the comforts of his home after receiving a call on his cell. He answered the unfamiliar number on his home screen. It was a woman at the other end notifying him he had been preselected for the trial study. He was informed he'd have to present himself at their local facility as soon as possible to begin the process. He was given the opportunity to choose a time that best suited his agenda. He picked the time later in the evening when his wife would be home and able to care for Jr. The woman asked if he had any questions or concerns to which he replied, "How much will I get paid and when?"

The caller informed him, "You'll receive your first payment at the end of the week if the test results we obtain from you are concrete for candidacy." Speaking of blood and hair follicle exams they'd be performing on him when he'd show up to their facility, she continued, "You will be granted three hundred dollars per day of enrollment to the study, whether you are physically present each day or not. As long as you don't miss any appointments we make for you—excluding weekends as productive days. There's a bonus of ten thousand dollars after successfully concluding the study and not interfering with any of our requirements or annotated dates for exams."

Jesus uttered, "Wow! So there's a possibility of making some good cash with you guys, huh? That's great; now I'll be able to afford my BBL and hair implant procedure. Would you happen to know how long the study will take?"

The woman uttered, "Since you will form part of the first group and there has never been another, I can't give you an actual time frame, which is why the monetary reward for your cooperation and participation is high."

He commented, "Well, I'll be there later on to begin clocking in those three hundred per day. Thank you very much, and I'll see you there later."

The caller stated, "You're welcome, but you won't be seeing me there later on. I'm outside of your geographical location. Please call this number if you're unable to make it to your appointment, to cancel or postpone it. If there's anything else I could assist you with, please let me know now before we end the call."

He said, "OK, no, I have no further questions or concerns. Thank you very much and have a great day too." The call was disconnected as he turned on his television to watch the FEMNS Network channel.

Danny woke up feeling much better from his injury. He went to his kitchen to cook some eggs and bacon for breakfast. He observed several unread texts on his phone and began replying to several women, including Lucia as the food cooked over the stove's flame. Josefina woke up to the smell in the air and walked to the kitchen. She said, "Good morning, Pops. Smells good; what're you cooking?"

Dan replied, "Good morning, *mija.* I've got some eggs and bacon coming up. You're going to eat, right?"

Josefina answered, "Yes, I'm hungry and have a slight headache from last night."

He uttered, "Take some medication for the headache before you eat. About last night, what was all the commotion you had in your room?" She grabbed some pills from the kitchen cabinet and served herself a cup of water to take it.

Josefina responded, "I came home with a guy I met online last night. Sorry if I woke you up."

Danny stated, "No worries, but tell me how it went with this guy. Was he masculine?"

She commented, "It went horrible. He pretended well all through the night, and that's why I brought him back. He also told me he lived with his mother, so we couldn't go to his place. He was wearing a chest weave, can you believe that?"

Dan chuckled and said, "Are you serious? No way, you mean to tell me they sell chest weaves now for these pansies?"

She replied, "I am serious, Dad. I guess so, or either he made it himself. Anyhow, when we were in my room, I tried getting him excited, but he wouldn't. Then he told me he was half a virgin and was scared to lose it. He did mention he'd tried anal before, didn't specify if with another man or woman. That's probably when you woke up, because I kicked him out of the house. Since he put himself in the position for me to introduce something up his rectum."

Dan was cracking up and uttered, "That sounds like the kind of story to tell someone who needs some cheering up. Wow, these guys are hysterically entertaining in their attempt to fool women into believing they're macho." He began to serve them food and took a seat to eat.

Josefina thanked him for breakfast and responded, "I'm getting tired of searching for a real man, literally. Like whatever happened to being macho?"

Danny commented as he ate, "Well, that's a good question to ask. Your sister's husband hopefully will have an answer to this crisis. Heard he was enrolling in the government studies to find out just why. In a way, I don't mind myself that there's a surplus of pansies. I'm enjoying being in high demand, picking them as they come. But I know it's affecting my daughters, so therefore, I want this to be solved and see you two happy."

Chris was in class, joking around with his peers. One of them told him, "Hey, bro, so do your two moms get along at home? Or are they always fighting over who washes your sharted boxers?"

Chris replied, "Better than yours, buddy. I bet back in your house there's a battle for dominance where they measure each other's clitoris to see which one's longer. Then they settle their differences over a glass of wine and a deep conversation on insecurity."

The kid uttered, "Bet at yours they don't even fight. They just scissor up in bed and cut the bullshit. No need for competition when the dick is missing." They both began to laugh at their words.

Chris responded, "Look, bro, I know you brought it up because deep inside you want to get with my stepdad. You probably want to suck and chew on his micro pipi. I'll let him know of your interest for him, and by tomorrow, I'll clear your doubts."

His pal commented, "Yeah, bro, let him know I'm interested in pleasing your mom while you and he watch. I want each one of you to be holding one of my nuts so I won't bang them up on your mom's ass. Then I want your stepfather to put some ice in your mom's anus because I'm going to heat things up at home."

Chris stated, "I wouldn't doubt it my mom's clit is bigger than your dick, and she won't even feel enticed to entertain the thought of letting you bang her. I'll let her know your parents want her to go over and fuck them both in the butt with her overgrown clit. I'm sure she won't mind settling both their differences with an experimental threesome to humble your mom and dad by tearing both their asses apart. Then she'll probably wipe off the fecal matter on your fucking face in hopes it helps eliminate all those pimples you've got."

They both chuckled, which grabbed their teacher's attention, who told them, "Pay attention to the class or go home!"

Josefina got dressed and took off with her friends to go look for men at the stores. She figured they may be able to steal a married or taken one from an unsuspecting partner who had become complacent. They knew most men now stayed at home and did their shopping during the day. So they went to a grocery store to search at their first stop. They exited the vehicle and walked inside. The store was filled with men, but it was hard to distinguish the real ones from the fake ones, so they came up with a plan. They decided to try and argue with their targets and see their reaction in order to make a determination. Josefina's friend was the first to experiment with that tactic. She walked up to a guy who was looking at some tools. She bumped into the man and didn't apologize. She instead told him, "What're you looking at, you sissy? Better turn that gaze elsewhere before you ask for more trouble than you can bargain with." The man ran away from her believing her warning, which proved he wasn't macho.

Josefina took the next initiative and walked up to a guy who was browsing through the beer selection. She bumped into him and said, "Hand me a case of cold ones in front of you since you're in my way." The man looked at her and grabbed her request to hand it to her, failing her test as she walked away, leaving him with the brew in hand.

The last friend walked up to a guy who was trying to make up his mind whether to take mesquite charcoal with lighter fluid or the generic version that was self-lit. She ran up on him and smacked the lighter fluid out of his hands. The man looked at her with tears running down the side of his face and fear in his eyes. All three women knew then they had to go elsewhere to find a hard masculine man because the ones at the store were obviously soft and feminine. They left the store and got back into the car to drive to another location.

The three females decided to pay a visit to a local hardware store, hoping they'd find some real men there. They drove up to the parking lot, and as they exited the car, they saw a bunch of women loading up their trucks with building material they had bought. They walked through the front doors and looked around the store, observing that a large number of women were shopping there.

As they strolled through several aisles, they spotted a man looking at cement products. Josefina approached him with the same tactic in mind. She bumped into him and told him, "Watch where you're going, asshole."

The man turned to her and said, "You watch where you're going. I'm here minding my own business while you're just trying to compete to see who's manlier in a battle not intended for a soft female like yourself."

Josefina knew then she had found one. She stated, "I'm sorry, please forgive my clumsiness. I thought you were part of the feminine type. What's your name?" Her friends' eyebrows rose up in disbelief as they witnessed her finding a diamond in the rough.

The man uttered, "Part of the feminine type? I would rather cut my own balls off than have them shrink in the absence of testosterone. My name is Salvador; what's yours?"

She replied, "My name is Josefina. Do you need any help with those bags of cement? I could pay for them if you'd like."

The guy responded, "Josefina? That name sounds masculine. No, I don't need your help or money. I've got this all under control, thanks."

Josefina commented, "Well, I like what I see. Just look at those muscles under your clothes. Your broad shoulders are intriguing to watch. Can I touch you?"

The man said, "You're funny. You and the rest of the women in the city are desperate to find a real man, and at the first interaction with one, you begin a sexual pursuit. No, you can't touch me, and leave me alone before I break your heart."

Josefina said, "Break my heart if you want. Matter-of-fact, break it while breaking my bed. Let me take you home, and you can stop working. I'll take good care of you and treasure your existence."

The man said, "No, thanks. I don't want to be supported and kept at home like a dog. Now, you and your friends move out of my way so I can pay for this." He proceeded to the cash registers with a few cement bags. Josefina and her friends had a smile on their faces as they followed him at a distance to watch him pay for his material.

He observed them stalking him and so did a robust woman who was in the line behind him. The woman told Josefina and her friends, "You girls run along and leave this man alone. It's clear he's not interested in any of you, and you're just making fools of yourselves by stalking him. Have some dignity and accept his rejection." Josefina and her friends hadn't realized they had grabbed the attention of a bunch of butch female shoppers who had mean looks on their faces. So they took the advice and left the store. Her friends dropped off Josefina, and she got ready to go to work.

Mercedes had got back from her job and entered her home. Jesus was waiting for her to arrive so he could go check in at the study facility. He told her he was leaving for his appointment and left in his car. When he got to the location, he had a hard time finding a parking spot. There were a ton of cars there and a long line of guys waiting to be tested and officially selected. He found a spot from a candidate who was leaving and parked his vehicle. He then got out and walked over to check in. There was a sign-in book inside, and he filled out his name in it; then he took a seat in the lobby next to a bunch of guys who were there for the same purpose. While waiting to be called, he heard a conversation where one guy was telling another, "I've heard that companies are selling counterfeit testosterone, and it's killing consumers."

The other man stated, "I wouldn't doubt it. You know what I heard? That a sure way to increase testosterone is by ingesting semen from a macho man. Only thing is, they won't just hand it out to you if you'd ask for it."

The first guy uttered, "So how would you go about doing that? I mean, it might work if you offer them money for their semen like a sperm bank."

The other replied, "True, but I think they'd get offended and suspect you may use it for resale or to impregnate a woman, and then he'd have to pay child support or something."

The first guy responded, "Well, you can also maybe contact the wife or partner to see if she'd be willing to share or sell it to you."

Jesus butted in, "What if you just hit up on her and suck it out of her vagina? Will that work?"

Both guys turned to look at him, and the second guy uttered, "Well, it might work, but then again I think it will be easier to buy it than using your method."

Jesus inquired, "Does it have to be human male semen or could you just get a dog and milk it?"

The first guy replied, "That's a good question. Do you know if it's possible?" He looked at the second guy.

The man uttered, "I don't think it's possible. To be exact, I'd rather try it from a human than a dog or any animal."

Jesus commented, "Well, that's something to think about. You guys just gave me some ideas to try myself. Hopefully my attempt isn't in vain and it works." He then heard his name being called for the first exam and excused himself as he walked toward the voice calling him.

Josefina was at her worksite, observing the machine assigned to her—she did quality sewing on the garments her factory produced. She was approached by her male supervisor who had been trying to get with her for weeks. Her manager told her, "Hello, beautiful. How're you doing today? You look stunning. When are you going to let me take you on a date?"

Josefina said, "Thanks, but I've told you before you're not my type. I can't accept your offer due to that reason."

Her boss stated, "Can you be more specific on what you're looking for? I mean it would help me in my intent if I knew what kind of guys you're attracted to."

Josefina uttered, "Well, for one, I like real men with masculine features. Broad shoulders and a deep voice, as explained in the book I've been reading called *A Guide to Get the Guy* by Amador Amado."

Her supervisor uttered, "I have broad shoulders and a deep voice. I'm just what you're searching for, honey. Look no more."

Josefina replied, "You don't have broad shoulders; you pop them out to appear as if you did. You also don't have a deep voice; you just make it sound deeper to disguise your little feminine one."

Her manager commented, "You're very wrong about me. I don't pretend to be anything I'm not."

She responded, "Look, Gil, I don't want to upset you or hurt your feelings. Please drop it and let me work in peace. Nothing you tell me will change my mind about how I feel and think about you. It's not a debate since my mind and perception of you have been made and remain the same."

He said, "Just give me a shot, girl. I promise I won't disappoint you."

She fumed, "A shot of what? Testosterone? No! You've already disappointed me by continuing to pursue me while I reject you. That's a sign you're not masculine enough for me. I also saw how Jenny beat you up outside of work the other day. You got your ass beat by a woman, and then you had her fired for telling the facility manager about it. I also heard she beat you up because you kept insisting for her to date you. That day I saw your shoulders at their normal position and heard your little feminine voice. I don't want that scenario to recur with you and me, so just leave me alone already." He was about to rebut it but knew it would be best if he'd walk away and take the L.

Danny had Carla at his house. She had volunteered to go over and cook for him since she felt guilty for hurting his pecker. She was in his kitchen making some shredded beef sopes. Danny was sitting, observing her and replying to her conversation. The front doorbell rang, and he got up to check who it was. Lucia was standing outside, waiting for him to open the door. Dan opened the door and asked her, "Hey, what're you doing here?"

Lucia replied, "Josefina told me to come by and grab some shoes of hers she wanted to drop at the cobbler since she didn't find the place I had told her about."

Danny told her, "Did she tell you where she left them for you?"

Lucia uttered, "She said she'd leave them on her bed; if not, she may have forgotten and has them in her closet."

Dan stated, "Well, wait here, and I'll go get them for you."

Lucia pushed the door in, wondering why he was acting erratically.

Danny told her, "Look, I have a visitor, and I don't want any problems like last time when you tried fighting my ex off."

Lucia responded, "I won't cause any issues with you. I'm just here for the shoes, and I'll be on my way." Dan let her inside as he walked to Josefina's room to get the shoes.

Lucia saw Carla and introduced herself, "Hi, I'm Lucia, Danny's ex-wife." She was immediately jealous of Carla since she was younger and better looking than her.

Carla said, "Oh, nice to meet you. I'm Carla, Danny's girlfriend."

Lucia told her, "I'm surprised he even has a girlfriend. I left him as he has a small package and acts feminine. Plus, he snores at night and has homosexual tendencies." None of what she said was true, but her intention was to scare her away.

Carla commented, "Well, I've seen his package and it's not small. I don't care if he snores, and I know for sure he's homophobic and doesn't like men at all. I don't see why you would be degrading him like that to me. Could it be that you still like him and are jealous?"

Lucia replied, "It could be. I mean, look at you and look at me. I will be honest with you; we still have sex every now and then."

Carla uttered, "Well, that's no reason to dishonestly try and belittle him. I also don't care if you two have sex. Have you not seen how hard it is out there to find a real man like him? Women, including myself, are willing to share these rare creatures. I've even known a few who'll fight for theirs. So we're either going to have to share him willingly and get along with each other or we're going to give him problems to where he'll eventually replace us both with four more women for his collection."

Lucia stated, "You have a good point. I mean if you at your age and with your looks are having a hard time, I can only imagine myself, although, even if he was to get rid of us, I'd still be part of his life since I'm the mother of his daughters."

Carla told her, "You're right, but it doesn't mean he'll be seeing you as anything else other than his daughters' mother. Just as he does now. How about we call a truce and stop this nonsense already? You're interrupting my cooking."

Lucia stuck her hand out and said, "Fine, guess we'll be friends and associates. Who knows for how long, but if you're willing to share him, then so am I. What're you cooking there?"

Danny came back right in time to not see them argue. He informed Lucia he couldn't find the shoes and asked her to get them. Lucia walked to her daughter's room, after Carla told her she was cooking sopes, and went through her closet. She found the shoes, and then she said goodbye to Dan and told Carla, "It was very nice to meet you, Carla. See you around." As she left the house, she had cooled down a bit and got rid of the thought of using violence against her.

Jesus filled some vials for blood work, and then he was told to take a seat back in the lobby. He followed the personnel back to the waiting lobby and sat in his previous chair. The two guys he'd talked to before were seated in their same places and continued to discuss rumors they'd heard about increasing testosterone levels naturally. The first guy said, "I've heard many guys say Ashwagandha, onions, and other things work. They did say it was only temporary, so I don't know of any product out in the market with good long-term reviews."

The second dude replied, "Me neither. The only thing that makes sense other than administering a dosage that is hard to find and expensive would be getting a natural dosage from a man with high volumes of testosterone."

Jesus told them, "I know a few real guys out there. For one, my father-in-law is macho. Maybe I could ask him for a sample?"

The first dude uttered, "Imagine how much your father-in-law will feel violated should you bring it up to his attention. Or the embarrassment he'll face if he assists you. I don't think it would be a good idea. Then there's the other source available, which would be an actual sperm bank. But they're hard to come by due to the lack of women who want to bring a child into this world and run the risk of it being a feminine male. So where else could one find some macho man semen?"

The second guy said, "How about placing an ad online and offering a reward for the exchange of sperm? I have a feeling that would work, don't you, guys?"

The first dude responded, "The macho men out there have money to begin with. And now that they're not pursuing women, they have plenty to spare. Why would they be interested in selling their fluids? They're not even giving them for free to the women chasing them."

Jesus stated, "I seriously believe it would work if you'd fool a woman who has a real man. Just think about it. Women are just getting accustomed to this change. Most of them are having difficulties determining who is who. There are so many of us out there, fooling females still. If the only possibility of raising our testosterone levels is by consuming human sperm, then that would be the easiest and most effective way. I still would consider utilizing animal semen though." He fixed his wig.

The second guy retorted, "It wouldn't work with animal semen. It would be ineffective to even consider it. The person who shared this finding with me advised me not to try animal sperm. I too had that idea in mind at the time."

Jesus uttered, "Well, I guess I'll be dipping the bucket into the water well." The men's names were called, and they went in for their final exam.

Jesus took the time to text his wife and have her ask her father if he'd be willing to donate some of his sperm. She texted back, "You're funny. You actually think my dad would want to share his semen with you? I'm sure even asking him for it would make him lose more respect for you. Just imagine what he'll tell you when he sees you. Hey, what does my cum taste like, you cum bucket? No, I'm not going to bother him with that nonsense. If you want to ask, you ask him yourself."

Jesus wrote back, "You're right. Never mind, I'll just figure out another way."

Josefina was still at work, and she was on her online dating application, searching for her soulmate during lunchtime. She was reading about a guy who had an impressive bio on his listing. He stated, "I'm looking for a woman who can handle a real man. Not looking for a mother figure to provide and support me. I am always working and don't have much time to go out. I can make an exception for the right female who's on the same page as I. My perfect mate would have to be very feminine, loving, caring, and beautiful. I enjoy taking time off from my busy life to travel and create new experiences. I enjoy trying new places to dine at, hunting, off roading, fishing, and hiking. I love the outdoors and getting away from civilization. My preferred date would include anything we both agree on."

Josefina sent him a message and hoped for the best. He was online at the moment and responded to her faster than she could finish her meal. He wrote, "Hey, you too have a desired description on yours. How long have you had your listing up for without any luck?"

Josefina responded, "Thanks, well, I've had it up for a little over a year. Took it down a couple of times because all I caught were duds. It's a never-ending adventure to find a macho nowadays. I'm sure it's kinda similar for you with being catfished by butchy females pretending to be feminine, right?"

The guy replied, "Lol, yeah, you got that right. So are you catfishing? I know I mentioned I like fishing but not that kind of fish. Are your pictures updated and official or have you manipulated them for bait?"

Josefina wrote, "That's how I really look. The one where I'm wearing a red dress was like three weeks ago. I'd consider myself very feminine. I don't work at a construction site or anything like that. I also don't know how to fix things around the house or cars.

I still get my hair and nails done too. How about you? How manly are you really?"

The guy commented, "Is that so? Well, just what I'm looking for. I'm manly enough to fight for what's mine. I enjoy fixing things around my house and cars. So far you seem to be the one here I'm more interested in. Maybe we could set something up should you not slip up, lol. Anyhow, I have to get back to what I was doing. Talk to you later."

She texted, "You sound and look extremely manly. I'll have to take your word for now. That's rare to find nowadays, a man who still enjoys working on his house and cars. I look forward to hearing from you later because I too have to get back to work myself." She finished her food and clocked back in to work.

Jesus had gotten out of the facility. They had informed him his blood work would be reviewed and they'd get back to him as soon as they received the results to let him know if he was suited for candidacy. He walked over to his vehicle and got in. By then the parking lot had cleared out. There were only a few remaining test subjects left after him. He turned on the ignition and drove out of there—headed back home. He was driving while listening to Cardi B music at high volume. As he got to his first stop at a red light, he noticed some guy next to him looking at him strangely. He turned to look at him but didn't recognize him. So he turned around to face forward as the light turned green. He continued to drive while texting his wife back, who was hurrying him up to get home. Suddenly the guy who was gazing at him at the traffic stop cut him off and hit his brakes in front of him. Jesus almost hit the back of his car, and then the guy sped up and pulled to the right and so did Jesus. By the time Jesus pulled out of traffic, the guy had gotten out of his car. He ran up to Jesus's ride and opened his door. The man grabbed Jesus's long hair and pulled off his wig; he then grabbed him out of his vehicle. Jesus and the man began pulling each other's hair and yelling obscenities at each other. The man shouted, "You fucking moron! You almost made me crash into you as you pulled out of the building while texting! Then you did it again just before I cut you off!"

Jesus replied, "That's no reason to get violent. I'm sorry I got distracted. Let go of the little hair that remains and I'll let go of yours, so we can talk this out like feminine men." They both let go of each other's hair.

The man said, "You shouldn't be texting and driving. It's dangerous and a crime if caught by police."

Jesus uttered, "I know, and I'm very ashamed and sorry I did. It's just my wife is on my ass to get home fast, and I don't want to disappoint her or get her mad." He picked up his wig from the ground and placed it back over his head.

The guy responded, "My wife too has been on mine to get home, which is why I was frustrated before you cut me off. Guess this talk helped us both to figure out why we're in a bad mood. I'm sorry I assaulted you. Will you forgive me? Maybe we could go have some margaritas together some day and vent about our wives?"

Jesus said, "Yeah, we sure have a lot in common to understand each other. Sure, bro, I love margaritas. Let me get your number and we could plan something for this weekend or next." They exchanged numbers, got back in their cars, and drove to their demanding wives.

Josefina got another message from the guy later on, and they continued to talk more. They ended up making plans for the night after she'd get off work. She was excited. She texted her friends to let them know she believed she had struck gold with a real man.

They congratulated her and asked her to update them on how her date had turned out. They also asked if she'd keep them in mind if he was a real man and hook them up with his single macho friends. She assured them she would and continued to text him while she was working. Gil—her supervisor—walked past her and observed her using her phone, which was a company violation. He told her, "Get off your phone so you can see if the machine needs readjusting on its sewing pattern. You know I could write you up for it, right?"

Josefina replied, "I'm sorry. It won't happen again." She put her phone inside her pant pocket and kept her eye on the machine's production.

Gil uttered, "I can let this one slide if you send me a nude of your ass."

She fumed, "That's sexual harassment, and I refuse to work under these conditions!"

Gil stated, "Well, first you'd have to prove it. I'm just going to write you up then."

She informed him, "Well, proving won't be hard to do since I actually turned my phone's voice recorder on. That's what I was doing with my phone when I saw you walking my way."

Gil commented, "You sneaky little punk. Show me your phone and the recording of my voice."

Josefina said, "Nope, I'm going to use it as leverage should you write me up in retaliation to my rejections. You can either take my word or call my bluff." Gil decided to not write her up and walked away.

Jesus had gotten back home, and Mercedes was watching a movie in the living room, waiting for him. She saw him walk in, and she got up from the couch and ran toward him. She grabbed him by his wig and pulled it off; then she grabbed his hair and asked, "Why'd you take long to come back? Did you really go to get tested or were you at your mom's house gossiping?"

Jesus said, "Ouch! Let go of my hair, please. My scalp already hurts from getting into an altercation with another motorist experiencing road rage. I did go to the test site; look at the paperwork I have in my hand. My mom doesn't want me around much anymore because she says I'm too feminine and I always ask her for money to buy stupid things."

Mercedes grabbed the paperwork in his hands and told him, "Let me find out you're lying to me and I'll send you back to your mother's house with all your shit packed. Damn, your head is balding too much." She then let go of his hair, handing him the follicles she had ripped off.

Jesus started crying and ran to their bedroom. He took off his clothes and crawled into bed. Moments later, Mercedes walked in and tried consoling him. She offered him sex, but he stated he had a headache and rolled over to the other side to face away from her, falling asleep.

CHAPTER 4

SEARCHING FOR A SOURCE

Mercedes woke up, and as she was getting ready, she heard a strange noise coming from outside the bathroom window. She thought of calling Jesus to check but remembered he was feminine and would wait on her to go check first before anything. Their dog, Mut, who was half rottweiler and half husky, was barking. She opened the window and saw some stray cats were fighting and told Mut to shut up. She then closed the window up and hopped in the shower. When she finished, she woke up her kids to get ready to go to school. She made some quick breakfast for them, egg and cheese burritos, to devour on their ride to their destinations. When Danniel and Chris were ready, she went to Jr.'s room and saw him sound asleep just like his dad, lying on his stomach—ass popping out with his thumb in his mouth. She went to him and took his thumb out, but he whimpered and placed it back in. She then strolled through the house to the living area and took off to drop the kids at school and head to her jobsite.

As she was dropping off her kids at school, she observed just how many feminine men were there to do the same, still wearing their sleeping clothes. Things sure had changed through the years, and she was beginning to see no hope. She had thought by now there'd be flying cars, but with the lack of machos willing to risk their lives, those plans were put on hold. Most men were now afraid of their own shadows, let alone fly in an automobile across the sky. Women were actually not interested in aircraft, so when the first company produced their product, it didn't sell enough to keep the company afloat. The company went bankrupt, and all projects were canceled due to the lack of consumers. The owner of the company invested his remaining assets on testosterone supplements and was now their leading distributor. He was able to bounce right back from his loss, so it turned out alright for him.

Arriving at work, Mercedes walked into the building. She went to get some coffee and ran into one of the other floor managers who told her, "Good morning. Have you been getting multiple requests for feminine men packages? My people are going berserk with the idea, and I ran it by the management. If they make a decision on it and begin to offer it, I'll be getting a bonus for the new customers it attracts. I'll be using the money to buy some testosterone for my husband, so he may be one of the few guys out there to make a full recovery from his feminine curse." Mercedes had brought it up to the management as well and wondered who had done it first to see who was actually getting the bonus.

> She asked her colleague, "When did you submit your idea?"
>
> Her coworker said, "Just yesterday. Hopefully they like it and make a move that'll make the company profit."

Mercedes was relieved since she had submitted the same idea a few days before her. She replied, "Yeah, I hope so too. Where would you get the testosterone from and how much does it cost?"

> She responded, "I'd get it from the leading manufacturer in natural testosterone (TEST1), and it runs about a thousand per month supply."

Mercedes uttered, "Wow, it's expensive, huh? That's like a car payment."

Her colleague explained, "It isn't a swap meet product though. It's been proven effective in as short as three months to reverse the male structure back into becoming masculine. Well, good talking to you. I've got to get to work now." She left, and Mercedes quickly googled the product and made a link for it in hopes she'd get the bonus and be able to get it for Jesus.

Jesus was woken up by Jr., who told him, "Dad, I peed on myself."

Jesus replied, "I told you to stop sitting down to pee. I know you were born with a micro pipi, but you need to make an effort in standing up without peeing on yourself. One way or another, you have to find out how not to piss on yourself. Go change into some clean clothes while I get up to make us breakfast." Jr. ran to his room to change. Jesus got out of bed and headed to the kitchen. He had begun making some eggs with chorizo when Jr. showed up to the kitchen wearing a new set of clothes. Jesus asked him, "Did you clean up any mess you made in the restroom?"

Jr. stated, "I didn't get any on the floor mat, just on my pants." Jesus uttered, "OK, well, sit down to watch TV while I finish cooking."

Jesus then remembered what those two guys at the facility had been saying about consuming semen, and he got on his phone to search for women he knew who had a macho male. He found a few on his social network application and contacted them in a flirtatious manner. He thought to himself, *If their husbands get mad and they approach me, I'll ask to blow them in return and get it straight from them instead—without getting my ass beat.* The food was ready, and he served himself and his son a plate. As they both sat down at the table to eat, he imagined how it would be to eat out a woman and suck up sperm from her vagina. He was grossed out about putting his mouth on a pussy but was alright with swallowing semen. As he drank some milk, he imagined himself gulping down some macho fluid. His son was looking at him, and he asked, “Why’re you smiling while drinking milk, Dad?”

Jesus replied, “It’s delicious, isn’t it? That’s why I’m smiling, thankful for the cows that provide it.”

Jr. commented, “I’d rather have it with strawberry syrup. I don’t like regular milk.” They continued to eat and discuss their differences and preferences.

Danny was awake at home. Carla was there making him breakfast before she headed to work. Josefina woke up and went to the kitchen after hearing an unfamiliar voice. Danny introduced them to each other, and they had a lot to talk about since they were only a few years apart in age. Danny interrupted their conversation by asking Josefina, “How’d it go last night? I heard you coming in late. Did you catch yourself a macho?”

Josefina said, “You won’t believe me. I went out with this guy who seemed to have the right stuff. We met at a restaurant for a late dinner. He was wearing a tight spandex shirt, and I kept noticing his muscles were off. I met him online, and he seemed to be very manly in writing, and he pretended well in person also. We seemed to be hitting it off, then his bicep ended up on the side of his arm halfway through the meal. I asked him what was wrong with his arm, and he told me he had a bicep implant because he had blown it a few years ago in a weightlifting competition and his real one was unable to grow properly. I kinda believed him, but then his other arm’s triceps began connecting with his bicep, and his pectorals moved around as well. Turns out he had modified his body with muscle implants to appear muscular since he was unable to obtain the results he desired. I knew then he was faking macho and walked out, leaving him the bill to pay."

Danny was cracking up, unable to stop. He said as he chuckled, "These pansies are getting muscular augmentations to deceive you all now? Ha, ha, that's fucking funny. Ha, ha, oh my God, I can't believe it. First the chest weave and now the muscle implants. That's hilarious, ha, ha, ha!"

Josefina told Carla, "Yeah, you're lucky to have found my dad. It's a feeding frenzy out there with these feminine men who want women to take care of them."

Carla stated, "I know how lucky I am, believe me." She kissed Danny on the cheek. Danny told Josefina, "Why don't you come to the gym with me in a bit? So you can maybe find yourself a good real man there."

Josefina inquired, "You think I'll find one there? How come I hadn't thought of that?"

Dan replied, "Yeah, you'll find one there for sure. You'll also find a few sissies, but you'll be able to tell the difference by looking at their physics. These feminine pansies can't grow big muscles unless they're using testosterone. You'll find them in the aerobic classes and a few hurting themselves by attempting to pick something too heavy."

Carla told Josefina, "Your dad is right about that. I hope you find yourself a real man there. It was nice meeting you. I've got to go to work now." She said bye to Dan and Josefina and walked out of their residence as Danny and Josefina ate what she had made.

Jesus had gotten a few responses from the women he had messaged. One had warned him about her husband, and the other was happy to hear from him since she hadn't seen him since high school. She told him, "I remember you were a dork who couldn't get girls. Now you're actually married. I'm surprised to hear that coming from you. I hadn't even noticed you posting pictures of her before, just now that I'm going through your profile."

Jesus wrote to the other girl first, "Tell your husband I don't care. I want to eat you out and fuck you doggy style." He pretended to be macho for his plot as he sat in the toilet releasing his fluids.

He then replied to the other one, "Yeah, I've been married for some time now. I'm kinda getting bored of her though. She's becoming masculine, and we fight all the time. She doesn't know how to dress to my standards. I come home from work and find her trying to use my exercise equipment. I think she's taking testosterone. Anyhow, maybe we could link up some day and catch up? I'm sure by now you're losing interest in being married too and would be searching for a macho like me, if you knew of one."

The old friend responded, "I might just take you on your offer. My husband has become a bit soft, and I don't know how to tell apart a feminine from macho. I'm still very feminine myself though. So you tell me when and where we could meet up?"

Jesus heard the front door open, and he threw his phone in the sink, believing it was his wife back early from work. It was his stepson Chris who had felt ill and ditched the rest of his classes. He then picked up his phone from the sink and replied, "I'll let you know later, girl. I've got to go to work now." He ended the conversation just as Chris grabbed some medication from the fridge and went to his room.

Danny and Josefina took off after finishing their meal. They arrived at the gym and got out of the car. As they entered, there was a woman at the front counter who greeted Danny, "Hi. Are you back for more gains? I still can't believe you look so good for your age, you GILF."

Dan said, "Hey! Thanks, it's all in the hard work and dedication I've put in over the years. This is my daughter, Josefina. She'll be joining me today as a guest."

The employee replied, "Oh, hi, nice to meet you. You've got such an amazing father. You guys go right ahead. Your father will show you where things are and what to do."

Danny and Josefina strolled through the gym, heading toward the back where the free weights were located. Danny told Josefina, "I'm going to get my first set in, so you can either go check out the guys or work out with me."

Josefina stated, "I'll just sit down on this bench and look. If I see someone, I'll ask you for your opinion and then take it from there."

Danny grabbed some fifty-pound dumbbells and began curling them after his stretch. He put his headphones in his ears to listen to rock as he exercised. Josefina observed her father lifting while scanning around for a macho man. She noticed a few guys nearby who didn't really attract her much. A group of three were squatting lite, spotting each other while gossiping and being touchy with themselves. She then extended her gaze and observed two guys walk in through the front door. She found one kinda enticing, but then changed her mind as she saw he and his pal enter the aerobics class. She turned to her left and witnessed a strong guy benching heavy. He looked like he was in his late thirties to early forties. She was impressed and decided to walk by him to get a closer look at his face. As she passed by him, she saw he wasn't bad looking. She went back to her dad to ask him if he knew the guy. Danny removed his ear pieces and replied, "That guy is macho, sweety. He isn't a fake. He has been coming here as long as I have. Thing about him is he isn't interested in women and turns down just about every single one who approaches him. Give it a try though, tell him I sent you." He placed his ear pieces back on and continued with his reps.

Josefina walked over to the guy and introduced herself, "Hi, my father, Danny, tells me you're a real macho."

The man dropped the bar on the bench and got up to see who was talking to him, then replied, "Danny is your dad?"

She uttered, "Yeah, do you know him?"

He stated, "Yes, he's a good guy. Always here working out. I've had a few conversations with him. But I don't understand why you're here asking me if I know him. Because he said I was macho?"

She responded, "Well, I'd like to get to know you. I find you attractive, and I'm looking for a man in my life."

He commented, "I don't know about that. See, I've been focusing on myself for some time and enjoy being alone. I wouldn't want to have a woman ruin my peace and happiness again."

She mentioned, "I won't ruin your peace and happiness. All you have to do is get to know who I really am."

He said, "I'm going to pass. Sorry, but I'm not looking for a woman right now." She was embarrassed he had turned her down, but she understood and walked back to her father's location.

Jesus got himself and his son ready, and they took off for his mother's house. Jesus rang the doorbell, but his stepfather was hesitant to open the door since he always felt his attention was threatened by Jesus. His mother walked over to the front door and pushed her husband out of the way. She opened the door and greeted her son and grandchild, letting them in, and they took a seat on the living room couch. His mother asked, "What brings you here? I don't have any money to loan you and I haven't made food yet either."

Jesus replied, "Don't worry, Mom. I'm just here to share some good news with you. I've been preselected to take part in the research on feminine men. I will soon make you proud by becoming masculine again."

It had somewhat to do with how he was now as compared to how he had been brought up. His stepfather had married his mother when he was about five years old. His stepfather was feminine himself and had been unable to raise Jesus correctly. Jesus also had an older sister; she and their mom would treat him femininely. They babied him too much and treated him as their own kind. The stepdad had been always working and hadn't cared to raise a son that wasn't his. So he was left with no other alternative but to see his mother and sister as role models. He dressed in their clothes and high-heeled shoes and wore makeup while playing. Kinda like his son, who was reliving his childhood. His biological father had run out on them for the same reason. He was ashamed to have given birth to a sissy. He would drink heavily and beat his mom up. He then found something better since his mother wasn't quite attractive enough to hold down a man with options. His stepfather, Tito, had gone to his room as he talked with his mom, Hilda. She was replying to him in reference to his good news, "Hey, *mijo,* you know I don't think it was meant for you to be masculine. That's why you've always struggled with women and played with your sister's dolls. You are a great dancer though, all because your sister and I would make you dance with us. You're lucky to have found yourself a wife and had a kid. You know you're not attractive or smart. Just look at your receding hairline, your thin hair, which evidently is falling off. Your big ears, your little scrawny body, your big teeth, and your little feminine voice. Don't forget the little pecker you came with. I feel sometimes you're a transgender who got lucky enough to grow a small winnie."

Jesus was listening to his mom offend him and uttered, "OK, Mom, I get it. You're not proud of me now and might never be. You believe I'm just a girl stuck in a man's body. I, on the other hand, have high hopes of becoming masculine and making my wife happy." He got up from the couch and grabbed his son to depart his mother's house.

When they exited the house and got to his car, the husband of the woman he had messaged spotted him. He got out of his car and approached him. Jesus knew then he was facing problems his cowardly self could not bear. The husband, angered by his disrespect, was about to beat his ass when his stepfather walked out and said, "Whatever you want with him, take it outside of my property." He closed the front gate to his driveway.

Jesus began walking backward as he argued, "But why? Why do you want to hit me?"

The man said, "You know damn well why, you fucking pussy!"

Jesus tried apologizing, and the man stopped as he got a chance to think about what he was doing. He realized he was at Jesus's family's residence and believed Jesus would call the police if he got beaten by him. He foresaw all this just by Jesus's cowardly actions of not wanting to fight. That would make him look bad and get arrested not only for the assault but also because he had gone to his family's home looking for trouble. So the guy left while Jesus and his stepdad almost shit their pants. Jesus and his son got in his car ,and Jr. asked him, "Who was that dad and why did you scream like he was going to kill you?"

Jesus replied, "He was some guy who wanted to rob you. So if you ever see him again, run from him like I just did." That caused his son to worry.

Josefina had gone back to her dad and informed him of what had happened with the guy benching. Danny told her, "See, I told you he wasn't interested in women. He's not gay; he just doesn't want to deal with females anymore. Check out that guy over there; he might be interested. He's coming out of a relationship. I've never had a word with him, but he seems like a good guy. Why don't you go talk to him while I continue my sets?" Josefina walked toward the guy her father had pointed out.

As she walked up to him, she saw he was drinking some pre-workout supplement and getting ready to exercise. Josefina said, "Hi, are you new here?"

The guy replied, "No, but you are. I've never seen you around." She extended her hand to him and introduced herself.

The guy stated, "Nice to meet you. Do you want me to show you how to work out or something?"

She uttered, "Yes, would you be kind enough to let me work out with you?"

He commented, "Sure, I'm working out my legs today. So follow me and do as I do." She acted in accordance with his routine.

They did a few sets of squats. Then they did some leg extensions and leg curls, followed by some calf raises. She tried her best to keep up with the guy as she got to know him a little. He had informed her he was single and had just broken up with his girlfriend of six months because she was trying to dominate him. She told the guy, "That's too bad. Good thing is, there are plenty of women out here looking for men like you, for instance myself."

The guy said, "Well, I'm here and available to entertain the thought of having another girl, as long as she's not bossy, manipulative, and lazy."

Josefina responded, "That's not me at all. Why don't you let me get your phone number so I can talk to you more?" The guy gave her his number as Danny walked over toward them to let her know he was done and heading out.

As Jesus drove back home, he kept looking into his rearview mirror—hoping the guy wasn't following him. His rectal muscles had tightened due to the fright and anxiety he had faced. He thought to himself, *I'm such a pussy to be messing with a guy like that. How did I even make such a stupid decision?* He got to his house and looked around to make sure the guy wasn't around.

His son noticed his nervousness and inquired, "Why do you look scared, Dad? Is everything alright?"

Jesus said, "I am scared of your mom being mad because we went to go visit your grandmother. She doesn't like me going over there because she says every time I come back I act more feminine."

Jr. replied, "There's nothing wrong with being feminine, Dad. I saw this video online where a grown man was saying that it's the new norm."

They got out of the car and walked into the house. Mercedes asked them, "Where were you two?"

Jr. uttered, "We went to visit grandma, and before you start being mean to dad, let him tell you how he stood up to this guy who was trying to rob me."

Mercedes turned to Jesus and asked, "Is that true? I doubt it because I know you're a pansy."

Jesus told her, "Yes, it's true. This guy was trying to kidnap Jr., and I stopped him. He ran away, and so did we. I think the testosterone you've been putting in my drink at night is starting to work."

Mercedes observed how sweat was running down his face, and he had a startled-deer look in his eyes. She responded, "Sounds like a load of shit, and you look like shit too. Why didn't you take Chris with you?"

Jesus commented, "He didn't want to come and was asleep as he had got back from school." Mercedes slapped him across his face, causing him to dart to the restroom to hide there.

She followed him to the restroom and banged on the door, shouting, "Come out and stand up to me too like you said you did to some guy! I know you're lying because you're a coward who won't even stand up for himself. Stop pretending you're some macho with those little raisins between your legs." She walked away to cool off, knowing very well his story didn't make sense.

Jesus remained trapped in the restroom, not wanting to come out because he was afraid she might hit him again. He was no match for her. She overpowered him physically and mentally. So he stayed there until Danniel got back from school, and they left to watch a movie at the theater.

Josefina and her dad had gone back home, and she got ready to head off to work. Her legs kept buckling because they were shot from the workout. She walked out of her house mimicking the stanky leg dance. She got in her car and drove off to work while texting the guy from the gym. She hadn't lost all hope in men and felt this guy would surpass the rest she had encountered. When she arrived at her jobsite, she tried getting out of her car but fell face-first. Her legs had locked up on her. Gil was there to witness the event and giggled, but he went over to help her up. She was bleeding from her nose and grabbed some tissue from her car to stop the bleeding as Gil picked her up. He told her, "I knew you'd fall for me eventually. It was only a matter of time before you bled your heart out."

Josefina replied, "Thanks for helping me up, but I didn't even know you were around to fall for you like you're saying."

Right then, Jenny—the girl he had gotten fired—showed up and began to beat his ass. Jenny punched Gil in the mouth and broke his tooth. She then grabbed him, tossed him to the ground, and began unleashing a fury of fists at his face. Gil screamed like a coward, "Help! Help! Someone please get this man off me!"

Josefina told Jenny, "Beat him for me, girl. Hit him hard enough to make him stop harassing women at work."

Gil shouted, "Help me, Josefina! I helped you right now; just get her off me!"

Josefina responded, "But I thought you said you were really masculine and had a deep voice? You don't sound the same when you're getting your ass beat. I told you, you were just faking it." A small crowd had gathered to observe him getting his ass beat and chanted for Jenny.

Then Jenny got up and ran away from the scene, leaving Gil with the shame of getting up and walking to work on his own. Josefina and the rest of the spectators followed him through the front door, laughing at him. Josefina removed the piece of paper from her nose after it ceased bleeding and went to her work station.

Mercedes, her children, and Jesus arrived at the cinemas. They went inside after she purchased some tickets for a horror film that the kids wanted to see. They waited in the lobby while she got them popcorn and drinks. From there, they headed to theater number ten as indicated on their tickets. Jesus walked behind them with Jr. holding his hand. He didn't really want to see the film because he was frightened by the previews. Jr. also was terrified, but they headed in and took a seat. Mercedes shouted at him, "Don't sit next to me! Go sit at the end of the row." The people in the theater heard that and laughed at Jesus.

Jesus and his son walked over to the seats at the other end and sat down. The movie began, and the viewers became silent to enjoy the show. There was a creepy scene in which a dead woman walked on some building walls, chasing a guy she was trying to kill. Jesus and Jr. tucked their heads into their knees as they did not want to watch. Then the crowd yelled, and Jesus and his son ran over to Mercedes and hugged her for safety. Mercedes embraced her son but pushed Jesus away, pointing him back to the end of the row of seats. He didn't leave but instead hugged Chris, who was sitting beside him. Chris shoved him off and told his mom to tell him something. Jesus ended up walking out of the theater and waiting for them in the restroom while they watched the film. When the movie ended and they walked out, they ran into Jesus sitting in the lobby. Mercedes told him, "You're such a sissy. I can't believe you were terrified of a movie, enough to not want to sit alone and instead walk out. What a fucking pansy." Chris and Danniel laughed at him, and they then got in their mom's ride to head back home.

Jesus and Jr. had a hard time sleeping later that night. Jr. slept in his parents' bed; he and his dad held each other tightly with their blankets over their heads, while keeping one eye open the whole night. This time they shoved their thumbs up their anus instead of their mouths.

CHAPTER 5
UNATTAINABLE CURE

The following day, Jesus continued messaging his female friend from high school. She had asked him to loan her money for gas to last her the whole week before she got paid. He retrieved some cash from his savings. He was saving to get himself a BBL and hair implants among other physical modifications he had in mind for himself. He was to meet up with this woman at a park around nine thirty. He was going to try and show dominance in order to suck sperm from her vaginal cavity. He dropped off Jr. at his mom's home with the excuse he had a doctor's appointment to check if one of his rectum veins had burst open. He drove down to the spot she had picked. When he got there, he saw her waiting for him in her car. Jesus drove behind her and parked. He got out of his vehicle and walked over to her driver's side window. He asked her, "Have you been waiting for me for a while?"

She replied, "Not really. I thought you were going to bail on me."

He commented, "Nope, I came to make you mine. I want to eat you out and fuck you doggy style."

She giggled and asked, "Did you bring the money you were going to loan me?" He took it out of his pocket and said, "It's right here, baby."

Suddenly, a man snuck up on him and punched him. The man grabbed his loot and took off. He got inside a car and sped away just as Jesus got up from the ground he had fallen on after being struck. He asked the woman, "What was that? Did you see who punched me and ran with my money?" He wanted to sob but held it inside, sticking to his macho role.

She responded, "I saw some chick that kinda looked like your wife. Maybe she came to teach you a lesson?"

He rubbed his hand on the affected area and uttered, "If it were my wife, she'd go after you probably and not me. Damn, I can't believe I got robbed."

The woman pretended to get a call on her phone and then said, "It's my husband, I have to go because he's heading home and thinks I'm there. I'll text you later, OK?"

He told her, "Wait, let me lick your pussy really fast." But she had taken off before he could finish. He then got back in his car to cry there before going back to pick up his son.

Danny and Josefina had gone back home after the gym following another day of hard work. She took a shower and headed out with her new target. Dan had the twenty-seven-year-old chick at his house. He was ripping that ass apart. He had her slouched over his bed while he rammed her. His doorbell rang, and he popped his dick out of her to go check who it was. He walked over to the door and saw it was Carla. He had forgotten she had told him she'd be there to cook for him again. He wasn't going to open the door, but she called him and heard his phone ringing inside. He cracked the door open and peeked. She asked, "Why don't you let me in? Are you with someone else? I didn't come all the way over here to not cook for you, so just open the door and go finish whatever it is you were doing."

He let her inside his home and went back to his room to get dressed. Alejandra, the twenty-seven-year-old chick, was still waiting for him slumped over. She heard him get back in the room but didn't continue to plow her, so she turned around and asked, "Is everything alright, daddy? Did I poop on your dick and turn you off or something?"

Danny said, "No, baby, you didn't turn me off or poop on me. My other girl is here to cook for me, and I don't want to cause her trauma by continuing to fuck you while she's here. So we're going to have to resume this another day."

Alejandra went to the restroom and cleaned herself up and then got dressed. She walked over to the kitchen and found Carla there. She argued, "So who the fuck are you? Don't you know how to respect other women's men?"

Carla replied, "First of all, sweety, I'm not here to fight or argue with you over anything. You do you and I'll do me. It's not my fault we have to share Danny. I don't mind, but it seems like you sure do. So you're going to have to make up your mind right now and do what you have to do because I'm not going anywhere." She was getting some ingredients from the pantry to start cooking as she spoke.

Danny had jumped in the shower meanwhile as his gals got acquainted. Alejandra didn't want to share him, so she got closer to Carla and swung at her. They began fighting in the kitchen, throwing all the produce to be cooked out. Carla grabbed a frying pan and threw it at Alejandra. Alejandra ducked, missing getting hit by the pan. She grabbed a chair and tossed it at Carla, who avoided the object by bobbing out of its way. They then came into close range and began swinging punches at each other. Danny got out of the shower, listening to the commotion in his kitchen. He ran over there and saw what was going on. He tried to separate them. Carla grabbed his towel and managed to remove it off his nude body. Alejandra grabbed his dick and said, "This is mine! Not yours!"

Carla grabbed it too, stating, "It's mine! Find your own!"

Danny was in pain because they both were squeezing his penis in their tight grasp. He tried shouting but couldn't. Alejandra grabbed his ass and told Carla, "You can have this, but his cock is mine!"

Carla grabbed his chest and replied, "This is mine! All mine!" As they battled over his body parts, their other hand was still attached to each other's hair—tugging.

Danny had to intervene and pull them apart. He told them both, "You two shouldn't be fighting over daddy. I belong to you both, but you must learn to share. Look at the mess y'all made in my kitchen."

Carla uttered, "I'm sorry, daddy. I didn't want any problems. I tried explaining to her we'd have to share you while I was trying to cook, but she attacked me."

Alejandra responded, "I don't want to share you with anyone, daddy."

Danny commented, "Well, if you want to be with me, you have no choice. A man like me is in high demand, and having two or three at once isn't as bad as the plenty more I can have. So if you want me to continue being your daddy, apologize and shake hands with Carla." Alejandra shook Carla's hand and said she was sorry.

Danny then told them both to clean up the mess they made in his kitchen and get acquainted while he got dressed. He strolled back to the restroom as they began to pick up. When he got back, they had finished cleaning up and had begun to cook for him together like the best of friends.

Jesus went to pick up his son at his mother's house, looking constantly over his shoulder because the fierce husband was looking for him. He had almost decided to send an Uber for Jr. in order to avoid more violence. He ran inside his mom's house and then went to the window to peek if he was out there. His mom asked, "What're you looking at? If it's the neighbor, tell her I'm not here. If it's the cops, don't open the door."

Jesus inquired, "Have you noticed any unusual activity since I left yesterday? Like maybe some car circling around the block."

His mother stated, "No, why? Do you owe someone money?"

Jesus responded, "It's because some guy is trying to beat me up for bothering his wife."

Hilda uttered, "Are you fucking stupid, Son? Why would you mess with someone else's wife? Didn't I tell you when you were younger to never mess with another man since you're a coward and can't fight?"

Jesus commented, "I know, Mom. I wish I had listened to you. Now this guy is looking for me."

Hilda told him, "Get your son and leave my house before you bring your problems to me! Get your scary ass out there and run or hide if you have to but not in my house."

He replied, "But, Mom, help me out. If you see anyone beating me up, at least call the cops."

She said, "Call the cops? No way! I don't want any law enforcement on my property. I've been living in this country illegally for decades, and I don't want to be sent back to Mexico. Now get going before I tell your wife you're over here getting into trouble and complaining to me about it."

Jesus got Jr. and told him, "We're going to have to run to my car, OK? Just in case the guy from yesterday tries to kidnap you again. Close your eyes and don't open them till I tell you to."

They ran out of the residence and to his car. They jumped inside, and he turned on the ignition. He took off as he watched his mother lock her front doors and close her blinds.

Josefina had gone hiking with the guy she had met at the gym. Her legs were sore, but she didn't fuss about it. He was leading the way up the mountain side. The scenery was spectacular from her perspective. She was stunned by the natural beauty in their backyard. She was also admiring the guy's rear end in front of her. Her stomach began bubbling up and she felt a gas exiting. It was pretty quiet, and she didn't want to scare the guy away, so she managed to push it back in. He asked her about her job, and she informed him about Gil's unwelcome advances. They followed a path up to a cave in the mountains. He advised her, "You should probably file a complaint on him. If he's gotten his ass beat by some girl and hasn't learned his lesson yet, then he needs a different form of punishment. Like getting fired or reprimanded."

She said, "You're right, but then again, he has connections in the management office. I feel like if I complain, it'll turn around on me."

He stated, "If that happens, you could ask around to see if there're more victims, which I'm sure there is, and you all can bring up your separate cases."

She replied, "You have a good point there. Maybe I should do that first so we could all file at the same time."

Just then, he observed a rock squirrel run across right in front of him. He halted and then saw a rattlesnake chasing it. The snake slithered down toward them, and he split his legs to allow it through. Josefina spotted danger and screamed, which caused her to lose grip on her gas. It came out—it was long and loud. The snake managed to go around her, continuing its hunt. The guy was in shock and asked, "Did you just fart or was it my imagination?"

She responded, "I'm sorry. I was holding it in for the same reason. I didn't want to gross you out."

He uttered, "You didn't gross me out. In fact I'm impressed. Never heard a lady fart so long and loud. Good thing we're out here in the open, and I didn't catch a whiff of it. Remind me when we're done to stop at a store to get you something for that."

She questioned, "Something for that? Like what?"

He replied, "Something for gas or maybe a cork? How about a fan that'll blow it back to you, with an air freshener mist attached to it?" He began laughing and so did she.

Jesus had gotten back home with his son. He was paranoid the woman's husband was following him and only felt half safe inside a structure. He messaged the other woman and asked her if everything was alright—mainly because he didn't want another man after him. He was fixated on the idea of consuming semen to address his issue, which he couldn't get out of his head. He went outside in search of Mut. He found his dog in his doghouse and stuck his hand inside, telling him, "Come here, boy. I need to milk your male tit so I can become masculine."

Mut was excited to see him. He jumped up and began licking his face. Jesus pushed him away, and Mut started running around, believing he wanted to play with him. Jesus chased after him with a cup in his hand. Jr. came outside and asked, "Dad, why're you running after Mut with a cup in your hand?"

Jesus replied, "I'm trying to collect a poop sample from him so I can take it to the vet and have it analyzed to see if he has parasites."

Jr. uttered, "Let me help you then." They both followed Mut around the backyard as he avoided being tagged.

Jesus was running when his feet got tangled up in the water hose, and he fell straight into their portable swimming pool and instinctively popped right out. He shouted, "Help! I can't swim, I can't swim!"

Jr. told him, "You're not even inside. It was just your head and shoulders anyway."

He looked at his surroundings and realized his son was right. Only his shoulders and head had been submerged in the pool for a second or so. He went inside to change as his son continued to pursue Mut. Jesus changed into a dry shirt as Mercedes walked in. She asked him, "What're you doing? And why's Jr. out in the backyard chasing Mut?"

Jesus responded, "I was changing because I fell in the pool chasing after Mut. We were playing with him, and I left Jr. out there to continue while I swapped clothes."

Jr. ran inside the house and handed his father the cup, saying, "Look, Dad, I was able to get some poop. Now you could take it to the vet and get it checked."

Mercedes and Jesus gagged as he uttered, "Great job, Son. Let me take that from you." Feces was sliding off the side of the cup, so Jesus ran with it to put it in a bag.

Jr. ran after him and helped him open the bag up to place the cup inside. He had some shit in his hands, which he smeared on his dad's wrist. Jesus gagged as he tied up the bag. He dropped the bag on the ground and ran to the sink to get it off his hands and asked Jr. to do the same. Jesus was cleaning his hands, he couldn't hold it in any longer and spewed. Mercedes heard him and yelled, "You freaking pansy!"

Josefina and the guy had gone up to the cave, and then they walked back down to their car. They got in and drove down to a pharmacy where he looked around for some medication for her gas problem. She was ashamed and didn't think she required medicine for just farting. As they walked through the gastrointestinal section, a man rushed in with his pregnant wife who was in labor. He demanded the pharmacist assist in delivering his baby. The man was hysterical, screaming and shouting as he grabbed a bag of chips from the counter and began eating them. The pharmacist argued, "I'm not a doctor and can't help you. Let me call an ambulance instead."

The man grabbed the pharmacist and yelled, "Get my baby out in one piece or I'll sue you for malpractice." The man then ran to grab some beach towels while his wife lay on the ground with her legs spread apart, experiencing labored breathing.

Josefina sat down next to the woman and held her hand. Her date tried calming down the soon-to-be father, but he insisted, "I need a doctor. My wife is in labor, and I feel like I'm going to faint. Hold me in your arms and tell me everything will be fine." The gym guy pushed him away as he tried to embrace him.

An older Black woman who was at the store shouted, "He needs some milk!" But no one paid any attention to her as the pharmacist came back with his phone in hand, talking to an emergency operator.

Josefina heard the woman say, "I'm fine; it's just my husband making a big deal about it and getting paranoid. This is actually our fifth child. He's acted the same way every birth. I don't know why he hasn't learned by now. He took me to the veterinary clinic for our first birth, then to an odontologist's office for the second. The third was at an optometrist locale. The fourth was with a shrink. Just smack him for me please."

Josefina told her date, "She said to smack him." The guy slapped the man on his face.

The man started to cry and said, "Why'd you hit me? Can't you see I'm in a lot of pain already? My wife is having a child, and my empathy feels her pain." The paramedics arrived to attend to the woman who was crowning.

Josefina felt her date grab her hand and say, "Quick, let's get out of here before he presses charges for slapping him." They darted outside to his car, and he drove her home so she could get ready and head off to work.

Mercedes informed Jesus, "Don't forget we have a quinceañera to attend today. So better start getting ready now since it takes you several hours to do so."

Jesus replied, "I don't have anything to wear though. I feel fat and my clothes don't fit right. Why can't you just pay for me to get plastic surgery? It would help me out a lot if you did."

Mercedes said, "Why can't you just be a man and suck it up?"

Jesus asked, "Suck my gut up? Do you know how uncomfortable that would feel?"

She responded, "Not your gut but the feelings you have bothering you. Get your stupid ass in the shower and start getting ready before I suck your soul out of your penis!"

Before showering, Jesus went to their bedroom and opened his closet to see what he could wear. He grabbed one of her dresses and put it on. He walked to the living area where Mercedes was eating leftovers and asked her, "Do I look pretty in this?"

Jr. told him, "You look beautiful, Dad. Can I wear a dress too?"

Mercedes fumed, "Take my dress off and find some pants and a shirt of yours to wear! Look what you're causing. Our son wants to wear a dress too."

Jesus walked back to the room and took the dress off. He then grabbed himself some leggings he had bought online. He pulled them over his legs and waist. They fit tight on him and his little Lemur leaf frog toes protruded; he walked to Mercedes to tell her, "I'm wearing this then."

Mercedes responded, "No, you're not! I can see your little frog toe, and no one wants to witness such a tragedy at a party."

Jr. ran out of his room wearing one of his dolls' dresses, shouting, "Look, Mom, don't I look pretty?"

She fumed, "Both of you feminine, little pipi guys, stop it and go find yourselves something masculine to wear." They each went to their room to change.

Moments later, Mercedes went to the bedroom and found Jesus whining in the closet. She grabbed a pair of pants and shirt for him and uttered, "You're wearing this without exceptions. Now get in the fucking shower, sissy!"

Jesus replied, "I'm not going." But she grabbed him and forced him into the shower.

Alejandra and Carla had left Danny's pad. He was watching a documentary about modern feminine men. It was very entertaining for him as he laughed at how the guys being interviewed were demonstrating their daily activities. A guy was explaining his penis had begun to mutate into a clitoris and his nut sack had sunk in and opened up like a vagina. He also mentioned his wife was growing chest hair and her clit was getting larger while her breasts decreased in size. Danny was cracking up at the show, unable to contain his humor. Lucia went over to visit, and he let her inside. She took a seat in the living room and watched the doc series with him. He told her, "Look, check this pansy out. He's explaining how his manhood is transforming into a woman's pussy."

Lucia replied, "Is that what's happening to you? That's why you haven't banged me in about a week?"

He uttered, "You know damn well that's not happening to me. It's just that every time I fuck you, you complain something hurts. You start whining you're not flexible and that I should take it slow."

Lucia responded, "Well, I'm not in my twenties or thirties like your little girlfriends who let you manhandle them. I don't work out like you either. My body is aging and it's normal."

Danny commented, "OK there, delicate. Why don't you go grab me a beer from the fridge and bring it here? Don't forget you're ensure while you're there. By the way, I got you a walking stick so you won't fall. It's next to the fridge."

Lucia said, "You're such an asshole. I don't need those things. Plus, this is a broom, not a walking stick." She grabbed him a beer and got one for herself, then handed him his.

Dan informed her, "It's a multipurpose female walking stick. Helps you get around the house while you clean." He giggled.

The documentary was now showing this guy who had been spending all of his money on beauty products. He had become a hoarder, saving numerous female articles and products in his bachelor home. Danny cracked up and told Lucia, "That's how Jesus is going to end up one day, if he doesn't grow his balls back. I wouldn't doubt it if he asks our daughter to penetrate him instead of him penetrating her." Just as he finished, Lucia, who had chugged her beer, got liquid courage.

She jumped on top of him and told him, "Let me have that cock of yours. The beer made my body nimble and agile, so let's see if you can hang this time." She tore off his clothes and began riding him like a bull rider.

Danny was startled by her actions but let her take control. He never saw it coming or that she'd remove her pants. She jumped up and down on his crotch, rubbing her breasts on his face. She took the TV remote from his hands and put it between her butt cheeks. She was moaning and moaning like there was a camera around filming them and she wanted to get an Oscar for her performance. Then she had an orgasm, which seemed to make her melt in his lap. Danny saw her eyes roll back and then forward as she gasped for air. When he observed she was done, he asked her, "You never even put my dick inside you. Is that how horny you were? Wow, that's a first."

Lucia replied, "I thought I did. That's how excited you get me, Danny. Take me to your room and do to me what you do to your little girls." Danny listened, escorting her to his room as she shouted, "Not through the back door!" He removed the TV remote out of the way.

Jesus had gotten out of the shower and was doing his hair. Mercedes was hurrying up Chris and Danniel who had gotten back from school. She was also helping Jr. get ready. She told Jr., "Put this on and don't give me a hard time." She then went to get her clothes to wear after the shower.

They were ready to leave when Jesus told them to wait really quick. He tried getting some of Mut's sauce before taking off, but he ran away from him again. He eventually gave up and went back inside just as they were all leaving.

When they arrived at the dance hall, the place was packed. Jesus made his way in, dancing to the music and greeting random people he didn't know. Mercedes said hello to the birthday girl, who was Danniel's friend from school. Danniel left her family to hang out with her friends. Chris took a seat at their reserved table and munched on the appetizers available. Jr. followed his father to the dance floor, where they both had a dance-off with the court. Mercedes ended up taking a seat next to her son Chris and told him, "And he said he didn't want to come. Look at him dancing on the floor like he was a stripper."

The dance floor had a bunch of feminine men showing off their moves as the women accompanying them sat down at their tables and drank beer. The guys fired up the hall with their dancing all night long. A few women would randomly go up to some and ask to dance, but the guys would refuse to share the spotlight and fun. They were dancing to "La Macarena" when they were suddenly interrupted by the event staff DJ, who announced the court entrance. Jesus didn't want to take a seat and neither did Jr.

Mercedes had to go get them both so that they wouldn't disturb the event. Jesus got up from his seat and went over to the bar to get a margarita. He grabbed two actually and downed one right then and there, taking the other back to his table.

He then left the drink at the table and went to the restroom, where there was a long line waiting outside. Feminine men were inside, fixing their hair and drying their body parts after the exhaustion of dancing. Jesus eventually used the restroom and took a seat to piss. He then walked back to their table, shouting and waving his hands over his head, "Whoo! Whoo! Happy birthday!"

Mercedes grabbed him and pulled him to his chair, stating, "Sit down and stop making a fool of yourself. You've only had one margarita so far, and you're acting like a drama queen." He tried getting back up, but she restrained him.

The lights went out again, and the dance floor was wide open. Jesus grabbed Jr., and they both went back to dancing their butts off. Once again, the feminine men ruled the dance. Mercedes saw another female looking at Jesus, who was shouting happily, and then she turned to look at her, shaking her head at her for not being able to control him. Mercedes asked a waiter passing by if he could bring her a pitcher of beer for the long night ahead. She went outside to get away from the drama the men had going on in there. She saw another woman outside smoking a cigarette and asked, "Excuse me. Would you happen to have an extra smoke for me?"

The woman replied, "Sure. Here you are." She handed her one and lit it up for her too. She then asked Mercedes, "Are you out here trying to get away from the commotion inside?"

Mercedes uttered, "Yeah, I wish things were back to normal and we women danced instead of men."

The woman commented, "I miss those days myself. Now I have to sit down and watch my husband dance his ass off. I'm now getting to see how they felt before this change took place."

Mercedes said, "Right. I remember that was us back then and now it's backward, and we're the ones getting drunk, feeling annoyed, and wanting to go home early." They both chuckled.

The woman put her cigarette out and said, "Well, I'll see you later. Heading back inside to babysit my drunk, jolly husband."

Mercedes told her, "OK, thanks for the smoke. I'll be in there soon myself to do the same."

When the party came to an end, Jesus refused to leave, so she had to drag his ass home and put him to bed. He nagged that he was starving but didn't know what to eat. She offered him her snatch, but he suddenly fell asleep.

CHAPTER 6
THE WEAK MEND

Jesus was woken up by Jr. who stated, "Dad, wake Mom up. She promised to take me to Slip-E's Water Park."

Jesus turned around, removing his thumb from his oral cavity, and shook Mercedes, saying, "Jr. says you promised to take him to the water park." And he dozed off afterward.

Mercedes awoke from her sleep and looked at Jr. standing by their bed, and she asked him, "You really want to go? That place is going to be full and the rides suck."

Jr. said, "I like going there to sunbathe, Mom. I also like the Winnie Creek that goes around the park."

Mercedes replied, "Alright, go wake your brother and sister up and y'all get ready." She ordered Jesus to wake up and get going as she got up from the bed.

Jesus woke up immediately after she told him and began getting his swimwear. He grabbed his pink bottom, pink floats, pink towel, pink shades, pink goggles, pink sandals, and pink shower cap because he didn't want his long thin hair to get damaged. Mercedes grabbed her stuff, then got the ice chest, some sandwich items, and some beer to drink. The kids were thrilled they were going to the water park. They left the house in Mercedes's vehicle.

When they arrived at the park's entrance, there was a long line. Jesus began to complain about it and about the way he looked. Mercedes told him, "This is why I hardly take you anywhere. You're always nagging about one thing or another."

Jesus said, "I'm hungry."

She replied, "So am I and I bet the kids are too. Right now when we get in, you could make yourself a sandwich with the stuff I brought."

Jesus uttered, "But I don't want to eat a sandwich."

Mercedes asked, "So what does the princes want to eat then?"

Jesus responded, "I don't know what I'm hungry for, but it's not a sandwich."

Mercedes looked at him as she said, "You're lucky all these people are here right now because I just feel like punching you in the face." The line began to move rapidly, and they made their way to the ticket office to purchase their entry passes.

Josefina went with the guy from the gym to a museum. They walked around learning history. She kinda felt the guy wasn't as masculine as he appeared but didn't know how she could prove it before she fell for him. She distracted herself in her thoughts as she pondered over a solution. As they were reading the educational literature next to the displays, she came up with the idea to have an arm wrestling match between them to identify what type of male he really was. She shared her suggestion with him without letting him know why. He agreed, and they gathered across a table and placed their arms over it. They grabbed each other's hands and put their elbows in a comfortable position. He counted to three, and they began to arm wrestle. She pushed her force into him, and he did the same. Then she got leverage and started to make his arm retract. She submitted his arm down eventually and asked, "How is that I beat you if you work out and have all those muscles?"

He said, "I let you beat me, sweety. I don't want to break your arm trying to be more masculine than you."

She contested, "No, no, let's do it again, and this time I want you to use all your force, you pansy." They locked hands again for a rematch.

Josefina beat him again, and she became more concerned. She inquired, "Do you take testosterone or steroid cycles?"

The guy responded, "I've taken some but not all the time. Why?"

She questioned, "Why did you and your ex-girlfriend break up?"

He mentioned, "She broke up with me because she felt I was becoming feminine. I really wasn't though, but she found some guy who she believed was more masculine and left me for him." Josefina put two and two together and realized he was a FEMNS fan.

Josefina had taken her car, so she ran out of the museum toward it. He followed her and whimpered as he saw her get in and lock the car. He asked, standing next to her door window, "What's wrong? Are you ditching me?"

She told him, "I can't believe you fooled me. You're not a masculine man. You're just a feminine one taking testosterone and working out. I don't want you calling me ever again, you sissy." She then drove off, almost running him over as she left him behind.

Mercedes and her family made it through the front doors. They searched for a table to set up their temporary camp site and found one next to the female restroom. Jesus didn't help her carry anything since he was useless. He took a seat and began to put sunblock on his skin while he ate a sandwich he made himself. He put some sunblock on Jr. too. He placed his shower cap on and followed Jr. to the creek. Mercedes took her beer out and began to sip on it peacefully, without Jesus being around to ruin her peace.

Chris and Danniel took off to the water slides. Moments later, Jesus returned whimpering. He said, "My shower cap fell because this kid pushed me in the water. Now my hair is going to be ruined. I want to go home." Jr. came running right behind him.

Mercedes said, "I don't care about your hair. It's falling off anyhow. Let me drink my beer in peace and go cry somewhere else!"

Jr. uttered, "But, Mom, you should go beat the kid up who bullied dad."

Mercedes replied, "Why would I do such a thing? If he can't fend for himself, then that's his problem not mine."

Jesus told her, "You just don't love me anymore. I can see it in your eyes and feel it at your touch."

Mercedes ignored him and commented to Jr., "Go play, *papi*. You wanted to come here to have fun, so go on and have fun. I'll watch you from here."

Jr. looked at his father sitting down and said, "I'll be back, Dad. You stay here where you're safe with mom." He then ran back to the creek.

Jesus moved away from Mercedes and lay on the ground to get a tan; he had tossed the reminder of his sandwich in the trash because his appetite was ruined. He faced down with his small saggy ass sticking out. Mercedes looked over at him and saw something unusual on his back. She asked, "Is that shit on your thong?"

Jesus looked back and realized he had shit on himself because of the kid and cried, "Oh no! I shit myself!" He got up and ran to the restroom to clean up as Mercedes laughed at him.

When Jesus returned from addressing his accident, he lay back down again to get a tan while he used his phone for entertainment. He watched some videos on how to control his feminine emotions. He then recalled he may have gotten paid for his participation in the study. He checked his bank account on his mobile app, and he saw he had money. He rose from the ground and went to the concession stand to get himself a plate of brisket with potato salad and macaroni.

As he stood in line, he observed some little girls pointing at him and saying, "That's the guy who got beat up by a little kid at the creek. He also pooped himself."

The bully kid's father walked up behind him and turned him around, divulging, "Are you the guy who was messing with my kid over at the creek? He tells me you wanted to touch his winnie, you sick fuck!"

Jesus replied, "That is a lie. Your son was bullying me and threw me in the water, and I would have almost drowned had I not had my floaties. If I touched him, it was accidental as I tried to rescue myself. Also, don't assume I'm a guy. I prefer being called pink daddy she."

The man picked him up since he was taller and masculine strong, saying, "Are you calling my son a bully and a liar?"

One of the girls in line who had witnessed the event shouted, "Mister, he's not lying. Your son was and still is going around punching people. He's not making it up. Your son also made him shit himself."

The man dropped Jesus, shouting, "Ew! You've got feces!" And he walked away. Jesus looked back at the girls and told them, "Thanks for helping me out."

One of them replied, "No problem. Thought it would be better we did that than have you pooping here near the food." Jesus was next to order; he did so and went back to Mercedes, while the people in line laughed at what the girl had said.

Danny was at his house asleep when the doorbell rang. He got up and let Carla in. She was there to cook for him again. He was on his way back to his bed when the bell caught his attention again.

He walked back to see who it was. Alejandra was there to wash his clothes, so he allowed her entry. He strolled back to his room, and just before he could lie in bed, the doorbell made him head back to the door once more. This time it was Lucia who was there to clean up his residence. He opened the door and let her inside. He heard them all talking and knew he wouldn't be able to go back to sleep, so he instead sat in the living area to watch TV. He felt like a king in his castle, observing his three women getting along and doing his chores. Josefina woke up and came out to see who was there. She had gone to bed when she returned from her failed date. She greeted everyone and sat down to eat what Carla had made. Danny got up from the couch and sat next to his daughter. Lucia, Carla, and Alejandra sat down to eat too. All four women engaged in conversation, which was beginning to irritate Dan. There was too much female chatter in his home, and he wasn't used to it. He hurried up to eat and went to his room to watch TV there. All four women finished eating and then got back to what they were doing. Carla and Josefina helped Lucia clean up the house. Then Alejandra informed them there wasn't enough detergent to finish washing and that she was heading to the store to get some more. They all wanted to go, so they told Dan they'd be back. When they left, he felt at ease.

They drove to the store, and when they got there, they walked around shopping for some things they needed for themselves. An older woman in her eighties approached Lucia and told her, "You have a beautiful family. All your daughters are gorgeous. I have two sons searching for love around their ages in case you're interested."

Lucia giggled, replying, "Only one of them is my daughter. The other two are my ex's girlfriends. I wouldn't mind if they'd hook up with your sons though. Let me go tell them." She felt embarrassed because the elderly woman had made her feel old but informed them of what she had offered.

Alejandra stated, "No, thank you, lady. I'm fine with my macho man."

Carla uttered, "Same here, miss. Hope you find your sons some good women though." Josefina responded, "I appreciate the offer, but I'm looking for some masculine men, so if your sons aren't that, then I'll just pass."

The older woman commented, "Wow, the guy you all share must be some macho hunk. My sons aren't all that masculine, to be honest. One of them is a manicurist at a salon and the other collects disability for being feminine. They both live at home with me. I just want them to go to a happy house because I'm only getting older and have no grandkids or daughters-in-law. When my honey, Bill, passed away, I just wanted to be alone at the house. But my sons never left the nest. I'd hate to see them remain single the rest of their lives. Bill and I had them when we were older since we had fun together till we hit forty. I sure miss my Billy." A tear ran down her eye.

Lucia responded, "I'm sorry to hear your husband is no longer with you." The older woman uttered, "Same to you."

Josefina, Carla, and Alejandra gave the women their condolences, and they all got back to shopping for what they were there for. When they had got everything, they paid and departed to head back to Danny's.

Jesus got back to the table, and Mercedes saw he had a plate of food. She asked, "Where'd you get that and with what money?"

He said, "I got it from the food stand over there. I got paid for my participation in the study today. You want some?"

She uttered, "It does look good, but I don't want some of yours. You probably didn't wash your hands when you cleaned the shit off your back."

He mentioned, "I sure did wash my hands for your information. If you want a plate, I can go get you one."

Mercedes commented, "Hand over the one you're eating and go get yourself one." She chugged the beer in her hand, then took the plate from him.

Jesus wanted to mend his broken relationship. He hadn't found a cure for his feminine ways, but he felt it would help if he wouldn't give her any more problems. So he gave her his plate of food and went to go get himself another one. As he got in line, he saw the bully kid was in front of him.

He turned to see Jesus and shouted, "You freaking sissy! You got me in trouble with my dad, snitch!"

Jesus informed him, "I had no choice but to tell him what you did. He scared me into spilling the beans."

The kid yelled, "You sure spilled the beans, didn't you?" He told the guy at the concession stand, "Watch out for this guy, man. He defecated all over himself and didn't wash his hands." He grabbed his food and left.

The park employee looked at Jesus and told him, "Sorry, sir, but you'll have to wash your hands before I serve you anything to eat. You could contaminate the rest of the merchandise."

Jesus questioned, "Sir? My preferred pronouns are pink daddy she."

Jesus waited in line for nothing and threw a small fit before heading back to the table. He was on his way there when he saw Jr. coming back whimpering. He asked him, "What's wrong?"

Jr. stated, "All the kids found out you're my dad and keep making fun of me. They're calling me poop dad's kid."

Jesus grabbed him and said, "Let's go tell your mother so she can go tell the kids something."

They got to Mercedes, and Jesus mentioned, "They didn't want to serve me more food and some kids are bothering our son."

Mercedes responded, "Well, I already ate your food. And why are some kids bugging Jr.?"

Jesus uttered, "They're calling him poop dad's kid."

Mercedes said, "It's not like they're lying. Anyhow, why don't you go defend him?" Jesus replied, "If I do, they'll only make more fun of him."

Mercedes uttered, "Then don't go and stay here. Why don't you have a beer and stop being such a bitch? That's why Jr. is the way he is too. He gets it from you, not from me."

Jesus responded, "I don't want a beer, but fine, I'll just make myself another sandwich and sit here with our son." He made them a sandwich each, and they sat down to eat.

Chris and Danniel had come back, and they asked Jesus, "Hey, we heard you shit yourself. Are you alright?" They giggled as they made themselves a sandwich too.

The ladies went back to Danny's house, and Lucia shared the conversation they had with the older woman with him. Dan started laughing and told her, "You do look like their mother. You can't blame the lady for the assumption."

Lucia responded, "I know, but it was embarrassing. She even told me she felt sorry for my loss as in losing you to them."

He chuckled and uttered, "Damn! I wish I was there to hear her say that. Anyhow, did you already clean up my house?"

Lucia uttered, "We're almost done. Is there anything else you need?"

He replied, "Yeah, can you go tell your daughters to keep it down? I'm trying to watch a movie here." He laughed as she walked away mad.

Lucia walked back to the living area and informed the ladies that Danny wanted them to quiet down. They all lowered their voices as they continued to clean up the house. Lucia walked outside to get some fresh air and forget what Danny had told her. She was about to head back in when the door opened, and Alejandra tossed a bag full of trash out, not knowing she was there. Alejandra then saw her and that she had some dust all over her face. Alejandra apologized and helped her clean off the dust. She then threw the trash in the bin outside, and they went back inside to prepare lunch for Danny and themselves.

Jr. had a water balloon in his possession, which he said he had found in the creek. He and Jesus began tossing it back and forth to each other. Chris and Danniel had eaten and taken off back to the slides. Mercedes was drinking her tenth beer and just sitting there watching Jesus and Jr. play. She looked over at the other tables and saw a bunch of women doing the same thing she was. Jesus caught the balloon and put his mouth to the tip and told Jr., "I'm going to bite the jellyfish." They were pretending it was a sea creature that was attacking them, kinda like playing hot potato with a twist.

Mercedes got up and went to the restroom. Jesus and their son continued playing. When she got back, she observed they were playing with a condom filled with water and told Jesus, "Are you stupid or something? You haven't noticed? That isn't a water balloon, but instead a cock sleeve."

Jesus looked at her as the balloon hit the side of his face and asked, "What's a cock sleeve?"

Mercedes informed him, "A condom, you sissy bastard! And it just hit your silly face. Who knows if it's been used or not."

Jesus saw the balloon on the ground and said, "Oh, shucks. It is a condom, ew! Jr., let's go wash our hands."

Jr. inquired, "What's a condom?"

Jesus told him, "It's a babyproof vest, Son. Something to avoid having babies with." He and Jr. went to the restroom to wash their hands while Mercedes cracked up at how dumb her husband really was.

When they got back from washing their hands, Chris and Danniel were there helping their mom gather their things. They were heading back home. Chris kicked the condom toward Jesus and told him, "Catch it with your mouth again, why don't you?"

Jesus chuckled and jumped out of the object's way. He then grabbed his towel from the floor, and they exited the park.

Josefina showered and got dressed, as she was headed to some party her friends had invited her to. She kissed her dad goodbye, as well as her mom and her dad's girlfriends who'd stayed back. She jumped into her friend's ride, and they took off. When they arrived at the party, it was still a bit early. They greeted the person hosting it, which was their other friend Hellen—who was the one who had taken a burrito to her face at the construction site. The other one who drove Josefina to Hellen's was Veronica. Veronica asked Hellen, "Where are the beers, girl? And when are your cousins coming so we can meet them?"

Hellen replied, "The beers are in the cooler right behind you. I don't know if my cousins are coming after all. They said they were going to watch some program on the FEMNS Network."

Veronica stated, "Well, good. You know if they're watching that channel, they're feminine. I thought you said they were masculine?"

Josefina said, "Yeah, Hellen. You made me get all dressed up to meet your macho cousins, and now they're not coming and they're feminine to top it off? You really disappoint me."

Hellen uttered, "I'm sorry, ladies. I seriously thought y'all would find a match in my family. I really haven't seen them in such a long time to know for sure they're not feminine. Maybe y'all will hit it off with one of my uncles. They are heading down here, for sure. They're married, but I can't complain if y'all attract them into infidelity."

Josefina and Veronica grabbed a beer and sat down next to her while she grilled. Hellen's father came out and greeted her friends. Her mother followed him and told him, "Go take the trash out and wash the dishes before the guests arrive." They were celebrating his birthday, but he had become feminine without authority.

Hellen's mom told Hellen, "Let me show you how to grill, girl. Move out of the way because the chef is here. Hand me a beer. That is the first lesson." Hellen got her a beer and watched her grill some carne asada.

Josefina asked Hellen, "You don't have any non-light beer? I don't like drinking this watered-down feminine piss." Hellen chuckled and went to go check if she had any regular brew inside.

When Mercedes and her family got home, they all went to take a shower. The only one who didn't wash was Jesus. He told Mercedes, "Since I got paid, let me take your car to the carwash and clean it up for you, as a small token for taking care of me." She agreed and hopped in the shower.

Jesus drove her vehicle to the manual car wash center. He got off and looked around at the women who were there washing their cars. He walked to the machine and read the functions. He looked at the hose and brush and wondered how exactly to use it. One woman asked him, "Is this your first time washing a car?"

Jesus said, "Yes, do you know how to use these machines?"

She informed him, "You're going to have to place some quarters in it. About seven dollars so you can have sufficient time to wash it right. If you don't have change, there's a change machine over there." She pointed at the currency dispenser.

Jesus thanked her and walked over to the change dispenser. He stuck in a ten-dollar bill he had and got quarters in return. He then walked back to the machine and inserted seven dollars' worth of quarters. He heard the brush and hose give off pressure, and he then grabbed the hose as the woman advised him, "You're going to rinse the whole car and then grab the brush and start brushing. When you're done brushing, you'll grab the hose again and rinse off the soap. Then you'll dry it."

Jesus followed her instructions and started washing Mercedes's car. He was coming around the front grill when he slipped, falling on his ass and spraying water on himself. The woman who had given him instructions laughed and walked away, knowing he'd eventually ask her to help him wash the car or ask her to do it for him. Jesus got up from the ground and continued to rinse the vehicle. The machine began beeping, and he thought he had broken it or it was going to explode, so he backed away until it stopped. He then remembered he needed to brush the car. So he grabbed the brush and brushed the exterior without any soap. When he believed he was finished, he grabbed the hose and tried rinsing it, but it wasn't spraying water. He looked at the hose end and observed that nothing was coming out. He then went to the coin operator and inserted more quarters. He heard the hose and brush turn on again, and so he grabbed the brush and brushed the exterior. He wasn't even halfway done with brushing when the machine stopped. He went back to the coin operator and placed more quarters. He kept doing that until he had finished brushing and rinsing the ride, which took him about two hours to accomplish. After that, he took about another hour to half ass dry the car.

When he believed he was done, he got into the car and was about to leave when the husband of the woman he had harassed showed up there and saw him. As he confronted him, Jesus turned the car on and drove off yelling, as if it was required to survive. The man got into his vehicle and chased after him. Jesus swerved in and out of the traffic, trying to lose the man. He finally pulled up to the police precinct and began honking, and the man following him saw him do that and left. Some police officers came out to see what was going on, and they walked up to his car and asked, "Why're you honking?"

Jesus replied, "There was some guy chasing me, and he wanted to beat me up, Officers. I'm scared to go home. Can one of you escort me to my house please?"

One of the officers responded, "We can't. We have bigger issues to deal with. You could spend the night here if you'd like and sleep in your car. Seems like being here is off-limits for the guy chasing you."

Jesus was whimpering but uttered, "Alright, I'll just hang out here a bit longer until I feel he's long gone." The police officers walked back into their office as Jesus scattered his vision around, looking to see if he could spot the man.

Hellen's party was a disaster. When her family finally showed up, there were none but feminine men. Josefina and Veronica were a little upset, but they had grown accustomed to the scarcity of machos. They were buzzing off the beers they drank as they observed Hellen's dad and uncles dance and sing. All the women had gathered at one table to socialize while sipping their brews. The FEMNS drank piña coladas as they danced, sang, and gossiped about each other. Josefina got up to go inside Hellen's home. She walked over to the restroom, and as the door wasn't locked, she went ahead and swung it open. Hellen's father was in there, sitting down and peeing; he told her, "Close the door, sweety. Daddy's peeing. I'll be out shortly."

Hellen shut the door and laughed. She then went to the other restroom. The restroom was available, and so she locked the door and took a massive shit. Veronica went looking for her, thinking she had gone home. She did the same and walked in on Hellen's dad and apologized. She then went to the other restroom and knocked. She heard Josefina and told her, "I thought you had left the party, girl. Hurry up there so we could go stop at a bar or something. Unless you want to stay here with Hellen?"

Josefina replied, "I'm taking a shit. I don't want to go to a bar. There's free beer here, and if you really think about it, we may go to a bar and not find any machos and still have to pay for our drinks and theirs."

Veronica uttered, "You have a good point. I'll be outside then. You don't push too hard or you might get a hernia." They giggled and Veronica left.

When Josefina came out, she sat down to continue drinking and enjoying the show the FEMNS put on. Eventually, the party came to an end, leaving a few women drunk, who did not want to go home. Josefina and Veronica took off around three in the morning after they watched Hellen's uncle cry to his wife and ask for them to go home. It was funny. They both made it to their homes safely and called it a night.

Jesus remained at the police parking lot until like midnight. Mercedes had gotten out of the shower, taken a nap, and woken up, and he still wasn't back. So she called his ass and told him to get home. He told her he was still washing her car, not wanting to be honest about his situation. He eventually took off, and when he got back, Mercedes beat his ass because he had taken too long and hadn't washed her car properly. She sent him to bed early while she and the kids stayed up playing board games.

CHAPTER 7
THE COCK-OUT

Josefina called Mercedes to see what she was doing later on in the day. Mercedes said, "Nothing, sister. I feel like eating some carne asada, but I also don't feel like grilling."

Josefina stated, "That's what I ate yesterday at my friend's dad's birthday party. It was really good. If you want, I could come over and help you cook some. I want to spend some time with my nephews and niece."

Mercedes told her, "OK, let me invite Dad and Mom over too then, so we could have a little family cookout."

Josefina questioned, "Do you need me to take anything?"

Mercedes responded, "If you can stop at the store and get some beers, that would be great."

Josefina replied, "No problem. So I'll see you there in about an hour or so."

Mercedes uttered, "Deal, see you then." They hung up, and Mercedes got out of bed.

She went to the fridge to see what they had and what they needed. She began making a list for the store. When she had the list ready, she left to go get it. Jesus woke up while she was gone and began sobbing. He thought she had left him. He looked around the room to see if he could see a note she may have left behind explaining her reasons. He didn't find any trace, and then she called him on his cell. He answered the call and told her, "Please don't leave me. I love you. You mean the world to me."

Mercedes questioned, "What're you talking about? I just came to the store because I'm going to grill and my family is coming over later on." Jesus was relieved as he heard her continue, "I need you to check if we have any mayo for some hot dogs." He wiped off his tears.

Jesus went to check and informed her, "There's a little bit but probably not enough for hot dogs. Can I invite some friends over for the cookout?"

Mercedes replied, "If they bring something and not just come over to freeload."

Jesus assured her, "I'll make sure they bring you some beer. Thanks, honey." She then hung up on him since she was about to pay.

Danny had received the invite from Mercedes, and he started getting ready. He called Alejandra and Carla to invite them so they could meet his family. They both agreed, so he gave them Mercedes's address and told them to get some drinks and snacks. He jumped in the shower, interrupting Josefina who was showering also. When he turned on the hot water, it cut off the hot water in her shower, and it shot cold, making her yelp. She shut off the water and heard her dad singing in his shower. She still had some soap lathered on her body. She wanted to rinse off but knew she'd have to wait till he was done; otherwise, she'd have to rinse with cold water. She got out and grabbed her towel instead. She dried herself and put lotion on her skin. She then put her clothes on and brushed her teeth. When she exited the shower, she remembered that if the kitchen sink was turned on hot, it would cancel the hot water in her dad's shower. She ran to the sink and turned it on. She then heard her dad yelp, "Ah, it's cold! Josefina, I'm in the shower! Turn off the water so I can finish!"

She walked over to his bedroom and asked, "What was that, Daddy? I couldn't hear you."

He shouted, "Turn off the water so I can finish showering, *mija*!"

She replied, "Oh, OK." And she went to turn off the kitchen sink.

After about thirty minutes, Josefina and her dad took off for Mercedes's house. They stopped by at the store to get some things. Danny was hit on by several women at the market. Josefina had to pretend she was with him so they'd leave him alone. Even the cashier, who was a feminine guy, began flirting with Danny as he scanned his items. Josefina told him, "He's with me. So leave him alone and do your job because we're in a hurry." The employee apologized and checked them out faster.

Jesus was on the phone, calling his friend Sam and his neighbor Nick to invite them to the cookout. Sam asked, "Can I bring my wife? You know that'll be the only way I'd be able to go. Otherwise she won't let me."

Jesus replied, "Yeah, of course. Tell her to come too; bring your kids as well. Just make sure you bring some beer and snacks."

Nick was the next caller to be invited over. He too was informed to bring beer and snacks and not to forget his wife. Nick questioned, "Should I bring some tequila and margarita mix?"

Jesus responded, "Yeah! Otherwise we'll have to drink beer, ew."

Nick uttered, "Alright then, bro. I'll start getting ready and head to the store as well, to get some stuff. I'll tell my wife to do the same. Even if she doesn't want to, once she smells the carne asada, she'll get motivated. So I'll be over in a few." They hung up.

Jesus woke up Jr. and told him to get in the shower. Chris and Danniel woke up and were informed of the situation, so they too began getting ready. By the time Mercedes got back from the store, Chris, Danniel, and Jr. were ready—Jesus was almost.

Danny and Josefina arrived shortly after at Mercedes's house. Mercedes had just gotten back from the store herself. She and Josefina turned on the charcoal grill and began preparing a potato salad and some charro beans. Danny saw Jesus and asked him, "How's it going? Any luck finding out why you're so feminine yet?"

Jesus replied, "No, not yet. But when I do, I'll probably be more macho than you."

Dan uttered, "I doubt it, buddy. I don't think there's a cure out there for guys like you, to be honest."

Jesus told him, "Well, I have high hopes for my son and me. You just watch how we'll come out of this crisis as if we were masculine this whole time."

Danny commented, "So are you going to get drunk today and wear your wife's clothes by the end of the night again?"

Jesus fumed, "I don't do that ever. If I do, it's probably because I was dared or lost a bet. Anyhow, I need to go wash the dishes." Danny laughed and went over to his grandkids' rooms to say hello.

Lucia showed up with some sodas. She put them in the refrigerator and went out to the backyard to greet her daughters. Carla and Alejandra showed up not long after with some things of their own. Carla had got some macaroni salad and some chips. Alejandra had brought some dip and a cake for dessert. Danny took them outside to meet his elder daughter. Mercedes felt awkward to see her father with multiple women in her mom's presence, who seemed unaffected. She asked Carla and Alejandra, "Are you gals thirsty? There are sodas in the fridge and beer in the cooler. The food is on its way. You can take a seat anywhere you like."

Carla asked, "Where are your children? I'd like to meet them." Alejandra agreed as they both sat down on a patio set.

Mercedes replied, "They're inside being lazy. They should be out here soon though." Danny told them, "Let's go inside so they could meet you two. Come on; follow me." They got up and were guided inside.

Danny introduced them to Jesus who was washing the dishes, stating, "This is Mercedes's wife, I mean husband, Jesus. Jesus, these are my girlfriends Carla and Alejandra."

Jesus was rinsing a cup as he responded, "Nice to meet you two lovely ladies. I'd shake your hands, but my hands are wet as you can see. You're more than welcome to grab anything to eat or drink." Danny pulled them away so they could follow him to his grandkids' rooms.

Alejandra inquired, "Is Jesus feminine?"

Danny uttered, "Can't you tell? It's really obvious, isn't it? His son Jr. is the same way."

They went to Jr.'s room first and found him playing with dolls. Danny hugged him, picking him up in his arms. He then turned around and told him, "Look, *mijo,* these are my girlfriends Carla and Alejandra."

Jr. asked, "Are they my grandmothers too?" Carla and Alejandra found him irresistibly cute as they greeted him and listened to him talk.

Danny told him, "Not necessarily, *mijo.* I'm not married to anyone who could be officially called your grandmother other than your grandma Lucia, because she's your mom's mom."

Danny put Jr. down, and he followed them to his siblings' rooms. Danny walked into Danniel's bedroom and found her putting on makeup while also doing her hair. Danny introduced them to each other, and Carla complimented Danniel, "I love your hair.

It's so beautiful, and the hairstyle you're going for makes it look even better. I wish I had your hair."

Danniel said, "Thank you. I could do your hair too if you'd like."

Carla responded, "I'd love that but not right now since you're getting yourself ready." They left her room to head into Chris's room.

They got to his room and found his door locked, so Danny knocked. Chris asked, "Who is it?"

Dan said, "It's Grandpa, *mijo*. I'd like you to meet my girlfriends. We could come back if you're busy though."

Chris opened his door and replied, "Gramps, hi, how've you been? Girlfriends, you say, as in plural? Wow, impressive, good job there. I have things to learn from you, don't I?" He allowed them into his room but stopped Jr., telling him, "You can't come in here, little bro. There are no dresses or dolls here for you, and you always grab my things without permission." Jr. was upset and took off running, whimpering to inform his dad of the occurrence.

Chris introduced himself to Carla and Alejandra. They told him he looked a lot like his grandfather as they figured he resembled Dan in his early days. Danny told them, "He gets that a lot. I've got some pictures of me around his age, and when you see them, you'll think it's him."

Sam showed up with his family of seven—him, his wife, and five kids. Two males and three females, who were all feminine—around the same age as Mercedes's kids. Sam had some beer and a party platter of veggies with cold cuts in his hands. Mercedes greeted him cordially, although unwillingly, since she wasn't quite fond of him. She had him set the platter on top of one of the tables and the beer inside the cooler. Mercedes's kids came out of the house to hang out with Sam's. Mercedes asked Sam's wife, "Hi, how've you been? Haven't seen you in a while. What's new with you?"

Sam headed inside with Jesus while Sam's wife replied to Mercedes, "Hi, I've been alright, you know. Same, same, just hanging in. And yes, it's been long since I saw you too. I mean last time was at a similar event where our husbands ended up drunk off margaritas, dancing naked, touching dicks, remember?"

Mercedes responded, "You're right, and it makes sense why we haven't seen each other since. I'm sure you want to avoid such embarrassment recurring, right?"

> Sally, Sam's wife, asked, "Do you have any beer to calm my nerves?" Mercedes pointed at the cooler and told her to help herself, which she did and cracked one open; then she continued, "I didn't want to come for the same reason, since last time was overwhelming, but then again I thought it would be best if I come. That way I could control my guy instead of letting you address them both on your own."

Mercedes uttered, "Well, let's not let them have margaritas today. Why don't we work together on that now that we've concluded it is upsetting to us both?" Sally agreed and sat down to drink her beer while Mercedes, Josefina, and Lucia grilled some steaks, burgers, and hot dogs.

Josefina got a call from her friend Veronica, who told her, "Hey, girl, Hellen and I are going to a Chippendale show tonight. Want to come?"

She replied, "At what time? Because I'm at my sister's house right now having a cookout."

Vero said, "In an hour or so we'll be headed out there and could maybe meet up with you there or pick you up?"

Josefina uttered, "Yeah, I'll go if you guys pick me up because I came with my dad." Vero commented, "Alright, see you in about an hour."

They hung up, and Jr. walked over to greet her, "Hi, *tia,* I missed you. Why haven't you visited me?"

She informed him, "I've been working throughout the week and hanging out with my friends looking for your *tio.*"

He responded, "I have a *tio* now?"

She mentioned, "No, silly. I'm still single, but what I meant by it was that I'm looking for a boyfriend who may hopefully turn into my husband one day." Chris and Danniel came over to greet her and Lucia since they hadn't known they were there already.

The steaks, burgers, and hot dogs started coming off the grill, and everyone began serving themselves. They took seats at the patio tables in Mercedes's backyard. The smaller kids, who were three—including Jr., sat at a little table. The five older ones sat at their own table. The women sat together and congregated. Sam and Jesus came out of the house with margarita cups in their hands and a smile on their faces. There was some clattering as Mercedes and Sally got up to confront them. Mercedes asked them, "Are those margaritas?"

Jesus replied, "How'd you guess, honey? I've been dying to have one with Sam for such a long time."

Mercedes uttered, "Give me that. I don't want you drinking margaritas tonight." Sally suggested the same to Sam.

Both FEMNS were upset and inquired, "How come we can't have margaritas but y'all can have those disgusting beers?"

Mercedes stated, "Well, you said it yourself. You've been dying to drink one with each other, but do you recall the last time and what happened?"

Jesus commented, "I sure don't."

Sam didn't either, and they weren't going to make a public statement of the past events, so Mercedes told them, "Just have that one only, and we'll explain to you two later in private."

Josefina had finished eating, and she got a text from Vero who informed her, "We're outside; let's go have some fun, girl. Bring some beers for the pregame."

Josefina told her, "OK, I'm on my way." She said bye to everyone and grabbed three beers from the cooler and headed out.

Just as Josefina walked through the front gate on her way to Veronica's car, Nick walked in with a bottle of tequila and margarita mix. They greeted each other, and she got in the car as he walked into the backyard. When he got to the gathering, he raised the bottles in the air and shouted, "Guess it's going to be a fun party, guys!"

Jesus and Sam cheered as Mercedes and Sally yelled, "Nope! Take that back to your house, Nick. Margaritas are prohibited in this home for the rest of our lives."

Nick exclaimed, "But why? I don't see the issue. Y'all just don't want us having fun; that's all, right? Party poopers."

Mercedes got up and walked toward him, not allowing him to get any closer and informed him, "Margaritas are going to make Jesus and Sam get so drunk and make fools of themselves, so take it back to your house and don't let them have any more than they have in their cups right now."

Nick replied, "Come on, how bad can things get with some margaritas? I don't see the issue, Mercedes; stop acting like my wife and lighten up."

Mercedes uttered, "Last time these two had some, they got drunk and stripped down to their birthday suits, dancing all night femininely and fondling with each other. We had to send the kids to bed early because they did not care or listen to us. They would have almost had sex with each other had we not stopped them."

Nick commented, "Oh, I see now. Well, let me take this back to my house then." Jesus and Sam booed him as he left to return the banned beverage back to his place.

Josefina and her friends arrived at the club hosting the Chippendale show. They paid their entrance fee after waiting in a long line—trailing outside the establishment—filled with horny desperate women in search of machos. They made their way to a table in the VIP section, which Hellen had reserved. They were approached by a waiter who took their drink orders and headed to the bar to get them. They were excited to be there, as well as the rest of the females who were attending the show. The waiter came back with their drinks as the host got on stage to inform them of the rules of the show before introducing the first dancer. To summarize what he had said, they weren't allowed to touch the guys or attempt to have sex with them. If they exceeded the first warnings, they'd be kicked out with no reimbursement. No objects were to be thrown at the dancers other than dollar bills. There was zero tolerance for soliciting prostitution. The host then called out over the microphone, "Ladies . . . get ready for the hour y'all been waiting for! Brought to you in part by FEMNS Network, in collaboration with Test1 incorporated! Our first performer of the night . . . get your dollars ready for Darell, aka Chocolate Thunder!" A six-foot plus Black man wearing a white suit came out from behind the curtains, dancing to "Pony" by Ginuwine.

The crowd of spectators cheered as the dancer moved provocatively on stage. He ripped off his suit, underneath which he had a white thong. He began making his way off the stage to give the women a more personal experience. They roared in return for his performance. Josefina and her friends chanted, "Take it off! Take it off!" They were referring to his last garment.

Darell grabbed his thong at the waist as he stood in front of a group of women located next to Hellen's table, and he ripped it off. He was well endowed, and one of the women at the table jumped out of her seat and began fondling him. She received a warning from the dancer himself and the security staff that came to his rescue.

Nick had gotten back from his house after dropping off the margarita mix and tequila. Jesus argued, "Why'd you listen to my wife, bro? Bring it back here so we can party." Sam agreed.

Nick said, "I don't want any trouble. I too want some, so let's do this. I'll fill up y'all's cups when they're empty, at my place, and bring them back full. That way no one notices or suspects." Jesus and Sam congratulated him with a hug for his outstanding plan.

Jesus and Sam gave him their cups, as he prepared a plate to take for his wife since she didn't want to attend the gathering. When the plate was ready, he walked to his house and handed it to her. Then he refilled their cups with the contraband while she watched sports on television. He went back next door and gave his pals their vice. Mercedes and Sally saw nothing out of the ordinary as they were keeping their eyes not only on their husbands but also on their kids and holding conversations with each other. The kids were playing and getting along just fine. Jr. and Sam's two youngest had gone inside to play on his game console. The older ones were outside, playing around with Mut. Jesus and Sam chugged their cups' contents and asked for more, so Nick requested a beer for his wife in exchange. He received a beer and headed back to his place.

He gave his wife the beer and served another round of margaritas for himself and his buds. He went back to the cookout and gave them their cups. The guys were gossiping about many things in general. Danny took Alejandra to the back of the house and banged her. He then went to get Carla and did the same. Lucia was the last to enjoy sexual healing. Jesus and Sam began getting loud, but Mercedes and Sally thought it was normal since they assumed they had not been drinking. Jesus shouted, "Yeah! Yeah!" He could hear one of his favorite Cardi B songs play over a Bluetooth speaker they had taken out to the backyard.

Sam too began acting a bit wild under the influence. He went over to his wife and started dancing on her lap. The rest of the women laughed at his poor performance. They had no idea what was about to come as they discreetly continued to down margaritas.

Josefina and her friends were having the night of their life. There were three other dancers other than Darell on the stage floor, going around the tables to get their tips. The guy in front of theirs was dancing on top of Veronica. He was swinging his hips into her abdomen while she had her hands out to her sides as requested by the man. Hellen smacked the guy's ass, and he turned around to look at her, swinging his index finger side to side, silently letting her know not to do that again. The guy then hopped off Vero and walked behind the ladies. He got in front of Josefina and placed one leg over her lap and swung his crotch at her, guided by the rhythm of the music playing. The security staff were busy escorting out patrons who had been noncompliant with their rules. Josefina had an urge to grab the guy's dick, and she mustered the courage to do so. The guy silently swung his finger in her face and got off her. He then went to another table since they were not following the regulations. Josefina was bothered but knew it was better he had left instead of them getting kicked out. Next a guy who was extremely muscular came to their table. He was Hispanic and had most of the characteristics as explained in the guide Josefina had read about obtaining a macho man. The guy began dancing on top of Josefina first, and she quickly took out some dollar bills from her purse to place in his thong. The guy jumped on top of their table and began humping it while moving in coordination with the song playing. Josefina smacked his butt, and the guy slapped her face. She quickly got some money out of her purse and handed it to him so he wouldn't leave their table or get offended. The dancer stuck around, hoping they were high rollers and would tip him well. Hellen and Veronica gave him some money as well, and he started dancing on their laps.

The margaritas had hit Jesus and Sam, and the next thing everyone knew, they're getting naked. Chris was the first to point out and said, "Mom! Jesus and his gay friend are stripping already!"

Mercedes turned to see what they were doing and witnessed they had removed their shirts and were dancing with their bodies close to each other, rubbing their nipples against one another. Nick too had begun to remove his shirt. Sally got up and raced toward them as the women who had been distracted became aware of the situation. Sally grabbed Sam and told him, "Let's go now! You were drinking margaritas, huh? Where'd you get them from?"

Sam replied, "You go home. I'm having fun. Don't you worry about me drinking." She smacked him and began racing off, calling out her kids' names to leave with her.

Danny got up from his chair and said, "It's time to go now. I don't want to see these pansies acting drunk again. I knew this would happen." He said bye to his daughter, his ex, and the kids and left with Carla and Alejandra.

Nick and Jesus removed their pants and began touching their dicks right as he was departing. He turned to see them and uttered, "So much for the cookout, which turned out to be a cock-out."

Lucia asked Mercedes, "Aren't you going to put your man in check?" But she was laughing and recording them.

Mercedes yelled at Jesus, "Hey! You better knock that out, you drunk pansy! Put your clothes back on. Nobody wants to see your little winnie!" Jesus and Nick ignored her.

The kids went inside to avoid seeing something that would terrify them for the rest of their lives. Mercedes then got up and began beating up Jesus, ordering Nick to leave. Nick listened to her and departed the party. Jesus made a big deal but was forcibly convinced to stop his nonsense. Mercedes sent him inside to go to sleep. Lucia informed her she was heading out as well and left after saying bye to the kids. Mercedes couldn't believe what had happened and went inside to continue beating Jesus for the scene he had caused. When she went to the room, Danny was proved correct. Jesus was putting on one of her dresses, about to run outside in it. Mercedes put an end to his bullshit by knocking him unconscious with the Bluetooth speaker they had outside. She removed her dress off him as he lay on the floor, where he fell asleep.

⟿⟾

The dancer was up on the table dancing, and Veronica tried putting his penis in her mouth. The guy got mad and asked her, "What's wrong with you? Why would you even want to put my dick in your mouth if you don't know where it's been?" He covered it with his hands.

Veronica replied, "I don't care where it's been. I want it to be in my mouth; now come here and give me your sausage, hunk!"

The guy informed her, "I'm gay and sodomized my boyfriend prior to coming out here, which means you'll get feces in your mouth if you continue to try and suck it." She thought about it and gagged, wiping the tip of her tongue with a napkin and took a shot, since she had licked it slightly.

Hellen grabbed the guy's ass, and he slapped her. He then called the security staff over right away as all three of them ganged up on him to grope his body. Four of the security personnel responded and grabbed the girls. They then began kicking them out, making their way toward the entrance. Josefina shouted, "This is bullshit! We can't help our emotions and feelings having naked men in front of us! Your rules are strict and suck. It's like teasing a fat kid with a piece of cake and not letting him take a bite!"

One of the security guards told her just before they were shoved out of the front entrance, "Rules are rules, and if you're not going to follow them, we will."

The security at the door took over and told them to leave. They warned them that if they didn't, they'd call the police to come remove them and possibly take them to jail for disorderly conduct.

They weren't the only ones out there. Other women who had gotten kicked out earlier were screaming obscenities at the staff across the street. A marked unit showed up to address the crowd across the street. The girls saw that and sprinted toward their car. Hellen fell halfway there as her shoe flew off while running away. She got up, and they continued to head to the vehicle before the cops took them in. Once at the ride, they got in and fled from the area. They dropped off Josefina, and she fell asleep immediately since she was quite intoxicated and tired. Her friends did too once they got to their homes safely. It was a night for everyone in their circle to remember.

CHAPTER 8

VIRAL MOCKERY

Jesus woke up lying on the floor—butt naked—with the worst hangover he'd ever experienced and his thumb up his anus. He got up from the floor in his bedroom with a massive headache. He put on some clothes and headed to the restroom to find some medication for his ache. He gulped down some pills and rinsed his mouth in the restroom sink. He then went back into his room to look for his cell phone. When he found it under the bed, he noticed he had received an email from the study. The email notified him he'd have to go in later that day to have more tests administered on him. He was to make an appointment as soon as possible. He logged into their virtual registry and set up an appointment for after his wife got back from work. He then logged into his social media platform and discovered his video from last night had gone viral. Everyone was making fun of him and his pals. Someone had also dug up his video that Danniel had recorded of him getting electrocuted, which was also circulating online. To top it off, someone had recorded him at the water park full of shit as well and uploaded it to the web. He had become a celebrity overnight. He got off his phone and went to drink some more water in the kitchen. Jr. woke up as he heard him grunting since he felt like shit. He walked up to him and said, "Hi, Dad, did you have fun last night? I heard you were dancing naked."

Jesus replied, "Yeah, I had fun last night, but I'm not right now, Son. How about you? Did you enjoy last night?"

Jr. uttered, "I did. I like playing with Sam's kids."

Jesus responded, "Well, I'm glad you had fun." Jr. got his tablet, and they walked to the living area.

Jesus asked Jr. if he was hungry, and he told him he was, so he began making breakfast. Jr. was watching videos online when he came across one of his dad's. He asked his father, "Is this you? It seems like it's going viral and everyone is making fun of you, Dad. Why are there parts of you blurred?"

Jesus stated, "I saw that already. Guess I'm the talk of the town now after having one wild night with the boys. Just don't look at any other videos of me you may find circulating, Son."

Jr. commented, "OK, Dad." He put his tablet away and turned the TV on.

Jesus got a text from his wife, and it read, "Hope you haven't seen the videos of you going around, but then again I hope you do. Maybe that way you'll learn your lesson that you act inappropriately when drunk. Good thing my coworkers don't know you. Otherwise they'd make fun of me for being with you. I want you to clean up the house and the restroom in the hall. Someone threw up all over it, and I have a feeling it was you." He asked her if she knew who had shared the footage, but she didn't reply.

Jesus got a text from his mother that read, "*Mijo,* are you alright? I can't believe I just saw a video of you acting immaturely and making a fool of yourself. I can only imagine what your *tias* will tell me if they see. You've really done it this time with your ways. Please don't come by my house for some time, at least till things settle and your dad cools off. He's not very happy seeing his stepson online acting a fool." He continued to get messages from people in his circle regarding the videos spreading like wildfire.

Mercedes was called into the boss's office. She left the floor in a hurry not knowing what it was about. She did hope it had nothing to do with someone recognizing her husband in one of the videos streaming. When she got to the boss's office, she knocked, and her boss said, "Come in. Hello, Mercedes, I'm so happy to see you; please take a seat." Mercedes sat down in one of the chairs in front of Mrs. Santiago's—her boss's—desk.

Mrs. Santiago said, "I just wanted to inform you that the channel package you brought up to my attention has been approved by the corporate office. The idea has increased the company's revenue in its first day of availability to the public for purchase, for which they sent me this bonus for you to receive." She handed her an envelope with a check inside.

Mercedes had a wide smile on her face as she thanked her boss. Mrs. Santiago told her, "I'm very content to have you on our team. Keep up the good work, and if you come across any more ideas, please let me know. The package has been named 'The Mercedes Deal' in your bright honor."

Mercedes was pleased, and she replied, "Thank you for believing in my idea. And yes, if I get any more, I'll come and share them with you."

She got up from the chair and was making her way out when Mrs. Santiago asked, "So what're you going to do with your bonus money?"

Mercedes turned around and uttered, "Well, I think I'm going to invest on some testosterone for my husband."

Her boss responded, "That's great. I just hope the video circulating online of someone's husband dancing nude with another guy—fencing—isn't your husband. I wouldn't waste my money on a lost cause like that."

Mercedes giggled and commented, "Nope, that's not my husband, and if it was, I agree with you about the lost cause and waste of money it would be." She then walked out of her boss's office, seriously reconsidering wasting her money on a treatment for Jesus.

Danny was going around sharing the shit out of Jesus's videos online. He thought it may increase his follower subscriptions and make him some extra cash, not that he needed it, but it wouldn't hurt him either. He was in his bedroom fixed to his phone, spreading the videos with his friends and family. He then got a message from Lucia, which read, "Hi, Danny, Hope you woke up feeling great today. I saw you've been sharing Jesus's videos online. I know he's an embarrassment to us and to our daughter who's his wife. I don't want to sound rude or demanding, but don't you think it's a bit selfish to burn him? He may be a feminine idiot we both don't like, but he's still Mercedes's husband and the father of our grandkids. Think of them and not of him and consider taking down those videos and stop sharing them."

Danny texted back, "You're right, but it's still funny to watch and know he's getting recognized for being a fag dork. I'll remove the videos off my social network and stop sharing them right now. I just don't think it'll help any since I'm not the only one sharing or reposting them. Anyhow, hope you have a good day yourself."

As soon as Josefina woke up, she went to the restroom. She began gagging and spewing out her night's alcohol intake. Dan inquired,

"*Mija*, are you alright? You must have seen your brother-in-law's video, huh? That's why you're throwing up? You missed it after you left."

She replied, "What videos? I had a rough party with the girls last night." She rinsed her mouth and exited the restroom as she resumed her convo, "We went to this Chippendale show and drank excessively, then we got kicked out. But what videos are you talking about?"

Danny told her, "Come take a look before I take them down." He showed her Jesus's videos.

She was in shock as she witnessed Jesus nude and stated, "What the fuck! Is that his little dick making contact with his friends? Oh my gosh! This is embarrassing; what a fucking pathetic feminine man he turned out to be." She gagged some more and ran toward the toilet again.

Danny was cracking up at her reaction. She threw up, and then she went through the medicine cabinets searching for something to get rid of her headache. She found some and took one capsule; then she walked to her room where she had a bottle of water. She swallowed the pill and sent a text to Mercedes just in case she was unaware of the videos. She realized the severity of it when she logged into her social media platforms and discovered how viral the videos had managed to become.

Mercedes was walking by her team's cubicles when she noticed the phone lines were ringing off the hook. All male customers were requesting for "The Mercedes Deal," and she smiled out of joy, forgetting the videos of her husband. Then the other manager—who believed she had come up with the idea—approached her. Vicky was her name, and she confronted Mercedes, "How did you steal my idea and get credit for it?"

Mercedes said, "I never stole your idea. I simply had it and shared it with the boss a few days prior to you telling me you had done the same."

Vicky replied, "That's not possible, otherwise she would have informed me you had already brought it up to her attention when I did!"

Mercedes uttered, "Why don't you lower your tone and attitude and go ask her right now yourself before you continue falsely accusing me?"

Vicky responded, "I will. I'm going to get to the bottom of this and find out if there has been a mistake. I was really counting on that bonus." She then walked away headed to the boss's office.

Mercedes walked away and sat at her desk. She was a bit rattled about being confronted, but she knew she was the one with the idea in the first place. It of course was suggested by some customers, but she was the one who pushed it up the ladder. She sipped on her cup of coffee and checked her work emails. All the personnel at the corporate office had sent her an email congratulating her. She then opened the envelope containing her bonus. The check was written under her name for ten racks. She opened her bank application and took some pictures to virtually deposit it into her account. When she looked up, Vicky was walking back toward her desk. Vicky told her, "I'm sorry to have falsely accused you of stealing my idea. She told me it was you who brought it up first. So you won fair and square."

Mercedes commented, "Apology accepted. I told you so." Vicky walked away and headed back to her section.

Due to the videos, Chris and Danniel had received some unwanted attention at their schools. They were both sent to the principal's office to address the confusion if any. Chris's high school principal asked him, "Is that really your dad on the videos everyone is making fun of?"

Chris said, "Unfortunately it is, but he's not my real dad; he's my stepdad. I know this has disrupted several of my classes, but I have no control of the web. I didn't upload any of those videos or partook in sharing or showing them to anyone. I'm actually embarrassed of them myself."

The principal replied, "You're right about not having control on what circulates on the internet. I'll have a word with your teachers to let them know they should put an end immediately to anyone making fun of you. If anyone disobeys my orders, I'll have them sent to my office to be disciplined. You're free to go back to class. and thank you for your honesty."

Chris uttered, "No problem, sir." As he walked out of the office, the principal showed his secretary the video, and they both cracked up.

Danniel had a similar situation, but she was sent to the middle school counselor's office. The counselor inquired, "Why are all the kids making fun of you and interfering with the class lessons?"

Danniel said, "Last night we had a cookout at our home, and my stepfather got a bit carried away while drunk. He was acting inappropriately. Someone filmed him and spread the video online. The video has become popular overnight, and the kids are making fun of me because of it."

The counselor raised her eyebrow and took her phone out, questioning, "Is this the video you're referring to?" She played the video.

Danniel stated, "Yup, that's the one. Sorry about it, but at least it wasn't me. It's not my fault my stepdad made a mockery of himself."

The counselor was about to burst into laughter but held it in, saying, "Excuse me really quick." She stepped out of her office and chuckled with her hands covering her mouth. She then stepped back in and replied to her, "You're right about it not being your fault. I will advise all your teachers of the situation so they can protect you in case someone bullies you. I will also discuss this with the principal so we can find a resolution. You can go back to class now. Hope you have a good day." Danniel departed, and she heard the counselor laughing out loud as soon as she turned the corner to head back to her classroom.

Sam and Nick contacted Jesus about the videos. Nick was first and said, "Did you see we became famous? We look so cool in the videos. Our butts look perky, and we look masculine, bro. Hopefully someone wants to interview us so I can promote my product that I've been working on for the past year."

Jesus replied, "I saw, and everyone is mad and upset at me. I too think we look kick ass, and you're right about our butts, now that you've mentioned it. What product have you been working on?"

Nick told him, "I've been developing a butt lift underwear for men that has a cell phone pocket, and it also has a bump in the front to make it seem like the junk is huge. If anyone asks me to go have an interview for TV, I'm definitely wearing it and going to promote it there."

Jesus uttered, "Let me call you back because Sam is calling me on the other line."

Jesus answered Sam's call and heard him saying while sobbing, "My wife is so angry at me. She doesn't even want to talk or look at me. Do you know who uploaded the videos? Sally is disgusted with me, and I think I overheard her talking to a divorce attorney. She told me everyone at the apartments we live at have been making fun of her because of me. She said even some old lady who she's never seen before called her a lesbian while she was washing our clothes in the laundry room."

Jesus told him, "I don't know who uploaded the videos, but we look cool, don't we? We will soon be so famous that we will never have to work in our lives ever again."

Sam said, "Sally beat the shit out of me, bro. My face looks like a semi ran me over. I don't care about being famous or having anything do with publicity. I have social anxiety as is, and it'll only worsen with fame. Plus, my kids are probably going through hell in school right now because of the video." And they were, similar to Jesus's stepchildren.

Jesus replied, "You're right, and yeah, if you feel that way, it's best you don't become famous."

Sam began shouting, "I'm sorry! OK, I'll hang up and never talk to him again, honey!" He then hung up on Jesus as Sally assaulted him once more.

Jesus called Nick back and informed him, "Sam got his ass beat, and his wife might be divorcing him due to the video. She also told him to never talk to me again, and I think he blocked me. Is your wife mad at you or anything? How's she taking this so far? I hope Mercedes doesn't ask for a divorce right now. I'd have nowhere to go. My mom told me she doesn't want me anywhere near her house because of the videos."

Nick uttered, "That sucks for Sam, bro. Damn, his wife is very unforgiving and abusive. My wife hasn't told me anything about it. I don't think she's seen it. She doesn't have any social media accounts. I'm sure she won't ask for a divorce though. She feels she can't get anyone better than me since she's older. Anyhow, I'll talk to you later because I'm heading out to my appointment for the study." They hung up, and Jesus finished eating his breakfast while watching the FEMNS Network, as Jr. went to the restroom.

Vicky had gone back to her desk feeling bitter and wanting revenge. She had been hoping and counting on the bonus check to help her husband become masculine by manually increasing his testosterone productivity. She observed Mercedes at her desk from afar, appearing happy and content, which she began to envy. Her husband was at home and sent her a text message with a link to Jesus's videos. She opened the link and witnessed the video. She squinted and saw a resemblance of someone familiar. She just couldn't recall where she had seen one of the guys in the video. She thought for a second, clearing her mind of negativity. She remembered Mercedes had a picture of her and her husband on top of her desk, and that's where she had seen the guy from the video. She got up from her desk and went over to Mercedes's desk. When she got closer, she noticed the picture was no longer there. She walked up to Mercedes, who was sitting at her desk doing paperwork, and asked her, "Whatever happened to the picture you had here of you and your husband?"

Mercedes had removed it earlier when she realized he had become a celebrity but replied, "I don't know what you're talking about, Vicky. I've never had a picture on top of my desk of my husband and I." She pushed it deeper into her purse with her foot, which was sitting on the floor next to her.

Vicky uttered, "I could've sworn you did have it there. Do you have a photo of him on you by any chance? I thought I'd seen him the other day at the store and wanted to make sure it was him."

Mercedes told her, "You're probably confusing me with the boss. She has one of hers and her husband on her desk. And no, I don't have a picture of him around. What store do you believe you ran into him at?"

Vicky stated, "I probably am confusing him, huh? You don't have one on your phone? Everyone has pictures on their phone of all their family members. Why don't you look for one there to show me?"

Mercedes rebutted, "I cleaned out all my pictures on my phone over the weekend and saved some to a USB, printed out the rest to add to a photo album, and hung some up in the house. Sorry, girl, but you're a bit late on that too."

Vicky responded sarcastically, "Bummer, late to my own party again, huh? You must have some of him on one of your social media accounts. Which one and what's your user name so I could search you?"

Mercedes told her, "I don't have any social media accounts. If you find any, they're fake, and I'm warning you ahead of time it's not me or mine."

Vicky said, "Alright, well, just forget about it. Sorry for intruding into your personal life. Just wanted to make sure it was your husband I saw at the store with another woman." She tried creating jealousy as her final leverage attempt.

Mercedes uttered, "My husband doesn't go to the store by himself, let alone with another female. You've never met him, and if you've seen him in pictures, he doesn't look the same in person. I assure you; you're confusing him with someone else. Anyhow, it's time to go home, so I'll see you tomorrow, Vicky. Have a great afternoon and don't show up home late or you might find your husband with another woman at the store." She winked at her and walked toward the front door.

Jesus had showered and gotten dressed while he waited for his wife to get back home so he could go to his appointment. When she walked in through the front door, she didn't even turn his way or talk to him. She even ignored him as he stepped outside, telling her he'd be back. He walked to his car and got in, heading to the study facility to check in. When he arrived, he had a hard time finding a spot to park again. Then a guy who had just parked saw him and walked up to his car, telling him, "Hey! You're the famous pipi poop man going viral online. I've got to admit those videos are funny, bro. Let me move my car out so your highness can take my space." He jumped back in his vehicle and moved it out as Jesus drove into it, and he took a photo with him.

Jesus got out of his ride and walked into the building to sign in. When he entered, he heard his fans chanting, who were happy to see him. Nick was there too, and they made fun of them both as they asked for their autographs and took pictures with them. When everyone calmed down, Jesus took a seat next to Nick. Nick told him, "You see, bro, we have followers now, and they're talking about making a group page about us. I see money raining on us soon."

Jesus told him, "They're making fun of us though. I feel like leaving and never coming back. My wife didn't even want to speak to me right now."

Nick said, "Bad publicity is still good publicity, bro. It's all on how you perceive it. I'm telling you, brother, this is the chance I've been waiting for all my life. I know someone is going to want to interview me soon and I'll be able to market my idea." They then called his name, and he left to go inside.

Jesus was alone when the two guys who had mentioned to him about semen consumption as a form to increase male testosterone sat next to him. They told him, "Did you try the semen supplement already?"

Jesus informed them, "No, I haven't gotten lucky. I was even going to try it with my dog, but he keeps running away from me. How about you guys?"

One of them said, "I got some from this bum who lives under a bridge up the street from my house. I'm starting to feel more masculine already. I told you not to try it from an animal though."

The other guy uttered, "Hey, so is it really you in those videos going around online? Let me take a picture with you, bro." He leaned over and took his phone out to take a photo.

The other guy commented, "Hey, bro, I was thinking since you've become an overnight celebrity, maybe you could be the face of my product for the company I plan on starting? I'm going to begin mass-producing semen capsules for us feminine men to take, and it would help to spread your fame toward the product. Look at it this way; you'll have a lifetime supply for free just by endorsing my merchandise. What do you say, bro?" Jesus pondered the idea as his name was called, so he told him he'd get back to him and left.

Nick got out of his appointment and headed out the door. A bunch of other guys recognized him and requested him for pictures and autographs. He ran outside and into his car. There was a mob following him, and he made a quick escape. He almost ran them over as he darted out of there and headed home. When he got home, his wife was still unaware he had become famous. She just asked him, "Did they find a cure for you, baby?"

Nick said, "No, not yet. Hopefully soon. I mean it's still early to be having negative thoughts. I'm remaining positive that they will and I'll be a macho again."

His wife kissed him, saying, "I hope you understand I don't care if you do or don't. I love you either way. I'm already in my sixties, and at this age, all that matters is keeping good company and not so much having a freak in bed."

Nick replied, "I love you too, honey, and appreciate all you've done and continue doing for me." He kissed her back, and he went to sit in the kitchen to try and contact some investors for his product.

Jesus managed to get out of his exams and ran out. By the time he got out, most of the participants had left. There were only a few who recognized him, but he covered his face as he jetted to his vehicle. He jumped inside and drove off. He was a bit paranoid about his unwanted fame. He grabbed a hat from the back of his car, which his son had left behind, and put it on. He was almost home when a car began following him. He made a quick stop at the gas station to fill up his automobile. He didn't notice he had company nearby. He got out of his car and paid for the gas with his fingerprint. He inserted the nozzle, then sat inside his car. He was on his phone watching videos when all of a sudden he heard someone scream, "Get out and fight like a man, you pussy ass motherfucker!" He felt his ride jolting and heard a crackling noise coming from the back.

When he looked back to see what was going on, he discovered it was the angered husband of the woman he had chased online. He had broken his taillight and was walking to his window, ordering him to get out and fight. Jesus looked around his vehicle to see if he could grab a weapon. He found a box cutter and exited the car, knowing he'd have to remove the nozzle in order to leave anyhow. The man observed him brandishing a knife and took a firearm from his waist. He pointed it at Jesus, and Jesus shouted, "Oh shit! Wait! Wait! Oh shit, wait!" He hopped on one foot, foreseeing the man shooting at him while he danced the bunny hop.

The man yelled, "Put that weapon away and fight me like a man, you fucking coward!"

Jesus closed the knife in his hand and uttered, "I'm not going to fight you. I'm just a feminine man who made a mistake. I go by pink daddy she. I'll suck your dick if you'd like me to make it up to you." He grabbed the nozzle and put it back in its spot.

The man was confused; his rage had calmed down, which had almost led him to shoot Jesus, and he said, "Fucking pussy! That's what I thought; just acting alpha, but you're a beta bitch!" He observed people looking at him and got back into his car and left.

Jesus had shit himself and pissed his pants. The people around him recognized him from his videos and began recording the scene to upload it online to add to the preexisting collection. He got in his car and sped off, heading home. He didn't even mind the feces running down the back of his leg. All he wanted to do was get home safely, and he did. When he got to his residence, he had complaints waiting for him. He ran to the restroom to clean off the shit and piss and change before showing his face to address the concerns.

CHAPTER 9
BROSKI-WEAR

The next morning, Jesus woke up to someone ringing the front doorbell. He got up out of bed and walked to the door to see who it was. A crowd had gathered outside, including a group of news reporters. He observed Nick giving an interview but decided he'd stay inside and not cooperate. He instead shut his window blinds and curtains. His son woke up and asked, "Who is it, Daddy? Who keeps ringing the doorbell?"

Jesus replied, "It's the Jehovah's Witness, Son. Shush, be quiet so they can think no one is home and leave."

They continued to knock and ring his doorbell as he and Jr. remained silent. Nick, on the other hand, utilized his fifteen minutes of fame by promoting his invention. He told the news reporters, "Yeah, well, we were drunk and having a good time. We actually did it on purpose to make some funny novelty videos, most importantly, so I could get this kind of reaction to promote my product." He raised his hand with his first concept and explained, "This here is the Broski-Wear, a discreetly comfortable garment that visually enlarges the crotch and buttocks. It has multiple layers of padding that promote relaxation in a soft breathable material. It has an integrated pocket to place your cell phone. It comes in two colors, white and black. If you're not using the Broski-Wear, you're using a women's bra and underwear! It'll be available to the public for sale in a few weeks, so be on the lookout or have bad luck and miss out!"

The reporter stated, "Wow, that was an impressive demonstration on your underwear, but tell me. Were you wearing this prior to the recorded encounter? Is this the reason why you and another man were groping each other? Our viewers are in suspense as to how you and the other gentleman got together and filmed the video, as well as what happened afterward. Did you two elope?"

Nick replied, "No, as I previously mentioned, it was an acting performance to promote my product. At this time, I refuse to answer any more of your questions and would kindly appreciate it if y'all left my property and gave me my privacy to return to my normal macho life." He walked away and went inside his house as the crowd remained outside.

Vicky had accomplished her task and found incriminating evidence online on Mercedes's social media. She began sharing it with her team, and they passed it onto the rest of the employees. Mercedes had begun her day as usual, not knowing about the rumors. She did start catching employees looking at her and pointing. Then one of the ladies on her team asked, "Have you seen the video of two guys fondling each other at a cookout?"

She acted surprised and replied, "No, I haven't. Why, is it funny or something?"

The girl said, "It's going viral. How could you haven't seen it yet? It's super funny but disgusting at the same time."

She stated, "I hardly get on my phone for entertainment purposes. So I don't even know what's hip or hop right now." The girl showed her the video. Mercedes looked at it and uttered, "Wow! That is funny, huh? Thanks for showing it to me, but we have a ton of work to do, so please get back to your seat and attend to customers' needs."

The girl commented, "Before I do, I just wanted to let you know everyone is saying one of those guys is your husband. They're also going around with a picture of you and the guy in reference." She showed her the text with the photo and walked away.

Mercedes was furious at this point. She got up from her chair and went outside to catch some fresh air. When she came back inside, Mrs. Santiago called her to her office. Mercedes walked in, and the boss told her, "Please take a seat. Now I don't know if you've noticed, but there's a rumor going around that one of the guys in the viral video is your husband. This is affecting the workplace, distracting everyone from their objective. I'd like to give you the opportunity to clear the rumors with me before it gets out of hand and reaches the corporate office. What do you have to say in your defense?"

Mercedes told her, "I'm sorry about the problem a video of my brother-in-law has caused. I assure you that's not my husband but in fact his twin brother. I'm not going around causing any problems in the workplace. I have reason to believe Vicky is responsible for this mishap. She confronted me yesterday about the new deal we're offering and wanted to take credit for it. I also believe she's the culprit behind this nonsense. I say this because after she accused me of stealing her idea and finding out from you that it was originally mine, she came back to my desk, persistently requesting to see a picture of my husband."

The boss uttered, "I see, so this is her retaliating at you for the deal. Well, thank you for confirming your side of this story. I will take your word at face value since you've been a part of this team longer than I have without previous incidents. I'll have a word with her shortly to order her to stop her games."

Mercedes responded, "Thank you very much for assisting me in this unwanted issue, also for taking my word. I promise if you stop her, this will not happen again." As she walked out of the office, she heard Mrs. Santiago calling Vicky in.

Jesus kept peeking out through his windows to see if the news reporters and the crowd had vanished. He also was looking to see if the angered husband was out there in the crowd. He slowly watched the group of spectators and news reporters dissipate. Once they cleared out, he hugged his son for reassurance and safety. He knew he had people looking for him and didn't know when or where they would catch him. He didn't want to go outside for the rest of his life, as he felt embarrassed and terrified. He got some bowls and served himself and Jr. some oatmeal. He had quick oats, which he poured into each bowl. He then added water and placed them in the microwave for one minute. When they came out, he added cinnamon, honey, and peanut butter, then he mixed them up. He and Jr. started eating, watching television—specifically the FEMNS Network. Nick's interview aired on TV, and he watched to see what he had said. After listening to the interview, he prayed and hoped the attention would cease. Jr. asked him, "Did you ever take Mut's poop sample to the vet? What did they say? Is he sick, pregnant, or something?"

Jesus said, "I did take it, but they haven't given me the results yet. I hope he's not sick, and he can't be pregnant since he's a male."

Jr. replied, as he continued to eat his oatmeal, "Oh, well, I hope he's not sick too. Did the Jehovah's Witness already leave?"

Jesus uttered, "Yeah, they left already, but stay inside and don't go out just in case they circle back the block."

Jr. responded, "OK, Dad, I won't go outside."

Vicky walked into Mrs. Santiago's office, and Mrs. Santiago shut the door to reprimand Vicky. The boss told her, "I hear you're the one causing ruckus on my watch. What seems to be the problem other than envy? How could you be going around making false allegations of Mercedes's husband when she just told me it's not him?" She took a seat back at her desk.

Vicky rebutted, "I'm not doing or saying nothing, ma'am. I don't know what you're talking about. I come here to work and not to gossip."

The boss responded, "One thing I hate the most besides an evil nosy person is a lying coward. I've gone ahead and reviewed the footage of you showing everyone a picture from your cell phone, which began a chain reaction of rumors. You don't have to admit to it, but you will have to clear up your desk, turn in your company-issued equipment, and leave this building since I'm terminating you in this instance."

Vicky argued, "But why? I'm sorry. I'll stop, clear the story up, and behave. Please don't fire me. I won't create any more problems, I promise."

Mrs. Santiago commented, "Too late for pity and excuses. I want you to leave my office and this building as soon as possible." Vicky's head was down as she walked out and headed to her desk to clear it.

Her coworkers saw her clearing up her belongings and putting them away in a box. They knew what had happened, and then they saw the boss come out of her office and grab everyone's attention. She told them, "From now on, I don't want anyone spreading rumors or gossip about anyone else here! This is a healthy working environment and shall remain that way as long as I'm in charge! Those who don't listen and disrupt the production will be fired on the spot!" She then walked back inside her office, setting a clear example to everyone of what happens to those who oppose her rules.

Vicky was later escorted off the property by the security officer on the ground. She was advised not to return; otherwise, she'd be subjected to a trespassing violation. Everyone else had stopped gossiping about Mercedes and had returned to their jobs without further incident.

Danny was in the gym working out when a group of women came and sat on the empty benches next to him to watch him exercise. He observed them and racked the bar. He asked, "May I help you, ladies?"

"Hi!" one of them replied, giggling.

He said, "Hi to you too." He lay back onto the bench to continue his routine.

The females giggled, smiles on their faces as they stared at Danny. He had his headphones on and did not listen to what they were discussing. They awkwardly continued to admire him. One of them made a hand gesture for him to remove his ear pieces. Danny racked the bar once more, removing his headphones and inquiring, "How may I help you?"

The woman responded, "Are you taken or married? My friends and I have a bet going on as to whether you are or aren't."

Dan uttered, "Whoever bet that I'm feminine won. Now please, if it isn't too much to ask, go away and let me finish my exercise." He placed his headphones back on and resumed his session.

The females chuckled and continued gossiping, then the same one stated, "I know you're not feminine. I can tell because at your age, even if you took testosterone or steroids, you wouldn't be as developed."

He had his music on a volume low enough to hear but pretended he wasn't listening. He finished his last rep and racked the bar. He then got up and began putting the plates back in their places and headed to the chest fly machine. The women followed him to the machine. He sat down after locking in his desired weight and began working out. The same female told him, "I know you could hear me. I want to be your slave, mister, for you to do as you please with me. I don't care if you have multiple women. I want to be a part of your most intimate desires. You could put a leash on me and tie me up in your backyard. You could make me your punching bag and cum bucket. You could just call me whenever you want sex and ignore me the rest of the time. You could throw shit at me while I'm tied up to your restroom. You could dick slap me all day while you eat the breakfast I cook."

Danny began cracking up and commented, "What is wrong with you? How could you volunteer for that type of treatment? And where in the hell did you get those ideas from?"

The woman told him, "Those are the things I'm willing to do and sacrifice for a real macho like you. There aren't many left, and even my friends agree to do the same. You could have us all at once. We've been looking for a man like you together, and we can't find one. Please take us with you so we don't waste any more time searching with no success."

Danny said, "Alright then, just let me finish my set here in peace and show me you all are house trained." The females listened and kept quiet. They were attentive in wiping off his sweat and handing him water as he worked out.

When he was finished, he told them, "Thank you ladies for all your help and support. I want you to go wait for me in the restroom so you can shower my body." They got up to run over there as he made his way out of the front door.

Jesus had continued talking to his old friend from school—Olivia. She was actually the one pursuing him. She had asked him to meet up with her at a car wash. He was hesitant because he didn't want more trouble than he already had on his plate, but he wanted to suck her punani dry of semen. When Mercedes arrived home from work, he was waiting to leave with the excuse he had more studies to attend. Mercedes informed him, "I almost lost my job today because of you. I had to lie to my boss and tell her it was your twin brother in the video going viral. You've seriously become a disgrace to this family. If it wasn't that I don't want to bother anyone with taking care of Jr. while I'm at work, I would kick you out of my house."

Jesus said, "That's why I don't do anything right in my life. You're always criticizing and judging me. You make me feel so insecure and ashamed of myself. How am I responsible for a video I didn't record or upload on the web? For all I know, it was probably your mom or dad who are accountable. Anyhow, I made some food for us to eat. I'll be back; hopefully, soon I can make you proud."

He exited the dwelling and got in his car. He was wearing a costume so no one would recognize him. He had on a hat and some baggy clothing to resemble a gangbanger. He drove to the car wash and saw some women washing their cars. He also saw a guy drying his truck at the end. He texted Olivia to ask her where she was. She told him she was right around the corner. When she arrived, he hopped out of his ride to greet her. She asked, "Have you been here for a while? I'm sorry; it's because I ran into some traffic."

Jesus replied, "Not too long. Don't worry about being late; it's OK. I was wondering if you would like to go somewhere more private to talk?"

She asked, "How come we can't talk here? I don't see an issue unless you're scared of someone or something and aren't the macho you claim to be."

He uttered, "What?! Nothing like that. I just want to eat you out and fuck you doggy style."

She responded, "Yeah, you've told me that before, but isn't there something else you'd like to do to me? I mean, I'm kinda getting bored of hearing you say the same thing like those are the only things you know how to do. By the way, could I borrow some money? I'm short about one hundred for my rent."

Jesus took a hundred-dollar bill out of his pocket and handed it to her, then he uttered, "You already owe me from last time. Why don't you forget about your debt and let me eat you out and fuck you doggy style instead?"

She replied, "Sure, Daddy, where do you want to go and do that to me?"

Jesus was happy knowing he was going to be able to suck some semen out of her. During their conversations, he had secretly touched the subject, and she had informed him her husband would cum inside her as she was on birth control. As he pointed at an alley nearby, she picked up her cell and told him, "Oh shit, it's my husband, and he said he knows where I'm at." He then felt a solid punch land on his chin. He fell to the ground, and when he regained consciousness, he saw several women around him, checking if he was alright. He got up and observed Olivia was gone and so was the man washing his truck. Then he noticed the angered husband pulling into the carwash. Jesus ran to his car and took off as the guy chased him. He was petrified and squeezed his butt cheeks tight, feeling as if he was about to defecate. The man continued pursuing him as he once again drove to the police station and began honking like a coward. The man kept on driving, leaving the area as he did not want to get into any legal issues.

Danny made it home without having the group of hungry women chase him. He got out of his truck and headed inside. He entered through the front door and observed his daughter dancing in the living room with her headphones on. She hadn't noticed he was back from the gym, so she began singing the song she was dancing and listening to. It was "Como la flor" by Selena. Danny walked up to her and tapped her on her shoulders. She was startled and tossed the dildo in her hand away, which she simulated to be a microphone. She removed her headphones off and greeted her father. Danny asked her, "Why're you so happy today? Did you finally score a macho?"

Josefina said, "I have a date with hopefully one tonight. He rides a motorcycle and seems rugged. Just the type I might husband up." She giggled as she grabbed and hid her sex toy from her dad.

Dan replied, "I'm happy for you. I hope he's the one so you could stop wasting your time searching and spend it birthing my grandkids." She chuckled.

She was about to head back to her room to put away her fake microphone when her dad informed her, "Guess what happened at the gym today?"

She uttered, "The guy I went on a date with took his boyfriend, and they got into a fight over you?"

Dan responded, "Close but not quite so. I haven't seen him around lately. I think he may have killed himself or skipped town to become a Chippendale. But anyhow, a group of girls thought of going to the gym to find a macho, just like you. They approached me and were stalking me throughout my workout. They offered to be my slaves, all three of them at the same time. Said I could make them my sex toys all at once. I was a bit creeped out because they seemed to have a high level of sexual frustration since they probably hadn't had sex in some time. I had to fool them in order to get away from them. I told them I was going to shower in the restroom and wanted them to go wait for me there. Then I ran the hell out of there."

Josefina commented, "You're mean, Dad. How could you ditch them?" They both laughed.

He stated, "I tried telling them nicely I wasn't interested, but they insisted. I had to trick them to escape."

She inquired, "Why didn't you just add them to your collection of admirers instead?"

He informed her, "No way! I've got three women already; plus, I deal with you, your sister, her wife, and two daughters. I've got too many women in my life to want more. Sometimes I feel like running away when y'all get together. It irritates me to be around too much estrogen. I don't know exactly how to explain it. I also don't mean to offend anyone by expressing myself. Anyhow, I'm going to cook me something because I told the girls to not come to my house today and let me rest. Do you want some omelets?"

She uttered, "No worries, Dad. No offense taken, and sure, I'll have some omelets before I head to work." She fled to her room, not noticing her dildo had fallen out of her pocket.

Danny called her back and told her, "Honey, you dropped some weird-looking microphone over here. You might want to come pick it up and take it to your room before it goes in the trash."

She walked back embarrassed and said, "Thanks, Dad. Sorry about that. I'll take it to my room."

Jesus had finally made it back home after being kicked out of the police parking lot. He ran inside and was only greeted by his youngest son, who was happy to see him. Everyone else in the house was upset at what his video had caused them over the past few days. He went to the restroom to clean himself from the beating he had sustained earlier. He noticed he had a bruise on his chin and began sobbing. He called himself derogatory names, putting himself down. His son knocked at the door and asked if he was alright. Jesus told him, "Yes, I'm fine, Son. Just brushing my teeth and fixing my hair."

When he exited the restroom, Chris was standing outside, waiting for him to get out. He looked at him with disgust and shoved him out of his way to enter the restroom. Danniel was in her room, and when she saw him outside her room, she rushed toward the door and shut it. Mercedes had grabbed a cold beer from the fridge and was sitting outside in their backyard—avoiding him too. Jesus undressed and put on some lounge clothes, a long shirt that covered only half his ass. He walked to the backyard, pondering to chase Mut down to get a free sample of semen. When he made it to the porch, he saw his wife out there, who didn't bother to turn and see who had come out. She drank her beer as she listened to music, attempting to cope with her misfortune in choosing the wrong man to spend the rest of her life with. Jesus went back inside the house since his plan had been compromised. Jr. came up to him and asked, "Dad, can you help me put on this dress so I could play princess? I can't zip it behind me."

Jesus said, "Let's see, turn around so I can zip it up for you. " He did so and then inquired, "Can I play with you? No one in the house seems to be happy to see me other than you, Son. I feel lonely and sad." He started weeping and continued, "I also feel fat and unattractive. I can't seem to raise my self-esteem. I've started peeing on myself like you, and my hair . . . it won't stop falling out."

Jr. replied, "Sure, Dad. Come play with me. Don't feel bad and cry. You're the most beautiful dad in the world. Come on, let's go to my room and pretend we're beautiful princesses." They both headed to his room to play.

Josefina had gone to work and then went on her date. Her date had arrived in a loud rumble of metal, wearing a leather jacket that had a skull logo on the back. She was impressed but was caught off guard as he slightly ran over her foot pulling up in front of her. She shouted, "FUCK! You ran over my foot!"

He immediately moved back to release her foot from under his bike's tire and said, "I'm so sorry about that. Please forgive me." He turned off his bike, got off, and helped her sit down on a bench.

They had met up downtown and were supposed to go together to some restaurant that had upgraded in technology and had received good reviews. She told him, "I don't think my foot is broken. It just kinda hurts a little. Mainly feels numb."

He replied, "I'm truly sorry about that. Are you alright to head off on our date, or would you like to postpone it?"

She uttered, "I'm alright. Let's go because I'm really hungry." She stood up from the bench.

He uttered, "How about you drive my bike down there? Do you know how to drive one?"

She stated, "OK, yes, I know how to. My dad had one and taught me when I was younger. I haven't been on one let alone drive it in such a long time, but I'll give it a shot."

Josefina hopped onto the motorcycle, and he handed her his helmet. He then sat behind her, and they drove over to the restaurant. They arrived within minutes and parked the bike outside. They then got off and walked inside. There wasn't a human host, waiter, or cooks. Everything was run by AI. They read a sign that stated they should have a seat and look over the menu and then pick something from the touch screen tablet. They took a seat and grabbed the tablet. They looked around and saw that others were enjoying their night out. They glanced through the menu and selected their course as well as the beverage. A bot came and dropped off their drinks. They had small talk summarizing their last conversation. She asked him, "Why don't you remove your jacket? Aren't you hot?"

He said, "I never take off my colors, and I'm not hot. I've gotten used to always wearing it."

She inquired, "So you belong to a bike gang?"

He replied, "Yup, I'm a bad boy like the rest of my brothers." The robot came to their table to drop off their meals.

Josefina began eating hers as if she hadn't eaten in days. He took his time with his and drank a beer. He belched loudly, catching everyone's attention there. Josefina was a bit shocked, but she took it as he was just full of testosterone. They continued eating and talking about different topics. Then when they finished, he told her to pay and got up from his seat. He headed outside to smoke a cigar. Josefina paid the bill via facial recognition on the table and walked outside after him. She thought he had ditched her but was relieved he hadn't. She asked him, "So how many push-ups can you do?"

He responded, "Probably twice as many as you. What's with the question though?"

She uttered, "I want to know just how masculine you really are."

He stated, "So you're trying to test a bike gang member to see if he's a real man? You think just any sissy rides with my brothers and I? We are exclusively a macho club and don't allow pansies in."

She responded, "OK, you don't have to get offended. It was just my overthinking and worries from past experiences."

He commented, "So what do you want to do next? Want to go back to my place and fuck?"

She got wet with the question but said, "I don't know. How about we arm wrestle it out? If you win, we'll go to your place. But if I win, you'll take me to the movies."

He told her, "Arm wrestle? I'd rather have a push-up competition with you since you're so worried I'm not a real man." She agreed, and they both dropped to the ground and began the competition.

It had been about a minute or so, and she had done a total of sixty push-ups. He had only managed to do twenty when his knees touched the floor and he stopped trying. She had figured then he was faking it. To confirm her suspicion, five members of his bike gang arrived and confronted him. They told him, "What're you doing on our side of town wearing our colors if you're not part of the club? We made it clear to you when we kicked you out because you were posing to be macho."

He got up from the floor and said, "Hey there, Rex. How've you been, man? I'm on a date right now, and you're embarrassing me by saying lies. Please tell her I'm part of the club so she can rest assured."

Rex swung at the imposter, and his brothers joined in the beating. When they finished with him, he was naked, lying on the ground covering his crotch and man boobs, crying like a little girl. Josefina was stunned yet not surprised he too had been fooling her. She told Rex, "Hey, can you give me sixty bucks from his wallet since he fooled me into being macho to get a free meal?" He tossed the guy's wallet at her and left with his pals to a bar down the street.

Josefina grabbed a hundred-dollar bill out and threw his wallet back at him. She then kicked him in the face and told him, "You should be ashamed of yourself. Acting all macho and rude all to get your ass beat by the same club you said you belonged to." She walked away, calling Hellen to pick her up.

Chris, Danniel, and Jr. had been put to bed, and Jesus lay in his bed. Mercedes walked over and was a bit drunk from earlier. She hadn't had sex in weeks with Jesus, and frankly, she didn't want to. But she was stressed and horny, so she tried getting him in the mood. She hugged him and grabbed his penis from behind. He began to moan and turned around to face her. He told her, "Do you want to eat my ass? I just shaved it today, and it's nice and clean."

She said, "No! I don't want to eat your ass. I want you inside me right now, relieving my stress."

He replied, "How about I eat you out, and hopefully you've been cheating on me with a macho so I could suck out his semen and ingest his testosterone?"

She asked, "What did you just say?"

He responded, "Nothing, it was a joke. But seriously do you have another man's semen inside you right now?"

She uttered, "No, I don't. Are you going to please me or not? I'm giving you an opportunity to make it up to me for the long hard day I had because of your little stunt."

He stated, "OK, let me make it up to you then." He kneeled on top of the bed, pulled down his shorts, and bent over, waiting for her to fuck him.

She took off her clothes and pulled him onto her, saying, "Come, make me feel like a woman, Jesus."

He tried slipping in his small penis inside her, but it had shrunk even more since the last time they had been intimate. He told her, "Let me turn off the lights so it could feel better."

He got up to turn off the lights and grabbed a water bottle he had on top of his nightstand. He inserted the bottle inside her as she stated, "Oh, Jesus. I think the testosterone-infused drinks I've been giving you are working. You feel big and thick." And she moaned and came.

As soon as she was done, she rolled over and fell asleep. Jesus tried to hug her, but she removed his arm from her side. Jesus tried going down on her as she slept in the hope she had some macho semen inside her vagina. When he came close to licking its surface, she farted on his face, and he began to gag. He lay back on his side and just fell asleep.

CHAPTER 10
NEW RIDE

Nick had received multiple offers from investors regarding his Broski-Wear, and he had signed a contract with one of them. The investor had begun mass-producing his product overnight. Nick was extremely proud of himself for turning around a bad scenario and having a good outcome of it. He also found out it was his wife who had recorded him and Jesus dancing and posted the video online. He was upset and had lost trust in her, and as he had made himself enough money, he decided to leave her. She begged him not to go, saying, "I'm sorry, Nick! Don't leave me. I had no bad intentions about recording you and posting it. I just wanted to show everyone how happy and fun you are."

He said, "Thank you for attracting attention for me, but this is the end of the road for us. You're too old for me, and I need to get rid of the old to let in the new." He gathered his belongings and placed them inside his new Corvette he had just gotten back from acquiring.

His wife shouted, "No! Don't leave me! Please don't go; I won't be able to live without you, Nick! I'll do anything you ask, anything. Just don't leave me!" But he was determined to get away from her as soon as possible.

Jesus woke up at the commotion and thought the news reporters and crowd had gathered again outside. He got up from his bed and went to close the blinds and curtains. As he looked outside, he noticed there wasn't a crowd. So he wondered where the yelling was coming from. He opened the front door and saw there was a brand-new Corvette in Nick's driveway. He exited his residence, following the yelling. He stood outside, observing Nick's wife pleading him not to go as he kept going in and out of the house with his stuff in hand. Jesus walked over to Nick and asked, "What's going on, bro?"

Nick informed him. "She's the one who recorded us, broskie, and posted the video online."

Jesus inquired, "Are you serious? Where'd you get this car from anyhow?"

Nick replied, "I just bought it with the money I received from the investor who signed a contract for production and distribution of my Broski-Wear. I have enough money to live on my own now, especially since I can no longer trust her."

Jesus questioned, "And where are you going to go?"

Nick uttered, "I'm going to go buy me my own house, broskie. Live life to the fullest and watch my business grow. You should have listened to me about taking advantage of the spotlight."

Jesus asked, "Can I go with you, broski?"

Nick stated, "Sorry, bro, but I've been dreaming of living alone and won't be able to take you with me. Besides, you have kids to look out for and a wife who cares about you unlike me."

Jesus pleaded with him, "Take me, Nick! Don't leave without me!" He joined Nick's wife in begging Nick.

Jr. came outside and shouted at Jesus, "Dad! What're you doing over there?"

Jesus uttered, "I'm leaving, Son. You take good care of yourself and make me proud." He got into Nick's car.

Nick came back outside with the last of his most important stuff. He saw Jesus in the passenger's side and pulled him out.

He told him, "You can't follow me on this ride, broskie. Go back home and take care of your son." He then jumped into his ride and darted out of there, as his wife ran behind him for about a block before she got tired and went back to her dwelling.

Jesus and she embraced as they sobbed for Nick. Jr. walked to them and hugged them too. All three held each other and cried. Then the postman passed by and tossed a package. The package hit Jesus in the face, and he let go of Nick's wife. He grabbed Jr.'s hand, and they went back inside their home.

Mercedes was at her workplace, taking care of business. Her boss called her into her office, and Mercedes went in to see what she wanted. When she walked in, Mrs. Santiago was shopping online for something for her husband. She showed Mercedes a pair of Broski-Wear underwear and asked her, "What do you think about this? You think my hubby will like them?"

Mercedes inquired, "Is that a pipi pouch to make it seem as if the one who wears it has a big crotch?"

Her boss said, "Yeah, it's pretty nifty and crafty, huh, don't you agree?"

She replied, "Yes, it is. Who would've thought of such a design to sell? I think your husband will love it."

Mrs. Santiago then mentioned, "Oh well, sorry, this isn't why I called you into my office. The reason why you're here is because I have a proposition for you. I'd like to make you the assistant coordinator at our building. The job is easy; you'll be right under me and will only report to me. It comes with a rewarding incentive—a fifty-percent raise from your current salary. What do you say, Mercedes? Do you want the job?"

Mercedes was delighted and responded right away, "Yes! Yes, I'll take the offer. I've been waiting several years for a promotion since I became the floor boss."

Her boss told her, "Good, I'm glad you accepted my proposal. You will start training next week. So I've assigned two new floor managers to replace you and Vicky, and you will be guiding them during and after training."

Mercedes uttered, "Great, no problem. I'll make sure they learn the correct way." She was so excited that when she rose from her chair she released a fart, and as she excused herself out of her boss's office, she heard Mrs. Santiago spraying some air freshener.

Danny had woken up early and was at the gym again when he noticed the three ladies were back. They entered the building and spotted him right away. They then walked over to where he was curling some dumbbells and stared at him. The one who had spoken to him the previous day inquired, "Where'd you go yesterday, Daddy? We were waiting for you naked in the showers all day until they closed and kicked us out."

Dan said, "I'm sorry about that. I had a family emergency and had to leave in a hurry. Since I didn't have any of your numbers, I couldn't let y'all know what had happened."

The woman replied, "I hope your family member is well and not in any danger. Here, let me input our numbers in your cell for next time." She grabbed his phone and jotted their numbers in it.

Danny continued to exercise, and while doing so, he thought of another plan to get rid of them. He finished doing his curls and left to do some triceps press downs. The women followed him to his location and continued staring at him. A guy approached them and asked, "Are y'all using this machine you're sitting on? I need to use it." They got up and allowed him to get his workout in.

Once again, they had some towels in their hands, and they wiped the sweat off Dan's forehead. They also gave him water from a sports bottle with a straw. The guy who had begun using the machine next to them asked, "Are you three with him? What a lucky guy."

Danny told him, "No, bro, they're yours if you want them." The guy uttered, "Really? I'll take the brunette."

The brunette responded, "Nope, you can't have me or any of us. We do belong to him. He's just trying to get rid of us. But we're staying with him even if it's against his own will."

Danny said, "Come on, baby. Go with this guy and be free and happy with him." The females refused to leave his side.

Danny finished his exercises and went to get some dumbbells to do some forearm roll-ups. The ladies followed him. They continued to make sure he was doing alright. He started working out and saw they were putting away his equipment back in their places. He found them useful and realized he could make something work out with them. When he finished exercising, he took them to the store to get some buckets, rags, and soap. He then took them back to the gym parking lot and had them wash some cars. They didn't refuse his orders, and by half a day, they had managed to earn some extra income for Danny.

Mercedes arrived at her house with her car overheating. She was frustrated and happy at the same time. Jesus came out of the house looking around his surroundings to make sure danger wasn't lurking nearby. He saw the coast was clear, so he walked up to Mercedes's ride and offered to take a look at it. He had also begun spreading rumors about Nick and his wife, and Mercedes told him she didn't want to hear gossip. Mercedes confided in him and allowed him access to her vehicle. He opened the hood and gazed away. He didn't put the safety hood prop rod, and the hood fell on his head. Mercedes laughed at him as he massaged his dome and fixed his error. He then heard the radiator cap boiling under pressure. He figured he'd open it to release the pressure, and when he did, the hot antifreeze burned his hand and splashed all over his clothes. Mercedes asked him, as he complained about his ache and burns, "Are you sure you know what you're doing there?"

Jesus said, "Yes, honey, it's just that I haven't messed with cars in a while. Just give me some time to figure this out." She walked inside and left him out there checking her car.

Moments later, he came back and stated, "I think your engine is gone. I found some water mixed with oil on the dipstick. The online mechanic I spoke to said you'll definitely need a new head. He said it's not a quick fix and may take someone a few days to replace if you find the parts available today."

Mercedes recalled she had her bonus, which she wasn't going to invest it on testosterone anymore, so she told Jesus, "Why don't we go look at some new cars at a dealer and worry about my car later? I'm getting a promotion and will be making enough money to afford a new one."

Jesus congratulated her, saying, "That's great news, honey. Maybe now with your promotion, you could pay for my plastic surgeries. The first thing I want is a BBL and hair implants."

She uttered, "Maybe or maybe not. Why don't we get ready and leave for the dealers now before we waste more time? I'll leave the back door open for Chris and Danniel. I'll send them a text to inform them on our way to the dealer."

Jesus stated, "Sure, let me grab my purse and car keys. Jr., we're leaving, come on!" They then took off for the car dealerships to search for their new ride.

Danny had the three females working their butts off. He went to buy them some drinks and came back. Their clients were mainly women who drove their sports cars and trucks into the lot. One of the girls asked Danny, "Can we take a break? We're hungry and have been working in the hot sun all day."

Danny said, "I thought you'd do anything for me? Like sacrificing your lives too? Just kidding, sure, take a break. All three of you go grab something to eat. Here's some money." He handed them some cash and watched them walk into a burger joint nearby.

They had no clients waiting for their cars at the time, and since it wasn't a professional or well-known establishment, no one was driving up to get their cars washed. Danny sat in his truck, texting back to his other three ladies. They were concerned he hadn't been back from the gym by then. He let them know he was alright and told them not to worry. He was handling some business. The three females came back really quick with their bellies full and ready to get back to work. So they did, as more cars were flagged down to get washed. Danny stuck around until the manager of the gym came out and said, "Hey! Do you guys have a permit for that? Who authorized you all to wash cars on our property?"

Dan said, "Look, Karen, why don't you head back inside and worry about the gym? We don't need a permit to wash cars on public property. It's for a good cause. We're raising funds for feminine men awareness, and all proceedings will go toward the research to find a natural form of testosterone."

The gym manager replied, "In that case, can y'all wash my car too? I'd love to help and contribute to finding a cure to the high levels of estrogen running through my body."

Dan responded, "Sure, bro, bring your car right over, and we'll have it ready before you're off work."

The manager pointed at his car that was a few feet away in front of them and said, "That's my ride right there. How much for the wash?"

Danny uttered, "Tell you what, it's going to be free for you, and you can give a donation if you'd like or not?"

The manager commented, "Alright, thanks, but here's twenty bucks to help fight feminine traits in men." He then headed back inside to continue working.

Mercedes, Jesus, and Jr. had arrived at a car lot. They parked and started walking around, looking at the vast selection of new and pre-owned vehicles. Mercedes was attracted to the sports cars and asked Jesus, "What do you think about me getting one of those?"

Jesus said, "To be honest, those cars are too fast and waste too much gas. Plus, since they're fast, you run the risk of getting into an accident, which is why your insurance premium will also go up if you get one."

He convinced her not to get a sports car. So they went over to the midsize cars section. There she found a nice white one she fell in love with. She asked Jesus, "What do you think about this one?"

Jesus stated, "Well, to be honest, I think a larger vehicle would be better for our family to ride in comfortably in case we want to go on a trip."

Mercedes replied, "Yeah, you're right. Let's go look at the SUVs."

When they got to the SUV section, a full size caught her eye, and she checked it out. She opened the doors to look inside. She climbed into the driver's side and sat in the seat. She felt that was the one, and asked Jesus, "What about this one? I love this one myself. It's very spacious and comfortable for long trips."

Jesus uttered, "Well, I don't know. I mean it's expensive, almost the same as a house. Why not just invest in another property and fix your car?"

She then inquired, "So what kind of car do you think I should get then, since you don't seem to like any of the ones I picked?"

Jesus pointed at the minivans and mentioned, "One of those. If it were my money, I'd get a minivan. They're affordable, spacious, comfortable, great on gas, and reliable."

Mercedes replied, "Are you serious, Jesus? A minivan? Come on, I'd rather get a muscle car than a minivan. Everyone will be making fun of us if we get one. What do you think, Jr.? What car would you get?"

Jr. said, "The minivan, Mom. I like them too. They remind me of the pink one I play with."

Mercedes stated as a sales agent approached them, "Alright, I guess it'll be the minivan then."

They ended up picking a gray one and began the buying process, which took them several hours of negotiation, during which the sales agent racked up the price with aftermarket add-ons and even sold them powertrain warranty, which was free. All this happened because Mercedes allowed Jesus to talk to the salesman, who deceived Jesus because of his inexperience and illogical thinking. She handed over her bonus, never realizing it hadn't paid off anything and only became the salesman's commission bonus instead.

The three women had finished up their day washing cars. Danny was pleased with their performance and decided to take them home after all. When they arrived at his house, the ladies got in the shower, and so did he. They all showered together, and Danny felt like a king. The ladies were actually washing him, which he realized took them less time than it would if he'd shower himself. All three women began kissing him and touching his skin. They began getting freaky with him, expressing passion and desire. He bent the brunette over and stuck his penis in her. As he banged her, he kissed the blonde, and the Black girl massaged the back of his neck while kissing it. Just as he was going to switch penetrating partners, the brunette—named Denise—turned around as he physically disconnected with her and accidentally pushed him out of the shower. Danny plunged through the glass door, which Miya—the Black one—had opened to use the restroom. He was on the ground covered in water and lying at Miya's feet as she pooped and looked at him while ripping it up. Heather—the blonde—got out, and so did Denise. They tried picking him up, but they started sliding all over the shiny tile on the restroom floor. Heather grabbed Miya, attempting to hold her balance on to her, and caused Miya to fall out of the toilet seat. She then defecated on Danny's face, who broke her landing. Danny asked, "Did you have papaya? Smells like papaya." Then he spewed.

Denise puked all over them after getting some feces on her arm. Heather was grossed out and barfed as well. Danny's restroom had become a disaster. They eventually cleaned up the fluids and solids on the floor with towels, and the three women wiped down their mess as Danny got back in the shower alone. When the trio was done, they got back in the shower, and Danny got out. He dried himself up, put on his underwear, and lathered lotion on himself before heading to his room.

Jesus, Mercedes, and Jr. drove off the lot in their new minivan. They were hungry, so they went to grab some pizzas. When they arrived at the drive-thru, Mercedes ordered, "Yes, I'll have one large pepperoni with jalapenos; a large with pepperoni, ham, bacon, and sausage; and a medium cheese pizza. Can you also add a three-liter cola and fifteen buffalo wings?"

The employee uttered, "Let me run that order back to you. You said you want an extra-large pepperoni with jalapenos."

"No! I said large, not extra-large," replied Mercedes.

The employee mentioned, "OK, a large pepperoni with jalapenos. A large meat, medium no-cheese pizza."

Mercedes interrupted him again, "I said a medium cheese pizza with cheese."

The employee commented, "A medium cheese pizza, OK. You also ordered a three-liter cola and fifteen barbeque wings. Will that complete your order?"

"Fifteen hot buffalo wings I said, not barbeque," corrected Mercedes.

The employee responded, "I made all the changes to your order. It'll be forty-eight with ninety-seven cents. Please drive up to the window."

Mercedes pulled up to the window and observed three young employees working in the back. She then witnessed one cutting up their pizza and taking out a slice. Mercedes knocked on the window that the drive-thru attendant had closed to charge her. The attendant opened the window and asked, "Yes, ma'am? Here's your card."

Mercedes stated, "I just saw one of you take a slice out of one of the pizzas I ordered." The employee looked at his coworkers and inquired, "Did any of you take a slice out of one of this lady's pizzas? She's claiming she saw one of you do so."

The other two guys replied, "Nope, we didn't take a slice out of her pizzas." The employee faced Mercedes and told her, "They both said they didn't."

She uttered, "But I just saw them do it. Anyhow, we're very hungry, so just give me my pizzas so we can go home and eat."

The attendant handed her the order through the window, and she drove off. She asked Jesus to check if they had handed her the right order. He opened up the first box and found it was an extra-large pepperoni with no jalapenos. The one under it was correct, and the last one was a plain pizza with no cheese, only marinara sauce. He also discovered they had given them fifteen barbeque wings. Mercedes was furious; she made a U-turn and sped back to the restaurant. When she got there, she told Jesus, "Go take that inside and tell them to give you your money back."

Jesus replied, "But it's not my money, and I'm embarrassed to get off and complain."

Mercedes smacked him and uttered, "Give me that then, you sorry ass guy!"

She got off the van with the pizzas in her hand and went inside. She threw the pizzas at the cashier, who thought she was there to place a new order. The kid was terrified as he heard her say, "I want my money back! This isn't what I ordered!"

The kid opened the cash register and handed all the money in it to her. He said, "Please don't kill me. I have a cat at home waiting for me." He somehow believed she was robbing the place.

Mercedes took her exact refund and left the rest there, telling him, "You freaking incompetent coward!" And she bit one of the wings and tossed what remained at his face. She walked out and got into her van. From there, they just went to grab some burgers instead before heading home to eat.

Miya, Heather, and Denise had finished showering and were lying in Danny's bed. They were grooming him and catering to his needs. Denise propped his legs up by placing pillows under him. Miya went to the kitchen to grab him a beer, and Heather massaged his arms so his muscles could heal from his workout. Danny asked them, "Hey, so do you ladies work or something? Because I don't want to be supporting y'all the rest of your lives."

Denise told him, "We actually own some men's beauty salons around the city. Miya has several rental properties, Heather has a car lot and body shop, and I have another business that counsels feminine men to accept their emotions and lifestyles."

Dan was surprised to hear these women were well-off and asked, "You think you could give my son-in-law a discount on some counseling? He hasn't been able to cope with the fact he's not producing enough testosterone."

Denise replied, "Yeah, I could help him out. Unless he's one of those two guys that went viral due to their extremely affectionate bromance. From what I can tell, those two aren't ever coming back from the pink side."

Dan uttered, "One of them actually is him. Sorry I even asked. You're right, there's no hope in making a man out of him ever again."

Miya commented, "Wow! You actually know one of those guys? You think I can get an autograph?"

Danny mentioned, "Why would you even want an autograph? He's nothing special, to be honest. My daughter who's married to him is fed up with his behavior. The other guy in the video is actually his neighbor, so technically I know them both."

They kept on talking through the night and eventually fell asleep. The trio of women hugged Dan and made his body temperature rise during his sleep. He eventually kicked them out of his bed and made them sleep on the floor.

Mercedes, her wife, and their kid got back home. They got off their new van, and Chris ran out of the house, saying, "What the hell is that? You got a minivan, Mom? Um, please make sure to never pick me up or drop me off at school. I'd rather walk a thousand miles to my destination than be caught getting on or off that tennis shoe looking thing."

Mercedes told him, "Your brother and father picked it. So blame them for it, not me." She handed him the food to take inside.

Chris told Jr., "Why would you tell mom to get that? Do you have any idea what it is and what other people think of it?"

Jr. replied, "It's a van like the pink one in my room. I like it. Dad and I are not going to be embarrassed of riding in that when we go get our nails done."

Chris burst into laughter and uttered, "Yeah, sounds like minivan passengers alright." He then laughed in Jesus's face as they sat at the table to begin eating.

Mercedes shouted, "Danniel! Come and eat; the food is here!"

Danniel came out of her room, and they all sat down to enjoy some cheese burgers, fries, and drinks. Jesus asked Chris, "How'd it go in school today?"

Chris said, "Better than it go being stuck at home with you trying to turn me feminine like Jr." He chuckled, and so did Danniel.

Mercedes uttered, "No more talking about feminine men while we eat. I don't want my appetite ruined over that conversation. Jr., could you please not do your nails while you eat here? That's not very hygienic, and you're going to end up getting some all over your food, which isn't good."

Jr. replied, "How come Dad gets to do it and not me? I don't see the difference."

Mercedes ordered him and Jesus, "Alright! Both you sissies, go eat somewhere else. I didn't spend my money on buying food and not being able to enjoy it properly."

Chris and Danniel laughed as they both went to sit on the living room floor and eat. Danniel later found out her mom had gotten a minivan and complained to her too. She repeated what Chris had told her and ran to her room to continue talking to her friends. After everyone ate, they rested a little and then went to bed because they had a whole new day ahead of them after sunbreak.

CHAPTER 11
TOYS' DAY

Sam called Jesus in the morning, waking him up. He told him, "Hey, bro, let's go out of town and get away from the bullshit in the city this weekend. I heard of this luxury resort a few hours from here. They have spas, manicures and pedicures, arts and crafts classes, and a bunch of other things for us feminine men. I think we'll have a great time over there. What do you say?"

Jesus replied, "How are you going to be able to go if Sally is strict with you? And where are you going to get the money to go?"

Sam said, "She's the one encouraging me to go. It was her idea, and she's even paying for it."

Jesus uttered, "Are you sure? Sounds like a test or scheme, don't you think? Like why all of sudden she's paying for you to go to some resort?"

Sam replied, "I don't think so. She just wants me out of the house, probably so she can relax in my absence. Anyhow, do you want to go or not?"

Jesus commented, "Yeah, I'm in. I don't think Mercedes would be bothered if I tag along. I'm sure she too would rest with me not being here."

Sam stated, "Great! I'll send you a link so you can check it out. I'll have her book us a room together, and you'll just have to drive us over there. They offer free cuisine, so we won't have to worry about food. We'll be over there Friday night through Sunday noon when we'll return home. Sounds like a deal?"

Jesus responded, "Yeah, we have ourselves a deal."

Sam said, "Good, talk to you soon then, bro, and can't wait to be at the resort with my best pal. See you, bye." He hung up.

Jesus got out of bed, and as he placed some waffles in the toaster, he sent a text to Mercedes regarding his weekend plans. She replied, "I don't mind. Go right ahead, so I can relax on the weekend with the kids and take them somewhere where we won't be embarrassed by you."

Jesus texted back with a bunch of heart and kiss emojis, "Thanks, honey. I appreciate it."

Jesus then went to get the house cleaned up and cook for his wife and stepkids. He first went to clean up the bathroom in the hallway. He got all the chemicals to do so and got to it. From there, he went to clean the one in their bedroom. He saw the toilet seat was down and threw a small fit, saying, "Damn it, I keep telling her to not leave the seat down. This woman is so stubborn, and she also left a bunch of toilet paper full of stinky shit in the trash instead of flushing it down, gross." He managed to clean it out and went to do some laundry.

He walked into the laundry room to find a stack of dirty linens there. He began washing Chris's first. As he put the pile in the washer, one of his boxers fell to the ground. Jesus picked it up and brought it to his nose. He took a long whiff, hoping maybe somehow he'd get a small dose of testosterone from its odor. Jr. came out of his bedroom and saw him sniffing his older brother's drawers and asked, "What're you doing with Chris's underwear, Dad?"

Jesus quickly tossed them into the washer and turned it on as he replied, "I thought I smelled waffles on his clothes and checked which one smelled delicious, but I was wrong. I forgot I made some earlier for us to eat. That's where the smell came from. Smell that?"

Jr. uttered, "You're funny, Dad. How could you forget you made waffles and thought you smelled that on Chris's stinky drawers?"

Jesus said, "I cleaned out the toilets just before I started washing, so it may have something to do with smelling shit and then smelling something delicious. Anyhow, why don't you go on and eat some waffles while I finish my chores?" Jr. left to eat, and he continued to wash.

Later, Jesus took Chris's wet clothes out of the washer and placed them into the dryer. He then grabbed Mercedes's clothing and began placing them inside to wash. He found some socks that were turned inside out and began complaining about that too since he had previously brought it up to her attention. In the meantime, he turned on the TV set to watch some FEMNS Network programs.

Danny had woken up to find Josefina fighting with Heather. She wasn't aware they had company and thought Heather had broken in to steal or rape her father in order to conceive a child. She saw Heather in the kitchen making coffee and confronted her, "Who the fuck are you, and what're you doing in my house?" She walked up to her and grabbed her in a headlock.

Josefina then began pulling her out of her house as Heather tried explaining, "Wait! I'm here with Danny!"

Josefina was about to toss her out when she heard her father say, "Stop! She's one of the three women from the gym, sweety! Don't kick her out."

Josefina halted her eviction and replied, "She's one of those three chicks you told me about? Oh, I'm very sorry for the misunderstanding." She released Heather from her grasp and introduced herself.

Danny was cracking up. He couldn't contain his laughter as the other two females ran out of his bedroom to see what the commotion was. When they were in the living area, Danny said, "Look, honey, these two are here with malice intentions, get them!" He started laughing, and so did Josefina and Heather.

Miya asked, "What's going on here? Why're y'all laughing? Is it an inside joke?"

Josefina introduced herself and explained, "I thought Heather was breaking into the house and attacked her. That's why Dad said that."

"Oh," responded Miya.

Danny had the girls make him breakfast, and they chatted with Josefina. Dan began getting triggered just as he had tried explaining to his daughter. The high-pitched burlesque sound coming out of their mouths was bothering him. So he asked them if they'd be kind enough to settle down. They obeyed him and talked in a lower tone as he sat in the living area further away from them. He turned on the television set and watched a feminine men documentary. A guy was explaining he had begun leaking milk from his breasts and his girlfriend was more sexually active than he is now. He also mentioned she would experience outbursts of anger and frustration just as he would have episodes of sadness and depression when he felt insignificant and unworthy. Dan started laughing and shared the news with the females at his home. They laughed too but were concerned that it may happen to them as well as they themselves had begun experiencing hormonal changes and hair growth spurs. Danny got back to watching the documentary after a special news release interrupted his program. The authorities were searching for a band of females who had been going around robbing banks. He wasn't able to tell if they were his new chicks or not because in the photos they presented, they wore masks. He began to wonder if these chicks were capable of conducting an armed robbery.

Mercedes was at work when her boss, Mrs. Santiago, called her into her office. Mrs. Santiago addressed her, "Mercedes, I was wondering if it would be too much to ask of you if you could somehow have your brother-in-law sign this sex toy for my husband?" She held a double-headed dildo with vibrators included, which was turned to the highest setting.

Mercedes found it strange but said, "I could take it home and ask my husband to ask him. I'm sure he'll John Hancock it without issue." She took the toy from her and wrapped it in some tissue, feeling awkward as she thought it hadn't been cleaned after its last use, and turned it off.

Mrs. Santiago replied, "Thank you very much. How's everything here at work? Any issues with the rumors anymore?"

Mercedes uttered, "Everything is good here, ma'am. No issues with production, and the rumors seemed to have vanished into thin air."

Mrs. Santiago commented, "I'm glad to hear that the issue was resolved with minimal effort and attention. How about at home? How're things at home?"

Mercedes wished she could be honest about her private life but instead mentioned, "Things couldn't be better at home. My family is doing great. My husband is extraordinary. We went shopping for a new car yesterday and had burgers for dinner."

Mrs. Santiago told her, "I'm glad to hear your family is doing well. Since you'll be attached to me at work, we're going to get to know each other a little better. Burgers you say, from where? And what car did you choose after all?"

Mercedes answered, "Thank you, and I can't wait to work right under you. We had burgers from Happy Burger, and I picked out a minivan."

Mrs. Santiago questioned, "A minivan? I perceived you more as the sports car type. Why'd you go with a minivan?"

Mercedes said, "Well, my husband and my younger son went with me to help me pick. That's what they recommended to me. I actually was fascinated with some sports cars but had to make a decision favoring the family and not just me."

Mrs. Santiago replied, "Good logic in thinking of the family first for your decision." Her phone rang, and she excused herself to answer it. Mercedes waved at her and made her way out of her office.

Mrs. Santiago put the phone on mute and said, "Mercedes, I almost forgot, before you leave, could you have your brother-in-law sign this too, please?" She picked up her leg from her chair and removed a small vibrator she had well hidden in her underwear.

She turned it off and handed it to her. Mercedes grabbed another tissue and wrapped it around the object, which was wet. She then exited her office and went to grab some latex gloves to stick the items in before placing them in a plastic bag. She made sure to wash her hands once she had accomplished the task.

Jesus had finished washing, sweeping, and mopping at his residence. He took a break from his hard work and got on his social media applications. He had various friend requests and a bunch of women liking his pictures on his public profile, mostly the ones he had posted a while back in some provocative wardrobe. Women were also sending him messages because they recognized him from the viral video. Mercedes was on her lunch break and called him. She told him, "Why are you posting pictures online and having all these bitches liking them and sending you messages?"

Jesus said, "I'm just noticing that too, but the pictures are old ones. I haven't replied to any of the women sending me messages. You don't have to be so mean to me. Why can't you understand I have feelings too and you always hurt them? You're being toxic and controlling."

Mercedes ordered, "You better take those pictures down from your account. Stop being so sensitive because if you didn't like my reactions and responses to your behavior, you would have changed your ways by now. I hope the government finds a cure for your lack of testosterone because I'm getting tired of having a woman as my partner instead of the man I thought you were when I met you."

Jesus started crying and uttered, "I'll just erase my account since it bothers you. For once in my life, people are following me and I've become famous. You're just hating on me."

Mercedes responded, "You're famous because your video went viral not because you have some type of extraordinary talent. They're only responding to a video where you and your pals made asses of yourselves. Go ahead and erase it right now, and I'll see you later." She hung up on him.

Jesus was sobbing uncontrollably, as he erased all his accounts online. His son came over to console him as he commented, "It's OK, Dad. Nick will be back to visit sometime soon."

Jesus began to cry some more as he remembered Nick was gone, and he told Jr., "I wasn't crying because of that, but now that you reminded me, I am. Your mom was being cruel to me on the phone right now. She made me erase my social media accounts and was verbally abusing and degrading me."

Jr. uttered, "Don't pay attention to her, Dad. I've seen how she's mean to you. She does it because you let her. She probably forgot the wave of emotions she felt when she was more feminine. Ever since she began growing hair on her face and back, she's turned into a bitter man."

Jesus mentioned, "You're right, Son. Thank you for making me feel better. You're my only true friend in this world who's seen how your mom treats me and understands how I feel about it." They hugged and kissed each other's foreheads.

Danny shut his television set and asked the ladies if they wanted to go to the store with him. All three agreed. Josefina wasn't able to since she had to get ready to go to work. They got in his truck and drove to a sporting goods retailer. They got off and walked into the building. As they entered, Dan noticed them paying attention to the guns on display. They stopped to look at them. Danny recalled the emergency broadcast on TV and started wondering even more whether they were the ones the authorities were searching for. He asked Heather, "Have you ever shot a gun before? Maybe held one in your hands at some point in your life?"

Heather said, "Only when I was younger. My dad took me hunting with him once, but I didn't do good, and he never took me again."

Danny then questioned Denise, "How about you?"

Denise replied, "Nope, I'm petrified of firearms. My grandfather shot himself with a rifle like that one there." She pointed at a shotgun.

Dan chuckled and said, "That's not a rifle. That's a shotgun. How about you, Miya? Do you have experience with firearms?"

She answered, "Never in my life. I do find them interesting though. If you have any, I'd love it if you'd take me shooting with you so I could learn."

Danny told her, "I do. So maybe someday I'll take you with me so you can take your first shot at something."

Danny then told them to follow him since he wasn't there to buy any guns. He walked to the back of the store over by the toy aisle. He was looking for an RC helicopter to purchase for Jr. since he had promised him one a while back. He was looking at a few when a man came around toward them. The man had heard

Denise's voice and thought he'd recognized it from somewhere. The man then looked at Dan with a blank stare in his eyes and then at Denise. Dan looked at him and asked, "May I help you, bro? Are you alright or something?"

The man pointed at Denise and ran out of the store, yelling, "Help! Somebody, help me! They're here in the store, and they're going to rob it!"

One of the employees shouted back, "Get the fuck out of the store, you fucking weirdo! I've told you before to not come here again, you schizo!" The man left the store in a hurry.

Danny asked the females, "What's wrong with that guy?" But they shrugged their shoulders.

Danny made his decision on the remote-operated chopper and went to the cash register to pay. The female worker noticed the girls with him, and she began to act a bit flirtatious with Dan. She asked him, "Did you find everything alright in today's visit?" She emphasized her lips by running her fingers over them.

Danny uttered, "Besides the deranged individual who ran out of here screaming, yes, I did."

She had a smile on her face as she scanned his item and played with her hair. She then answered Danny, "I apologize for that man. He's been that way since he was a hostage in a bank robbery last week. But anyhow, I like your shirt. It fits you well."

Dan replied, "Thank you. I appreciate it. I like yours too; it fits you well also." He then giggled.

The cashier told him, "It's just my uniform shirt. You should see how I look in plain clothes though, and without them too." She winked at him.

Denise interrupted, "Why don't you check us out and stop flirting with our man before I tell your manager how disrespectful this experience has been for us?" Heather felt like jumping over the counter and beating her up, but she held her composure and smiled instead.

The worker commented, “I’m sorry. Please forgive my offense; you’re right, I shouldn’t be flirting with customers.” She charged him and bagged his purchase, and they left.

Jesus was doing some online shopping as he cooked some enchiladas, Spanish rice, and refried beans. He was immaturely attempting to waste his first payment for his participation in the study. He knew he would be getting paid the following day, and he had an itch to get rid of his money before the next payment came in. He then received a call from an operator representing the study. She informed him, “We need you to come in today if possible to retest you. There were some abnormalities in your samples, which we need to verify if it was an error in our process or a non-favorable result for candidacy.”

Jesus said, “I can be there in a few hours, the usual time I sign in. Does this mean I’m not getting paid for this week?”

The operator replied, “No, you’re still getting paid. So you’ll be there today at your usual time? Sounds good; thank you and enjoy the rest of your day.”

Jesus uttered, “That is correct. I’ll be there today later on and you’re welcome.” They hung up.

He had forgotten he had been rolling up the enchiladas and had removed the latex gloves he had used to not get his fingernails dirty. He had some red chili sauce on his wrist, and he swiped it over his eyes, unaware it was there. Soon after, he felt an immense burning sensation in his eyes. He ran to the kitchen sink to try and rinse it off under the tap. It didn’t work, so he opened the fridge and poured some milk over his eye. That didn’t work either, so he went outside and rubbed Mut’s penis over his eye. Nobody knows why he even considered that would work, but it failed as well. Mut actually got turned on and chased him around the yard, trying to hump him. Jr. ran outside and yelled at Mut, "Leave my dad alone! Bad dog!" He chased them both, trying to stop Mut.

Jesus was yelping for someone to rescue him. He tried jumping over the gate separating Nick's wife's property and theirs. He got caught in the fence and hung by his legs on their side. Mut caught up to him and began humping his face. Jr. ran up on them and tried removing Mut off, but Mut overpowered him. Jesus noticed Mut was coming, and he opened his mouth to catch some of it. He then gulped his ejaculation, and Jr. asked, "Did you just eat some of his pipi milk, Dad?"

Jesus said, "Is that what that was? I don't know, but I accidentally swallowed something very salty." Mut had walked away, and he went inside his dog house to fall asleep.

Jr. helped him untangle himself from the fence, and then they headed back inside. Jesus's eyes had stopped burning, and he had consumed some semen after all. He got back to cooking, and his son went back to playing tea party with his female life-size dolls.

Danny got back to his house and found Carla waiting for him outside. She crossed her hands as she observed he had company. He tried introducing them to her, but she instead started fighting with Miya. Heather and Denise were about to jump in when Miya told them, "It's a one on one. Let me handle her on my own."

Dan tried separating them, but Heather and Denise grabbed him and told him not to get in. Carla was throwing calculated punches at Miya, but Miya had some fight in her as well. They looked like two professional boxers going at it. Heather and Denise cheered their friend as they beat the shit out of each other. Carla dropped Miya on the ground, got on top of her, and continued striking her in the face. Then Alejandra showed up and joined in the fight. She grabbed Denise, and they started combating with each other. The next thing, Lucia drove up, got out of her car, and jumped on Heather. Danny watched all six of his women fighting. He went inside to grab a beer. He then went back outside and took a seat in his lawn chair to watch the show. Carla grabbed Dan's water hose and wrapped it around Miya's neck. She began choking her. Alejandra pushed Denise into a small apple tree growing in Danny's front yard. Denise hit her face but caught her balance. She started yanking apples from the tree and throwing them at Alejandra. Lucia was smacking the shit out of Heather with a plate of food she had in her hands, which she'd brought for Dan. All of a sudden, Danny's neighbor came out of his house shouting, "No! Stop, ladies! This is not the place to cause drama! I don't want my property value to decrease since I'm trying to sell my home!" The women weren't listening to him, so he turned to Danny and said, "Don't just sit there; do something, man!"

Danny told him, "Mind your own business, Tom, and get the fuck off my landscape rocks!"

Tom responded, "Sure, sorry about that. I won't call the cops, but please control these savage women." Danny flipped him off as Tom walked back inside his residence.

Mercedes entered her house after getting off work. She smelled the food and went to her room to change before sitting down to eat. When she swung the door open, she observed Jesus wearing some flamboyant attire. He had on a bright purple shirt with dark maroon pants, a maroon light scarf, black combat boots, and purple shades. She asked him, "Why're you dressed like that? Where are you going?"

Jesus said, "I'm going for my appointment for the study. They called me earlier to go back and retake my tests. And last time I was there, I had a ton of attention, so I dressed like a celebrity."

Mercedes laughed and stated, "I already told you, you're not a celebrity; you're more like a famous idiot of whom people make fun behind his back to not hurt his feelings."

Jesus grunted and took off for his appointment. He wasn't about to let Mercedes ruin his status. He got in his car and drove over there. On his way, the angered husband spotted him and gave chase. Jesus noticed him and went to the police station again. The husband drove away as some officers came out of their station to kick Jesus out. One officer asked Jesus, "Why're you dressed like an idiot and honking outside our station?"

Jesus answered, "I'm a celebrity in danger. I need you all to serve as my personal bodyguards and escort me to my appointment." The cops laughed.

Another officer inquired, "And just who are you, Mr. Superstar?"

Jesus said, "Haven't you guys seen my video circulating online? You may refer to me as pink daddy she."

One of the officers questioned, "Are you one of those two pansies dancing naked and touching dicks?"

Jesus replied, "That's right, I am. Now please get in your cars and escort me to my appointment safely." The cops laughed at him.

The officer responded, "You're not a celebrity. You're just some dumbass wanting attention like your pal who's now selling some Broski-Wear. Matter-of-fact, we can't escort you because there's no immediate danger present for us to do so. Now get your feminine ass out of here before we arrest you for disorderly conduct." They walked back inside as Jesus sobbed inside his car.

Jesus then wiped the tears from his eyes and headed for his appointment. When he reached there, he added some zing to his step. He walked into the building and signed in, then he took a seat, waiting to be called. It wasn't as packed as the other days, but there were some candidates present. No one seemed to recognize him, so he got up on top of his chair and shouted, "Excuse me! Can I have your attention please?! I'm the famous guy in the video that has gone viral. If anyone wants to take a picture with me or get an autograph, please form a line here." He pointed in front of him, but no one seemed interested in lining up at all.

He cleared his throat and retorted his speech. One of the ladies at the front counter told him, "Sir, we don't care who you are. No one's going to line up for no autograph or pictures, so please sit down and wait your turn."

Jesus told her, "Ma'am, please don't scare away my fans. And my preferred pronouns are pink daddy she!"

She replied, "Look, you fucking clown! Take a seat in your chair and shut up! You're disrupting our duties and worrying our feminine clients who are paranoid as is. If you don't obey, I'm going to have you removed from here and taken off the candidacy list." Jesus took a seat in his chair and shut up, still wondering why no one wanted his autograph or picture.

Over at Danny's place, the girls had finally stopped engaging in combat. Lucia, Alejandra, and Carla got up with their battle wounds and departed from the area. Denise, Heather, and Miya had got the best of them, and they went inside to clean themselves up. Danny finished his beer and entered his home. The girls asked him, "Who were those chicks?"

Danny told them, "Those are my other three girls who y'all just met." Heather questioned, "Was the oldest one their mother?"

Danny answered, "Ha! No, she's actually my ex-wife, Josefina's mother."

Heather stated, "Damn! She could fight. She beat me up pretty good. Just look at my face."

Dan said, "Yeah, she's pretty feisty."

His plate of food had been scattered all over his front yard. So since he hadn't cooked, Denise offered to make him something to eat. She had already started cooking the main dish earlier. He allowed the ladies to finish preparing a late lunch, as he sat on his sofa and continued watching the documentary he had been watching. Once again, the special alert was broadcasted, interrupting his program. He flipped the channel, and he saw some women teaching mechanics to the viewers tuning in. He changed the channel again and came across a program where they flipped houses. All the construction workers were masculine women who were doing the job. He flipped the channel once more back to the documentary. The special alert had concluded, and the documentary was back on. He watched a woman share her story of being able to lift heavier weights at the gym and that she had more physical endurance as well. She claimed to have gained muscle mass and had grown a fair amount of anal hair. She also stated her breasts as well as her nipples had shrunk in size. Danny laughed as they showed her picking up her husband in her arms, and he was smiling as if he was the happiest man in the world. His wife then put him down and kissed him on his forehead, which made him blush. Danny was cracking up, and the ladies asked if he was alright. Dan uttered, "Yeah, it's just that this TV show is hilarious to watch. I don't know how these sissies aren't embarrassed to admit they're becoming women. I know I probably would. Good thing is I'm not."

Denise told him, "That is funny, you're right if you really think about it. Food is ready, Daddy. Come eat with us."

Danny turned the TV set toward the kitchen table and went to sit in front of a beef stew and mac and cheese. He grabbed a spoonful of the stew and placed it in his mouth. His taste buds rejoiced, and he was content. The emergency broadcast came on again, and he noticed the girls saw it and acted a bit strange. Heather asked, "I wonder who those chicks are that they're looking for. They've got some balls to pull that off." Her friends agreed as they devoured their meals.

Jesus left the study facility after getting retested. He was heading home but had to stop by at the store to get Mercedes some snacks she had ordered him to grab. He got off and went inside. This particular convenience store had no actual clerk. All their items were inside metal and plexiglass dispensers, where you had to tap on the item and pay right then and there before getting it in your hands. He entered and made his way toward the snack section. He grabbed her a bag of birria flavored chips and a can of watermelon chili lime flavored soda. Once he retrieved the items, he departed the building and got back in his vehicle. Just as he was getting in, a random chick walked up to him and told him, "Hey! You're that guy from the video, right?"

He answered, "Yes, that's me. My preferred pronouns are pink daddy she. Do you want my autograph?"

She said, "Pronoun? Whatever ha, I love the way you cook those meals on your page. I've learned a ton of recipes from just watching you cook."

He replied, "I don't have a cooking channel though. I think you're confusing me with someone else."

She uttered, "Really? Well, please forgive me then." She walked away as he started up his ride.

Jesus was upset she had mistaken him for someone else. He in fact was hoping she was a fan and would want to take a picture with him or something. He drove back home and made it there without any interruptions. When he got out of his car, the angered husband drove by and saw him. Jesus ran like a little bitch to the front door of his home, taking his keys out to try and open it. He was nervous since the guy had circled around the block and was heading back toward him. Jesus dropped his keys on the ground, and he became so terrified he began banging on the door, hoping someone would open it for him. Just as the guy parked in front of his pad, Jr. opened the door for him. He ran inside screaming, "Mercedes! Mercedes! Everyone, hide under your beds right now! There's a mad man outside!"

Mercedes ran toward the living area where he was shouting and asked him, "What the hell are you talking about? Who's outside or what?"

Jesus responded, "There's some crazy guy outside who's trying to hurt me and possibly you guys too! Run for your lives!" He darted to his restroom and locked himself in.

Mercedes peeked out the window and saw no one out there and nothing out of the ordinary. She shouted at Jesus, "There's no one outside, you little paranoid coward!" He didn't reply, so she sat down to eat her snacks and drink her pop.

A few hours later, they went to bed. Jesus hadn't wanted to leave the safety of his restroom. Mercedes had to pry the door open and take him out of the shower, where he had barricaded himself. He had also armed himself with the toilet bowl plunger, which he swung at her when she opened up the shower curtain. She slapped him and made him get out so she could take a dump before going to bed. When she got out feeling lighter, she tried getting some sexual intercourse out of him, but he told her his pipi hurt and he didn't want to do anything. He stuck his thumb in his mouth and fell asleep.

CHAPTER 12
FEMNS-ORT

Mercedes woke up in the morning and found Jesus under the bed in a fetal position. He had heard some noises during the night and believed it was the enraged husband looking for him. So he fell out of bed and went under it to sleep, feeling a bit safer there. She kneeled down and pulled him out. He woke up and got out from under the bed and lay back on it. She then began getting ready to head to her job. Jesus remained asleep with his thumb in his mouth. When he finally woke up, she and his stepkids were gone. He remembered he and Sam were heading out to the resort, so he began getting his things ready for the weekend trip. It took him about two hours to finally pack all his shit into three full-size suitcases. Jr. woke up and asked him if he could cook him some *huevos montados* with the leftover enchiladas. He prepared both of them some, and they sat down to eat while they watched these feminine men cartoons called "The Sissies." Jr. was laughing and eating when Jesus got a call from Sam asking him if he was ready and still going. Jesus told him, "Yeah, bro, are you?"

Sam answered, "I'm almost done packing, but I can't find my curling iron. Did you pack yours?"

Jesus said, "Yeah, you can borrow it if you don't find yours. I'm so excited; hopefully, we'll have a blast, buddy."

Sam uttered, "Thanks for letting me borrow it. I'm thrilled too, bro. I heard they have a slushy margarita machine that pours the perfect blend with unlimited refills."

Jesus replied, "Hell, yeah! That sounds refreshing right now to me. Can't wait to have some."

Sally began shouting at Sam in the background, "What was that I heard? Did you say something about a margarita machine? You better not drink any margaritas over there and get kicked out early and have to come back home before Sunday!"

Sam told her, "OK, I won't, honey. Stop embarrassing me while I talk to Jesus."

Sally slapped him, saying, "Show me some fucking respect, motherfucker! Who the fuck do you think you're talking to? I pay the bills around here and feed your sorry ass! Don't you forget who makes the rules here!"

Sam informed Jesus, as he flinched at Sally's words repeatedly., "I'll just see you later, bro. I have to take care of some things before we leave."

Jesus responded, "Sure, no worries. See you soon." They then hung up the call.

Jesus got a call from Olivia, who asked him, "Do you want to meet up right now?"

Jesus told her, "I can't right now. I'm a little busy. I'm getting ready to travel on a weekend trip. Is there something you need though?"

She uttered, "Oh, that sucks because I wanted you to eat me out and fuck me doggy style."

He said, "Damn! Wish I could help you with that right now, but I've got a bunch of things to do before heading out this evening. How about we reschedule it for when I get back?"

She answered, "OK, have a safe trip, *papi*. Talk to you soon. I love you."

He was flattered to hear her tell him she loved him, so he commented, "Aw, you're so sweet. I love you too, baby. Thanks for your warm wishes, and I'll see you in a few days." They then hung up.

Jr. had heard him tell someone he loved them too, so he inquired, "Who were you talking to, Dad, and told them you love them too? I know it wasn't Mom because she never tells you she loves you. She actually tells you she hates you."

Jesus answered him, "I was talking to ... to your grandma, Hilda. I told her I was going on a trip and she told me to be safe and that she loves me."

"Oh," said Jr.

Jesus thought that Mut's semen was not making him feel any different. Guess those two guys were right about that. He sat down to watch some TV while counting down the time for his departure.

Danny woke up and found the girls had left. He couldn't find them anywhere in his house. He even checked outside, but they weren't there either. He was about to call Denise when he heard his doorbell ring. It was them. When he opened the door, they said they had gone to get some burritos to have for breakfast. They went inside, and they all sat down to eat. Josefina woke up too and walked to the kitchen table. Danny asked them, "How'd you girls go to get them if y'all don't have your cars here?"

Denise answered, "We took an uber, and I also went to pick up my car. It's parked outside your house. We didn't want to wake you up since you looked so comfortable."

Danny said, "Oh, well, thank you for not waking me up. It's kinda my pet peeve."

Josefina had found out they had a rumble yesterday while she was at work and inquired, "So who won yesterday's fight?" She walked into the kitchen and greeted them.

Heather replied, "Your mom really knows how to fight. She beat me up. Can't you tell by the way my face looks?" She had a partial black eye and her lip was busted open.

Josefina stated, "Yeah, I know she does. She used to fight a lot when she was in high school and with her brothers whose souls rest in peace,"

Denise commented, "Those three girls messed us up a bit. No offense, but even though they won the fight, we won the battle since we're still here with your dad."

Josefina responded, "Yeah, well, I wouldn't count that as a win. My daddy here gets a lot of girls, and he might just replace y'all with another group of three when you least expect it." The three of them were in shock that she had bluntly shared that information.

Danny told Josefina, "Honey, don't start trouble. These three women have been nothing but good to me so far."

Josefina uttered, "I'm not trying to start a dilemma. I'm only being honest. I mean nothing personal about it since they've been pretty cool with me too." They continued eating.

Danny finished his burrito and told them he'd be back as he was going to the gym. The girls wanted to go with him, but he told them, "Why don't you three stay here and clean up my home before I get back?" They unwillingly agreed since they didn't want to appear clingy or needy to him.

Dan got up to get ready. Josefina jumped in the shower as the three started cleaning up the residence. When Danny was ready, he told them he'd be back soon and left. They were sad but hoped he wouldn't return with their replacements so soon. Denise peeked through the window to see him drive off, then went to find something to clean up. Miya and Heather were cleaning up his room. Josefina got out of the shower and found Denise in her room. She politely told her, "Could you please leave my room so I could change?"

Denise said, "Oh, I'm sorry. I was going to clean up your room."

Josefina uttered, "I really appreciate the offer, but I like to clean it myself and don't like anyone going through my things."

Denise commented, "Is it because you have something to hide? Maybe a dead body in your closet or how about a sex toy collection under your bed?"

Josefina questioned, "Were you going through my stuff? Please get out of my room. I already asked you nicely." Denise left her room and closed the door, wondering which guess she had gotten correct.

Josefina got dressed and took off to work. The trio stayed there cleaning up Danny's house, and when they finished, they cooked him some food to have when he got back from the gym. Meanwhile they were alone, and they waited for his return, patiently sitting on his couch and watching some films on his TV set.

Mercedes was at work when Mrs. Santiago called her to her office. Mrs. Santiago asked her, "Were you able to get those items signed?"

Mercedes said, "Yes, I almost forgot. Let me go get them from my vehicle. I'll be right back."

She then walked out of the building and went to her minivan. She opened the door and searched for them. Then she remembered she had put them in the glove box. She opened the box and took them out. She grabbed a marker she had on her person and signed them herself. She wasn't about to request her husband to sign them because he'd be more flattered and act conceited. Besides, he didn't have a twin brother who would sign them either. After she signed them, she closed up her van and walked back inside. She went to Mrs. Santiago's office and handed her the toys with a false signature, wrapped up in a plastic bag. Mrs. Santiago asked, "Why're they all wrapped up in this bag? Did they gross you out or something? Are you a germaphobe?"

Mercedes answered, "No, I'm not a germaphobe. My husband's brother actually wrapped them up that way so his signature could remain preserved."

Mrs. Santiago uttered, "Oh, that's so thoughtful of him. Would you do me another favor and hand him this to sign too, please?" She got up from her chair and removed her boxer briefs, then handed them to Mercedes.

Mercedes was grossed out by her boss's request. She didn't want to offend her and place her new position in jeopardy, so she took her marker out from her pocket and picked her drawers up with it. She asked her for a bag, and Mrs. Santiago grabbed one from her desk and handed it to her. She also told her, "You think it's possible he could sign this picture for me too?" She removed a picture from her desk drawer and handed it to Mercedes.

Mercedes looked at the picture and was disturbed by it. Mrs. Santiago was wearing a leather suit, and her husband was butt naked with a gag ball in his mouth as she stood on top of him introducing a huge dildo in his anal cavity. They both were facing the camera in the photo. Mercedes put it away really fast to not pay more attention to the details. She told her boss, "I'll have him sign this too. Well, gotta go and get back to work." She got up and went to her desk.

When Mercedes got to her desk, she sat in shock as she could not believe just how wild her boss was. She was not even shy or embarrassed about her sexual deeds. She put the picture and drawer away in her desk and made sure they didn't come out until she was headed home. In the meantime, she got back to her paperwork after getting up and making a quick run through her floor to see if any of her employees needed assistance with a call, but they were all doing well without requiring help.

Danny was at the gym working out his legs. He had wrapped up four sets of squats. He was headed to the leg curls machine when he saw a butch woman benching excessive weight. The bar fell on her chest, and she was unable to push it up anymore. The guys at the gym noticed it, but they didn't want to intervene since years before it had been established that women turned their good deeds around to supposedly sexual advances. The butchy female was grunting and looking around to see if anyone would help her. She noticed Dan walking by and asked, "Can you please help me? I'm stuck." Danny ignored her as she yelped, "Someone! Help!"

The other guys there turned the other way, pretending they hadn't seen anything. The gym manager came running since it was his duty to ensure the safety of his clients. He got behind her, standing above where her head lay on the bench, and tried spotting her. The weight was too heavy for him also. He grunted, attempting to pick it up but couldn't. He released his breath and told her, "You need to push the bar as I pick it up. This requires teamwork." They tried it again.

They had managed to lift and pull the bar about halfway to rack it when he let out a gas. She lost her concentration, and the bar fell on her chest again. The manager apologized, and they tried it once more. The butchy woman pushed with all her strength and sharded, dropping the bar on her pecs. The manager looked around at all the guys there and shouted, "Guys! We need your help here!" But no one stepped up to play hero.

The manager then walked over to one of the bars' end and began removing the plates off it. He removed several forty-five pounders, and the bar swung the opposite way. There was a loud clunk. The bar hit the manager on its way up and sent him airborne. The butch didn't even thank the manager or help him up. He instead got up himself and looked around to see the guys there laughing since they had known what the outcome would be. He was lucky she didn't file for harassment. He walked back to his office, ashamed of his unappreciated effort.

Danny was laughing with another guy about the situation as they observed the masculine woman head over to the squat rack and place excessive weights on it too. Danny and the guy got back to their routines as the woman walked under the bar. She placed her feet parallel to her shoulders and dug them into the floor. Some of her fecal matter dripped down her left leg. She then grabbed the bar with her hands and twisted her wrists to get a good grip, placing it over the back of her neck. She picked up the bar, pressing down on her feet. She then took a step forward and bent her knees. She squatted down, but when it was time to push up, she froze. Her legs began to buckle, and she dropped the bar behind her to avoid another injury. All the guys there were staring at her as she shouted, "What are y'all looking at? I bet you've been through this yourselves, trying to lift something too heavy! We women are going to be stronger than y'all one day and will ignore your troubles too!" She then began making her way out of the gym.

When she was gone, the machos laughed at what she had said. The FEMNS were sad since they too believed women would out-strength them one day. Danny continued his exercise, and when he finished, he took off.

Jesus was inside his home hanging out with his son when he heard the doorbell ring. He got up from the floor where they had been playing with dolls and walked over to see who was outside. He peeked through the peephole and observed the angered husband standing outside, who appeared furious. Jesus turned to look at Jr. and placed his index finger over his lips, telling him to not make a sound. Jesus slowly walked away from the door and grabbed Jr.

They went to hide from the man. Jesus was praying the guy would leave and never return. They were hiding under Jr.'s bed when they heard another ring. Jesus covered his son's mouth with his hands and shushed him. Jesus had placed a call to the police but didn't speak after the operator answered. The operator kept saying, "If this is an emergency, please let us know."

Jesus didn't respond but instead blew into the mic, hoping the operator knew something was wrong and would dispatch a unit to his location. He then heard someone walking in their backyard as Mut barked. Then Mut stopped barking, and they heard the back door being opened. Jesus softly whispered to the operator, "Help. There's a guy breaking into my home, and he's going to rape me and my son. He's masculine; we need help."

The operator said, "OK, I'm sending help. Please stay on the line."

Jesus heard her directing any available unit to his location for a possible home invasion. Jr. and he closed their eyes as they heard footsteps inside their home. The footsteps started getting closer to them. He whispered to the operator, "He's inside the house now. Please get here fast. I don't know how to fight, and my son and I are scared."

The operator answered, "Help is on its way now. You just hang in tight there. Try and grab a weapon if you see one. If the subject makes contact with you, you must fight for your life with anything and everything at your disposal."

Jesus inquired, "What if he tries to rape me? What will I do then? Should I offer him a blowjob while the cops get here?" The call was dropped due to network service issues in the area.

Jesus bit his fingernails, and then he heard sirens at a far distance. Then he saw some feet heading into his son's room as the door opened. He shut his eyes and kept quiet. The person in their home kneeled down to look under Jr.'s bed, then grabbed Jesus's arm to remove his hands covering his face. Jesus screamed and wiggled his way out from under the bed. He tossed his cell phone at the person and took off running, leaving his son behind as collateral. He ran out of his house and saw the police driving up the street. He flagged them down to his location. Then Jr. came out and told him, "Dad, Dad, it's Danniel! She's back from school early!"

Jesus was relieved to hear it wasn't the mad husband and turned to look at his home's front door where Danniel stood watching him. The cops got there, and Jesus informed them he had made a mistake. He explained what had happened, and the reporting officer told him, "Look, mister, we have very important calls coming in all day. If you don't have an actual emergency, don't interfere. Instigating trouble and being a coward isn't one. Please don't call nine one one." The officer then left, and Jesus and Jr. went back inside their residence.

Sometime later, Mercedes walked into her home, receiving the news from Jr. that the police had been there earlier. Mercedes asked, "How come they came? Who called them?"

Jr. said, "Daddy called them because he said there was a man outside trying to break in and rape us."

Mercedes replied, "What? Jesus, get your stupid ass over here and explain to me why you called the cops."

Jesus walked over and inquired, "What was that, honey?"

Mercedes fumed, "Why did you call the police and tell Jr. some man was trying to break in and rape you?"

Jesus uttered, "Oh, there was a man outside, and he looked like he wanted to rape us after breaking down the door. I called the police because Jr. and I were terrified he'd manage to come in and hurt us."

Mercedes questioned, "How exactly did you know his intentions? What if he just wanted to sell you some testosterone or maybe even give you some because he heard you're too feminine?"

Jesus commented, "I know because ever since I became famous he's been following me around."

Mercedes slapped him and mentioned, "Quit that delusional talk! I already told you, you aren't as famous as you presume! Matter-of-fact, weren't you leaving today for your weekend trip?"

Jesus told her, "I am a star! You're just jealous like the rest. Yes, I am leaving in a few hours. Why?"

Mercedes answered, "Because I can't wait for you to take off so I could have some peace. You know what? Why don't you grab your stuff and get going earlier?" She walked to their room and grabbed his luggage, then threw it outside.

Jesus was next to be tossed out. She shut the door behind him as he banged on it, shouting, "It's not time yet! Let me back in! I don't even have my keys on me!"

As soon as he said that, Mercedes opened the door, replying, "Here are your keys. No more excuses." She closed the door on his face.

Jesus started crying, wondering why he had married such a short-tempered woman. He grabbed his suitcases and took them one by one to his car. He scanned the area to make sure the mad husband wasn't around and it was clear of any threats. He finished putting all his luggage in the trunk of his car and got inside. He turned it on and felt the AC blowing cold in his face. He called Sam and asked him, "Hey, bro. Are you ready? My wife kicked me out of the house early, and I'm sitting in my car waiting for you to let me know when to pick you up."

Sam told him, "My wife kicked me out of the house too. I'm sitting outside, ready to go. Come pick me up so we can head out."

Jesus replied, "Alright, I'm on my way now. See you in a few." They hung up as Jesus drove over to Sam's.

Danny got back to his dwelling and walked inside. As he made his way in, the girls jumped up from the couch to hug and greet him. They were happy to see him there without their replacements.

Denise took his gym bag from his hands and took it to the garage. Miya walked behind him following his direction while massaging the back of his neck. Heather went to serve him a glass of water. She took it to him in his bedroom where he was taking off his clothes to jump in the shower. Denise got back and came to his bedroom. All three females began undressing and getting ready to shower with him too. They headed into his restroom, and Danny got in his shower. He told Miya, "Might as well use the restroom now if you have to. I don't want to repeat what happened the other day." He chuckled.

Lucia, Alejandra, and Carla had been blowing up his phone since the time they had met the three new ladies in his life. He had told them to give him space because he wasn't going to stay with them. He just didn't know how to get rid of them as he was growing accustomed to their presence. Danny began sharing the story about the masculine woman at the gym with the girls. They all laughed with him. All four were now in the shower. Danny had them scrubbing his body with soap. Denise was shampooing his scalp. Heather started scrubbing his male organ, and it started getting erect. Heather rinsed his penis and put it in her mouth. Miya had finished scrubbing his feet at the time and was about to place his leg back down when he got a cramp. His body jolted forward, pushing his dick in deeper in Heather's mouth. She gagged and pulled her head away. He grabbed Miya's tits to hold his balance, and she shouted, "Ah! It hurts!"

Some shampoo trickled down into his eyes, and they started burning. He released Miya's breasts and turned around to rinse out the shampoo in his eyeballs. He head-butted Denise while turning around and hit Miya with his elbow. Heather got up and tried helping him rinse his eyes off. She slipped and grabbed Miya, pulling her to the ground. Miya grabbed Denise, and Denise grabbed Danny. All four of them plunged to the shower floor. Danny had managed to clear the shampoo from his eyes. They all laughed as they lay on top of each other, then they began to get back up on their feet. Danny told them, "I don't think showering together is a good idea anymore." The women agreed, and since he was done, he got out to dry himself.

The woman showered their bodies and got out some minutes later. He was in his bed lying down when they came out. Miya was complaining about her nipples and head and Heather about her throat. They were making fun of the scenario, retelling it to each other. Then they lay down in bed with Danny. Denise and Heather started massaging his legs after he told them he had worked them out. Miya brought him a cold beer and held it for him so he wouldn't spill any on his bed. Moments later, they took turns riding Danny and then took a nap when they all had nutted.

Jesus pulled up to Sam's apartment. Sam was still sitting outside, and when he saw his pal, it put a smile on his face. Jesus drove up to a parking space in front of him. Sam got up and came over to him and said hello. They then began putting Sam's stuff in the back seat since there wasn't any room for them in the trunk. Sally came out of the apartment and shouted, "You forgot this!" She threw at Sam his nightgown, which he had left on the bed after removing it in the morning to shower.

Jesus said hello to Sally, but she ignored him and shut the door. They then got inside the vehicle and began their road trip. Jesus put on his favorite artist, Cardi B, and exited the apartment complex. They stopped at a red traffic light where a bum started dancing to the song they were listening to. The vagrant ran up to them and asked for some spare change. But Jesus hit the gas, observing the man chasing after his car. Sam yelled, "Call the cops, bro! Let them know there's some crazy guy dancing in the street and chasing cars!"

Jesus said, "I can't call them again. I already called them earlier, and they lectured me about it."

Sam questioned, "Why'd you call them?"

Jesus began telling his story. Sam was laughing at him because he didn't believe it and thought he was just paranoid. Jesus went into detail on why the bothered husband was after him. Sam was astonished and told him, "That's why you don't mess with other guys. You never know how strong, crazy, and determined they are."

Jesus replied, as they got on the freeway, "I know that now."

They were traveling west bound when they came up behind a semi driven by a masculine woman. They were about to pass her on the left-hand side when another truck came out of nowhere, almost colliding with them. Jesus swerved his vehicle and went off the pavement, picking up dust. Sam screamed for his dear life as Jesus maneuvered the car back to the pavement. A state trooper witnessed their incident and pulled them over. As she got out of the car and approached theirs, Jesus lowered the music down. She came up to the driver's side window and asked for his driver's license and insurance. He handed it to her, and then she looked at the passenger. She asked, "Hey, aren't you two the guys who went viral online?"

Jesus answered, "Yes, we are. My preferred pronouns are pink daddy she, but how'd you recognize us?"

She said, "It wasn't hard to recognize you two. There's not too many fruit cakes traveling the roads right now. Where are y'all headed to anyway?"

Sam replied, "We're going to a resort to spend the weekend together."

She inquired, "So, you two are together, together?"

Jesus smiled and uttered, "No, not at all. We're married."

The trooper responded, “I don’t get it. Y’all aren’t together, but y’all are married? So are y’all getting a divorce or something?”

Sam commented, “No, ha, ha, we’re not a couple. We both have wives at home.”

She told them, “Honestly, I thought you two were gay. You guys sure were acting that way in the video.”

Jesus mentioned, “We’re not homosexuals. Not at all. Would you like to take a picture with us and maybe get an autograph?”

She said, “No thanks. I’d rather not. Here’s your documents. Y’all be safe on the road now.” She then headed back to her unit and cleaned her hands with hand sanitizer as Jesus and Sam got back on the road.

Mercedes took her kids to visit her mom. She had found out she had gotten into a scuffle and wanted to check in on her. They went inside and sat down as Lucia shared her story with Mercedes. After she was informed in detail of the incident, they left to go get some ice cream and walk around the mall. Jr. wanted his mother to buy him some nail polish and some hair bands since he claimed his hair was getting longer and he couldn’t see. Lucia suggested he cut it off instead so he wouldn’t turn out like his dad. Chris and Danniel laughed at him, and he threw a fit, saying, “Stop making fun of my dad. He may be feminine, but he’s a good guy. I hope I grow up to be just like him. But I’m not getting married to a mean woman like you, Mom.” He took off running, and they chased him down.

Mercedes eventually purchased the items he had requested in order to calm him down. They returned to Lucia’s residence, and Jr. started playing with Josefina’s old dolls. They ate dinner and hung out till the sun went down. Then Mercedes took her family back home. Lucia went with them and spent the night over at Mercedes’s home.

Sam kept seeing a sign on the highway for a fortune teller and card readings. He insisted they stop and fuel up there. Jesus had to pee, so he exited the highway when that particular exit came up. They drove to the gas station where the psychic was located. Jesus pulled into the fuel pumps and handed his wallet to Sam, telling him to fuel up and wait for him before getting his palms read. Jesus ran inside the store and found a masculine woman at the counter. He asked for the restrooms, and she told him, "Sorry, but they're closed for repair. Try the next exit."

Jesus ran out of the store and toward the back. He saw a small pond and decided to pee there. He didn't want to pee standing up since he hadn't been able to do so properly in some weeks. So he removed his flip-flops and took off his shorts and thong. He then walked into the pond and squatted down. He felt his little testicles submerge in the water, including the tip of his little dick and cheeks. He released his body fluids with a sigh of relief. When he finished, he felt something clamp and tug at his micro penis. He stood up and found a bass clinging on his oversized clitoris. He yelled out of panic and started slapping the fish. He was able to pry the bass off and tossed it back in the water. He then made his way to his dry clothes and put them on. As he got dressed, a wild woman crept up on him. She had a pet raccoon on a leash, but she looked like a vagrant. She asked him, "Hey, are you looking to have a good time? I can eat your ass out while I jerk you off."

Jesus screamed, "Ah! Hell no, get away from me, lady!" He ran back to his car.

Sam had filled up the car by the time Jesus got back. Jesus told Sam, "Let's get out of here! There's some wild woman in the back trying to eat ass and jerk off any dude willing to."

Sam said, "Bro! Calm down. You're letting the fame get to you. She probably meant that in a good way. Besides, I really want to get my palms read and future told. If you don't want to come, just wait for me here. I'll be back really fast." Jesus stayed in the car as his pal went inside the little office next to the fuel store. Moments later, he came back with a smile on his face. He stated, "She told me I was going to become masculine again. That my wife is going to be happy and things will go back to how they once were."

Jesus uttered, "That's great buddy, now let's get out of here."

Sam got back in the car as Jesus sped off. Sam told Jesus, "Oh, and she had a really nice raccoon pet. I think she's the one you ran into behind the store. She offered to eat my ass and jack me off, but unlike you, I let her. She said the card reading was free, so I didn't have to pay. Isn't that kick ass, bro?"

Jesus answered, "No, not really. If it was the same woman, she looked like she hadn't bathed in months or brushed her teeth, which means your ass is going to have bad breath on it."

Sam commented, "Oh no! You might be right. Why don't you smell my ass and see if it stinks?" He got up in his seat and started pulling down his shorts.

Jesus responded, "What're you doing? No, man! Sit back down and buckle up; it's the law! I don't want to smell your butt hole!" Sam stayed mute the rest of the way, embarrassed and discouraged.

Sally dropped off her kids at her sister's house, then left on a date with a guy who had been hitting up on her. She too was heading out on a weekend trip with him to a small historical town a few hours away. She got in his car, and they darted out of the city. She wanted to forget about Sam at least for a few days. They were traveling on the highway when he got a flat tire. He called for roadside assistance since he wasn't masculine enough to change his own tire. She then started having second thoughts of the whole rendezvous. When the service crew arrived, they changed out his tire and got them back on the road. But Sally made up an excuse to head back, and the guy dropped her back at her sister's home. He then asked her if she could cover for the travel expenses. She claimed, "What expenses?"

He said, "The tire repair." He stuck his hand out, waiting for her to refund him for the service.

She replied, "You're not even a real macho like you claimed to be, and now you want me to pay for your flat tire? You better get out of here before I call my brother-in-law so he can show you what a real man is."

The guy uttered, "Well, bring him out then. That way he could pay me."

Sally shouted out his name, and he came out of her sister's home as Sally yelled, "This feminine man is bugging me and said you're not going to do anything about it!" Her brother-in-law rushed the man's vehicle, causing him to take off—frightened by a real macho man.

CHAPTER 13

SAT HER DATE

Jesus and Sam checked in late at the resort. Sam had failed to inform Jesus that the psychic had told him they'd get a flat tire and would spend several hours changing it because they were too feminine to do so themselves until some masculine woman would pull over to help. When they arrived at the resort, they had some frozen margaritas, and then they fell asleep. When they woke up, they made their way to the diner where they were served breakfast while a woman played a grand piano on a stage located in the center of the room. She was playing Cardi B, and Jesus started moving in his chair and singing the words to the song. When the musician noticed he was stealing her attention, she stopped playing that song and played something else. Jesus and Sam finished their meals and headed to the spa.

When they entered the spa, they were greeted by the staff who suggested they change into some bathrobes. Jesus and Sam changed in the restroom, then went back to lie down on some massage tables. The staff inquired if they'd care for a frozen margarita, which they gladly accepted, as they got pampered. There were strawberries and cream incense burning in the room. The lights were dim, and the working area seemed cozy. One of the massage practitioners asked Jesus to turn over and lie on his back. He did so but covered his male breasts that had begun maturing. His nipples were sensitive, and every time the woman passed her hands over them, he'd moan. Sam was lying next to him a few feet away. He had propped his ass up and had requested a deep tissue anal massage as he sipped on his frozen drink. The staff then placed hot stones on the areas they had massaged. Sam jumped up when he felt the hot stone in his rear end. He then calmed down and allowed the employee to place it in correctly. Jesus turned around to see after hearing Sam grunt and told him, "You now can say you have a hot rock-hard ass." They both started giggling.

When the session concluded, Jesus and Sam walked over to the hot tubs. They were handed out some swimwear, into which they changed. Afterward, they entered the tub and sat in a comfortable position. There the staff placed eyelid covers on them so they could receive and enjoy the best experience possible. There was a drink holder in front of each one of them, which held their margaritas in place, close enough for them to tilt their heads forward and sip. Jesus felt something touching his ass. He thought it was Sam and said, "Quit it, bro. We haven't even had enough margaritas for you to start acting that way."

Sam said, "Huh? What are you talking about, bro? I haven't moved at all."

Jesus removed his eye cover and saw a butchy female next to him. She was a customer as well and was looking for a feminine man to sodomize with her growing urges. Jesus looked at her and asked, "Why're you grabbing my ass? Don't be disrespecting me like that while I'm here trying to relax."

The woman replied, "I am here to relax also, but I'm looking for a guy who wants to get pounded in the ass by a woman like me. Would you be interested?"

Jesus uttered, "No way! Now leave us alone and go find your own hot tub, lady."

Sam overheard the conversation and commented, "Are you really interested in what you said? I mean I could give it a try for fifty bucks. Maybe even for free with the right amount of margaritas in my system."

Jesus interrupted him, "Sam, no, don't start with that. You're a man at the end of the day, and men don't get their anus penetrated by women. Erase that thought from your head and just have a good time. As for you, hop over to another tub and don't bother us anymore or you'll have some trouble heading your way." He stared and pointed his finger at the female.

The woman responded as she was getting out of the tub, "Trouble? Are you threatening me, little pansy man? I will literally beat the shit out of both you sissies even while going through labor."

Jesus uttered, "No one threatened you with violence as a consequence for the trouble I'm referring to."

She said, "That's what I thought; you want to be a real man, but can't. Better keep those butt cheeks clenched after the right amount of margaritas, because I'm raping you then." She stared at Sam as she walked over to the next tub.

Jesus and Sam got out of the tub right after she did. They didn't want to be anywhere near her. They dried themselves with towels provided by the resort and put on their clothes. Then they walked out of the spa area, headed for their next activity.

Mercedes and her kids all woke up a little early and started getting ready to go visit an archeological museum. Lucia had already showered, and she started making them pancakes as she drank a cup of coffee. Jr. requested her to make him a pancake with a shape that would surprise him. She made him a dick-shaped one just for kicks. When Jr. got his pancake, he said, "Wow, you made mine look like an evil mushroom, Grandma, thanks." He poured syrup on it and devoured it.

Mercedes, Chris, and Danniel came over to eat, and when they finished, they left for the museum.

When they got to the museum, a security officer was patrolling outside on a hoverboard. Just then the battery charge on the board failed, causing it to halt, and he flew right across them, slamming into the museum's sign. His baton was holstered at the back of his duty belt, and it lodged in his ass, as he fell down. He yelled, "Ouch, that hurt!" They laughed as Jr. ran to help the guy up, removing the object out of his rear end.

The man thanked him, got back up to his feet, and took the hoverboard to be charged. As they entered the building, they were greeted by the same officer at his desk. He handed them pamphlets and allowed them to gaze around. They came across a display that showed the anatomy and evolution of men. Chris told Jr., "You see that, Jr.? You're not a man since you don't have one of those between your legs." He chuckled afterward.

Jr. stated, "This is a fake display. I'm going to talk to the guard at the front to let him know they need to update it."

Mercedes uttered, "Son, don't let your older brother get to you. He's only doing it to upset you."

Jr. said, "I know, Mom. I really miss Dad though. He's the only one who understands me, how I feel and think. Hope he's having fun at the resort."

Lucia commented, "I'm sure he's having fun out there. They cater to your kind, make you feel special in order to go back and spend more money. I heard they give discounts on the first trip and jack up the price on the following ones after they hook you in."

Chris responded, "Oh, they're hooking them alright, but not how we'd all imagine." He had an evil grin on his face.

A group of feminine men walked into the museum and looked at the display in question. They began to complain as they had similar beliefs as Jr. They called the officer over and informed him, "This display is a mockery to our ancestors. We need this reevaluated and recreated to fit our current changes. It's sexually biased, offensive, and repulsive to our sexual transformations." The security guard agreed since he too was feminine.

They all filed a formal complaint and dropped it inside the suggestion box. Mercedes and her family had walked away from there; otherwise, Jr. would have joined the petition by asking his mother to write his complaint for him.

Jesus and Sam walked over to the margarita bar and got a refill. They asked the bartender if there were bigger cups for them to use so they wouldn't have to refill those as much. The bartender said, "I don't have larger cups than those. Maybe you guys can bring your own if you find any. There aren't any rules just yet stating you can't bring your own cup."

Jesus told her, "My preferred pronouns are pink daddy she and not one of the guys. So we could bring our own cup, and there's no standards regulating the size? Come on, Sam, let's go find ourselves bigger cups. We'll be right back." They went in search of a bigger container around the resort.

Jesus and Sam looked at the pots outside that held plants in them. Jesus put his hand inside and tried to remove the plant from the soil. Sam said, "I think we'll get in trouble if we use these. They'll probably kick us out, and I can't go home early or Sally will be mad at me."

Jesus replied, "You're right. Come on, let's go look for something else." He placed the pot back in its original place and fixed the plant inside it to look as it had done before.

They came across some ashtrays outside, and Sam inquired, "How about this? I think it'll work."

Jesus uttered, "No, they're really dirty, and our margaritas will taste like ashes if we use those. Let's keep looking for something else."

They headed inside to their rooms. Sam had to pee anyhow, and when they were in their rooms, Jesus looked around to see if he could find anything there. He grabbed the trash can and smelled it. It didn't smell so bad, so he washed it in his sink with soap several times. He opened his room door on hearing Sam knock. He informed Sam he was going to use his trash can, and Sam went to his room to wash his as well. When he went back to Jesus, Sam said, "Now we need bigger straws because the ones they have won't reach the bottom of these margarita containers."

Jesus commented, "You're right; let me think here. Ah-ha! We could use our snorkels, buddy. We just have to remove the one-way valve and voila!" They took their snorkels apart and headed back to the bar.

When they got to the bar, the bartender chuckled and stated, "Are you two serious about using the trash cans as cups and snorkels as straws? No one has done that before, but as I mentioned earlier, it's not yet been prohibited."

Jesus and Sam handed her the trash cans as Jesus stated, "Hell yeah, we're serious, girl. We're the world's number one margarita fans. Please fill mine up to the top; there's a nice tip for your cooperation." When he received his trash-a-rita, he signed the cup he was using before and handed it to her, saying, "This will be worth gold one day. I'm a celebrity, but please don't let everyone know. I'd like my privacy to be respected while at the resort." The bartender took the cup and pretended to put it away but instead threw it in the trash under the bar.

Jesus and Sam had their trash cans filled up, and they walked away from the bar and headed toward the salon to get their manicures and pedicures done. As they walked in, the staff laughed at the size of their drinks. They took a seat in the pedi chairs and drank their margaritas in peace as the staff attended to their feet.

After Mercedes and her family left the museum, they went to the city's amusement park. Mercedes drove over there and parked her minivan. Lucia told her, as she took her time getting out, "Your new ride is very comfortable. I almost fell asleep."

They walked to the entrance of the park and formed a line to pay for the tickets. The park was owned by a masculine woman who despised feminine men. There was a sign at the entrance that made it clear: "No FEMNS allowed in the park." Chris told his little brother, "Guess you're going to have to stay in the car."

Mercedes said, "Jr., please try and act like a normal boy. I don't want to get kicked out of the park if you start acting like a little girl." The family was concerned Jr. might not be able to pull it off and they'd get removed from the park before riding all the rides.

They walked inside after purchasing their one-day passes. Chris and Danniel took off on their own as Mercedes, Lucia, and Jr. went their separate way. Jr. wanted to get on the merry-go-round, and so they walked toward it. When they got there, he insisted on hopping on a pink horse. Mercedes told him, "No, *mijo.* Ride something else. I told you to act like a normal boy, and if you don't, they're going to kick us out."

Jr. said, "I want to ride that one though. Why can't they just not be so mean? I want to go home. I don't like this park's rules."

Mercedes got him off the ride and took him aside to have some words with him. "Look now, Jr., I have paid for all our tickets, and they won't refund me that money if they remove us from the park. I made it very clear to you before we came inside. Why can't you just act normal and stop being like your father? For all you know, you're probably not really feminine but instead influenced by your dad's behavior. Now let's get back on the ride and don't ruin it for all of us, or I'm going to take you to the van and leave you there alone till the rest of us are done here."

Jr. uttered, "Fine, but you have to buy me a pink cotton candy right now." She agreed she would buy one after the ride was over, and they got on the merry-go-round.

When the ride started, Mercedes had to console Jr. because he began shouting he was scared. The ride attendant kept her eye on him, trying to figure out if he was in violation of the park's rules or not. Mercedes took him off the horse he was sitting on and made him sit with her and Lucia on a bench behind. When the ride came to a stop, Jr. opened his eyes and they got off. They headed to the snack shack to get him some cotton candy. Lucia asked for a beer since she knew it was going to be a long day. From there, they headed to the bumper carts and hoped Jr. wouldn't break character. After waiting in line for the next round, it was finally their turn. But Jr. tried running away from his mother and grandmother. They grabbed him and forced him to get on it with them. He was yelling so loud he caught the attention of the ride attendant there too. When the fun came to an end, there was a security officer waiting for them. She informed Mercedes, "Ma'am, would you please follow me?" She escorted them out of the park.

Lucia went searching for her other two grandkids, as Mercedes and Jr. were removed from the park. They went to the van to wait for the rest. Jr. was happy because he didn't have to ride anymore and he had gotten his cotton candy. He ate his treat while Mercedes sat in the driver's seat, displeased with his behavior.

Jesus and Sam walked out of the salon feeling like a million bucks. They had their hair done by the courteous staff, and they shook their heads, flaunting it back to let everyone know. Their nails looked flawless too. They walked toward the casino to try their luck. The other customers kept staring at them because of their massive cups, but Jesus believed it was because they were famous.

When they got to the casino, they sat at some slot machines, inserted credits, and jerked the lever down. They didn't win anything even after sitting there for about thirty minutes, so they walked to the card tables. They took a seat at the card pair game, and they placed their bets. Sam was getting lucky calling out the pairs of cards. He had racked up about three hundred bucks when they went over to play tic-tac-toe at another table. Jesus was on a roll, gathering about five hundred bucks himself. He was a tic-tac-toe expert, and the robot didn't know it. Their cups were halfway empty when they decided to sit over at the thumb wars table and try their luck there. Sam was first, and he grabbed a robotic hand and started playing. The robotic hand won the first match. Then as the second one took place, Jesus accidentally spilled some of his drink on the robot's computer. The hand malfunctioned and wouldn't let go of Sam's hand. It gripped Sam's hand even harder. Sam shouted for help and Jesus ran to go find someone. The casino manager ran over toward them and hit the emergency shutoff button. When the robot finally let go of Sam, his thumb was dislocated. Sam screamed in pain, and the manager offered to help him, but Sam refused. The butch woman from the hot tub walked over to him and pulled his thumb back into place. Sam thanked her, but she uttered, "Maybe later when you have sufficient margaritas under your belt, you could show me your gratitude." She then walked away.

Jesus recommended Sam to stick his thumb into his drink to minimize the swelling. Sam shoved it inside and said it was too cold. Jesus then suggested to him, "Well, you can stick it in your butt to warm it up."

Sam went ahead and kept shoving it from the trash can to his ass all throughout the day. They walked over to the bean bag toss stand in the casino. Jesus bet on the game and ended up losing all the money he had made so far. Sam took his turn and also forfeited his cash credits. They then entered a makeup competition.

Jesus won the first prize, making up for his loss. Sam was booed because he painted butterflies on his face that resembled penises with wings. Then they both heard there was going to be a beauty king contest and ran to get registered as contestants. They were taken backstage to pick out their wardrobe. Jesus grabbed a shiny gold suit dress that was in style, and Sam got himself a red one. They began dressing up, and when they were ready, the announcer informed the public to take their seats and enjoy the show.

Lucia met up with Chris and Danniel. They were informed Mercedes and Jr. had gotten kicked out. Chris said, "I knew that would happen, Grandma. Well, they can wait in the van while we have fun without them."

They formed a line to ride one of the park's scariest attractions. Lucia called Mercedes and informed the kids didn't want to leave just yet. Mercedes told her they'd wait for them outside in the van for an hour or so. All three got on the ride and buckled into their seats. Lucia had chugged beer before entering the ride. The ride attendant walked around, making sure everyone was safely secured to their seats. When he finished, he started the ride and sent it on its way. The group of carts took off and within seconds had picked up speed. They were headed upward in a spiraling course on the cart's rails. When they got to the top, the cart slowed down and then plummeted downward for about a minute at a fast rate of speed. Then the rails formed a vortex that made the carts spiral straight forward through the rail frame. Lucia got dizzy and felt nauseous. She spewed out her beer and breakfast from her intestines. Her barf managed to fly out of the ride's perimeter and splatter all over a group of kids who were sitting down there eating. This caused a chain reaction around the park, and everyone started throwing up. When the ride came to an end and they got off to walk toward the next ride, Chris told his grandma, "That was cool, Grandma. Look at all the people barfing because you vomited on those kids. Now the people who kicked Mom out are getting their karma." He giggled and walked to the next ride on their list.

Danniel spewed after she saw a fat guy throw up some dark fluids. She was grossed out because the man's expelled liquid reeked like shit. Chris gagged but didn't regurgitate like everyone else did. They made it safely to the next attraction and formed a line. They got on the ride, and even though it was exciting, it wasn't as nerve-wracking as the previous one. When they got off the ride, they noticed the security personnel chasing the obese man who had caused Danniel to vomit. He had stripped down to his red thong, which you could barely see under his belly that hung over his waist. It turned out he was a feminine male and had fooled the person at the ticket counter. The security officers ran after him as he charged through the tables where people were eating. He managed to grab a hold of a hot dog and a drink during his escape. He shoved the hot dog down his throat, all while running away from the security. He began drinking the soda and then tossed the cup back at one of the security guards pursuing him. Just as he made it to the park's exit, he turned around and vomited on the security officers. He then ran out of the park and over toward his car. Mercedes observed the man running through the parking lot. He stopped to rest in front of her van, placing one of his hands on the hood and gasping for air. Mercedes honked at him, and he jiggled his breasts at her, then ran to his vehicle. The man sped off in his ride, as Mercedes dialed Lucia to find out if they were safe.

Jesus was called out from backstage to make his entrance through the runway. He came out walking confidently and posed for the audience. He made a 360-degree turn and started walking backstage. Just before getting to the back, he froze and turned around to view the crowd once more. He then walked on tippy-toes, placing one foot in front of the other, and leaned in to blow a kiss at the spectators. He walked backstage and was happy to see his pal Sam up next. He told Sam, "Good luck out there. Give them a great show so they'll crown you or me king of the contest." He then smacked Sam's ass as he made his way toward the runway.

Sam came out also very confident, but as he made his way to the front edge of the stage, he tripped and flew over into the crowd. He landed on top of the butch woman from the hot tub. She hugged him in her arms and told him, "I knew your curiosity would bring you to me. Let's get out of here and head back to my room. Come on!" She got up from her chair and carried him out of there.

Jesus was backstage, bragging to the other contestants that he was going to win since he was famous. The rest of the participants took their turn on stage. Jesus never noticed Sam hadn't returned after his performance. When all the FEMNS had vogued, they were called back to the stage so the spectators could judge them and crown the king. Jesus walked out onto the stage and stood next to the others. The host walked around, pointing at each one of them and eliminating those who didn't get cheered. There were five guys left, and Jesus was one of them. The crowd eliminated two of the contestants and made their decision on the last three. Jesus was booed off the stage since he had become arrogant. He then ran backstage and changed. When he had suited back into his regular clothes, he searched for Sam. He called him on his phone, but it was turned off, and he was unable to get a hold of him. He went around asking everyone if they had seen him. No one even remembered him. He then walked out to the spectators and asked them. A woman replied, "He left with a masculine-looking woman. She was carrying him out of here in a hurry. I think I saw them leave through the front doors, and I may have overheard her saying she was taking him to some bar close by."

Jesus uttered, "Thank you very much, lady. I really appreciate your help." He ran toward the front entrance and caught a taxi ride to the bars nearby.

Lucia informed Mercedes they were fine and not to worry. She explained the reason behind the big man running around half naked and then hung up on her since they were about to get on another ride. Jr. had finished his cotton candy and was whining he was hungry. Mercedes told him, "You're going to have to wait till your brothers and grandmother get out of the park. I'm hungry also, but I have to be here with you since you couldn't act normal to save your life."

Jr. said, "Can't you just order something online and have it delivered here? I'm also bored and want to go home already so I can play with my dolls."

Mercedes replied, "I told you to wait; now be quiet, and don't irritate me anymore. I wish you'd be old enough so you could've gone with your dad and his friend."

Jr. uttered, "I wish so too so I could have my own house and not have to put up with you being mean to me anymore." He then opened the door and ran out of the van.

Mercedes exited her vehicle and chased after Jr. She saw him sprinting toward the fence. When she got to the fence line, she witnessed he had hopped over and was inside the park running toward the crowds. She immediately headed toward the entrance. When she got there, she informed the tickets sales representative about her situation. The employee told her, "So you mean to tell me that the feminine kid who was with you is back inside the park? That's not good, not good at all. Let me get a hold of security so they could be on the lookout." She notified the security over a two-way radio of the situation.

Mercedes questioned, "Can I go in and search for him?"

The female replied, "Absolutely not. You both got kicked out earlier, and if you weren't able to control him on your own, then you might not be able to control him in the park."

Mercedes uttered, "I could control him; it's just that he ran away while we were waiting for my other kids to come out."

The employee responded, "No, ma'am, you're not allowed back inside. The security staff will find him and bring him back out. You just wait here for them."

Mercedes commented, "Please don't hurt him. He's just scared and wants to be treated equally."

The woman said, "I'm not responsible if he gets hurt. The sign at the entrance makes it clear to everyone that feminine men or kids aren't allowed and will be physically removed off the property."

Mercedes answered, "OK, alright. I'll just wait here, and hopefully he'll come back unharmed."

Jr. was running around the park, looking for his family. He ran past some of the staff who were cleaning up the puke off the floor with the fat guy's clothes. He spotted his grandma and sprinted toward her. As he ran up to her, she saw him and asked, "How'd you get back in? Didn't they kick you and your mom out?"

Jr. told her, "I ran out of the van and jumped the fence back inside."

Lucia replied, "Why though? They're only going to kick you out again if they see you. Come on, let's go back to your mommy so she won't be worried." Chris and Danniel went with them.

When they got to the front entrance, they were intercepted by the security staff. One officer said, "Hey, kid. We made it clear you're not welcomed here when we removed you. Please leave the property so there won't be any more problems."

Lucia told him, "He's just a little boy. Leave him alone."

The security guard replied, "Look, ma'am, rules are rules, and there's no exceptions to them. Now you and your other companions will have to leave the park too. You guys are guilty of helping this boy back in the park. We don't want to see any of y'all back here again."

They exited the park and walked toward Mercedes who was still arguing with the ticket sales woman. When she saw her family, she left the ticket window and ran toward them. She grabbed Jr.'s hand and escorted him to her minivan. They all got in as Chris and Danniel complained. Mercedes told them she'd take them back some other day without Jr. and then drove them to a restaurant to grab a bite. From there, they went back home.

Jesus drove around the bars close to the resort. He got off to look for Sam inside the first one. He asked the taxi driver to wait for him outside. He entered the bar and went straight to the bartender and showed him a picture of Sam and himself on his cell phone. The bartender said, "I haven't seen that guy around here. Matter-of-fact, I haven't seen him in my life."

Jesus wrote down his number in a napkin and handed it to the bartender, then left. He got back inside the cab, and the driver asked, "Any luck finding your friend?"

Jesus replied, "No, not yet. The bartender said he's never seen him in his entire life. Could you take me to the next bar please?" The cab driver took off for the next stop.

Moments later, they arrived at another bar. Jesus got off the cab and walked inside. He cast his gaze around at the people in there but didn't spot Sam. He then walked over to the bartender to ask. He got the same response, and he left his number with him too. He then exited the bar and got back in the cab. They drove to the next place, and he got off again. He went inside and didn't find his pal there either. He got back in the taxi. The driver continued taking him around all the bars in the area. When they had gone through them all, the driver asked him, "So how're you going to pay for this ride? I've taken you to all the bars, and I'd like to get paid and go back home now."

Jesus told her, "I don't have cash on me right now, but if you take me to an ATM, I could make a withdrawal and pay you. Unless you have fingerprint pay or retina scan cash."

The masculine female driver replied, "No, we don't have any of those fancy systems here in town. How about you just let me perform some sexual activities on you?"

Jesus uttered, "No mam, I'm married, and unless you could prove you've had unprotected sex with a macho within the last two days, then I'm turning down your offer."

The woman replied, "What good will it do if I've had unprotected sex with a macho man within the past two days?"

Jesus answered, "Well, if you have done so, then I'm willing to eat you out and suck up all the masculine semen from you in order to get a dosage of testosterone."

The woman responded, "I have had sex with a macho man, and you can do what you said to me." She then parked her car in a dark alley and hopped onto the backseat with him.

Jesus was hesitant and pushed her away, telling her, "How can you prove what you say is true? I just want to find my friend and go back to the resort if you're lying."

She commented, "You're just going to have to take my word for it. Now come closer and kiss me. Relax, I won't hurt you. You'll enjoy whatever happens between us."

He told her, "Show me the inside of your vagina so I can make sure there's semen in there."

She removed her clothes, spread her legs, and said, "Take a good look at this pussy and suck it dry."

He spread her lips apart, examining her, and then uttered, "There's no sign of semen secretions inside of you. You're lying to me."

She immediately shoved his face into her vagina and replied, "Eat me out, motherfucker! You need to pay for the ride somehow!"

Jesus yelled for help and pushed her away. She then grabbed him and began licking his face. He tried opening the door, but it was locked. She hopped on top of him and tried getting his little dick out. She ripped off his shorts and had a hard time finding his penis. Jesus was terrified but was unable to defend himself since she was overpowering him. She tried inserting his cock inside her, but it wouldn't slip in. She then flipped him over and tried eating his ass to see if it would make his dick erect. That didn't work either, so she flipped him back again to face him and asked, "What's wrong with you? Am I not turning you on or something?"

He said, "How could I be turned on while being raped?"

She uttered, "You're just a fag trapped in a man's body. Get out of my car and get lost, you pansy!" She opened the door and shoved him out.

Jesus fell to the ground. He saw her put her clothes back on and get back in the driver's side. She sped off, leaving him there without anything to cover him from the waist down. He also had his ass all wet with saliva when she had licked it. He got up to his feet whimpering and started walking back to the resort. He tried calling Sam on his phone again, but it was still off. He thought about reaching out to Sally to see if Sam had contacted her but decided not to worry her. It took him about an hour to walk back to the resort. When he entered through the front doors, he yelled at the receptionist, "Help, I've been raped and my friend has been kidnapped!"

The receptionist handed him a towel to cover himself with and uttered, "Oh my gosh! Do you want me to call the police?"

Jesus was exhausted, and recalling his previous interactions with the law, he answered, "No, there's no need to call the police. Have you by any chance seen my friend around? I just want to find him." He displayed a photo to her.

She gazed at the picture and replied, "No, I'm sorry, but I haven't seen him around other than earlier when you two were walking around the place." He thanked the receptionist and walked to his room to call it a night.

Josefina had another date. She took about an hour and a half to get ready. She shaved her armpits, mustache, legs, privates, and even the thin hairs beginning to sprout on her chest. She dressed up really sexy in a short skirt and a tight top. She then headed out of her home, while talking to her date on the phone. He told her to meet him at some bar and grill. She got in her car and drove over to the location. When she arrived there, she headed inside and ordered two beers. She took a seat at the bar and texted the guy who was supposed to be on his way there. He texted back, "I'm almost there, baby. You keep that sweet ass seated comfortably before I tear it up later."

Josefina sipped her drink and watched the TV monitor in front of her. A women's basketball game was on. A random guy approached her and said, "Hey there, sweetheart. Looks like your date never came. I could take his place if you'd like me to. Let me know, and I'll show you a good time."

She told him, "My date is on his way now, and I just got here. Thanks for the offer, but I'm not interested at the moment." The guy walked away as she went through her date's online profile.

Josefina reviewed the guy's pictures and thought he wasn't good looking, but if he was man enough, she'd make an exception. She had been at the bar for about thirty minutes, and she texted the guy again. Her date texted back, "I'm sorry to be taking so long. There's a lot of traffic out tonight, and I'm stuck. I am on my way there though. You just be a good girl and wait for daddy."

She replied, "OK, well, please hurry because I'm already getting hit on by guys here." He responded, "Tell them your daddy is on his way, and if they're not as masculine as I am, they're in for a whole lot of trouble."

She giggled and wrote back, "OK, daddy."

She continued to watch the game and sip on his beer after she drank hers. The bartender asked her if she wanted another round, and she accepted. She kept going through the guy's pictures, hoping he'd get there soon and it was worth the wait. Some time had passed, and she had already gulped his beer and downed her second. She started drinking the fourth one, which was meant for him. She texted him again, but this time he didn't reply. She dialed his number, and he didn't answer either. The guy who had hit up on her earlier walked up to her and sat on the stool beside hers. He told her, "I was right, wasn't I? He's not coming? Let me buy you another beer, and we could chat and get to know each other." She agreed.

This guy at the bar began telling her he was very picky and needy. He requested her to pay all his bills, move him in with her, buy him a car, and pay for his gas and insurance. He wouldn't cook, clean, or work and would just stay home while she worked to provide for them both. She told the guy, "Are you fucking serious? You want me to do all of that for you and not get anything in return? You're clearly a feminine man. Why don't we just settle this now?"

The guy asked, "How're we going to settle this here?"

Josefina punched him in the face and began beating his ass up. The guy was unable to defend himself since he turned out to be feminine. She then left without a man since the other guy had stood her up and the one there wasn't her type. She had sat her date out all for nothing.

CHAPTER 14
ALMOST SCORED

Danny woke up and wanted to visit his daughter Mercedes and her kids. He showered and got dressed. Denise, Heather, and Miya asked if they could go with him, but he told them he wanted to go alone since his ex was over there. They didn't argue and instead started picking up his house as he walked out the front door. He drove over to a burrito joint to grab some breakfast for his family. When he got back to his truck with the food, he found a kid looking inside his truck, contemplating on breaking in and stealing the chopper he was taking to Jr. Danny shouted, "Get away from my truck before I beat the shit out of you!" The kid took off running.

Danny unlocked his truck and got in. He checked the back seat to make sure the helicopter was still there, and it was. He turned on his truck and drove to Mercedes's residence. When he arrived there, he got off and walked to the front door. They were all still asleep and woke up at the sound of the doorbell. Chris opened the door and let his grandfather inside. Jr. came out of his room and saw his grandpa there with a big box. He asked him, "What do you have there, Grandpa?"

Danny placed the bag of burritos down on the kitchen table and replied, "I have something for you. Hopefully you'll like it, and we can mess with it after breakfast. Come here and sit down to eat with me. Do y'all have anything to drink?" he asked.

Jr. walked over to the kitchen table and uttered, "I don't know, but for sure we have no beer if that's what you're looking for. Grandma drank it all yesterday."

Danny opened up the fridge and grabbed a pitcher of juice. He then poured himself a cup and sat next to Jr. He opened up the bag and handed him a bean and cheese burrito, then grabbed his.

Chris came from his room and sat with them. Mercedes, Danniel, and Lucia came afterward. They all munched on their food, and when Dan and Jr. finished, he opened up the box and showed him the helicopter he had got him, Jr. asked, "They didn't have it in pink, Grandpa? You know that's my favorite color."

Danny stated, "No, *mijo*. They didn't have it in pink. You should consider picking another color as your favorite. Pink is for girls, not boys. Come on, help me put the batteries in the VR headset remote."

While helping his grandpa, Jr. mentioned, "Pink is the new blue, didn't you know, Grandpa?"

Dan uttered, "No, it's not, son. Pink will always be pink, and blue will always be blue. Anyhow, there, now let's go fly this outside in your backyard."

They walked outside, and Mut came out to check what was going on. He tried humping Jr., and Danny had to push him away. He placed the chopper on the ground after switching it on. He then moved his headset to get it up in the air. He managed to get the chopper to hover around the yard, and Jr. was impressed with his new toy. When Dan got the hang of it, he passed the headset remote control to Jr. so he could learn how to use it. Jr. was a bit scared since he wasn't accustomed to playing with boy toys. He grabbed the remote in his hands as his grandpa showed him how to fit it properly to work the aircraft. Jr. got it up in the air and was doing well. Then Mut jumped on top of him and tried humping him again. The chopper flew over to the neighbor's yard. Nick's ex was in the backyard pulling out weeds from the vegetables she was growing. The chopper went down into her path and tore up her shirt and bra. She yelled, "Oh my gosh! What was that?" She stared at the flying object.

She got up from the ground and chased it down with a shovel she had picked up. She swung the shovel at the chopper. Danny and Jr. had no idea what had happened since the privacy fence was a bit high, and their attention was fixed on the helicopter, which was up in the air again. Jr. brought it back down, and it hovered right over her head. She swung the shovel at it but missed. The chopper headed back toward them, and she ran to the fence line, believing it was videotaping her and invading her privacy. She misjudged the fence and slammed right into it. Danny and Jr. heard the noise and went to go check what it was. When they came around the side of the house, they found her there without a shirt or bra. Her ptosis breasts were stuck through the fence. She was calling out for help. Danny was about to tell Jr. not to look at her cleavage but changed his mind as he figured it may help him become masculine. Dan walked up to her and asked if she could get her tits free. She exclaimed, "I don't know. I'm trying to pull them out, but they're pretty stuck. Did you guys see something flying around? I was trying to chase it since it was recording me." The chopper made a thud sound as it fell from the sky since it was not being controlled anymore.

Danny looked at Jr. and answered, "Nope, we haven't seen anything flying around. Let me help you get those titis unstuck." Mut came by and started licking her breasts that protruded on their side of the fence.

Danny tried pushing them back onto her side but was unable to, mainly because when he pushed, she complained it hurt. He told her, "If we can't push them out. I'm going to have to cut the fence in order to free them."

She whimpered and asked, "Is that really necessary? Let's just try and push them out manually."

Danny told Jr., "Go in the house and get some cooking oil and then bring it here to me." Jr. obeyed and ran inside.

She inquired, "What're you going to use the cooking oil on? I hope you're not planning on cooking my breasts, mister."

Dan chuckled and responded, "I'm not going to cook with it. I'm going to lubricate your tits and squeeze them out to freedom with it."

She commented, "Oh, OK, well, I hope it works because I don't want to call anyone to come free me. I hope no one's recording this either." She looked around to see if anyone was.

Jr. came back with the oil in his hands and handed it to his grandpa. Danny opened the bottle and poured some over her breasts and began wiggling them. Within a second, her tits were loose, and she thanked him, as she covered them up. Jr. was giggling, and Mut tried humping him again. She went inside her house to put on her shirt. Danny and Jr. walked inside the house with the helicopter and shared the story with the rest.

Jesus woke up in his bed with his ass all sticky. He had never cleaned off the saliva left behind by the cab driver. He grabbed his cell phone and called Sam. His phone rang and rang without being answered. He then sat up in the bed and decided to call Sally to give her the bad news. Just as he keyed in the last digit, he heard a knock at the door. He rose to his feet and went over to see who it was. He asked, "Who is it?"

Sam said, "It's me, bro, open up. I have to tell you something."

Jesus opened the door and saw his pal on the other side. He embraced him and asked, "Where were you? I was looking for you all night long."

Sam told him, "You remember the butch from the hot tub? Well, when I went on stage I tripped and fell on top of her. She then carried me to her room and raped me all night, bro. I feel violated. My dick hasn't been this sore since I let Mut suck it once."

Jesus replied, "Wait, what? Anyhow, I'm glad you're alive. I too was raped last night by the taxi driver who took me around the bars searching for you."

Sam entered his room and inquired, "Do you have any ice so I can put some on my cock?"

Jesus uttered, "I sure don't, but I left my margarita in the fridge and it should be cold still. Let me grab it for you." He took it out and handed it to Sam as he continued, "So you were in her room this whole time, bro?"

Sam took the trash can and placed it over his privates, then answered, "Yes, bro. She kidnapped me and kept me hostage in her room until this morning when I managed to escape as she fell asleep."

Jesus said, "Let's report her. Come on, grab the phone and call the receptionist desk."

Sam stated, "No, bro, I can't. I don't think anyone will buy my story. Besides, I took the money she had in her wallet. Figured I'd charge her somehow for the sexual pleasures. I'm just going to go shower in my room, and maybe we could hang out in the swimming pool before we head out. Glad no one saw my walk of shame over here."

Jesus replied, "Yeah, sounds like a plan. I too need to shower and get rid of the sticky slobber in my ass. I'll meet you down there when I'm done." Sam left for his room to shower, and he jumped into his.

When Danny went inside Mercedes's home with Jr., Lucia grabbed him and pulled him into the garage. She interrogated him about his new lovers. Danny told her, "They're still at my place. Don't know when they'll leave."

Lucia asked, "And are they pleasing you right? Or are they giving you a hard time?" Danny replied, "That's none of your concern, Lucia."

She then got on her knees and took his dick out. She put it in her mouth and began sucking it. Danny let go of himself, because he was never able to resist the way she gave him head. He was enjoying it and started buckling at his knees. Then Jr. walked into the garage, and she popped his dick out of her mouth and put it back inside his pants. Jr. questioned, "What're you doing, Grandma? Are you proposing to Grandpa?"

Lucia got up and said, "I was looking at your grandpa's belly button because he said it has been hurting him."

Jr. uttered, "That's funny, because I caught my mom doing the same to Dad once. You'll be alright, Grandpa. Dad never had to go to the hospital or even to see a doctor after Mom blew inside his belly button." Danny and Lucia laughed sheepishly.

They then went back inside the house, and Jr. told his mother about his grandparents doing the same thing she and Jesus had done a while back. Mercedes had an embarrassed look on her face, but then she realized what Jr. had caught her parents doing and turned it around on them. She told her mom, "Mom, why don't you just ask to blow dad's belly button in my room next time, so Jr. won't interrupt the medical procedure you try on Dad?"

Lucia replied, "I will next time, *mija*. Sorry about that."

Danny then headed to the restroom to fix his penis, and Lucia followed him in to finish her job. Just as Danny nutted inside her mouth, Chris opened the shower curtains, and he could not believe what he saw. Lucia got up from the floor and ran out, as Danny shook off his cock, pretending he had been pissing. Chris was gaslighted into believing he had imagined seeing his grandmother there. Danny walked out of the restroom and let Chris dry himself and get ready in his own privacy. Chris was unable to remove the vivid picture in his head of his grandmother giving his grandfather a blowjob. He was sure he hadn't fabricated it.

Jesus and Sam met up at the pool. Jesus had his shower cap and his goggles on, as well as his floaties inflated. Sam had his life jacket, shower cap, and diver's mask on. They entered the pool and sat at the edge to dip their feet and make sure it wasn't too cold to jump in. They both jumped up on realizing the water was frigid. The winning contestant from the beauty king show was there, and he started taunting them to get in. Jesus was jealous and pushed Sam in. He then jumped inside himself. Sam was a little upset Jesus had forced him in, but his body temperature started getting used to it, and he began to try and swim in the four-foot section. Jesus thought of a way to impress the winner, who was mocking him as he lay on one of the beach chairs sunbathing. He figured if he did some aquatic tricks it would get the job done. So he flipped in the pool, sticking out his feet in the air. But he farted and came back up to hear Sam and the winner laughing. Jesus then got out and stood by the pool's edge right in front of where the guy lay. He jumped in and splashed water on the guy who began to whine at that. Sam and Jesus laughed, telling him, "Maybe you should go get a tan elsewhere. The pool is for swimming and getting wet."

The guy got up and went to get the long pole and net used to take the debris out of the pool. He held it over Jesus's head and dropped it over him. Jesus was trapped, and he tried getting it off but was unable to do so. He then sank into the deep end and started drowning. Sam helped him back to the shallow end and removed the net off his head. Jesus saw the guy running off, and he got out of the water quick enough to grab his sandals from the floor and toss them at the guy, hitting him on the back of his head. The guy stopped running and sobbed, flipping Jesus and Sam off. Jesus and Sam cracked up in laughter. Then the butch woman came over, and Sam shut up. She told him, "Where'd my little sex toy go this morning? I woke up, and it was gone."

Jesus said, "Leave my friend alone. I warned you yesterday about it. He informed me you kidnapped him and raped him all night. You better get out of here before I call the police."

She turned to look at Jesus and uttered, "Mind your own business. I want my toy back, Sam. Give it back now!"

Jesus had no idea what was being discussed, then Sam mentioned, "I can't give it back."

She questioned, "Why not?"

Sam responded, "It's stuck inside me. You shoved it way deep in my ass, and I can't get it out. I also haven't been able to poop all day because it's blocking my rectum."

She stated, "Well, then let me try and take it out. Come on, get out of there and come here."

Sam uttered, "No, it'll hurt. Just wait and I'll see if I can remove it myself later on. If I do, I'll drop it off at your room." Jesus was in shock to find out his pal had something lodged in his ass and couldn't get it out.

She left back to go to her room, and Jesus asked Sam, "Do you want me to try and help you get that out of your ass?"

Sam said, "No, bro. I think it's really stuck inside and won't come out unless I have it surgically removed. It's not even bothering me much, so don't worry. And please don't tell anyone about it." Jesus promised not to tell, and they swam a little longer before they got ready to head back home.

Just when they were about to get out of the pool, the object came out of Sam's ass. It was a purple ten-inch dildo with rivets on its sides. The water must have relaxed Sam enough to release his grasp on it. It was floating on the surface of the pool when it struck Jesus on his face. He took off his mask to get a better look and realized what it was. He also noticed it had some feces stuck to it. Jesus screamed, "Ew!" He ran out of the pool.

Sam turned around to see what was going on and said, "There it is. I never even felt it coming out." He grabbed it, and they both left the pool.

Josefina woke up on hearing the sounds her father's ladies were making. She had got a text from Veronica, inviting her to go with her and Hellen in search of some real men. She jumped in the shower and got dressed afterward. When her friends reached there, they started honking. Tom, the neighbor, came out to tell them to stop. Veronica replied, "Ain't nobody here to visit you, so mind your own business! Why don't you just head back inside and eat your oatmeal?"

As Josefina walked out of her home, Tom confronted her, "You need to tell your friends to not be disturbing the rest of us."

Josefina said, "Look, Tom, you're the only neighbor who always has something to say. You're the problem, and you haven't realized it yet and never will. You can't control what happens outside of you and sometimes not even inside your house. My father has spoken to you before, and you don't seem to get it. Stay inside and shut your doors. Ignore anything that has nothing to do with you. Most importantly, mind your own business."

Josefina got into the car as she and her friends went hunting for real men. This time they planned on attending a church function in the hope they'd find machos there. They drove off and stopped to grab a bite before finding a church to visit. They went to eat at a restaurant that specialized in preparing and serving the best menudo in the city. They got out of the car once they parked outside the business and headed inside, going straight to pick out a table. They took a seat, and a waiter came by to hand them menus.

The waiter returned momentarily to ask for their drink orders. She then headed to the back to get their beverages. When she came back out with their drinks in hand, she overheard them talking about their plans. She told Josefina, "I go to this church right down the street, and let me tell you, there are some real men who attend, but they're married. You might want to try another one just in case that one was in your plans." She took their orders as Josefina pondered on which other church they could hunt in.

Some minutes passed, and the waiter came back out with the girls' food. They ate and handed her a tip before they left. They got back in the car and drove around in search of a church. They eventually found one and got off. They headed inside and took a seat before mass began. They looked around and saw there were a few candidates who could fit the criteria they desired. The pastor noticed them at the back and called them to the front, welcoming them as newcomers. They acted bashful as they were placed on the spot, but eventually they were convinced to take a closer seat to the front. There they looked around to see if any machos were staring at them. There was an older gentleman who appeared to be interested in Hellen.

He couldn't take his eyes off her. Josefina pointed it out to her, and Hellen took notice. After the sermon, the older man walked over to Hellen and introduced himself. He mentioned he was a widow. He must have been in his seventies or so. Hellen began to feel right at home for some reason. She felt the man was more than macho and of the old-fashioned kind with high values. He informed her he had three sons who were unmarried. Josefina asked him, "Why aren't they taken? Are they feminine?"

The old man said, "No, they're not feminine. They just haven't found the right one for them. They're always working and hardly go out in search."

Josefina gestured to Hellen as if to say, "Keep him interested so he can introduce his sons to us."

Hellen asked the man, "How long have you been a widow?"

The man responded, "About a decade or so. She fell ill and never made it." His dentures fell out of his mouth, and Hellen picked them up for him, while her friends were disgusted.

Hellen questioned, "You think you could introduce your sons to my friends? Do they come to church with you sometimes?"

The man placed his dentures back in and uttered, "Sure, I can introduce you all to each other. They used to come to church with me, but they've been working really hard, even on Sundays."

All of a sudden, four older women came over and interrupted the older man. They told the girls, "You girls stay away from our man. He's ours, and you can't have him."

Josefina answered, "We're not after him. You all can keep him. We're interested in his sons."

The women stated, "So are our daughters, so stay away from them too." The women then grabbed the man and took him away just as Hellen managed to get his number.

Jesus and Sam began getting their things ready in order to head back home. They met outside their rooms, which were adjacent to each other. They walked downstairs to Jesus's vehicle to place all their luggage inside. They then returned the keys to their rooms and filled up their trash cans with margaritas. The courtesy desk employee asked them, "Did you two enjoy your stay? I hope y'all had fun and will return some day."

Jesus said, "We did have fun and enjoyed our stay. I will definitely revisit some other time."

Sam uttered, "I had fun too, but I also had the worst experience of my life with one of the tenants. She raped me and held me hostage. I couldn't get away from her, and no one came to my rescue." He whimpered.

The girl replied, "I'm so sorry about that. If you let me know who it was and what room number they're in, I'll notify the manager and police."

Sam stated, "It's fine, no need to make it a big deal. I just wanted to point that out and vent. I will suggest y'all only allow feminine men into your resort because I'm sure there are plenty of masculine women out there like the one who attacked me staying here."

The staff member commented, "We don't allow any women other than staff to visit our resort. It's exclusively for feminine men. So if you were violated by a tenant here, it was a guy and most likely transformed into a female." The two dudes were in shock as they looked at each other.

They said goodbye to the worker and headed to the car. Just as they got in the car, the butch woman came out of nowhere and confronted Sam; the woman said, "Where are you going? Did you ever find my toy? You better not even think of leaving without returning it."

Sam told it, "I haven't found it. It never came out. I tried shitting it out, and it was impossible. You're just going to have to buy another one. And by the way, I know you're a man already."

The woman replied, "I'm not going to buy another one. You better try taking it out before you leave, or I'll find you and take it out myself. And I never said I was a female." Sam gagged.

Jesus shouted, "Leave my friend alone already, you fucking pervert! We already told the resort about you, and the police will be here any minute!" The guy was unimpressed.

Sam told Jesus, "Just go. Let's get out of here now." Jesus hit the accelerator as Sam removed something out of his rectum. Sam had reinserted the toy earlier, and as they sped away, he launched it at the guy's face. It splattered on his cheek. Fecal matter could be seen dripping off his visage from the toy. The guy ran after the moving vehicle as Sam and Jesus laughed out loud. He couldn't catch up to them as they hit the highway. Once they got on the road, they were long gone and headed back home.

Josefina and her friends departed the church and drove around the city. They still had an objective in mind and were determined to accomplish it by the end of the day. They drove down one of the city's busiest intersections and saw a group of guys walking. Josefina shouted, "Hey! You guys look cute! Let us take you out to eat!"

One of the guys shouted back, "No, thanks! We're good!"

Josefina replied, "Good call there, feminine men! I was just testing you all, and y'all failed big time!" The light turned green, and they proceeded forward.

They made it to a tire shop, and Josefina suggested they should stop there to see if there were any machos working there. They parked and got out of the car and walked over to see inside the shop; since, there were three female employees attending customers outside. One of the females asked them, "Have y'all been helped?"

Veronica said, "Not yet, but we were hoping one of the male workers could assist us."

The female replied, "Ha! Ha! There aren't any male workers here. The last one quit after we outworked him."

Veronica uttered, "OK, well, thank you, but we'll just go to another tire shop." They got in the vehicle and drove off.

They continued traveling down the main street and came across a fire department house. They noticed activity outside and drove in to check it out. People were washing fire trucks, and when they got closer, they observed they were all women. They then continued to hunt their prey down. They arrived at a car dealer and drove in to see if there were any males. Then they spotted one talking to a potential customer. Veronica got out of the car and approached the guy. She asked him, "Excuse me. When's your lunch break so I could take you out to eat?"

The guy replied, as he sobbed, "I don't get one. I'm mistreated here by the women who run this lot. They're always calling me names and belittling my existence."

Veronica knew then he wasn't macho and told him, "Grow some fucking balls, you sissy!" She ran back to her vehicle, having made the guy break down and cry more to the point he ran inside the building and quit his job.

They then drove to another busy street, keeping their eyes out for the prize. They came across a military recruiting office and parked in front of it. A woman came out running from inside to try and recruit them. She handed them some documents, and Josefina inquired, "If we enlist, what're the possibilities we'll find some machos in the service?"

The woman replied, "Extremely slim. All our new recruits have been females. No men have enlisted in a few years, and if that's all you're looking for, get in line because all the women I know are in search of real men as well. Even in other parts of the country and locations of the world, this crisis has reached them too. At first, we were bringing machos over from South America, but even there they're running scarce. There seems to be no real men out there anymore."

Veronica uttered, "Alright, well, thank you for the information. Good luck finding one."

The woman questioned, "So y'all don't want to sign up for the army?" They left her with the question unanswered since they had hit the throttle, and they got out of there before she could convince Hellen to enlist.

Jesus and Sam drove on the highway, sipping on their margaritas and making fun of the guy who had raped Sam. Jesus got a bit distracted and hit something. He swerved, but pressed the brakes and pulled over. He and Sam got out to go check what it was. They walked back to the location and saw a small fox dying on the road. Jesus began crying and shouting, "No! I just killed this poor creature. I won't be able to live with myself."

Sam too yelled, "You're a murderer! How could you have not seen it crossing the road?" He banged on Jesus's chest with his closed fists.

Jesus said, "What do I do? I can't leave it here dying all by itself."

Sam uttered, "Pick it up and place it on the soft ground so it won't die burning on top of the asphalt."

Jesus walked over to the creature, then gagged as he frantically debated whether he could pick it up or not. Sam handed him a plastic bag for him to pick it up without catching rabies. Jesus grabbed the bag and bent over to try and pick it up. Then he jolted up straight, saying, "I can't! I just can't; you pick it up." He handed the bag to Sam.

Sam turned it away, replying, "You ran it over. You pick it up."

While they argued who'd pick it up, a car pulled over to check on them. A guy got off and walked over toward them, frightening the two. Jesus and Sam stepped in front of the animal to cover up what they thought was a crime scene. The guy asked them, "You guys having car trouble?"

Sam said, "No, I just stopped to pee. Thank you though."

The guy replied, "Alright then, see you back on the road." As he walked away, he spotted the fox's tail between Sam's legs. He stopped and inquired, "Are you guys hunting out here or something?"

Jesus uttered, "No, not at all. Why would you ask such a thing?"

The guy responded, "What's that behind you two then? Looks like a dead raccoon or something."

Jesus and Sam confessed about their real reason for being there. The guy joined them in the argument as to who'd pick up the dead fox. All three were going nuts when the guy's passenger got out and helped them decide. It was a masculine female, and she grabbed the bag and went over to pick up the creature to move it to a better resting location. When she bent down and touched the fox, it jumped up and ran off. This whole time it had been playing dead in order to fool them, believing they were predators. The women told them, "You guys are something else. Come on honey, let's get going now." She and the guy walked back to their vehicle.

Jesus and Sam wiped off the tears from their eyes and got back in their car. They returned to the road and continued heading back home. They were embarrassed by the incident and didn't mention it again.

Josefina and her friends came to the realization there were no more machos left on earth. All the guys had turned feminine and they were in trouble. From their past experiences and the information they had gathered from the recruiting officer, it seemed all men had turned soft. They then recalled Hellen had gotten the old man's number. Josefina had Hellen call him to get his sons' phone numbers. She dialed the number, and he picked up, saying, "Hello, hello."

Hellen told him, "Hello, mister, we met earlier in church. Do you remember me?"

The old man said, "No, I didn't forget my fingers at church. I have them right on my hand and am staring at them right now."

Hellen giggled and replied, "No, I didn't say that. I'm Hellen, the girl you met at church. I'm calling to see if you could give me your sons' numbers so my friends and I can call them."

The man went silent for a second and uttered, "Who's this? Are you playing a joke on me? It's not funny; I'm an old man who can't hear a thing."

Hellen questioned, "How were you able to listen and reply to our conversation during church?"

He responded, "Yes, I went to church earlier, and now I'm home. Who is this though? I think you have the wrong number." Hellen then heard a woman's voice in the background telling him to use his hearing aid.

Hellen stated, "Put on your hearing device so you could understand me, sir."

The man put on his hearing aid and commented, "OK, I can hear you now. What was that you said?"

Hellen answered, "It's me, Hellen from church. I was calling to see if you'd be kind enough to let me get your sons' phone numbers please?"

The man told her, "Oh, hi, Hellen. Yes, let me go find where I have them written down so you could call them."

The woman in the background said, "It's that little bitch from church, isn't it? Don't give her your sons' phone numbers. You said you'd introduce them to my daughters. Hang up the phone and come finish your meal." And just like that, the phone call was disconnected.

Josefina and Veronica said, "Damn! What a bitch she is, and she's calling us bitches? Well that sucks. Now how're we going to find a mate?" Veronica and Hellen dropped off Josefina at her house and left in the direction of their own homes without luck, even though they had almost scored.

Jesus and Sam made it into the city. Jesus drove Sam home and dropped him off. Sally was happy to see him for some unknown reason. She must have missed him while he was gone. Sam told Jesus, "Thanks for accompanying me on this trip, bro. I had a good time. Even through the mishaps, I'd do it again."

Jesus said, "No problem. Thank you for inviting me and paying for my stay. I too wouldn't mind going over there again. Hopefully we can return in a few months or so." Sam shook his hand and headed into his house.

Jesus left the apartment complex and drove to his house. He was almost there when the angered husband reminded him someone was looking for him. The man drove behind him, but Jesus didn't notice him. When he got to his house, the man got out of his car and ran toward him. Jesus was about to get out of his car when he saw the man. He closed the door of his vehicle hurriedly, crushing his leg in the process. Jesus yelled and pulled his foot back inside, opening the door slightly. He then sped off toward the police station, which was the only way he could be able to get rid of this guy.

When he got there, the officers came out and ran him off again. He ended up going home afterward. When he walked in, Jr. was happy to see him. He jumped up in his arms and told him he had missed him. Mercedes didn't seem to pay any attention to his presence and headed off to bed. Jr. went to his room after listening to his dad's stories of what had happened over there and what it was like. Lucia and Danny had already gone home. Jesus walked into his bedroom and began taking out all his belongings from the suitcases. When he finished, he jumped into bed and fell asleep.

CHAPTER 15
BREAKING NEWS

Danny woke up in his bed and rolled over, only to not find any of his three chicks to hug. He thought it was weird, but it wasn't the first time. He believed they may have gone to get breakfast again. He got up and went to take a piss. Then he noticed the women had begun dropping their hairs all over his house. He had gone through that in the past with his daughters and ex-wife. It was a bit frustrating to him as he recalled one time he had a strand of hair wrapped around his penis, making him feel uncomfortable. There was another instance when he had one bugging him all day between his butt cheeks. He came back to the present and decided he'd have a word with his chicks when they got back. He wiggled his dick and cleaned off the remaining drip.

He then headed back to his room to change into his gym clothes. Josefina was still asleep, so he didn't bother waking her up. He was dressed and ready to go, but he waited a little longer to see if the girls would come back. He sat for about fifteen minutes and left after they didn't return. He got in his truck and took off.

When he got to the gym, he walked in and was greeted as usual by the front counter attendant. He walked over to the free weights and began to stretch. Then he began to work out. He noticed a group of guys walk into the gym and head toward the free weights. They were four guys, and they too began to stretch. Danny was minding his own business, lifting the dumbbells he had in his hands. One of the four guys asked him, "Hey, old man, are you done using those fifty-fives you've been babysitting for a while? I need to use them."

Danny said, "If you see them in my hands, it means I still am using them. When I'm done, I'll put them back on the rack for anyone to use." The other three smirked and laughed at their friend.

The guy felt intimidated and tried to gain his respect back by attempting to jerk them out of Danny's hands, saying, "Give them here and let me show you how to use them!"

The guy was unable to retract them from Danny's grip, and Danny told him, "Step the fuck away from me, you little pansy motherfucker, before I beat you and your fucking faggot bunch with the same dumbbells you're trying to take from me!"

All four guys were now threatened and wanted Dan to respect them, so they told him, "Look, geezer, we don't want to hurt you in front of everyone here, so just hand them over and get the fuck out of our way." He appeared smaller in height than he really was, and they came to find that out when he stood up.

Danny replied, "Which one of you four pussies is going to be my first victim?" As he held his dukes up.

The guy who wanted the dumbbells uttered, "How about we have a workout competition so you'll see for yourself you're the weak one out of us all?"

Danny responded, "I'll take all four of you in any contest any day except being fucking feminine. I could smell all four of your hormones and estrogen from a mile away. You may go around punking your kind into believing y'all are machos, but you ain't fooling a real one like me. So come on and let's fucking rumble, you bunch of sissies."

The guy stated, "We don't want to fight you, old man. Let's just solve this issue by working out and see who lasts longer."

Danny commented, "Let's do this then. Not even with all the fucking juice in your guys' system will it amount to the real natural testosterone pumping through my nuts."

They then began working out. One by one, Danny defeated them all just as he had warned them. They were drained, and the testosterone they had taken wasn't working well for them against a man who naturally produced more than they did all together. When Danny outlifted them, he then began slapping the shit out of them. He smacked them around, saying, "What happened to the fake courage y'all came in here with? Fucking feminine tarts." The guys took off running away from Danny's aggression, realizing he wasn't faking it like they were. They left the gym, and Danny drank some water, as the others exercising chanted his name.

Jesus woke up from a weird dream he was having about the taxi driver from the resort, who was fucking him in the ass with a crowbar. His phone rang, and he answered, "Hello."

A study representative was on the line telling him, "Hello, Mr. Jesus. I'm calling from our government study group database. I wanted to inform you that you have to schedule an appointment with us sometime this week. It's in reference to the tests we've performed on you."

Jesus said, "Is everything alright with my labs? Should I be concerned? Is there no cure for me?"

The representative replied, "I can't answer your questions over the phone, sir. But please make an appointment as soon as you can."

Jesus uttered, "OK, I'll do so as soon as we hang up. I'll schedule an appointment on y'all's automated system. Thank you for notifying me." They then hung up.

Jesus began to worry about his test results. He wondered if they had misplaced them or messed them up again and he'd have to go and get them redone, or even worse, they had taken him off because he was too feminine. He thought, *Oh well, more money as long as I'm still a candidate.*

He got out of bed and made an appointment for later that day. Just as he finished doing that, Olivia texted him, "Hi, are you back from your trip? I hope it went well. I just wanted to see you again. This time I'm going to let you do whatever you want to do to me. I'll be your good girl."

Jesus wrote back, "Hi, I got back last night. It went alright. I could probably meet you later on after I get off work. I'll text you then."

She replied, "OK, sounds good. Hope you're not mad. It kinda seems like you might be. Anyhow, I wish you a great day, my macho man."

He texted back, "Not mad, just busy at work. See you later."

He went to the front of the house and noticed the grass hadn't been watered since he had been gone. He went outside to water the grass and some flowers he had planted. While watering the grass, he observed a frog jumping his way. He frantically and exaggeratedly jumped out of its path and began shooting water at it. The frog was looking for water and found some. Jesus was terrified of any creepy crawlers, scaly reptiles, or slithery amphibians. He tried kicking the frog away but slipped and fell. Just as he was getting up, he noticed two kids who had ditched school walking by. They were goofing around, talking loudly and making fun of his fall. Jesus shouted, "Keep it down! There's people in the neighborhood trying to sleep!"

One of the boys said, "Man, fuck you, Karen! You just water your grass and shut the fuck up!"

Jesus replied, "Where are your manners, young man? My preferred pronouns are pink daddy she. I bet your parents wouldn't be so proud of you if they'd hear your dirty mouth right now."

The kid uttered, "My parents wouldn't even care as much as you do. Too bad you're Danniel's stepdad. Otherwise I'd beat your stupid ass right now."

Jesus responded, "So you know Danniel? Great, I'll ask her when she gets back home so I could go to your school and let the principal know you two were ditching school and causing trouble."

The kid stated, "Danniel was right. You are some fucking sorry ass feminine disgrace to her family." The kids kept on walking, and Jesus shut up since his feelings were compromised.

He continued to water the grass, crying a little once the kids were long gone. The frog jumped up onto his feet. He had forgotten all about it. He felt the frog on his foot and kicked it off. He then ran to turn off the water and went inside to wipe his tears.

Mercedes had forgotten all about the things Mrs. Santiago had given her to get signed. She had been following her around all morning, learning her new position. Mrs. Santiago was informing her how things should be and what to do when they're not. Mercedes was writing everything she found important, which she'd forget if she didn't. Mrs. Santiago asked her, "Are you getting it so far? It sounds more complicated than it really is. It'll take you adjusting to it just as with everything else in life."

Mercedes said, "It does sound complicated but only because I haven't been through it before. Just as you said, I'll get used to it, and it won't even worry me in a couple of days."

Mrs. Santiago questioned, "By the way, did you get my things signed by your brother-in-law?"

Mercedes replied, "I sure did. They're in my van. I can go get them for you right now if you'd like."

Mrs. Santiago stated, "No, it's OK. That could wait. I'm just glad you were able to get them autographed for me, thanks."

Mercedes uttered, a smile on her face, "OK, I'll bring them after my break. You're welcome, and it was nothing."

They continued walking around as her boss explained her new duties. They walked past an employee having a discussion with a client and stopped to listen. The customer representative said, "No, sir, we can't get you a discount for a penis enlargement surgery. We don't have any medical partners. We can offer you a discount on some of our premium channels though."

The man replied, "I want to talk to your manager. I'm sure y'all can get me a price reduction on getting my dick bigger."

The employee stated, "I'm sorry, sir, but my manager is busy at the moment. If you'd like to call back later and ask for her, it would be more convenient. If I can assist you with anything else, please let me know right now."

The man answered, "How about some testosterone supplements? Can y'all hook me up with any? I mean, I've been a loyal customer for decades, and I've gotten nothing out of y'all. I heard your company was bought out by Test1, and they have what I need, but it's more expensive than I could afford."

The representative commented, "I'm unaware if our company has been sold to someone else, but I can assure you that if it was and one day we have discounts, you'll be the first to know. In the meantime, I wish you luck in finding the best deal on your personal products. You enjoy the rest of your day, sir, goodbye."

Mercedes and Mrs. Santiago told the employee that she had handled that as best as possible and congratulated her for it. They then walked over to the break room. In the break room, they found a man going through the employee refrigerator. He appeared out of place. Mrs. Santiago asked, "May I help you?"

The guy turned around and said, "Yeah, you can give me some food and suck my cock."

Mercedes butted in, "Excuse me sir, but that foul language isn't tolerated around here. Let me see your employee badge."

The man replied, flipping her off, "Here's my badge."

Mercedes called security to have the man removed from the building. It turned out he was an unhoused individual who had just happened to piggyback behind someone entering the building. When the security officer showed up, he quickly escorted the man out of the break room. The man put up a fight, and the guard tackled him to the ground. The man grabbed a chocolate bar from his pockets, which he had stolen from the fridge, and said, "Look, I shit myself, and now you'll be my shit, buddy." He opened it and smeared it all over them both without the officer being aware of what it really was.

The security got pissed and dragged the guy out of the building, kicking him a few times. Once at the door, he tossed him out and followed him off the property. When they got far away from potential witnesses, he beat the guy up and left him there lying on the street.

Jesus was cooking and cleaning since no one had done so during the time he was on his trip. Jr. came out of his room and hugged him again. He said, "I really missed you, Dad. I got kicked out of the amusement park, and everyone in our family made fun of me. The weekend flew by, but I wish you would've been there."

Jesus told him, "I missed you too. I also had some good and bad times out there. Come here, and let's sit down to eat." They took a seat at the table and consumed what he had cooked.

Jesus heard some noise coming from outside the house. He had almost finished his food and got up to go check. When he looked outside the window, he observed Nick's Corvette parked in his ex's driveway. Jesus quickly went to the door and opened it. He ran outside and saw Nick had returned to get some of the things he had left behind. He looked distinguished. He had grown some muscle mass and facial hair, and his man boobs had decreased in size. Nick said, "Hey, Jesus! How've you been, man? Are things still the same since I left?" Jesus tried hugging him, but he pushed him away, stating, "Whoa! Broskis don't do that anymore."

Jesus replied, "Man, you've really changed. I can see it in your appearance and even in your voice. It sounds deeper. What have you been taking to achieve those results?"

Nick told him, "I've been taking some products from Test1. Now that I've got money, I can afford it." His ex came out of the house, sobbing for him to stay, but he uttered, "Stop crying, bitch! I'm not staying or coming back. I want nothing to do with you any longer. I'm too much macho for you to handle. I'd fucking hit you, but I don't want any trouble or scare Jesus here. Now shut your dick-sucking mouth." She apologized as Jesus stood in shock looking at the new Nick.

Nick finished gathering his things and told Jesus, "I've got to go now, bro. Good seeing you. You take care and try to buy some Test1 so you too could put your bitch in check." Sam got in his car and drove off as Jesus and his ex embraced, mending their broken hearts with each other.

Mercedes had gone for her lunch break, and she went to her vehicle after eating. She grabbed the articles her boss had handed her to be signed and signed them herself again with the permanent marker. She was a bit stressed not only because she had a new position to learn but also because she was still responsible for two groups while the new floor managers were undergoing training. She was sitting in her minivan when she saw the intruder from earlier walk up to her.

He told her, "Give me all your fucking money, bitch! Hand over all of your belongings and car keys!"

Mercedes handed him the things in her hands but not her money or keys and said, "Lower your tone, mister. You have no idea who you're messing with!"

The man picked up the boxer briefs, smelling them, and uttered, "Whose boxers are these? They smell like fish mixed with shit. And who signed them? Are these someone famous's drawers? I could probably sell them online and get some money. And who's this in the picture? Is it you and your husband or boyfriend? I could possibly get a buck or two for this from some weirdo. Why do these things have the same signature? Where's your money and car keys?"

Mercedes answered, "Those are worth top dollar. They belonged to some guy who went viral online for dancing naked with his friends. Take those, but I'm not handing over my money or keys."

The guy responded, "Do they belong to the fruitcake who touched nipples and foreskins with some dudes?"

Mercedes stated, "Yeah! Exactly who they belonged to. He autographed them for my son who's a fan of his."

The man commented, "Why would your son want this picture?" She informed him, "The picture was for me actually."

The man looked over the things in his hands and tossed the picture in her face and told her, "You keep that fucking picture with no value. I'll take these boxers, thanks." He walked away, leaving her alone.

Mercedes would have swung at the guy had he not left. He was shorter than her and scrawny, which reminded her of Jesus. So she wasn't about to get punked by him either. She locked her vehicle up and headed back into the building. She went to Mrs. Santiago's office and handed her the picture and explained what had just happened outside with the boxer briefs. Mrs. Santiago ran outside looking for the man, and when she spotted him across the street, she sprinted over there and kicked his ass. She was able to get her boxers back and left the guy knocked out on the ground, telling him, "Get your own celebrity memorabilia, motherfucker!"

Danny got back home from the gym and found Josefina and the girls eating some burritos at the kitchen table. There was one for him too, so he took a seat and enjoyed it with them. He didn't question their whereabouts since he figured that's where they had gone—to buy food. He got a bit irritated with their chatter and walked to his living area and turned on the television. He was about to watch his favorite show when a special emergency report came on. The reporter stated, "This morning once again the group of armed women have struck gold. They committed an armed robbery at this bank behind me in the south side of the city. This is already their tenth successful crime and their first of the week. Police are requesting the public if anyone has information leading up to an arrest they will receive a reward and their identity will remain anonymous."

Danny looked at the girls who had no clue of what he was watching on TV since they were talking to Josefina. He then asked Denise, "Hey, Denise, have you heard of the group of three females who've been robbing banks in the city?"

Denise said, "You mentioned it the other day. Why do you ask? Is there a reward for capturing them or something?"

Dan replied, "Apparently there is a reward. I'm just asking in case you know who they are."

Denise uttered, "Oh, how much is the reward? I want to know more now. I wouldn't mind catching them and getting compensated. But no, I don't know anyone who's committed an armed robbery, and if I did, I don't think they'd admit to it unless they've already served their time."

Danny agreed with her and left it alone after telling her what he knew so far about the robberies. All four women in his home were intrigued by the story. He began watching his favorite show. A masculine woman was being interviewed, and she was informing the interviewer how she had been feeling savagely horny and fucking every single guy who talked to her. She said she had even begun raping a few of the ones unwilling to cooperate. She had stopped getting her menstrual cycle. Then a guy came on and said he had been bleeding from his ass every month for the past three months. He also mentioned he had started experiencing a lower libido. Danny was historically cracking up, listening to what he was saying during his interview. He shared the story of the guys at the gym with the ladies and compared the guy on TV to them as an example. The show concluded, and he got up from the couch and headed outside to work in his backyard. He had some weeds to pull and some grass to mow. Heather followed him outside with a towel and a glass of water. She wiped off the sweat on his bare back since he had removed his shirt before getting started. He told her, "Can you take this to the trash bin?" He handed her a bunch of weeds he had pulled out of the soil in his yard.

As she grabbed them, she was pricked by the thorns in the weeds, but she said, "Yes, dear. Do you need anything else?"

He answered, "No, just that for now." He pulled on the lawn mower to get it started.

Heather came back to the yard as he was mowing the lawn. A small rock shot out from under the blades of the mower and hit Heather in the face. She yelled, "Ouch! What the hell was that?" She wondered what had hit her since she was a dingy blonde.

Heather then walked right behind Danny and wiped off the sweat on his back, but she got bit by ants on her feet since she was wearing flip-flops. Still, she bore the pain and continued to assist Dan with his duty. When Dan finished and looked at her, he saw she was bleeding from her forehead and had ant stings all over her feet and legs. But she had still not let go of the towel or the glass of water. He questioned, "Are you alright, baby? What happened to you?" She explained the scenario to him, and he giggled.

After he had raked the grass and put everything away, he took Heather with him in the shower. He took good care of her then. The other two women were busy cleaning up their hairs, which he had brought up to their attention.

Mercedes got back to her house after a long day at work. Jesus greeted her, but she took off her sweaty shoes and handed them to him without accepting his hug. She ordered him to take them to the room and let them air out. He did so, and once done, he left for the test site. As he drove there, he felt anxious about what the issue was.

He arrived and ran inside to sign in. He took a seat and waited his turn. When he was finally called, he followed a woman to the back. She took him to an examining room, and he removed all his clothing and put on a thin medical robe. Moments later, a doctor walked in and introduced himself to Jesus. The doctor told him, "Well, Jesus, I don't know if anyone had ever mentioned this to you, but your testosterone levels are really low. Matter-of-fact, I don't think your body is even producing any. There's an abnormal high level of estrogen surging through your body though."

Jesus inquired, "Does that mean I will never be masculine again? Oh no! I can't believe this." He started crying.

The doctor answered, "Well, I can't give you a firm answer to your question for now. It is inconclusive, to be honest. What I would like is for you to have more tests done so we could determine what's causing you to be different from the other candidates. We've gathered so far that there is a link between the rest. Those who ate Fruit Loops in high volumes during their developing stages and then drank Bud Light excessively as adults have been the ones we've been treating with high doses of testosterone donated by masculine women who've volunteered for the study. We also concluded that some who were affected drank tap water and ate GMO foods. You're the first of your kind so far to have these types of results, and therefore, I'd like to help you out."

Jesus replied, "I'll do anything, doctor, to become masculine again, anything. I actually didn't eat much cereal growing up. My mother fed me dog food with water instead. She said cereal wasn't healthy for me. I used to love Bud Light as I got older, up until a few years ago, when it didn't go with me anymore. It would bloat me and make me pee myself. I'd get so drunk I wouldn't remember how to get home. One time some guy even raped me after I passed out in the back of an alley."

The doctor stopped him from going into further details about his story by saying, "OK! Well, there's no need to share that irrelevant information with me. I'm going to have someone come and draw some semen samples and get a spinal tap as well. You wait here, and I'll see you next time with your results."

Jesus left the facility after having more tests done; his back was hurting him. He had a hard time getting into his car but managed to do so. He texted Olivia so they could meet up. He really needed testosterone after receiving the results that he had high estrogen levels. She replied, and they made plans to meet at a parking lot.

When he arrived, she was already there. Just as he was about to get out of his car, some guy ran up to him and beat his ass inside. He took his wallet and left him sobbing inside his ride. Olivia pulled up next to him and told him, "I can't believe you keep falling for it over and over. I thought you'd learn after the second time, but you haven't. The man who's been beating you every time we meet is my husband. We've been taking your money, and I'm starting to feel sorry for you, so that's why I'm letting you know."

Jesus asked, "Why though? What did I ever do to you? All I wanted was some masculine semen from you so I could increase my testosterone levels. Now what am I going to do?"

Olivia answered, "I knew you were feminine since the first day I saw you in school, also because of the pictures on your profile. It's nothing personal, to be honest. It was my husband's idea to make you learn to respect others' marriages. As far as getting your fix, I don't know, but it's pretty disgusting you're willing to eat out women just to suck up their partner's semen. I wish you luck in your life, and please don't ever contact me again." She then drove off as he continued to whimper.

Sam had only enjoyed being missed by his wife for a few hours. The illusion wore off on her, and she went back to mistreating him for being unmasculine. She had him clean up the entire house while she went to work. He also had to clean up the kids' rooms, organize her clothes in her drawers and closet, wash clothes, and cook. He was preoccupied when his doorbell rang. He walked to the door, and as soon as he opened it, he was punched on his face. He began to bleed and fell to the ground, as he saw a guy running away. He rose to his feet and ran after the man, catching up to him as he was getting inside his vehicle. Sam confronted him, "Hey! Who are you and why'd you hit me?"

The guy was the one Sally had gone on a date with and replied, "I thought you were Sally. Sorry, I don't want any trouble."

Sam replied, "Why would you want to punch my wife though? What did she do to you?"

The guy informed Sam about what had happened while he was out of town. Sam was a little upset that his wife had tried to cheat on him but happy she didn't leave him and kick him out of the house since he had nowhere else to go. They both got together and figured a plot for taking revenge on Sally. She had no idea what they were cooking. They exchanged numbers, and the man left in his car as Sam walked back inside his home to finish up his task at hand. Just as he was walking back into his apartment, a dude who was heading to the laundry room asked, "Are you washing by any chance? I've been waiting for the washers for about an hour or so. My girlfriend wants me to wash, and she's been on my ass all day about it. She doesn't understand I can't just remove others' clothes out and use the washers. It's unethical and rude. Plus, I run the risk of having some guy beat me up, and I don't even know how to fight or desire to get in a scuffle."

Sam told his neighbor, "It's my clothes, sorry. Let me head down there and place it in the dryer for you, so you won't get in more trouble with your girl." They both walked down there, gossiping about other residents, and Sam did what he said he would, then went back to his apartment to do what he had to do as his kids chilled in their rooms.

Jesus got back to his house, and Mercedes asked him, "What the hell happened to your face? You look like you got in a fight, and I know damn well you don't know how to or want to."

Jesus lied to her, "I got mugged coming out of my appointment."

She laughed at him and uttered, "That's what you get for going around pretending you're famous."

Jesus then walked to his bedroom to continue weeping over the incident and the bad news he had received. He hadn't even wanted to bring it up to Mercedes's attention for he knew she'd make fun of him. Mercedes walked into the room to ask him if he wanted her to get him something from the store. He wiped off the tears from his eyes and told her, "No, I'm OK."

She then left the room and took off with the kids for the store to grab them some snacks. When she got back, Jesus was in the kitchen looking for something to eat. He noticed she hadn't brought him back something and asked her, "How come you didn't get me anything?"

Mercedes answered, "I asked you if you wanted something and you said no."

He was expecting her to read his mind, and since she didn't, he felt upset and walked back to his room. He then took off his clothes and fell asleep, hoping tomorrow would be a better day for him.

CHAPTER 16

BUSTED

Tito and Hilda, Jesus's parents, woke up, and Tito was acting extremely emotional. He threw a tantrum and asked her to make him breakfast in bed. He also wanted her to do his nails and shave his ass. He said he felt sad inside. He needed something to cheer him up and fill his void. Hilda told Tito, "You're crazy. I'm not going to do your nails or shave your butt. Who do you think you are? You're the reason why my son turned out to be feminine. You failed my son in teaching him to be a real man."

Tito replied, "I had nothing to do with the way your son turned out to be. You're the one who probably picked the wrong man to conceive him with. It's a genetic issue that doesn't pertain to me since I'm not his biological father. I choose to be this way because I feel it's the least you could do since I've provided you with the resources to live a good life so far. All I want is a little bit of pink and purple polish on my toes after you cut my nails. Is that too much to ask for?"

Hilda responded, "How about you get that thought out of your head and go outside and fix the air conditioner? Besides, whether or not you're his biological father, you were his role model."

Tito uttered, "I guess . . . but it's too hot, and I don't want to get a sunburn or sweat. I hate being all sweaty and feeling yucky. Plus, I may break a nail out there, and it's going to hurt."

Hilda answered, "You're just a woman trapped in the body of a man. Had I known this ahead of time, I would've stayed single. All you guys who end up with single mothers end up becoming more feminine than the rest of the unmasculine guys out there."

Tito refuted, "That's not true. It takes a real man to father the children of those who were left behind."

Hilda told him, "That's false. Real men don't end up with single mothers. Real men would much rather find themselves a woman with no kids and that she'd be a virgin. It's you freaking feminine guys who're getting together with single women because y'all can't get anything better. I've been learning about this situation from a podcast. I agree with this information. Only weak men settle for less than they deserve. Now get your ass up on the roof before I make a man out of you!"

Tito jumped out of bed, saying, "Alright, alright, let me look for my shoes." He wanted to cry since she had managed to dominate him for over three decades.

Tito went outside and got the ladder to get up. As he was climbing up the ladder, Hilda came outside to hurry him. He got on top of the roof, and then Hilda removed the ladder, telling him, "Now you're going to stay up there till you come back down a real man."

Tito was crying and pleading, "Please put the ladder back. I don't want to be up here all day. Don't be mean to me. I've always been a good man to you."

Hilda laughed and stated, "You've been a beta this whole time. I was unaware of such a term. I thought all men were the same and some were just nicer than others, but it turns out I was wrong." She then got in her car and went to the store, leaving Tito up on top of the roof whimpering like a little girl.

Jesus woke up with a crust in his eyes, as he'd fallen asleep crying. His anus was also sore as he'd inserted his thumb into it instead of in his mouth. He hopped out of bed and walked into the restroom. He sat down to pee, and when he finished, he washed his hands. As he washed his hands, he looked at himself in the mirror and questioned why he was born a bitch. He saw he was just a sorry ass motherfucker with no wits, talent, or any trait or quality of high value. He began sobbing, slapping himself in the face, and pulling out his thin hair. He picked up his wife's razor blade and tried to slice his wrist. He was a failure even at that. He couldn't make contact with the razor on his skin without getting scared of the consequences. He was a terrified individual with no expectations other than misery—a true coward who had been disguising himself as a macho the whole time. He thought about his adolescence and realized he had always suffered from testosterone deficiency. He had had secret crushes on guys at school. He had always liked playing with dolls and dressing up as a woman. He had enjoyed partaking in gossip and the spread of rumors. He had dreamed of becoming a famous model. He had never liked himself or his body. He never knew what he wanted to eat although he was hungry all the time. He believed his partner should read his mind without him being up front. He had always hated to work or to use his weak strength. He loved drama and watching soap operas. He didn't like penetrating females with his little dick. He would much rather get his ass licked than eat pussy. He fantasized of having male organs in his mouth and anus. All his negative thoughts made him feel worthless. He tried another form of suicide. He tried hanging himself from the shower curtain. He tied a knot on it and wrapped it around his neck. He stood on top of the toilet next to the shower and threw himself forward. He thought the curtain holder would support his weight and allow him to hang from it until he met his death, but he was truly useless. As soon as he jumped off the toilet, the curtain pole snapped into two and made him fall straight into the shower knob. He broke a tooth and started bleeding. He couldn't believe his plan had failed. He got up to see in the mirror that he had a broken tooth and cried. Jr. woke up at the commotion and knocked on the restroom door. He said, "Dad, are you in there? Are you alright? I heard a loud noise, and it worried me." Jesus superglued his tooth back on and tossed his hair in the trash.

Jesus replied, "I'm OK, Son. I fell off the toilet because I was peeing on myself and was trying to avoid it." He had forgotten about his son being there and the chances that he'd find him dead if he so chose to continue. So he cleaned up his face and headed out of the restroom.

Hilda got back home from the store to find Tito hanging from the roof, yelling for help. His pants had fallen down to his ankles, and everyone could see he had on a purple thong that belonged to her. She asked, "Is that the thong I've been looking for? I knew you had it the whole time but didn't want to confront you knowing you'd deny it. Plus, I wouldn't want it back after you've used it. I could only imagine the shit stains you've left on it like you leave them on your underwear."

A concerned feminine guy walking by shouted, "Hang in there, pal. I'll save you. Let me just look for a real man for this job at hand." He took off running in search of a macho.

Hilda questioned Tito, "Did you at least fix the air conditioner?"

Tito answered, "I tried, but I don't know how to mess with this particular model. I'm used to messing with swamp coolers only. Please get me down from here. I'm begging you, honey."

Hilda went to grab the ladder and brought it back, saying, "Here you go, you pansy. I'm only letting you down because I don't want it in my conscience that you died because I left you up there."

Tito thanked her and began climbing down the ladder. He couldn't stop whimpering, and when he got down, he hugged

Hilda and told her, "I thought I was going to die. That's the worst fright of my life. Thank you for having mercy on my soul." He got on his knees and began kissing her shoes.

Hilda had him get all the groceries out of the trunk, take them inside, and put them away. She also made him put the ladder back where it was and had him call a professional to fix the air conditioner for them. She didn't paint his nails or shaved his ass. She didn't even make him breakfast and only made herself some while he sat and watched her eat. There was no going back from losing respect with a woman like that. He was lucky men were scarce and she was too old to find a replacement for him. So he went back to their bedroom to polish his own nails after trimming them and shaved his ass as well.

Danny woke up, and once again, the girls were gone. He turned on his television set and found out they had been arrested for the bank robberies while in the process of committing their eleventh one. He jumped out of his bed in shock that Denise, Heather, and Miya had accomplished what they were being accused of. He then began wondering what they had done with all the money they had stolen. He woke up Josefina to inform her of the news. Lucia, Alejandra, and Carla kept blowing up his phone to question him if it was really them on the news. No one could believe those three witty, innocent-looking chicks had managed to rob ten banks. Lucia, Alejandra, and Carla almost flew over to Dan's house. When they got there, they began asking him questions about the money. The news report had stated the cash hadn't been found other than the one they had in their possession after they got caught in the process of their eleventh heist. Danny began putting things together. He figured out the day he had met them they had just finished robbing a bank near the gym. His three remaining ladies kept confusing his thinking by interrupting him with the possibilities that they had left the money somewhere in his house. Lucia asked him, "Let's just say you were to find it. What would you do with all that money?"

Danny told her, "First of all, I doubt they left it in my house. Second of all, I don't know what I would do. If I were to find it, I probably wouldn't tell anyone, so that way I won't be turned into the authorities and charged with conspiracy to commit a crime."

Lucia questioned, "Would you buy me a new car and a house?"

Dan replied, "I didn't buy you that while we were married. What makes you think I would now?"

Carla and Alejandra were busy searching for the money all over his house. Josefina joined them in their search. Lucia left Dan in the living room watching the news regarding the capture of those three girls who had been living with him for the past week. All four women started treasure hunting in Dan's pad. Alejandra came into the living room with a chainsaw and was about to start cutting up his hardwood floor when Danny stopped her and said, "What the fuck are you doing? Give me that before you chop off your fucking hands or head."

Alejandra replied, "What if they hid it under your floor?"

Danny uttered, "Oh really? And then they installed back my wood flooring before Josefina and I noticed, right?"

He then heard some loud thuds coming from his garage. He got up and ran over to see what it was. Lucia had grabbed a sledgehammer and was trying to break the concrete floor. Danny took the sledgehammer away from her and told her, "Are you fucking stupid? How in the fuck do you think they excavated a hole to bury the money, then covered it up without Josefina and I realizing it?"

Then he heard some clunking noise outside. He ran over there and found Carla trying to break some landscape rocks in his backyard with a shovel. He ripped the shovel out of her hands and told her, "You too? I can't believe you women came over here to try to fuck up my house, thinking you're going to find the missing cash." He gathered all three of them and kicked them out, as he pondered on accepting the news that his temporary happiness was locked up.

Hilda had Tito do the dishes and cook for her, as she threatened him that she would leave his sorry ass if he didn't. Tito was terrified of ending up alone without a woman by his side. He, as most feminine men, believed they would die or be cursed without female companionship. So he did everything in his power to please her. He had previously allowed her to cheat on him in the past—with several partners. So by this point, she was in charge and showed no mercy or pity. Tito cooked up some tacos and served her a plate. He took it to her as she lay in bed watching her podcast show. He handed it to her, and Hilda told him, "Where's my drink?"

Tito said, "I'm going for it right now, baby. I just had to bring you your food first. Here you go. I'll be back with your drink to feed you, my queen." He then set the plate next to her as he went for her drink.

Tito came back within a few seconds with her beverage. By then she had inspected her food, and she criticized it, saying, "Those tacos look like they were cooked by an amateur. How do you expect me to eat that? I'd rather you go get me something from a restaurant like a shrimp cocktail."

Tito replied, "I'm sorry, honey. I didn't think you wouldn't like my cooking. Let me go get you that cocktail you want. I'll be right back." He grabbed the car keys and headed out of the door.

When Tito got back home with the cocktail, Hilda had already eaten the tacos. He handed her the cocktail and told her, "Here you are, my goddess queen."

She slapped the cocktail out of his hands, spilling it all over him, and said, "You took forever to bring it back. I had to eat your disgusting tacos and don't want it anymore. Now clean that fucking mess on the floor, you imbecile."

Tito ran to the kitchen to grab the broom and mop to clean up the spill. He ran back and started picking up as Hilda watched him. Hilda got up from her bed and kicked the dustpan in which he had already gathered the solids. Tito didn't contest and instead picked it right back up. He finished cleaning up the mess, and Hilda threw the plate of tacos at him, saying, "Now clean that up too."

Tito grabbed the broom since the plate had shattered on the floor. He picked up all the shards and then threw them in the trash. Then he grabbed the mop and cleaned up the grease on the tiles with a napkin before mopping. Hilda hurried him up as the doorbell rang, which saved him. It was the technician who was there to fix the air conditioner.

Danny was sitting alone in his living room after the women had left. Josefina had also taken off to work, while he had been at the gym. He had just come back from working out to clear up his mind a bit. Everyone there had asked him about those girls he had with him the other day. They remembered they had been following him around the gym, and then the next day, he had put them to washing cars in the parking lot. He told everyone he hadn't known they were on the run and had no clue what had happened to them after he went home the day they were washing cars. He had a lot on his mind, yet he still wondered if they had stashed the money inside his house. There was a knock at his front door. He got up and checked who it was. There were multiple police units blocking his driveway, and officers were scattered all over his front yard waiting for him to come out. Tom, his nosy neighbor, had called them over, believing he was involved in the robberies. He had recognized the three females on the news as being the ones who were staying with Dan. Danny came out with his hands up, and he turned around with his shirt lifted up as directed by the lead officer on site. He obeyed their commands and got on his knees. He was placed in handcuffs and asked if there was anyone else inside his home. He responded, "I am alone in there. My daughter has already left for work." The officer radioed in to obtain a search warrant and took him to the back of a squad car.

The cops asked him questions regarding the three female suspects they had under arrest for the aggravated armed robberies. He refused to speak to them without having a lawyer present. They took him down to the station to interrogate him on his role in the crimes committed by the women Tom identified as living with him. The police officers were granted the search warrant, and they went into his house. They searched through everything but didn't find anything incriminating him in participating in the robberies. One officer went through Josefina's belongings and found her extensive sex toy collection under her bed. He sniffed a few of her toys and even licked one. His partner told him to stop being a sick fuck when he opened the door and found him about to insert it in his rectum. He put the toys back, and they left her room intact. They eventually gave up and headed back to their duties.

Jesus was doing the same things his stepfather was doing, well, almost. Mercedes wasn't home to throw things at him and make him pick them up. But he was washing dishes and cooking for her. After all, he had learned to be a bitch from his stepfather. A feminine man can never be able to raise a macho himself. Jesus was living proof of that. His son was the continued curse of their female hierarchy and would more than likely grow up to be a coward himself—to sum up, more cowards into this world for their survival. Jr. asked him, "Dad, can you help me put on this dress? It keeps falling off."

Jesus stopped what he was doing and replied, "Sure, let me teach you a trick Tito taught me." He grabbed a pin and tightened up the waist with it.

Jr. was happy and stated, "Thanks, Dad, you're the best!" He ran off back into his room to play with his dolls.

Jesus got back to what he was doing. As he cooked some food, he imagined what it would be like to be a real man—a man of honor who was respected and feared by others. He then veered off, imagining him sucking Nick's dick. He almost burnt the food on the stove as he pondered with a smile on his face what it would be like to suction out all of Nick's new testosterone and become like him one day. He turned off the stove and let his beef soup simmer down. He sent a text to Nick's phone asking him if he'd be willing to donate or sell him some of his semen. Nick replied right away and told him, "Broskie, are you serious? Why would you want my cum and what for? Is my ex in this too? Is she trying to get pregnant at her old age or something? Tell her to leave me alone already."

Jesus texted back, "Yeah, bro, I'm serious. Your ex didn't put me up to this. I was informed by some other feminine guys, who can't afford Test1 like myself, that if I were to ingest the semen of a masculine man I too would become a macho. So would you be kind enough to help me out please?"

Nick wrote back, "No, bro. I don't believe that's true. I wouldn't want to help you by either selling or donating my semen to you. I'll just send you a bottle of Test1 so it could help you out."

Jesus replied, "Would you really? Awe man, you're really a good friend, bro. Thanks, I'd greatly appreciate it if you would send me some."

Nick never responded back to his text nor did he send him a bottle of Test1. He totally forgot about it since he was having intercourse with five very sexually desirable chicks when he got the texts. Jesus waited for the bottle to come in the mail, but it never did.

Dan was allowed to contact an attorney and was freed from their custody because of lack of evidence. The three bank robbers hadn't admitted they were staying at his place or that they knew him. As he was being released, he snatched some chips from the detective in charge of the case, the same one who was questioning him. He did it to prove dominance over him since the detective was unmasculine. The detective actually craved some sexual desire in the back of his underwear as his anus throbbed for Danny after he did that. Danny got picked up by Lucia and was driven back to his house after a few discomforting hours of being questioned and accused falsely.

When he got home, he went outside to drink a beer on his front porch and saw Tom out there acting strange. He had been informed by the detective that a neighbor of his had called them and told on him. Danny confronted Tom, "That's right, you fucking nosy feminine motherfucker! I'm free, and I know it was you who called the cops with false allegations! I'm glad your wife isn't around to feel the embarrassment of the bitch you've become!"

Tom said, "What're you talking about, Danny? I didn't call the police. Why would I do that?"

Danny uttered, "They told me one of my neighbors did, and who else is as nosy as you? You did it because you're a sorry ass bitch who's too attached to your feminine characteristics. Anyhow, I'm out now, and you're still alone with no woman while I have plenty to choose from. You would have realized you're the problem and not me if you had the nuts to use your head, but all you use is your ass to think, you fucking pussy." Tom ran inside his residence, as he felt Danny's aggression would blow up, and he'd eventually lay his hands on him.

Lucia came outside and offered Danny some sex. She said, "I know you were probably in need of a woman while you were locked up. I'm here to help you relieve any unwanted stress, daddy. Take me to your room and do as you please."

Dan uttered, "I wasn't even there long enough to crave sex, Lucia. You're just acting on the impulse of wanting me inside you since you haven't had any since who knows how long. But if you really want me to fuck you, do me a favor and go piss on Tom's front door."

Lucia ran over to Tom's front door and pissed as well as took a shit. He'd eventually step on it as he'd come out to water his grass late at night when it was dark and no one was around to irritate him. Lucia then went to Danny's restroom to wipe her ass. When she finished, she got under the bed sheets with him and relieved some of her frustrations.

When Mercedes got back home and had eaten, she asked Jesus to accompany her to the store to get some groceries. Mercedes, Jesus, and Jr. headed to the store. When they got there, Mercedes told Jesus, "I hope you don't bring it up to anyone's attention that you were in the video. Everyone has already forgotten about it since there were copycats who took your spotlight away."

Jesus replied, "But what if someone comes up to me and asks for my autograph or wants to take a picture with me?"

Mercedes replied, "You just deny it was you, but I highly doubt anyone will walk up to you to get a picture or autograph. Your fame is gone and only lasted a little. Now come on and push that cart so I can get the things we need."

Jesus and Jr. followed her around as she placed items in the cart. Jr. asked her, "Mom, can you get me these strawberry cream cookies? They come with a coupon for half of the price on a doll I've been wanting."

Mercedes responded, "No! You should stop playing with dolls, Son. I'd hate to see you grow up to be like your dad. You just don't get it yet, but when you get older, you'll realize your father was never a role model to begin with." Jr. tossed them in still when she wasn't looking.

They were over at the drinks aisle when the angered husband spotted Jesus. He saw he was heading to the restroom and followed him in. Jesus was in the toilet sitting down to pee when the door was kicked in. The man began beating the shit out of him. Jesus yelped for help, but no one could hear his cry. The man then picked him up and made him sip some of the water in the toilet. Jesus gulped it down without putting up a fight. The man then released him as he laughed. Jesus asked him, "Can I suck your dick, mister? I'd like to get some of the testosterone you have to help me become masculine. I'll even pay you for a dose." The man was grossed out and took off just in case Jesus wanted to call the cops.

Jesus had pissed on himself, so he began to dry his clothes under the hand dryer in the restroom. Mercedes noticed he had taken longer than usual and went over to get him. She took him out of the restroom, pulling him by his hair. Some of the other customers observed how he was all beat up and believed she had done the damage. A feminine guy said, "Hey! Leave him alone. You know us men have rights too. You can't just beat him up. He probably didn't do anything to deserve the pain you've inflicted on him."

Mercedes told him, "You should mind your own business. I didn't hit him, but I will hit you if you don't walk away." The guy ran out of there after telling Jesus he was on his own.

Mercedes then questioned Jesus, "Why're you all beat up if you just went to the restroom?"

Jesus answered, "I slipped and fell while I was going into the toilet. It had macho piss all over the floor, and I didn't see it. That's why I also smell like urine." She believed his story, and they headed over to pay and left the store.

Josefina had gotten back home from work. She found her mother and father butt naked in his room. They were asleep. She had no idea the police had arrested her father earlier that day. She had no dates to attend since she had come to the conclusion real men hardly existed any longer. She changed out of her work clothes out and put on some comfortable attire. She then grabbed some of her toys from under the bed. She made sure her door was locked before getting busy with her dildo. She inserted one into her vagina and was about to place another in her mouth when she thought it smelled funky. She took a closer whiff and realized it smelled like coffee and donuts. She stopped masturbating and wondered why the hell it had such an odor to it. She got up from her bed and grabbed another one. She had smelled it before, and that one hadn't smelled awkward, so she put it in her mouth and fondled herself with it. She imagined being with two macho men and began to orgasm. Just as she was splashing vaginal juices and moaning, Lucia opened her door. Lucia was shocked and told her, "Hey, *mija*, I didn't know you were busy. I'm sorry for not knocking. I feel bad for you for not having a man in your life to fulfill your sexual needs."

Josefina jolted off her bed and tossed her toys away; she was embarrassed and stated, "I'm sorry you caught me doing this, Mom. But you have no idea how lucky you are to even have a real man you have to share. I can't even find one myself who I could share with other women. All that's left out there are feminine pansies."

Lucia sat next to her and uttered, "I'm not going to judge you for what you're doing. It's very sad, but you're right. There aren't any machos anymore, and I do know how lucky I am to have to even share your father with other women. Good thing is we didn't lose him to those younger three that got caught. I was a bit worried about them, and so was Carla and Alejandra. We thought he was never going to want us back since it seemed he had replaced us. Anyhow, I just came to say goodbye. Your father doesn't want me spending the night in his house. He says I'll think he wants me back and start bringing my things little by little." She got up from the bed and found the dildo Josefina had tossed away, which was stuck to her pants.

Lucia tried removing it, but the saliva left behind by the police officer was sticky. Josefina chuckled and tried helping her. She was able to pry it off her mother but fell over onto the floor while doing so. She got up and asked her mother, "Something is wrong with this one. I got back and found it all sticky, and it smelled like coffee and donuts. Smell it."

Lucia said, "No thanks, *mija*. I don't want to smell your toy. I'll take your word for it. I know you are unaware, but the police came for your father earlier and took him in for questioning. Tom called them and accused him of participating in the bank heists. The cops got a warrant and searched the house while he was locked up. Maybe one of the cops messed with your toy?"

Josefina replied, "Dad went to jail? Wow, that's crazy. Fucking Tom, that guy needs to mind his own business. And it makes sense why this dildo smells like coffee and donuts, ew! I'm going to just throw it away." Lucia hugged her daughter and left as Josefina tossed the toy in the trash and went to bed.

CHAPTER 17

SWEET TARTS

Today was Jesus's birthday, and he woke up thinking his wife had left him a surprise present. He checked under the bed, in the closet, and all around his bedroom but found nothing. He exited his bedroom and walked into the kitchen to see if she had left him a gift there. When he got to the kitchen, the only thing there for him was a pile of dirty dishes. He opened the refrigerator to see if maybe there was a cake inside for him, but there wasn't one either. He still had high hopes and thought maybe she would get back from work and surprise him with mariachis singing him a happy birthday. Jr. woke up, and he too didn't remember it was his father's birthday. He simply asked to be fed so he could continue to play in his room. Jesus checked his phone to see if anyone had wished him a happy birthday, but no one had done so. His lips began to tremble and twitch as he started to cry. He ran back into the bedroom and lay in bed for a little longer. He felt like texting Mercedes to remind her it was his birthday but decided not to because he thought maybe she did remember and had something planned for him when she'd be back home. Not even his mother had texted him yet. He texted Sam to see what he was doing. Sam replied, "Hey, bro, I'm just here watching TV and talking to some dude who Sally was going to cheat on me with while we were out on our trip. How about you?"

Jesus wrote, "What? You must be kidding, right? Sally was going to cheat on you with some other guy? That sucks, but why're you talking to him? I'm just here lying in bed after waking up to find no one cares what today is."

Sam texted back, "Yeah, bro, she was. He and I are going to get back at her. We've been discussing a few things to do with her. He's actually a pretty cool dude like us. I met him the other day. He came by and punched me after I opened the door. He thought it was Sally who'd come to the door, and then he took off. I chased him and we became pals."

Jesus questioned, "Why would he punch you and then y'all are pals? Like, is that why you haven't texted me in a few days? Are you replacing me with him? Makes sense why my best friend didn't remember what today is."

Sam wrote back, "Weird how it happened. No, I'm not replacing you. I've just been busy talking to this guy and planning things against Sally. What is today, bro, besides it being Wednesday?"

Jesus texted, "Well, that's great you've made friends with the guy who wanted to bang your wife. I'm glad for you in an awkward way. Never mind about what today is. It's just another Wednesday. Text you later, bro." Sam didn't reply to him.

Jesus got up out of bed and remained positive even though no one had remembered his birthday. He showered and then washed the dishes. Afterward, he cooked for his family, as well as swept and mopped the house. He turned on the radio and heard the oldie "It's My Party" by Lesley Gore, then he started crying, mopping away his tears off the floor as they fell.

Danny woke up and headed to the gym right away. He had begun to miss those three young chicks and had to clear his head.

He got to the gym and ignored everyone there since he figured they'd only ask him the same questions as yesterday. He was in the middle of his routine when he started thinking of where the girls would have hidden the money in his house, if they had done so. He hurried and finished his workout and then rushed back home.

When he got to his house, he ran inside to begin looking for the cash since he didn't want anyone present if he'd find it. Josefina had left with her friends and would be back in about two hours before heading out to her job. He started looking through his closets. He then went to his garage and searched through the pile of things he had gathered over the years. He didn't find the money in his garage, so he went to the kitchen and searched through all the cabinets. He came empty-handed and checked the restrooms. There too he didn't find anything. Josefina came back with her friends, and they all asked him about his girls who had got popped for robbing banks. Hellen asked him, "You didn't know they were bank robbers? They didn't make it obvious to you they were committing armed robberies?"

Danny said, "Nope, not at all. They seemed like three normal nice young gals like yourselves."

Hellen thought he was flirting with her and uttered, "Stop, you're making me blush. You really think that of me?" She leaned in toward him.

Danny told her, "Yes, I do. I mean I've obviously known y'all for some time since y'all went to high school with my daughter. With them, I didn't know them long enough to be accurate in my determination of their true personality."

Hellen grabbed his arm and uttered, "I like you too, Danny, and have had a crush on you since I was in high school."

Danny removed his arm from her hands and responded, "I never said I like you that way, Hellen. You're my daughter's friend, and I've always seen you as a daughter too."

Josefina came back from her room and saw Hellen being touchy with her dad and said, "Hellen, stop trying to hit up on my dad. That's disrespectful, and I'm sure you wouldn't like it if I did it to you." Hellen got up from the chair as Veronica laughed.

Hellen stated, "I'm sorry, Josefina. You're right about that. I just got lost in the moment because your dad is a real macho. One of the few left in this world. I'll just talk to you later. Come on, Vero, let's go." The two departed the residence, as did Josefina also a few minutes later.

As soon as they all had left, Danny jumped in the shower. He continued to think of where the money was. He had a vision of the moments they had shared in the shower together and missed them even more. They had brought him some unexpected joy out of nowhere, and then it all fell apart. He wasn't in love with them, but he had grown some feelings for those three.

Sam and the guy his wife tried cheating on him with were getting along just fine, if not concerning good. They had come up with the idea to surprise her at work. They showed up at her job and called her outside to address the situation she'd hidden. Sally headed out of the facility where she was the head tool mechanic for machines that crafted beer at a local distillery. She was shocked to see them both outside together. Sam told her, "Hey, honey, I want you to meet my new friend. His name is Paul."

Sally shook Paul's hand and pretended she didn't know him, stating, "Hi, Paul, it's very nice to meet you, but what brings you two here to my job?"

Sam replied, "I can't believe you're acting like I don't know what's going on. He told me you tried cheating on me with him while I was out of town. Aren't you going to admit to it and accept accountability?"

Sally uttered, "Fine, yes, I did talk to him, and we were going to go and spend the weekend together. Until I realized he was as feminine as you and asked him to take me back home. Is that what you wanted to hear? Nothing happened, and that was that."

Sam answered, "Well, I'm glad you're being honest now, but now it's my turn. Paul and I are going to form a relationship, and I'm moving out with him to his mom's house."

Sally told him, "What? Are you for real? You're leaving me, your wife and mother of your kids, to start a new life with a man who I tried cheating on you with? That's insane."

Sam commented, "Yup, that's right, woman. I sure am dumping you for him, and I know he'll treat me better than you ever have. By the time you get off work, I'll be long gone. He's going to eat my ass like you've never been able to, and we're going to make so much love to each other that it'll erase all your assaults from my body."

Sally was confused as to how that had even happened. Sam and Paul left her puzzled as she saw them both drive away. She went back to work and kept thinking about what had occurred. She even got distracted and caught her fingers under some moving mechanical parts she was doing maintenance work on. She pulled her hand out and saw it was only the protective gloves she was wearing that had gotten stuck. She shut the machine off to remove the glove and got back to work.

She wondered if it was all a big joke. Was Sam pretending or was he serious? The only way she'd find out for sure was once she'd get out of work and go home. Until then, the doubts caused her anxiety, which would only be answered within time.

Danny got back to looking for the cash. He was up in his crawl space on his knees, searching through a pile of rubbish he had up there. He got a cramp on his calf and extended his leg out, then pulled his toes inward. That movement caused some dust to scatter in the air, causing him to sneeze. His leg cramp returned after sneezing, and he got stuck up there unable to get back down. He had left his cell phone in the house, he recalled, as he began searching for it in his pockets. He continued to pull on his toes. When the cramp faded, he laid there and began to crawl. He made it to the entry point of the crawl space located in the garage and fell out of there, unable to properly climb down the ladder he had used to enter. Luckily for him, he landed on top of some old punching bag he had. He was all sweaty and dusty. *Another failed attempt to locate the money*, he thought. Then he heard Tom outside. Tom was speaking to himself or someone on the phone since there wasn't a second voice responding to him. Danny got up and dusted himself and grabbed a towel to dry his sweat. He heard Tom say, "Yes, daddy, I'm going to do all those nasty things you want me to. No, I haven't told anyone about us. I will continue to keep our secret well hidden from the world. So I'll see you later tonight at my place? Sounds good, daddy. I can't wait; see you soon, bye."

Danny's garage was right next to his house, and he must have been watering his grass while engaging in a conversation with his boyfriend apparently. Danny had a smile on his face after listening to the conversation and finding out Tom had a boyfriend. It made sense why he was so unmasculine now. Danny hopped out into the living area and grabbed his water bottle. His doorbell rang, and he went over there to see who it was. Carla was outside, waiting for him to open the door. He let her in, and she asked him, "Why do you look all dirty? Have you eaten, daddy? I'm going to make you some delicious food."

Danny told her, "I was outside and fell on the ground; that's why I'm all full of dirt. OK, I'm going to go change clothes and wash up a bit." He walked toward his bedroom.

When he came back to the kitchen, he didn't see Carla there. Instead, he found her in the living area checking under the couch for the dough. Danny said, scaring her, "Really, Carla? You came to cook for me or to look for the money?"

Carla replied, "Well, both actually. I need some money to pay some of my school debt. I'm sorry. Will you forgive me?"

Dan uttered, "I'm starting to feel as if you've become a gold digger. Might have been the time I neglected you and the others for the bank robbing trio. Either way, you have to go." He grabbed her and kicked her out of his house.

Carla was begging him to not make her leave; she said, "Please, Danny, I want to stay and cook something for you. It's not the money I'm only interested in. I love you and want to be with you. Come on, let's go to your bedroom so I can suck your dick. I'd like for you to meet my kid and family too."

Tom was still outside, trimming his flowers, and told Dan, "Looks like you're having more girl problems, Danny."

Danny said, "Fuck you, Tom. I'd rather have issues with women than be begging some guy on the phone to come do whatever he wants to me."

Tom replied, "What's that supposed to mean?"

"You know exactly what I'm referring to. I overheard your conversation earlier while I was in the garage. 'Yes, daddy, I'm going to do all those nasty things you want me to,'" Danny stated, mimicking his voice.

Tom cleared his throat and responded, "It's not what you think it is. I was talking to my friend about—about this weird fantasy he has of me feeding him nasty food. Anyhow, why am I even bothering to explain myself to you?"

Dan answered, "It's called shameful guilt, Tom. That's why you're explaining yourself by giving false information. So why don't you just mind your own business, care for your fucking flowers, and stay the fuck out of my life, you senior queer cum pot?!"

Dan got back to getting rid of Carla, who had managed to head back inside his crib while he was arguing with Tom. Danny walked back into his residence and grabbed her as she was getting some things to prepare him a meal. He threw her ass out and told her, "You're fired!" He then shut and locked his door.

When Mercedes stepped foot in her home after work, she saw Jesus sitting in the living room all dressed up. She inquired, "Where are you going dressed that way? Do you have another appointment or maybe a celebrity photo shoot?" She giggled at her comment.

Jesus got up from the couch and walked toward her, telling her, "Today is a special day, my love. Have you forgotten already?" He tried hugging her, but she shoved him off.

Mercedes replied, "How is today a special day? Are you cured already and now have become the man I've always wanted you to be?"

A tear began to fall out of Jesus's eye as he uttered, "Never mind, I guess it's just another day for you and everyone else." He ran to his room and wept.

Mercedes walked into their bedroom to change. She changed her clothes as she listened to him sobbing. She told him, "Stop crying; why're you being so sensitive? Is it that time of the month or what?" Jesus didn't reply as he whimpered uncontrollably, unable to stop.

Mercedes ignored him and put on her shorts and shirt, then walked out of the room. She went to the kitchen and sat down to eat. Jesus was really hurt she hadn't remembered his birthday. He had been seriously hoping she'd come back from work and surprise him with a gift and possibly a serenade. When her older kids got back from school, she took all three of her children to go grab some ice cream without even asking Jesus if he would care to join.

Jesus tried calling Sam, but he didn't answer. He called his mom, and she too didn't pick up. He called Nick without any luck either. His last resort was to call a suicide hotline, and the person at the other end heard his story and sang happy birthday to him. Jesus thanked the woman on the line, but she told him, "No worries, it's my job to help those who call to resolve their issues and make them feel special." Jesus hung up on her, making sense of what she had told him.

He felt unwanted and unneeded. No one he knew had remembered his birthday. He walked outside to his backyard with a glass of margarita and took a seat in the patio set. Mut came over to him and started licking his tears off his face. Jesus allowed him to since it was the only attention he had received during the day. Mut then began humping his leg. Jesus didn't budge and just continued to drink his beverage.

Just then, Mercedes came back with the kids and went outside to drink a beer. She saw Mut humping Jesus and asked, "What the hell is wrong with you? You're allowing Mut to molest your leg. That's probably a form of animal cruelty since you're just teasing him." She closed the door and headed to the front yard to sip on her beer in silence.

Jesus didn't break his sadness, and he felt Mut leave him a present behind on his leg. Semen dripped down his calf, which he swept it up with his hands and put it in his mouth. Jesus then walked back inside to grab a refill. Chris and Danniel were at the kitchen table doing their homework. Chris told Jesus, "You might want to wipe that white stuff off the side of your lip there, buddy. It looks like you were milking Mut if you ask me."

Danniel uttered, "Ew! Did you perform oral sex on Mut? That is gross."

Jr. defended his father, "My dad wouldn't do that. You two are just being mean to him like Mom. It's probably just some saliva from him crying all day, right, Dad?"

Jesus replied, "Yes, Son, it's just saliva." He wiped it off with his tongue and headed back outside.

Sally got out of work and raced toward her home. She drove up to the apartment complex and parked her car in front. She got out of her car and ran in to discover all of Sam's things were gone. Her kids weren't there either. She grabbed her cell and called Sam, but he wouldn't answer. She then heard her phone ring. It was her mother notifying her that Sam had left her kids with her. Sally drove over to her mom's, and when she got there, she walked in to hear her children tell her they had seen Sam kissing another man. Her mother told Sally, "Come, follow me to my room. I want to talk to you." Sally went to her room, and she shut the door.

Her mom told her, "How do you explain this situation to me? What did you do to cause a man to leave his family for another man? Do you know how embarrassing it is to know your man left you for another guy?"

Sally said, "Look, Mom, we're not living back in your days where men were real men. I understand how shameful it would be to accept that in your era. In this era we're living in, men aren't really men. They're extremely feminine, and it shouldn't surprise you. Deep down inside, they're all gay, except for a few in whom nothing in this world could minimize their testosterone levels."

She then received a text from Sam. It was a video in which he and Paul were kissing and having sex. She showed the video to her mom and said, "See, this is what I should be ashamed of? He was a dick-loving bitch to begin with."

Her mother watched the video and asked, "How in the world is he alright with sending you this video of him getting penetrated by another man? And then they're kissing and sucking each other's nipples like it's normal. Wow, I never expected that from Sam."

Sally uttered, "You call that a real man? He was too feminine for me, and the weird thing about it, which you don't know, is that I was going to cheat on him with the guy he left me for."

Her mother questioned, "What? Wait a second, he was supposed to be your sidepiece, and he turned out stealing your man from you? Should I go grab some popcorn? This is beginning to sound like a good drama tale."

Sally replied, "I was talking to that guy and paid for Sam and his friend to go on a trip so I could have some time alone with him. When I met him in person, we were heading to our own little getaway. He got a flat on the road, and then I noticed from his actions he was just as feminine as Sam. I then told him to take me back home and cancel the trip. He tried getting me to pay for the road service, but I refused. He ended up dropping me off at Shelly's and took off. He was mad, but I didn't know he'd be so angry as to tell Sam and then convince him to leave me for him."

Her mother stated, "Let me write this down because I'm sure it'll make a good movie script for me to sell Hollywood."

Sally said, "Stop, Mom, you're making me feel bad when I shouldn't. Have you and the kids eaten already? I'm pretty hungry right now."

Her mother responded, "Let's go get something to eat then because we too haven't eaten anything since I was caught off guard when Sam dropped them off." They took off to eat as Sally continued to tell her mom in detail about the incidents while she wrote everything down.

Danny had gotten back to searching for the loot when he received a call from jail. It was Heather. She told him, "Hi, Danny, hope you're doing good. I just wanted to let you know I really miss you. So does Denise and Miya, but I think I do more. I want to apologize for not letting you know what we were doing without you being aware. I hope you understand we didn't tell you so you wouldn't be involved. During the course of our relationship, I fell in love with you. You're a great man, one of those hard-to-find kinds. I don't know what our future looks like. We still haven't gone to trial, but I know we won't be getting out of here any time soon."

Dan replied, "I miss you girls too. You three grew into my life and just left unexpectedly. I will admit I miss you the most, but don't tell the others that. You three really pulled it off for some time. I never guessed it although I did suspect, but when I did, I'd discard the possibilities just by observing y'all's behavior."

Heather uttered, "Hold on really quick. Denise is initiating someone into our gang." She dropped the phone and went to help jump some chick into their clique. Then she was back, grabbing the phone and gasping for air as she spoke, "So you miss me the most, huh? Why is that?"

Danny answered, "Well, I found you to be the most docile one out of the three. The most feminine one too. Plus, I saw how you were always there taking good care of me. You even got bit by some ants and didn't flinch or leave my sight. You're also the one calling me right now. I hope you girls don't get a long sentence. If I'm still alive and well when you get out, I'd like to get back to what we had."

Heather uttered, "Awe, you're so sweet, daddy. I too pray we don't get a lot of time. I'd love to be with you right now taking care of you rather than being here with all these women who're on high testosterone levels and creating an unsafe living environment."

Danny told her, "I'd like to ask you something regarding your charges, but I don't want to get involved with it. I've been going crazy thinking if y'all maybe left something in my house by any chance." Just as Heather was going to answer his doubts, she was struck by the phone next to her during a riot for dominance and control of the unit between her gang and another, and her call was cut off.

Danny put his phone away, and he had got back to searching for the money when he remembered the time they had gone to buy Jr. the helicopter. The crazy guy who had run out of there accusing them of being bandits was right. He had recognized their voices as he had been their hostage at one of their heists.

Jesus got up and out of the room and decided to go get drunk at a bar by himself. Today was daddy's night at all the pubs. He required not only the attention his wife didn't provide but also the assurance that he was attractive as well. He left without telling anyone in the house where he was headed. When he got to the bar, he walked in to find a bunch of masculine women there having beers after work. They all turned to look at him since he was the only guy there. He took a seat at the bar and ordered an extra-large margarita. The bartender handed him his drink, and he began chugging it down. A butch next to him asked, "What's the special occasion if any?"

He replied, "It's my birthday, and no one at home has wished me a happy birthday."

She told him, "Well, happy birthday to you!" And all the women at the bar sang along.

Jesus continued to drink and vent with the masculine woman next to him. He summarized basically all of his life over the course of thirty minutes. She questioned, "So you were the guy who went viral online, you say? I don't think I recall seeing you in any of the videos I saw circulating."

Jesus responded, "Yeah, well, it's because everyone else suddenly started copying my video, and I lost my fame that way." He got up to use the restroom.

Jesus walked into the filthy toilet and grabbed some soap and towels to clean it up before he took a seat to piss. Once he had washed it up and dried it with towels, he sat down and let his fluid out. He was reading some of the graffiti on the toilet wall left behind by guys who had visited the bar. One stood out. It read, "Watch out for the butch at the bar. She'll slip some rohypnol when you're not looking." Someone else had written their phone number, who was in search of a macho man. Jesus felt a bit tipsy and was carking up at what the dudes had written in the toilet. He went for the toilet paper and realized it had run out. He then wiggled his ass and hoped he hadn't wet his cheeks while urinating. He got up, picking up his pants, and went to wash his hands. He then exited the restroom and walked back to the barstool where he had been sitting. He took a seat, and the butch inquired, "Were you able to use the restroom in peace? Or did you piss on your butt cheeks?" She chuckled.

Jesus replied, "I actually think I did get my cheeks wet."

She became aroused by his response. She uttered, "Let me buy you another round after you chug that one down." She leaned in his ear and whispered, "Hopefully you'll let me lick the piss off your cheeks." Jesus shivered. He agreed to the beverage, and they both counted to three before drinking all that was in their cups. Several women walked up to him and asked him if he wanted to dance, which he refused. Some also hit up on him, but he turned them down as well. He wasn't there to hook up and in fact was just there to get wasted and forget no one had recalled today was his birthday. He was halfway into his third margarita when he began feeling dizzy. The room spun around on him, and he seemed to lose focus of where he was. He tried getting up but stumbled into the butch's arms. He then lost consciousness and had no idea what was going on or going to happen.

Sam and Paul were having the best time of their lives. They had gotten Paul's mother upset because they had a bunch of racket going on in his room. She was unaware they were a gay couple having sex. Paul came out of his room to grab them some margaritas. His mother asked, "What's all that noise you have going on in your room, Paul?"

Paul told her, "We're practicing some wrestling moves, Mom, that's all."

His mom replied, "It sounds like you guys are having too much fun in there. Hope you guys don't break anything."

Paul uttered, "We won't, Mom. Don't worry about us wrestling. Even if you hear strange noises that may sound like someone's moaning, it's all part of our wrestling performance. We're going to keep practicing all night long so we can try and join the professional leagues."

His mother said, "Alright, Son. You just behave, and hopefully you become a wrestler and find yourself a woman to have some kids with and settle down."

Paul answered, "Yes, Mom, but don't pressure me to find a woman. I've told you before how they're all masculine nowadays. Most of them also don't want to have children." He then stepped back into his room with the drinks in hand.

Sam grabbed his beverage from him, as he lay in bed with a sheet covering his naked body. Paul informed him of what his mother had said. They both laughed and kissed each other. They then put their drinks down and continued to piledrive one another. Paul was ramming Sam in the ass when Sam fell into the Sheetrock dividing Paul's and his mom's rooms. He broke through the other side and landed on her bed, where she lay watching a movie. She couldn't believe what she was seeing and yelled, "Ah! Paul, what the hell is going on? Why're you two naked, sweaty, and connected to each other?"

Sam told her, "Hello, Paul's mother. Sorry to meet you like this."

Paul replied, "We're practicing this wrestling move, Mom, called the CPR choke, in which instead of doing a hamlet maneuver you choke the guy out, watch." He wrapped his hands around Sam and strangled him.

Paul's mother was crying, unable to believe him as she stated, "Get out of my room and go practice all the wrestling moves you want in yours. I hope you're not lying to me. I don't ever want to see you like this again, whether it's a wrestling move or not." They both went back into Paul's bedroom and tried covering up the wall so she wouldn't see them again.

Paul handed Sam his clothes, and they both got dressed. Their plan was to wait till she fell asleep to resume where they had left off.

Jesus was out of it, and the masculine woman took him to her house. He could have avoided what came next had he believed in the message he had read at the bar's restroom. She sat him in her bed and began to undress him. When he was nude, she took out her toy collection and started experimenting with him. Jesus wasn't aware of all the objects she introduced in his ass during the night. She did all kinds of freaky shit to him and recorded her actions. She figured if he wanted to be famous, she'd make him famous then. She hung him over one of her chairs and used her robotic masturbating simulator that began thrusting a dildo up his ass. Meanwhile, she placed herself in front of his face and rubbed her vagina on it. She also put on a long rubber glove for washing dishes and stuck her arm inside his rectum. When she took her arm out, she had a small vibrator in her hand, which Jesus had probably forgotten was there since it had run out of batteries. Jesus was grunting but couldn't do anything since he was heavily sedated. The butch woman even turned his ass into a waterfall. She spat beer inside and watched his anus flush it out on its own. She also placed hard shell-covered chocolate pieces in his asshole and watched how he shot them right back out. She went to her restroom and brought the plunger out since one of the chocolates didn't want to come back out. She put the plunger on his butt and began pumping it until it came back out. She managed to retract some of his feces, but she just left it on him without caring to clean him up. At that point, she got grossed out and decided to get rid of him. She took him back to her car and tossed him in the back. She drove around, wondering where it would be a good spot to unload him at. She couldn't drop him at the bar since the last guy she had picked up had complained about her, and the bartender had given her a warning. She stopped and stretched her hand over to the back seat. She went through his pockets and retrieved his wallet. She looked through his documents and found his address listed on his driver's license. She then drove to his home.

When she got to his residence, all the lights were off because they all were asleep. Mut came over barking, but as soon as he smelled Jesus and saw him, he stopped. She then threw him over the fence in his backyard. Mut came over and smelled the dry shit in his ass and ran away. The masculine woman then hopped back into her car and drove back home without anyone seeing her. She left a sweet tart lodged in his ass, which Mut came by to eat later on. Jesus's day indeed ended without anyone from his circle wishing him a happy birthday. No one remembered or cared. The only gift he received was from the butch who removed the vibrator in his ass, which had begun bugging him every time he pooped.

CHAPTER 18
EVICTED

Mercedes had woken up and didn't even bother to notice her husband wasn't asleep next to her. She jumped in the shower and got dressed to head off to work. She dropped off Chris at his high school and Danniel at her middle school. She then raced through the traffic to get to work promptly. When she made it to the building and walked in, Mrs. Santiago told her, "Have you seen the new video circulating online of your brother-in-law? I think it's even better than the last ones. He really went overboard this time, and I can't wait to see what's next. I'm sure he's acting the scenes; there's no way some guy would do that on purpose." She showed Mercedes the video that had been uploaded to the web a few hours ago.

Mercedes couldn't believe her eyes and asked, "Are you sure this is my brother-in-law? I don't see how he'd let some woman sodomize him." She was skeptical.

Mrs. Santiago uttered, "Yeah, it is. I memorized the exact location of his butt dimple from the previous video. Even though this one is kinda dark, you could still tell it's him. I'm not the only one who recognized him. People are writing comments about it in agreement."

Mercedes handed her phone back and told her she had to go use the restroom. She ran into the restroom and called Jesus on his cell to find out what was going on. Jesus's phone was off, so he didn't pick up. He actually didn't wake up until Jr. came outside looking for him. Mut was humping him when Jr. found him. Jesus jumped up and answered Mercedes's tenth call. He heard her say, "What the fuck is wrong with you, Jesus? Another viral video of you, and this time some woman is shoving things up your anus?"

Jesus didn't know what she was talking about and questioned, "What video, Mercedes? And why did you kick me out of the house and made me sleep outside with the dog?"

Mercedes replied, "I didn't kick you out and made you sleep outside with the dog. There's another video of you going viral, Jesus; that's what I'm talking about."

Jesus uttered, "Stop it, Mut, stop humping me. So who in the hell left me outside in the backyard with my pants down and all shitted on? Last thing I remember was I was at the bar having some drinks and talking to some masculine woman. Then I went to the restroom, and I blacked out."

Mercedes responded, "So you went to the bar to find some other woman to cheat on me with? I've told you I didn't want you going to any bars alone. The masculine woman you're talking about is probably the one who's raping you in the video." She then hung up as Jesus got off the ground, feeling unstable, and he balanced himself with his son's help.

When Mercedes opened the door to the stall she used, Mrs. Santiago was standing there listening to her conversation. Mercedes pretended it was the girl in the next stall who had been talking, who at the time was also farting. They both walked out of the restroom after washing their hands and continued with their duties.

Jesus put his pants back on and stumbled into his home. He went into the restroom to wash up and threw his defecated clothing in the trash. He still couldn't remember what had happened the previous night.

Danny had to block Carla from calling him. She continued to beg him to take her back throughout the night. He woke up a little later than he had planned to start his day. He rose out of bed and went to get ready to hit the gym. He couldn't find any clean clothes to work out in. He realized he had gotten used to the women who catered to him by doing his laundry and keeping up with it. He placed his clothes in the washer and waited till it was being rinsed to add fabric softener. He then put on the clothes he had worn the previous day and headed to a sporting goods store to get a shirt and shorts to wear at the gym. When he arrived at the store, he began looking around the clothing section. A feminine man walked up to him and asked, "Do you think this swimsuit looks good on me?" He was wearing a one-piece woman's swimsuit.

Dan turned around to see him and uttered, "Yeah, it looks good on your little sissy self. I'm sure you'll have the rest of the FEMNS jealous of you at the pool." The guy thanked him and walked away, making a beeline to make his purchase.

Danny got back to looking through some muscle shirts. He was looking for a specific color of gray. He found some, but they had some designs on them that were not to his liking. A group of FEMNS walked into the store, who were obnoxiously loud. They walked over to where Dan was, and one of them said, "Hi there, macho man. Would you be kind enough to help us in selecting some gym clothing?"

Danny answered, "I don't work here. You'd be better off requesting assistance from an employee than from me."

Another FEMNS replied, "But we want your help because we want your opinion. See we're hoping to get some clothes that will attract a macho man like yourself."

Danny responded, "If you really want a macho man like me to pay any attention to you, then you'll have to act more masculine and not feminine. If you're able to score with a guy you feel is masculine, then he wasn't masculine to begin with. Besides, whatever happened to you pansies trying to marry women to support you while y'all stay at home?"

The guy stated, "Most women nowadays don't even want to provide for us. So there's more homosexuality being explored. I'd love to find a woman who'd let me stay at home, but most of them won't take us into consideration. They're not falling for the previous tactics of acting masculine anymore. They've been reading guides on how to pick guys, and unfortunately now that they're becoming educated, they no longer are easy to persuade."

Danny told him, "Well, that sounds like a personal problem. Like I said, if you lure a guy it's because he was feminine to start off. If y'all haven't been able to trick a chick, then you won't be able to subdue a dude." He grabbed one of the shirts he didn't really like and walked away.

As Dan paid for his clothing articles, the group of FEMNS created a commotion in the store. One of them fell to the ground claiming he had slipped on some of the store's products that were left out of place, posing a danger. These guys were clearly trying to catch a free ride somehow. The guy was yelling, pretending to be in great pain, as the manager ran to check what was going on. The other guys with him told him how the incident had unfolded. The guy on the floor uttered, "I think the fall broke my hymen, and I will no longer be a decent lady to my future husband."

Danny told the female cashier, "What a bunch of fags! Trying to live for free somehow since they're not man enough to provide for themselves." The cashier giggled and asked him for his number as she rang him up.

Danny refused to hand out his phone number and left the shop with his new clothes after telling her, "Sorry, but I don't have any more room for another damsel in distress." From there, he drove to the gym and had a great workout.

Mercedes was on her lunch break when Mrs. Santiago asked her, "Are you sure you weren't talking to your husband in the restroom? It seemed like you were telling him he's the one on the videos and not your brother-in-law."

Mercedes answered, "I wasn't on my phone. I was busy using the restroom. The girl who was next to me was the one on her phone, but I didn't pay any attention to her conversation, to be honest." Mrs. Santiago walked away with a doubt in her head.

Mercedes got up and was about to head outside to her vehicle when a delivery driver showed up with a package. The driver said, "I need someone to sign this delivery for me, please."

Mercedes replied, "Sure, I'm the one who does that now. Just place the box down there, and I'll sign it for you." The guy placed the package on the ground by the security desk and handed her his handheld device for her to sign with her fingerprint.

As she was signing, the delivery driver was trying to figure out where he had seen her before. He then asked her, "Hey, aren't you married to that guy who went viral online?"

She replied, "No way, I'd be embarrassed to be with a guy like that."

The guy uttered, "Yes, you are. I saw you two the other day at the store together with your little daughter."

Mercedes stated, "No, you're confusing me for someone else." She handed him his device and began to walk away in order to avoid further embarrassment.

The guy grabbed her shoulder and told her, "Look, I'm sorry if I'm putting you on the spot, but I'd like to talk to you about something your husband has been doing behind your back."

Mercedes turned to face him and questioned, "What is he doing behind my back?"

The driver told her, "He has been contacting my wife in order to obtain some of my semen. He and other feminine men have been desperately in search of macho sperm to increase their testosterone. He was hoping my wife would allow him to eat her out, and he could extract it from her to medicate himself."

Mercedes said, "Are you sure you're not confusing my husband? I mean, I don't think he has the guts to approach any females. Why would he be doing that behind my back though?" She had forgotten Jesus had brought it up to her attention when he had asked her if she could get some from her dad.

The guy uttered, "Yes, I'm sure it is your husband. Do you remember that day at the grocery store he went to the restroom and came back out all beat up? Well, that's because I fucked him up. I had been looking for him for some time already since he had disrespected my marriage. I understand this may seem wild to you, but it's true. See those types of feminine men have been hiding behind curtains, pretending to be masculine. They first started a while back talking shit to us real men with screen courage, and now they're hitting up on females they wouldn't have the balls to hit up on in person."

Mercedes stated, "He did come out of the restroom all beat up. I've always known he was a coward, but what can I do? I sometimes wish I had never met him."

The guy informed her, "Your keyboard warrior needs to be put in place. Why don't you let me get your number, and later on, we'll call him so you can see what his true nature is?" She let him take down her phone number and got back to work as he did too, since he had more deliveries to make.

Jesus got out of the shower and fed Jr. His anus was throbbing, and he couldn't recall why. He checked online to see what the web doctor could tell him. The doctor suggested he put an ice pack on his ass and take a break from any heavy lifting or strenuous activities. He also asked him, "Unless you're the guy who's on the video I just saw, getting his ass rammed by some butch woman?" Jesus thanked the doctor and exited the site to look for the video.

Jesus was shocked to find the video just as his wife and the doctor had mentioned. He viewed it and tightened his anus as he watched her insert objects into it. Clenching his rectum irritated his injury, and so he tried to relax as he continued to watch the footage. He could not believe his eyes, although he was amazed he had survived through the encounter. He then began to try and remember what had happened the previous night. He had a flashback of when he was in the restroom and the messages he had read, warnings that he had failed to comprehend. Jr. pretended to throw a doll at him so he could play with him, and the movement caused his ass to feel a sharp pain. He fell to the ground, and Jr. came over to check on him. He saw the video Jesus was playing on his phone and asked, "Is that you, Dad? What's the lady doing to you?"

Jesus shut his phone screen and replied, "That's not me, Son, and I think the woman was performing CPR on the man because he passed out after she began to violate him."

Jr. inquired, "What does that mean, violate?"

Jesus responded, "It's when someone does something to you that they shouldn't have had, against your will or best interest."

Jr. uttered, "So this morning when I found you outside getting humped by Mut, he was violating you?"

Jesus said, "Exactly, he was violating me, Son."

Jr. ran to this room, shouting, "My dad was violated by our dog!" He shared it in a group chat with other little boys, who were grossed out about that.

Jesus ignored him and finished watching the video. He saw how she removed something from inside his anus and said, "Thanks, lady. I didn't know that was there. No wonder why my stomach doesn't hurt today." He then started cleaning around the house and cooking.

Moments later, the news reporters were back at his house wanting to get an interview. Jesus shut the blinds and curtains and disregarded the activity taking place outside his home. He told Jr. to not open the door or go outside until the people had left. The news reporters were persistently trying to get him to talk on camera. One of them hopped into the backyard and tried opening the door to go inside. Mut charged at him and began humping him, which caused the rest to record what they were witnessing. One of the reporters was live and began saying, "It appears one of our colleagues is being victimized by the man's dog. The famous man in the viral videos must have taught his pet things after it has seen its owner engage in similar sexual activity. A sad reminder to those who believe our pets don't see what we do. The man still has not made a public appearance at the moment and might be making more videos inside his home." The guy getting humped by Mut ran to the fence and jumped over it, falling right behind the live reporter, screaming, "That dog must be a victim of animal cruelty and is giving signs in order to be helped or saved!"

Danny went back to his house after his gym session and made himself something to eat. As he sat down, Josefina got up and joined him at the table. She asked him, "Have the girls contacted you? I wonder if they're alright."

Danny told her, "I spoke to Heather yesterday. She said they're doing as best they could. They haven't been given an exact date for trial."

Josefina questioned, "Did she tell you if they hid their money here?"

Danny replied, "I was about to ask her, but the call cut off. She mentioned they're forming a gang there and probably got in a fight with some other gang, I guess."

Josefina uttered, "They're in a gang now? Wow, those three are my heroes. Robbing banks, getting locked up, and being part of a prison gang. They sound so unreal from the three chicks who were staying here with us."

Danny responded, "Yeah, who would have guessed they'd turn out to become what they have?" Josefina finished eating and jumped in the shower to get ready to go to work.

Danny waited for her to leave and then he got back to searching for the money. He climbed up the roof and checked behind the AC unit. He then came down and checked inside his tool shed in the backyard. He moved some things around but found nothing. He got tired of searching as he had run out of ideas where they may have hidden the cash. He went inside, put his clothes in the dryer, and showered. When he got out, he sat in his living room to watch his favorite documentary. Alejandra came over to his house to prepare him a meal, and as he opened the door for her, he observed a strange car parked outside Tom's driveway. He let Alejandra in, and as she began to cook, he crept outside to see if he would catch Tom with his boyfriend. Danny slowly walked onto Tom's property and went up to his window. He heard some moaning and grunting coming from inside the house. He looked through the window and observed Tom getting penetrated by some younger dude. This was his chance to finally get back at Tom. He took his phone out and started recording their sexual encounter. The guy fucking Tom noticed something outside the window and stopped. He walked over to the window and saw Danny crouched under, with his phone out. The guy informed Tom, and they both put on their clothes and ran outside. Danny found out they had discovered him, so he walked over to his front lawn.

Tom came out and ran over to his property and told him, "You better not have recorded our yoga session, Danny. Why're you depriving me of my privacy?"

The younger guy came out and said, "It's not what you thought it was. We were meditating. Please erase the video I saw you recording."

Danny responded, "Ha, ha! I've got you now, Tom. You thought you were perfect and judged me and my life up to the point of calling the cops, not minding your own business. Look at you now. I bet you wished you had not been so nosy, huh? I knew this day would come. What're you two going to do if I post this video online?" He blackmailed them.

Tom uttered, "I'm sorry, Dan, for all the trouble I've caused you. Please don't share that video and ruin this young man's reputation and mine. I'm begging you, I'll do anything. How about I pay you some cash for the footage?"

Danny inquired, "How much money are we talking about?"

Tom stated, "I've got about one hundred thousand in the bank right now. You can have it all; just don't share the video."

Danny commented, "Well, I'll be waiting in my home for you to get back from the bank with my cash. You've got thirty minutes before I post this video and make it go viral." He walked into his house as Tom sped to the bank.

Mercedes got out of work, and she called the delivery driver before she drove back home. He answered and told her, "Let me have your husband's phone number so I can call him and you can hear for yourself just what a queer he is." She shared Jesus's number with the guy.

The guy called Jesus from his phone and Jesus answered, "Hello."

The delivery driver said, "Jesus? This is the guy who beat you up in the grocery store restroom, husband of the woman you harassed online. I'm not calling to start any trouble with you. Are you alone and able to speak to me?"

Jesus replied, "How'd you get my phone number? Yes, I know who you are. I'm really sorry I messed with your wife. I've apologized to you before. Please forgive me. I'm just a feminine coward." He whimpered.

The guy uttered, "Don't worry, buddy. The reason why I'm calling is because I understand you're looking for some macho sperm to ingest in order to increase your testosterone levels and become masculine. Is that correct?"

Jesus responded, "Yes, I am looking for a macho semen donation or someone who could sell me some."

The guy stated, "I want to sell you some if you're interested. I'm short on cash for a trip I want to take, and we could help each other out. What do you say?"

Jesus told him, "Yeah! That would work for me if it works for you. How much do you want for the first dose?"

The guy answered, "Well, why don't you ask your wife what a fair price would be since she's on the phone listening to your faggot ass trying to purchase some sperm from me?"

Mercedes shouted, "Jesus, who the hell have you turned out to be? You've been hiding too many things from me now. I can't even explain how disappointed I am in you. You should be ashamed of yourself."

Jesus said, "I'm just kidding, Mercedes. I knew this was a prank call."

They guy hung up on Jesus and told Mercedes, "You see now just who really is your husband."

Mercedes replied, "Yes, thank you for clearing this up for me. I'm headed home to kick him out of my house. I'll talk to you later." She then hung up and sped toward her house.

When Mercedes drove up to her residence, she jumped out of the van and ran inside. The reporters were still outside, and they began recording and going live, presuming something was about to happen. She shut the door behind her and grabbed Jesus, beating him up. Jr. was in his room listening to music, since his dad hadn't cleared out the situation outside with the news reporters. He had no idea his mother was going to finally get rid of his feminine father. Jesus tried fighting back, but Mercedes overpowered him. She dragged him toward the front door and tossed him outside. She shut the door, and the news reporters flocked Jesus, asking him questions. Mercedes opened the door and began throwing his stuff out. One reporter asked, "How does it feel to have the most viewed videos online right now? Can you tell us a little more about the first ones? This last one you were in, was it part of the show when the woman removed something out from your anus? Can you tell our viewers what's going on right now? Why is this woman throwing all your stuff out and not letting you back in the house?" Jesus remained silent, and he sobbed as he banged on the door, hoping Mercedes would let him in.

Mercedes opened the door once again and tossed more of his belongings outside. She shouted, "You're being evicted for being a freaking feminine male who has no shame of being on online videos that aren't something to be proud of." A reporter tried putting a microphone closer to her so the audience could listen to what she was saying, but she slammed the door, leaving Jesus outside.

Jesus grabbed some of his things and ran to his car. The reporters followed him to his vehicle. He jumped in with his things and took off. He tried calling Mercedes, but she didn't answer. He drove around the city, hoping she'd calm down and let him back into her home. Back at the house, the news reporters had dispersed. Some of them took off following Jesus, and the others went back to the station to edit and release the footage they had obtained. A random bum who was in the crowd stuck around till the end and got lucky with some of Jesus's things, which he picked up from the front of the house.

Tom returned before the deadline and knocked on Danny's door. Alejandra opened the door and called Dan. Danny walked over to his front door and asked Tom, "So, do you have my cash?"

Tom answered, "Here it is. Do we have a deal then? You take the money and not post the video online?"

Danny looked past Tom and saw the young man biting his nails as he replied, "Sure, we have a deal. Just one more thing though."

Tom questioned, "What's that?"

Danny responded, "I want you to stop being so nosy and never ever fuck with me again."

Tom uttered, "OK, I'll mind my own business from now on. I'll fight my feminine urge to be nosy." Tom stuck his hand out to seal the deal, but Danny shut the door in his face and went inside his home with a bag full of dough.

Alejandra asked Dan, "What was that all about? I thought you and your neighbor didn't get along."

Danny told her, "We don't, at least I don't like that sissy ass motherfucker. I got back at him. He was with his boyfriend in his room getting fucked, and I recorded them. They offered me this money to me to not upload the video content on the world wide web." He chuckled.

Alejandra inquired, "So are you going to not share it online now?"

Dan stated, "Ha! I sure fucking am. Want to be the first to see it?" He let her watch after she agreed.

Danny immediately posted the video online from his cell phone after Alejandra had watched it. He had no reason to keep his word to a feminine guy who, per his convenience, wanted to cooperate with him. He figured he'd make some extra paper with views and likes. Danny took a seat back on his couch, feeling content about having won this battle. He continued watching the documentary, and Alejandra served him a plate of food. While he ate, he thought of using some of the money he had just made on purchasing himself a virtual reality headset to watch his favorite program from the comfort of his bed. He finished eating and took Alejandra to go get it and then took her to get an ice cream.

Jesus had driven up to the side of a park to sit in his car and wait for Mercedes to call him back. He was sobbing profusely as he went through the pictures of them both on his phone. He felt this was the end of their relationship and he had nothing else in his life worth living for. Once again he contemplated suicide, but he was scared to hurt himself physically, so he sat in his car texting those he knew. Nobody answered his messages. He watched as some women played with their kids at the park, and then a baseball broke through his window, shattering the glass and hitting him in the face. A grown masculine female and her daughter were responsible for the damage, but they hid the baseball bat and walked away as if nothing had happened. Jesus looked around to see if anyone was playing baseball who he could confront about his broken window, but by then, the mother and daughter were gone. He then witnessed a group of feminine men jogging past his car. They stopped and handed him a flier, encouraging him to participate in a FEMNS rally they were having in a few days to address male rights. He took the flier and wiped his boogers with it. He then placed it on the passenger seat as he received a call on his cell. He thought it was Mercedes, but it was the study group contacting him to present himself there to receive the results of his tests. He confirmed he'd be there later on and hung up. He looked at his phone, hoping his wife would call him, but she never did. When the group of FEMNS joggers came back around to his car, one of them asked him, "Hey, aren't you that guy from the videos online? I'm a fan of your work. Could I get an autograph and a picture?"

Jesus said, "Yeah, just let me wipe off my tears."

They took a photo, and the guy questioned him, "Why're you crying? You should be happy you're a star. I wish I was a star. The closest I'll get to the sky is a rainbow." Jesus shared his story with the guys.

They all began to cry with him and told him, "You'll be alright, buddy. That's how women are now—heartless. What did we ever do to deserve being treated this way by them?" They hugged him and calmed him down a little.

Then a group of masculine women came to break them up and told them to go do that in the privacy of their homes because there were children in the area. The group of FEMNS took off running from the females not waiting to get beat up, and Jesus drove away to his next temporary location.

When Danny got back to his house, Alejandra left. She had to go to hers because those were Dan's rules. He got back to looking for the cash. He began searching in the same spots he had already done so. The doorbell rang, and he paused his search to see who it was. It was Lucia, so he opened the door and asked, "What do you want? I'm a little busy rearranging my furniture."

Lucia answered, "I came to prepare your dinner. I won't get in the way, and I could even help you move the furniture around."

He hesitated to allow her entry but did so after telling her, "Just prepare my food. I'll fix the furniture myself."

Just as he was closing the door, Tom ran outside with his boyfriend, shouting, "You said you weren't going to put the video online! Why would you break your word? I want my money back, Danny!"

Lucia swung the door back open and went outside, replying, "Shut the fuck up and leave Danny alone already! You fucking lame excuse of a man!"

Tom was a few feet away from her and uttered, "Mind your own business, woman. This is a matter between two men."

Lucia responded, "I only see one, and you should mind yours! Since you're not a man, I'm going to handle this for Dan."

Lucia began swinging at Tom and his boyfriend. Tom tried pulling her hair, but she elbowed him in the face. His boyfriend jumped on top of her and tried choking her, but she swung him over her and dropped him on the ground. Tom charged at her, so she punched and kicked him. She struck her leg on his groin, but he didn't budge. His testicles had already descended into his pelvis as he was in the process of transforming. Lucia then pinched his sensitive nipples, causing him to yell in pain. She then grabbed the back of his head with both her hands and pulled it toward her knee. As soon as her knee made contact with his face, he became unconscious. His boyfriend got up and tried charging her again, but she made him flinch in pain. He stopped and picked up Tom from the ground and carried him back into his house. Lucia had defeated two FEMNS on her own. Danny had been watching the combat unfold and congratulated Lucia on her victory. They walked back into his residence. Danny fucked the shit out of her and then allowed her to cook. It had turned him on that she was willing to fight those guys for him. Not that he required her backup, but it made him feel appreciated and valued. Dan could've taken care of both on his own with less effort and in a shorter time frame.

Jesus arrived at his appointment and walked in. He was eventually called to the back to receive his test results. The doctor told him,

"I have some interesting news to share with you. I don't know if you were aware of it or not, but our studies indicate you were born a transgender—mainly female to be exact. Do you have any kids?"

Jesus answered, "Transgender? How is that possible? I do have a son, though."

The doctor replied, "Well, consider it luck if any, or you might want to get a DNA exam. Thing here is, we won't be able to make you masculine no matter how hard we try. Even if you'd have a surgical procedure done, you'd still be mostly a woman."

Jesus began to sob as he questioned, "So you're saying I'm a female and not male at all? What am I going to do now?"

The doctor stated, "Well, yes, that's what I'm saying. I don't know what else to tell you other than the truth, ma'am."

Jesus uttered, "It makes sense now why my whole life I've felt like a woman. It's going to take some time for me to adjust to being called ma'am."

The doctor told him, "Also, we're going to have to remove you from the program since you're not fit for candidacy. We need feminine males and masculine women to research. So, I wish you luck in life and see you some other time. This lady will be escorting you out of the facility." A butch came in the room and grabbed him by the arm to take him out.

Jesus was depressed and felt like shit after finding out he was born a woman. There wasn't anything he could do to turn into a man. He got in his car and called Mercedes, but she didn't answer. Before heading out of the parking lot, he called Sam, Nick, his mother, and his sister to see if he could spend the night at their place, but nobody picked up his calls. He fell asleep inside his car at the parking lot until the security officer swung by and kicked him off the property. He then drove around the city, in search of a place where he could park his car without an issue and rest up for the night.

CHAPTER 19

DESTINY'S COURSE

Jesus had no luck in getting ahold of anyone to spend the night at their place. He had gone to his mother's house, but she didn't answer the door. He also tried Sam's, but Sally came out and informed him of the bad news that he no longer lived there or that he wasn't with her either. She advised him to try seeking refuge at the homeless shelter. Jesus ended up sleeping in his car parked under a bridge. The unhoused in the area broke into his vehicle at night and took all his belongings. They raped him and stole his car. As he had no money, home, car, or food, he occupied one of the unhoused makeshift sleeping areas under the bridge for the night. When he woke up, he was assaulted by the person sleeping next to him since he hadn't been recognized as being part of the crowd that usually gathered there. Jesus was banned from the location, and they didn't even bother telling him where he could grab a bite for free. He walked along the most impoverished sectors of the city. All the people in the streets made fun of him after they realized he was the guy from the videos. One guy even came up to him and told him, "Hey! You're that guy, the one online in the sex tapes going viral. I thought you'd be rich by now. What're you doing over here? You're a celebrity, and you don't belong in these streets. Let me help you find a place to stay." He took him around the shelters, but as soon as they found out who he was, they denied him entry.

The unhoused eventually took him to his campsite and beat him. He also had him perform oral sex on him and recorded the event. The man uploaded a new video to the collection. Jesus roamed the streets all day panhandling, but no one offered him cash. He had to eat from the trash cans, and when he tried using his phone to call Mercedes, he found it had been disconnected and he no longer had service. He missed being back home with his family. At this point, he regretted all he had done that had led him up to this moment. As he walked along one of the streets, a car passed by and splashed water on him from a puddle that had formed from a broken septic drain.

Danny woke up to find Lucia next to him. He hurriedly woke her up and told her, "You need to go back to your place. You've broken my rule of not spending the night here."

Lucia said, "I'm sorry, Danny, but I was tired and you fell asleep, and so did I. Let me just rest a little longer and I'll leave, please."

Danny replied, "Hell no! Get your old ass up and go sleep in your bed. I have things to do."

Lucia uttered, "Like what, Danny? What do you have to do that me sleeping in your bed is going to be an issue?"

Danny responded, "I have to get ready and head off to the gym. If you're not going to leave, then go sleep in Josefina's room. By the time I get back, you better have made me breakfast and showered or left." He got up, got dressed, and took off for the gym.

Lucia got up and went to Josefina's room and crashed out with her in her bed. When Josefina woke up, she thought her mother was someone else and kicked her off her bed. Lucia got up from the floor and corrected her daughter. They both got up as they laughed at the situation and prepared a meal before Dan got back. They also searched around the house, looking for the fortune that could have been hidden there. They had no luck, so Lucia went home, and Josefina took a shower and left with her friends to buy some sex toys since they had no men to fulfill their needs.

Sam and Paul were kicked out of Paul's mom's house, as she found them showering together early in the morning using her conditioner bottle as a sex toy. They left his mother's dwelling with minimal personal belongings because Paul's car was a two-seater. Oddly enough, they went to Sally's house to see if she'd let them settle in while they found another place to live. Sally was shocked when she opened up the door and heard their request. She told Sam, "Are you on drugs? How in the world did you think I'm going to allow you and your boyfriend to stay here after you left me for him? I definitely don't want you back or have the kids see you two fornicating. Get lost and never come back here again, you cupcake with a cherry on top."

They took off from there and were allowed to stay at one of the homeless shelters. Later that evening, they showered together and were banned from the shelter as well. No one understood or cared they were in their honeymoon phase. They ended up spending the night on the streets.

When Danny got back home after the gym, Heather called him and gave him a clue as to where she had hidden her share of the money. Danny talked to her for a while until she got involved in a violent war inside her housing unit. Danny then went outside to dig up where the anthill was—the same one she had stood over while he was doing his yard work, where she got bit by the ants. He dug a few feet and found several duffle bags. He removed them, making sure nobody was watching, and he covered the hole back up. He hid the bags in the crawl space, and within a few weeks, he started a business after buying Tom's house and kicking him out. It turned out Tom had to borrow the one hundred thousand dollars from his home equity. He couldn't pay it back and lost his home, which Dan purchased to make sure he didn't get another pansy neighbor. Danny used some of the money to fund his grandson's testosterone treatment and turned him masculine as he aged. Danny continued his lenient relationship with Lucia and Alejandra. He made a boo-boo and got Hellen—Josefina's friend—pregnant. She took advantage of him one night at a family gathering since he was a little drunk and snuck him back to her place, where she got on top of him and took in his semen. She had finally found herself a macho, although not how she had planned. Danny took care of his son and left a legacy behind for him. He also hired the best criminal defense lawyer for Heather, and she was released as she cooperated with the state prosecutor on the case. Danny now had four women to take turns with him. He allowed Hellen, Heather, and Alejandra to move into Tom's old house. Not Lucia though, not only because she had her own property but also because he didn't want her old ass around bugging him all day since she had no life after he divorced her and was going through menopause.

Josefina eventually ran into the old man from church, with whom Hellen had spoken to. She got his number and met one of his sons—the only masculine one he had. They hit it off, got married, and eventually started a family of their own. She moved out of Dan's pad and gave her room to her new brother. All this caused her older sister to envy her since her family had separated. Josefina lived very happily with this guy who made sure she was safe in his arms at all times. Danny gave her a wedding gift and bought them a house. He also paid for his other daughter's home.

⟡

Sally got the divorce papers signed, and she remained single for a while. She and Veronica, Josefina's other friend, started hanging around together since they were the last singles of the pack. They ended up forming a tight bond, which led to a formal relationship. They got a discount on their wedding cost because Sam and Paul joined them. It was one of the most awkward weddings anyone could have attended. The church and hall were separated by a curtain, and attendees kept jumping in and out of each ceremony.

Sam and Paul went on to make sex tapes of their acts. They made a shitload of money from the amateur porn industry—something Sam's kids were so ashamed of. They hardly spoke to him after finding out about it, but Sam was OK with it. He and Paul got a cat, and they considered it their son. They now live in a big house, where they continue to break down walls since they were cheaply built by masculine women with novice experience.

⟡

Nick became one of the richest men in his city. He never got back with his old ex. He instead had several women living in his mansion. He got three of them pregnant and had a few kids of his own. All his boys were born masculine, and he was a happy father. His company continued selling billions of Broski-Wear worldwide. He even invented a new product that he named the Broski-suit. It was a slip-on bodysuit that made its users look like they worked out and were jacked. His main customers were FEMNS, who couldn't afford plastic surgery or testosterone treatments.

Chris and Daniel eventually graduated and moved out of the house as Jr. had become hostile because of the high testosterone levels surging through his body. He became physically strong and muscular before he was enrolled in middle school. He had a bunch of girls chasing after him and would sneak them into the house while his mother was at work. He made sure his mom was protected at all times, and she saw him differently once he was cured from the epidemic and gave him all the respect a real man deserved. He forgot about his father and didn't mention him in conversations. After becoming masculine, he lost respect for Jesus.

The government ran out of funds right after they began converting feminine men back to being masculine by using masculine women's testosterone. A few of the guys who were slightly low on testosterone made a comeback, while the rest became even more feminine. Women began developing muscle tone and restored most of the economy. The new norm persisted for another century or so, until both sexes were fully transformed into the opposite gender.

Tito and Hilda, Jesus's parents, never spoke to Jesus again. One day he showed up at their house as they were coming back from the market. Hilda told him to leave and walked inside their residence. Tito informed Jesus there was only room for one feminine man in the house and made it clear to him that he wasn't welcome. They ended up turning the home they rented back to its rightful owner and registered in a senior citizen housing center. Hilda eventually left Tito since he had never been able to please her. She moved to another center and took two semi-masculine old men with her, who replaced Tito. She was eventually extradited from the country for living illegally with a fake social security. Tito was the one who notified the federal agency that was responsible for her removal. She now lives in Mexico in a small village in a modest home with her pet donkey, who she blows for comfort.

Mercedes was devastated at the separation, but she kept in contact with the angered husband who had beaten up Jesus. He helped her through her sadness, and she became his sidepiece. The guy was a real macho unlike Jesus and was more than capable of satisfying his own wife and Mercedes. She finally had a real man on her side, even though she had to share him. To her, it was well worth it since she couldn't find another macho like him to keep for herself.

As for Jesus, no one took him in, and he gave up eventually. No one ever heard of him again. Some say he was still on the streets panhandling. Others say they had heard he had met up with a butch pimp and was prostituting himself to survive. A few informed he had gotten lice and had to cut off his remaining hair, and he gained some weight and looked more feminine than before. One thing was for sure, he never became the man he always wanted to be. His small fame dissipated. He remained the pathetic pansy he was meant to be and still prefers being referred to as pink daddy she.

The End

Made in the USA
Columbia, SC
03 October 2024

42935463R20167